ONE OF OURS

• THE BARNES & NOBLE LIBRARY OF ESSENTIAL READING •

ONE OF OURS

Willa Cather

Introduction by Angela M. Salas

BARNES & NOBLE

NEW YORK

THE BARNES & NOBLE
LIBRARY OF ESSENTIAL READING

For my mother
VIRGINIA CATHER

CONTENTS

INTRODUCTION

WILLA Cather's *One of Ours* (1922) tells the story of Claude Wheeler, a young Nebraskan who discovers his mettle and finds meaning to his life as a participant in World War I. Contemporary readers must come to their own conclusions about whether the novel ultimately valorizes or questions Claude's willingness to die in a foreign country for ideals he can barely articulate. *One of Ours* earned author Willa Cather the Pulitzer Prize for fiction in 1923; it also occasioned fierce controversy on the pages of newspapers, journals, and literary magazines. At issue in these debates were Cather's authority as a woman to write a war novel and whether her apparently positive attitude toward the Great War was in step with antiwar sentiments expressed by younger authors like John Dos Passos, e.e.cummings, and Ernest Hemingway. The ruckus marked the first time that professional critics and the reading public were at odds about the quality of Willa Cather's work, with a small but vocal set of critics dismissing *One of Ours* as sentimental, unrealistic, and overrated, and other critics, as well as many readers, defending the novel as forthright, uplifting, and compelling. So fierce was discussion about *One of Ours* that, for years, an uneasy silence fell around this novel, with readers and critics devoting their attention to less problematic works, such as *O Pioneers* (1913) and *My Ántonia* (1918); in more recent years, however, Cather scholars have called for a reexamination of the novel, and have suggested that it is a far more complex piece of writing than either supporters or detractors realized when they were so passionately debating its merits.

Renowned for such novels as *O Pioneers!* and *My Ántonia*, Willa Cather (1873–1947), is often thought to be exclusively a chronicler of the early days of Nebraska's settlement. Born in Winchester County, Virginia, and relocated to the town of Red Cloud, on the plains of Nebraska, at age nine, Cather graduated from a rigorous academic program at the University of Nebraska-Lincoln and moved to Pittsburgh in 1896. In Pittsburgh, Cather worked in journalism and, by age twenty-two, was made managing editor of *Home Monthly* magazine. Cather then worked for *McClure's*, publishing her own early prose and poetry in other magazines, until the author Sarah Orne Jewett counseled her to leave her job and devote herself to writing, as well as to turn her attention to the Nebraska and Virginia of her childhood. This advice to concern one's self with the terrain and populations of one's earliest environs is not unlike that which Edith Wharton received from Henry James, who wanted his young friend to turn her back on European themes and locales in order to plumb New York and its society in her work. Taking Jewett's advice made a decisive difference in Cather's career, as taking James' advice had made in Wharton's literary career; Willa Cather became one of the preeminent authors of her generation.

When she died in 1947, Willa Cather was still one of the most esteemed writers of her time, although she had been the target of disdain by some influential critics in the 1930s. Such critics decried what they considered to be Cather's lack of political engagement; however, one might argue that these critics simply misread her work, which is always concerned with such matters as environmental destruction, the pervasiveness of the profit motive in human interactions, the plight of immigrants, and the manner in which many of America's poorest and weakest inhabitants are, sometimes literally, ground up in the wheels of commerce and progress. Thus, despite the formal elegance and lucidity of her work, which in no way resembles the cruder muckraking work of some of her more clearly activist colleagues, Cather can readily be considered a politically engaged author, as well as one who questions, with love and fierce intellect, some of the most unexamined but cherished notions of the United States of America, such as the idea that deserving people, like cream, always rise to the top. In *One of Ours*, Claude Wheeler *is* the cream of his Nebraska town, and of his oppressive family. Bullied by his father, his brother, and by his wife, Claude enlists and becomes a leader of men, the sort of officer whose men will lay down their lives to earn his respect; however, his moment of transcendence is cut short when he, like his men, is mown down by enemy gunfire. Overlooked and criticized as being out of step with his father's and his town's notions of practicality and masculinity, Claude must flee the putative land of opportunity in order to become the man he is meant to be.

Regardless of critical slings and arrows, Cather produced provocative work throughout her career; indeed, her final novel, *Sapphira and the Slave Girl* (1940), a novel about slavery, evil, and complicity in evil, elicits passionate response over half a century after its publication, most notably in Nobel laureate Toni Morrison's volume of criticism *Playing in the Dark: Whiteness and the Literary Imagination* (1992). In recent years, scholars have called for a reappraisal of *One of Ours*, attempting to rescue it from the uneasiness that has surrounded it since the boisterous disagreement that reigned in the years immediately following its publication.

Among the ironies about the controversy surrounding both *One of Ours* and its subsequent award of the Pulitzer Prize for Fiction are that it was the first of Cather's novels to make the best-seller lists, and that it was a success with former soldiers and their families. The majority of those critics who disparaged *One of Ours* did so on the grounds that it was unrealistic; thus, the fact that ex-soldiers and their families purchased, read, and praised the novel is of some interest, since one would imagine that such readers would be among the first to object to an unrealistic or idealized depiction of the war in which they had so recently been embroiled. In fact, a perusal of contemporary reviews and responses to *One of Ours* reveals two startling facts: first, that the critics were evenly divided on the matter of the quality of

Cather's novel; second, that the readers of newspapers and magazines that published negative assessments of the novel felt moved to write stirring responses when the novel received poor reviews. Thus, a negative review would be followed by reader rebuttals, which were responded to by the initial reviewers, and which prompted more responses from readers. These interchanges could go on for weeks, highlighting both the range of opinion about the novel, and the contested nature of any attempts to impose meaning upon the war itself, since such epistolary battles generally focused upon whether Cather's narrative was appropriate or accurate to particular readers' experience of World War I.

It is equally worth noting that the matter of women's qualifications to write about war loomed large, if generally unspoken, in some of the more negative reviews. Ernest Hemingway famously alleged that Cather had written her war scenes from footage of the film *Birth of a Nation*, writing "Poor woman she has got to get her war experience somewhere." In truth, Cather had done meticulous research about the war and individual battles of the war, and had also lived in France for two months to get a feel for the country that occupies a third of her novel; nonetheless, the allegation that she had needed to crib from the cinema to pen a battle scene stuck, taking some of the luster from her accomplishment.

As we begin the twenty-first century, Cummings' *The Enormous Room* (1922), Hemingway's *The Sun Also Rises* (1926) and Dos Passos' *Three Soldiers* (1921) are among the novels people think of when grasping for the titles of works about World War I. That this has occurred despite the fact that Edith Wharton's *A Son at the Front* (1923) and Cather's *One of Ours* were the more highly respected works at the time they were published suggests that men such as Hemingway were successful in arguing that men, not women, are singularly equipped to speak the truth about war. In addition to being penned by men, the three aforementioned works are vigorously anti-war, while Wharton's and Cather's novels accept the premise that the war was necessary, and that it was fought to preserve goodness and liberty from German authoritarianism. Thus, several things were at stake in the debate over the merits of the novel, and the actual literary quality of Cather's, or even Wharton's, work, was not always chief among them. Rather, who had the authority to comment upon war, and how they earned that authority was of singular importance.

Literary critic Merrill Maguire Skaggs describes *One of Ours* as the story of "a young man who has everything who feels little but failure until the moment of his heroic and therefore fulfilling death." Claude, the novel's protagonist, is not ungrateful and unmoored from the realities of life; rather, he is, despite his incipient greatness, treated as a mere cog in his family's machine. He wishes to attend college at the University of Nebraska in Lincoln, but his parents, afraid of the influence the university's more worldly faculty and students might have on him, send him, instead, to a third-rate church-affiliated college, which transmits accepted knowledge to its students, rather than encouraging them to ask questions, push intellectual boundaries, or even do original research. When Claude is finally able to take courses at the university and to undertake an independent research project — on Joan of Arc — he begins to realize his intellectual potential. Scholarship, he finds, is exciting, and the act of sifting through information to find the answers to a question that vexes him gives him his first sense of mastery in his life. However, as befits Claude's dreadful luck, his intellectual revelation coincides with his father's decision to withdraw him from college altogether, on the premise that he needs Claude's labor on the family farm more than Claude needs an expensive and impractical education. Furious at once again being at his father's capricious beck and call, Claude nonetheless returns to the farm and suffers his father's and brothers' scorn for what they see as intellectual pretensions. He absorbs their amused contempt and never notices what Cather's narrator tells us: that Claude is a comfort to his mother and their housekeeper, and that his generous willingness to fix the things that break around their house makes him a source of wonderment and pride to them.

Lonely and in need of companionship, Claude decides to marry Enid Royce, a young woman whose own father warns Claude against marrying her. A staunch romantic, Claude proposes to Enid anyway, on the premise that marriage will change her from a "cool, self-satisfied girl" into a loving wife. He builds a house for them to live in, and, despite evidence to the contrary, he assumes that Enid will be the first person in his life to truly love and treasure him and his ideals. Enid, however, prefers a world of ideas to a world of flesh, and, although she marries him, she refuses to consummate their relationship, or to treat Claude as anything other than a male housemate whose attitudes and actions she hopes to improve through lectures and good example. The two pursue separate lives in the house Claude has built until Enid leaves Claude to do missionary work in China. With all this behind him, it is not hard to fathom why Claude Wheeler, a vigorous and unappreciated young man who feels himself condemned to toil in his father's fields for the rest of his life, might decide it important to enlist in the American Expeditionary Force and defend France, the land of Joan of Arc, whose life kindled the first stirrings of emotional and intellectual intensity in his otherwise stifled life.

Some of the less enthusiastic reviews of *One of Ours* suggest that the novel romanticizes war, and that the view Cather paints of the destruction of the war, and the loss of life it entailed, was sentimental and idealized. More recent scholars, however, suggest that this supposed weakness is really an indicator of Cather's ability to imagine the perspective of her protagonist. Deborah Lindsay Williams suggests that Claude Wheeler, not Willa Cather, is an unrepentant romantic, and that Cather simply depicts his ideals and observations, with little authorial meddling. For instance, Cather carefully describes the ravaged French countryside that greets Claude and his fellow soldiers; Claude, however, only notices the discipline and fortitude of his men, and he misses entirely the wreckage that Cather shows her reader. Thus, the ravages of war are present in the novel, and only readers who identify too closely with Claude, or who are too deeply alienated from Cather, will miss them. Merrill Maguire Skaggs suggests that *One of Ours* is "saturated in irony," and neither sentimentalizes war nor underestimates its costs.

While the opinions of scholars and critics can certainly be compelling and enlightening, it is ultimately the right of a careful and engaged reader to come to decisions for him or herself. This edition of Willa Cather's Pulitzer Prize-winning novel *One of Ours* will permit readers to acquaint themselves with Claude Wheeler, a young man who, for most of the novel has every material thing a person might want, but lacks a sense of meaning to his life. Having met Claude and seen his life through his eyes, as well as the more dispassionate eyes of Cather's narrator, readers will be able to formulate their own ideas about whether Claude's enlistment is a rush toward glory or a willful plunge towards death. They will, as well, be able to ruminate about the ways the issues Cather raises in *One of Ours* remain with us, over eighty years since its initial publication, and to come to their own conclusions about whether the book truly is one of the great neglected World War I novels, as some have suggested.

Angela M. Salas received her Ph.D. from the University of Nebraska-Lincoln. An associate professor of English at Clarke College, in Dubuque, Iowa, Salas has published about Willa Cather, Edith Wharton, Yusef Komunyakaa, and the Vietnam Veterans Memorial.

BOOK ONE

ON LOVELY CREEK

I

CLAUDE Wheeler opened his eyes before the sun was up and vigorously shook his younger brother, who lay in the other half of the same bed.

"Ralph, Ralph, get awake! Come down and help me wash the car."

"What for?"

"Why, aren't we going to the circus today?"

"Car's all right. Let me alone." The boy turned over and pulled the sheet up to his face, to shut out the light which was beginning to come through the curtainless windows.

Claude rose and dressed,—a simple operation which took very little time. He crept down two flights of stairs, feeling his way in the dusk, his red hair standing up in peaks, like a cock's comb. He went through the kitchen into the adjoining washroom, which held two porcelain stands with running water. Everybody had washed before going to bed, apparently, and the bowls were ringed with a dark sediment which the hard, alkaline water had not dissolved. Shutting the door on this disorder, he turned back to the kitchen, took Mahailey's tin basin, doused his face and head in cold water, and began to plaster down his wet hair.

Old Mahailey herself came in from the yard, with her apron full of corn-cobs to start a fire in the kitchen stove. She smiled at him in the foolish fond way she often had with him when they were alone.

"What air you gittin' up for a-ready, boy? You goin' to the circus before breakfast? Don't you make no noise, else you'll have 'em all down here before I git my fire a-goin'."

"All right, Mahailey." Claude caught up his cap and ran out of doors, down the hillside toward the barn. The sun popped up over the edge of the prairie like a broad, smiling face; the light poured across the close-cropped August pastures and the hilly, timbered windings of Lovely Creek,—a clear little stream with a sand bottom, that curled and twisted playfully about through the south section of the big Wheeler ranch. It was a fine day to go to the circus at Frankfort, a fine day to do anything; the sort of day that must, somehow, turn out well.

Claude backed the little Ford car out of its shed, ran it up to the horse-tank, and began to throw water on the mud-crusted wheels and windshield. While he was at work the two hired men, Dan and Jerry, came shambling down the hill to feed the stock. Jerry was grumbling and swearing about something, but Claude wrung out his wet rags and, beyond a nod, paid no attention to them. Somehow his father always managed to have the roughest and dirtiest hired men in the country working for him. Claude had a grievance against Jerry just now, because of his treatment of one of the horses.

Molly was a faithful old mare, the mother of many colts; Claude and his younger brother had learned to ride on her. This man Jerry, taking her out to work one morning, let her step on a board with a nail sticking up in it. He pulled the nail out of her foot, said nothing to anybody, and drove her to the cultivator all day. Now she had been standing in her stall for weeks, patiently suffering, her body wretchedly thin, and her leg swollen until it looked like an elephant's. She would have to stand there, the veterinary said, until her hoof came off and she grew a new one, and she would always be stiff. Jerry had not been discharged, and he exhibited the poor animal as if she were a credit to him.

Mahailey came out on the hilltop and rang the breakfast bell. After the hired men went up to the house, Claude slipped into the barn to see that Molly had got her share of oats. She was eating quietly, her head hanging, and her scaly, dead-looking foot lifted just a little from the ground. When he stroked her neck and talked to her she stopped grinding and gazed at him mournfully. She knew him, and wrinkled her nose and drew her upper lip back from her worn teeth, to show that she liked being petted. She let him touch her foot and examine her leg.

When Claude reached the kitchen, his mother was sitting at one end of the breakfast table, pouring weak coffee, his brother and Dan and Jerry were in their chairs, and Mahailey was baking griddle cakes at the stove. A moment later Mr. Wheeler came down the enclosed stairway and walked the length of the table to his own place. He was a very large man, taller and broader than any of his neighbours. He seldom wore a coat in summer, and his rumpled shirt bulged out carelessly over the belt of his trousers. His florid face was clean shaven, likely to be a trifle tobacco-stained about the mouth, and it was conspicuous both for good-nature and coarse humour, and for an imperturbable physical composure. Nobody in the county had ever seen Nat Wheeler flustered about anything, and nobody had ever heard him speak with complete seriousness. He kept up his easy-going, jocular affability even with his own family.

As soon as he was seated, Mr. Wheeler reached for the two-pint sugar bowl and began to pour sugar into his coffee. Ralph asked him if he were going to the circus. Mr. Wheeler winked.

"I shouldn't wonder if I happened in town sometime before the elephants get away." He spoke very deliberately, with a State-of-Maine drawl, and his voice was smooth and agreeable. "You boys better start in early, though. You can take the wagon and the mules, and load in the cowhides. The butcher has agreed to take them."

Claude put down his knife. "Can't we have the car? I've washed it on purpose."

"And what about Dan and Jerry? They want to see the circus just as much as you do, and I want the hides should go in; they're bringing a good price now. I don't mind about your washing the car; mud preserves the paint, they say, but it'll be all right this time, Claude."

The hired men haw-hawed and Ralph giggled. Claude's freckled face got very red. The pancake grew stiff and heavy in his mouth and was hard to swallow. His father knew he hated to drive the mules to town, and knew how he hated to go any-where with Dan and Jerry. As for the hides, they were the skins of four steers that had perished in the blizzard last winter through the wanton carelessness of these same hired men, and the price they would bring would not half pay for the time his father had spent in stripping and curing them. They had lain in a shed loft all summer, and the wagon had been to town a dozen times. But today, when he wanted to go to Frankfort clean and care-free, he must take these stinking hides and two coarse-mouthed men, and drive a pair of mules that always brayed and balked and behaved ridiculously in a crowd. Probably his father had looked out of the window and seen him washing the car, and had put this up on him while he dressed. It was like his father's idea of a joke.

Mrs. Wheeler looked at Claude sympathetically, feeling that he was disappointed. Perhaps she, too, suspected a joke. She had learned that humour might wear almost any guise.

When Claude started for the barn after breakfast, she came running down the path, calling to him faintly,—hurrying always made her short of breath. Overtaking him, she looked up with solicitude, shading her eyes with her delicately formed hand. "If you want I should do up your linen coat, Claude, I can iron it while you're hitching," she said wistfully.

Claude stood kicking at a bunch of mottled feathers that had once been a young chicken. His shoulders were drawn high, his mother saw, and his figure suggested energy and determined self-control.

"You needn't mind, mother." He spoke rapidly, muttering his words. "I'd better wear my old clothes if I have to take the hides. They're greasy, and in the sun they'll smell worse than fertilizer."

"The men can handle the hides, I should think. Wouldn't you feel better in town to be dressed?" She was still blinking up at him.

"Don't bother about it. Put me out a clean coloured shirt, if you want to. That's all right."

He turned toward the barn, and his mother went slowly back the path up to the house. She was so plucky and so stooped, his dear mother! He guessed if she could stand having these men about, could cook and wash for them, he could drive them to town!

Half an hour after the wagon left, Nat Wheeler put on an alpaca coat and went off in the rattling buckboard in which, though he kept two automobiles, he still drove about the country. He said nothing to his wife; it was her business to guess whether or not he would be home for dinner. She and Mahailey could have a good time scrubbing and sweeping all day, with no men around to bother them.

There were few days in the year when Wheeler did not drive off somewhere; to an auction sale, or a political convention, or a meeting of the Farmers' Telephone directors;—to see how his neighbours were getting on with their work, if there was nothing else to look after. He preferred his buckboard to a car because it was light, went easily over heavy or rough roads, and was so rickety that he never felt he must suggest his wife's accompanying him. Besides he could see the country better when he didn't have to keep his mind on the road. He had come to this part of Nebraska when the Indians and the buffalo were still about, remembered the grasshopper year and the big cyclone, had watched the farms emerge one by one from the great rolling page where once only the wind wrote its story. He had encouraged new settlers to take up homesteads, urged on courtships, loaned young fellows the money to marry on, seen families grow and prosper; until he felt a little as if all this were his own enterprise. The changes, not only those the years made, but those the seasons made, were interesting to him.

People recognized Nat Wheeler and his cart a mile away. He sat massive and comfortable, weighing down one end of the slanting seat, his driving hand lying on his knee. Even his German neighbours, the Yoeders, who hated to stop work for a quarter of an hour on any account, were glad to see him coming. The merchants in the little towns about the county missed him if he didn't drop in once a week or so. He was active in politics; never ran for an office himself, but often took up the cause of a friend and conducted his campaign for him.

The French saying, "Joy of the street, sorrow of the home," was exemplified in Mr. Wheeler, though not at all in the French way. His own affairs were of secondary importance to him. In the early days he had homesteaded and bought and leased enough land to make him rich. Now he had only to rent it out to good farmers who liked to work—he didn't, and of that he made no secret. When he was at home, he usually sat upstairs in the living room, reading newspapers. He subscribed for a dozen or more—the list included a weekly devoted to scandal—and he was well informed about what was going on in the world. He had magnificent health, and illness in himself or in other people struck him as humorous. To be sure, he never suffered from anything more perplexing than toothache or boils, or an occasional bilious attack.

Wheeler gave liberally to churches and charities, was always ready to lend money or machinery to a neighbour who was short of anything. He liked to tease and shock diffident people, and had an inexhaustible supply of funny stories. Everybody marvelled that he got on so well with his oldest son, Bayliss Wheeler. Not that Bayliss was exactly diffident, but he was a narrow-gauge fellow, the sort of prudent young man one wouldn't expect Nat Wheeler to like.

Bayliss had a farm implement business in Frankfort, and though he was still under thirty he had made a very considerable financial success. Perhaps Wheeler was proud of his son's business acumen. At any rate, he drove to town to see Bayliss several times a week, went to sales and stock exhibits with him, and sat about his store for hours at a stretch, joking with the farmers who came in. Wheeler had been a heavy drinker in his day, and was still a heavy feeder. Bayliss was thin and dyspeptic, and a virulent Prohibitionist; he would have liked to regulate everybody's diet by his own feeble constitution. Even Mrs. Wheeler, who took the men God had apportioned her for granted, wondered how

Bayliss and his father could go off to conventions together and have a good time, since their ideas of what made a good time were so different.

Once every few years, Mr. Wheeler bought a new suit and a dozen stiff shirts and went back to Maine to visit his brothers and sisters, who were very quiet, conventional people. But he was always glad to get home to his old clothes, his big farm, his buckboard, and Bayliss.

Mrs. Wheeler had come out from Vermont to be Principal of the High School, when Frankfort was a frontier town and Nat Wheeler was a prosperous bachelor. He must have fancied her for the same reason he liked his son Bayliss,—because she was so different. There was this to be said for Nat Wheeler, that he liked every sort of human creature; he liked good people and honest people, and he liked rascals and hypocrites almost to the point of loving them. If he heard that a neighbour had played a sharp trick or done something particularly mean, he was sure to drive over to see the man at once, as if he hadn't hitherto appreciated him.

There was a large, loafing dignity about Claude's father. He liked to provoke others to uncouth laughter, but he never laughed immoderately himself. In telling stories about him, people often tried to imitate his smooth, senatorial voice, robust but never loud. Even when he was hilariously delighted by anything,—as when poor Mahailey, undressing in the dark on a summer night, sat down on the sticky fly-paper,—he was not boisterous. He was a jolly, easy-going father, indeed, for a boy who was not thin-skinned.

CLAUDE and his mules rattled into Frankfort just as the calliope went screaming down Maine street at the head of the circus parade. Getting rid of his disagreeable freight and his uncongenial companions as soon as possible, he elbowed his way along the crowded sidewalk, looking for some of the neighbour boys. Mr. Wheeler was standing on the Farmer's Bank corner, towering a head above the throng, chaffing with a little hunchback who was setting up a shell-game. To avoid his father, Claude turned and went into his brother's store. The two big show windows were full of country children, their mothers standing behind them to watch the parade. Bayliss was seated in the little glass cage where he did his writing and bookkeeping. He nodded at Claude from his desk.

"Hello," said Claude, bustling in as if he were in a great hurry. "Have you seen Ernest Havel? I thought I might find him in here."

Bayliss swung round in his swivel chair to return a plough catalogue to the shelf. "What would he be in here for? Better look for him in the saloon." Nobody could put meaner insinuations into a slow, dry remark than Bayliss.

Claude's cheeks flamed with anger. As he turned away, he noticed something unusual about his brother's face, but he wasn't going to give him the satisfaction of asking him how he had got a black eye. Ernest Havel was a Bohemian, and he usually drank a glass of beer when he came to town; but he was sober and thoughtful beyond the wont of young men. From Bayliss' drawl one might have supposed that the boy was a drunken loafer.

At that very moment Claude saw his friend on the other side of the street, following the wagon of trained dogs that brought up the rear of the procession. He ran across, through a crowd of shouting youngsters, and caught Ernest by the arm.

"Hello, where are you off to?"

"I'm going to eat my lunch before show-time. I left my wagon out by the pumping station, on the creek. What about you?"

"I've got no program. Can I go along?"

Ernest smiled. "I expect. I've got enough lunch for two."

"Yes, I know. You always have. I'll join you later."

Claude would have liked to take Ernest to the hotel for dinner. He had more than enough money in his pockets; and his father was a rich farmer. In the Wheeler family a new thrasher or a new automobile was ordered without a question, but it was considered extravagant to go to a hotel for dinner. If his father or Bayliss heard that he had been there — and Bayliss heard everything — they would say he was putting on airs, and would get back at him. He tried to excuse his cowardice to himself by saying that he was dirty and smelled of the hides; but in his heart he knew that he did not ask Ernest to go to the hotel with him because he had been so brought up that it would be difficult for him to do this simple thing. He made some purchases at the fruit stand and the cigar counter, and then hurried out along the dusty road toward the pumping station. Ernest's wagon was standing under the shade of some willow trees, on a little sandy bottom half enclosed by a loop of the creek which curved like a horseshoe. Claude threw himself on the sand beside the stream and wiped the dust from his hot face. He felt he had now closed the door on his disagreeable morning.

Ernest produced his lunch basket.

"I got a couple bottles of beer cooling in the creek," he said. "I knew you wouldn't want to go in a saloon."

"Oh, forget it!" Claude muttered, ripping the cover off a jar of pickles. He was nineteen years old, and he was afraid to go into a saloon, and his friend knew he was afraid.

After lunch, Claude took out a handful of good cigars he had bought at the drugstore. Ernest, who couldn't afford cigars, was pleased. He lit one, and as he smoked he kept looking at it with an air of pride and turning it around between his fingers.

The horses stood with their heads over the wagon-box, munching their oats. The stream trickled by under the willow roots with a cool, persuasive sound. Claude and Ernest lay in the shade, their coats under their heads, talking very little. Occasionally a motor dashed along the road toward town, and a cloud of dust and a smell of gasoline blew in over the creek bottom; but for the most part the silence of the warm, lazy summer noon was undisturbed. Claude could usually forget his own vexations and chagrins when he was with Ernest. The Bohemian boy was never uncertain, was not pulled in two or three ways at once. He was simple and direct. He had a number of impersonal pre-occupations; was interested in politics and history and in new inventions. Claude felt that his friend lived in an atmosphere of mental liberty to which he himself could never hope to attain. After he had talked with Ernest for awhile, the things that did not go right on the farm seemed less important.

Claude's mother was almost as fond of Ernest as he was himself. When the two boys were going to high school, Ernest often came over in the evening to study with Claude, and while they worked at the long kitchen table Mrs. Wheeler brought her darning and sat near them, helping them with their Latin and algebra. Even old Mahailey was enlightened by their words of wisdom.

Mrs. Wheeler said she would never forget the night Ernest arrived from the Old Country. His brother, Joe Havel, had gone to Frankfort to meet him, and was to stop on the way home and leave some groceries for the Wheelers. The train from the east was late; it was ten o'clock that night when Mrs. Wheeler, waiting in the kitchen, heard Havel's wagon rumble across the little bridge over Lovely Creek. She opened the outside door, and presently Joe came in with a bucket of salt fish in one hand and a sack of flour on his shoulder. While he took the fish down to the cellar for her, another figure appeared in the doorway; a young boy, short, stooped, with a flat cap on his head and a great oilcloth valise, such as pedlars carry, strapped to his back. He had fallen asleep in the wagon, and on waking and finding his brother gone, he had supposed they were at home and scrambled for his pack. He stood in the doorway, blinking his eyes at the light, looking astonished but eager to do whatever was required of him. What if one of her own boys, Mrs. Wheeler thought. . . . She went up to him and put her arm around him, laughing a little and saying in her quiet voice, just as if he could understand her, "Why, you're only a little boy after all, aren't you?"

Ernest said afterwards that it was his first welcome to this country, though he had travelled so far, and had been pushed and hauled and shouted at for so many days, he had lost count of them. That night he and Claude only shook hands and looked at each other suspiciously, but ever since they had been good friends.

After their picnic the two boys went to the circus in a happy frame of mind. In the animal tent they met big Leonard Dawson, the oldest son of one of the Wheelers' near neighbours, and the three sat together for the performance. Leonard said he had come to town alone in his car; wouldn't Claude ride out with him? Claude was glad enough to turn the mules over to Ralph, who didn't mind the hired men as much as he did.

Leonard was a strapping brown fellow of twenty-five, with big hands and big feet, white teeth, and flashing eyes full of energy. He and his father and two brothers not only worked their own big farm, but rented a quarter section from Nat Wheeler. They were master farmers. If there was a dry summer and a failure, Leonard only laughed and stretched his long arms, and put in a bigger crop next year. Claude was always a little reserved with Leonard; he felt that the young man was rather contemptuous of the hap-hazard way in which things were done on the Wheeler place, and thought his going to college a waste of money. Leonard had not even gone through the Frankfort High School, and he was already a more successful man than Claude was ever likely to be. Leonard did think these things, but he was fond of Claude, all the same.

At sunset the car was speeding over a fine stretch of smooth road across the level country that lay between Frankfort and the rougher land along Lovely Creek. Leonard's attention was largely given up to admiring the faultless behaviour of his engine. Presently he chuckled to himself and turned to Claude.

"I wonder if you'd take it all right if I told you a joke on Bayliss?"

"I expect I would." Claude's tone was not at all eager.

"You saw Bayliss today? Notice anything queer about him, one eye a little off colour? Did he tell you how he got it?"

"No. I didn't ask him."

"Just as well. A lot of people did ask him, though, and he said he was hunting around his place for something in the dark and ran into a reaper. Well, I'm the reaper!"

Claude looked interested. "You mean to say Bayliss was in a fight?"

Leonard laughed. "Lord, no! Don't you know Bayliss? I went in there to pay a bill yesterday, and Susie Gray and another girl came in to sell tickets for the firemen's dinner. An advance man for this circus was hanging around, and he began talking a little smart, — nothing rough, but the way such fellows will. The girls handed it back to him, and sold him three tickets and shut him up. I couldn't see how Susie thought so quick what to say. The minute the girls went out Bayliss started knocking them; said all the country girls were getting too fresh and knew more than they ought to about managing sporty men — and right there I reached out and handed him one. I hit harder than I meant to. I meant to slap him, not to give him a black eye. But you can't always regulate things, and I was hot all over. I waited for him to come back at me. I'm bigger than he is, and I wanted to give him satisfaction. Well, sir, he never moved a muscle! He stood there getting redder and redder, and his eyes watered. I don't say he cried, but his eyes watered. 'All right, Bayliss,' said I. 'Slow with your fists, if that's your principle; but slow with your tongue, too,—especially when the parties mentioned aren't present.'"

"Bayliss will never get over that," was Claude's only comment.

"He don't have to!" Leonard threw up his head. "I'm a good customer; he can like it or lump it, till the price of binding twine goes down!"

For the next few minutes the driver was occupied with trying to get up a long, rough hill on high gear. Sometimes he could make that hill, and sometimes he couldn't, and he was not able to account for the difference. After he pulled the second lever with some disgust and let the car amble on as she would, he noticed that his companion was disconcerted.

"I'll tell you what, Leonard," Claude spoke in a strained voice, "I think the fair thing for you to do is to get out here by the road and give me a chance."

Leonard swung his steering wheel savagely to pass a wagon on the down side of the hill. "What the devil are you talking about, boy?"

"You think you've got our measure all right, but you ought to give me a chance first."

Leonard looked down in amazement at his own big brown hands, lying on the wheel. "You mortal fool kid, what would I be telling you all this for, if I didn't know you were another breed of cats? I never thought you got on too well with Bayliss yourself."

"I don't, but I won't have you thinking you can slap the men in my family whenever you feel like it." Claude knew that his explanation sounded foolish, and his voice, in spite of all he could do, was weak and angry.

Young Leonard Dawson saw he had hurt the boy's feelings. "Lord, Claude, I know you're a fighter. Bayliss never was. I went to school with him."

The ride ended amicably, but Claude wouldn't let Leonard take him home. He jumped out of the car with a curt goodnight, and ran across the dusky fields toward the light that shone from the house on the hill. At the little bridge over the creek, he stopped to get his breath and to be sure that he was outwardly composed before he went in to see his mother.

"Ran against a reaper in the dark!" he muttered aloud, clenching his fist.

Listening to the deep singing of the frogs, and to the distant barking of the dogs up at the house, he grew calmer. Nevertheless, he wondered why it was that one had sometimes to feel responsible for the behaviour of people whose natures were wholly antipathetic to one's own.

III

THE circus was on Saturday. The next morning Claude was standing at his dresser, shaving. His beard was already strong, a shade darker than his hair and not so red as his skin. His eyebrows and long lashes were a pale corn-colour—made his blue eyes seem lighter than they were, and, he thought, gave a look of shyness and weakness to the upper part of his face. He was exactly the sort of looking boy he didn't want to be. He especially hated his head,—so big that he had trouble in buying his hats, and uncompromisingly square in shape; a perfect block-head. His name was another source of humiliation. Claude: it was a "chump" name, like Elmer and Roy; a hayseed name trying to be fine. In country schools there was always a red-headed, warty-handed, runny-nosed little boy who was called Claude. His good physique he took for granted; smooth, muscular arms and legs, and strong shoulders, a farmer boy might be supposed to have. Unfortunately he had none of his father's physical repose, and his strength often asserted itself inharmoniously. The storms that went on in his mind sometimes made him rise, or sit down, or lift something, more violently than there was any apparent reason for his doing.

The household slept late on Sunday morning; even Mahailey did not get up until seven. The general signal for breakfast was the smell of doughnuts frying. This morning Ralph rolled out of bed at the last minute and callously put on his clean underwear without taking a bath. This cost him not one regret, though he took time to polish his new ox-blood shoes tenderly with a pocket

17

handkerchief. He reached the table when all the others were half through breakfast, and made his peace by genially asking his mother if she didn't want him to drive her to church in the car.

"I'd like to go if I can get the work done in time," she said, doubtfully glancing at the clock.

"Can't Mahailey tend to things for you this morning?"

Mrs. Wheeler hesitated. "Everything but the separator, she can. But she can't fit all the parts together. It's a good deal of work, you know."

"Now, Mother," said Ralph good-humouredly, as he emptied the syrup pitcher over his cakes, "you're prejudiced. Nobody ever thinks of skimming milk now-a-days. Every up-to-date farmer uses a separator."

Mrs. Wheeler's pale eyes twinkled. "Mahailey and I will never be quite up-to-date, Ralph. We're old-fashioned, and I don't know but you'd better let us be. I could see the advantage of a separator if we milked half-a-dozen cows. It's a very ingenious machine. But it's a great deal more work to scald it and fit it together than it was to take care of the milk in the old way."

"It won't be when you get used to it," Ralph assured her. He was the chief mechanic of the Wheeler farm, and when the farm implements and the automobiles did not give him enough to do, he went to town and bought machines for the house. As soon as Mahailey got used to a washing-machine or a churn, Ralph, to keep up with the bristling march of events, brought home a still newer one. The mechanical dish-washer she had never been able to use, and patent flat-irons and oil-stoves drove her wild.

Claude told his mother to go upstairs and dress; he would scald the separator while Ralph got the car ready. He was still working at it when his brother came in from the garage to wash his hands.

"You really oughtn't to load mother up with things like this, Ralph," he exclaimed fretfully. "Did you ever try washing this damned thing yourself?"

"Of course I have. If Mrs. Dawson can manage it, I should think mother could."

"Mrs. Dawson is a younger woman. Anyhow, there's no point in trying to make machinists of Mahailey and mother."

Ralph lifted his eyebrows to excuse Claude's bluntness. "See here," he said persuasively, "don't you go encouraging her into thinking she can't change her ways. Mother's entitled to all the labour-saving devices we can get her."

Claude rattled the thirty-odd graduated metal funnels which he was trying to fit together in their proper sequence. "Well, if this is labour-saving ——"

The younger boy giggled and ran upstairs for his panama hat. He never quarrelled. Mrs. Wheeler sometimes said it was wonderful, how much Ralph would take from Claude.

After Ralph and his mother had gone off in the car, Mr. Wheeler drove to see his German neighbour, Gus Yoeder, who had just bought a blooded bull. Dan and Jerry were pitching horseshoes down behind the barn. Claude told Mahailey he was going to the cellar to put up the swinging shelf she had been wanting, so that the rats couldn't get at her vegetables.

"Thank you, Mr. Claude. I don't know what does make the rats so bad. The cats catches one most every day, too."

"I guess they come up from the barn. I've got a nice wide board down at the garage for your shelf."

The cellar was cemented, cool and dry, with deep closets for canned fruit and flour and groceries, bins for coal and cobs, and a dark-room full of photographer's apparatus. Claude took his place at the carpenter's bench under one of the square windows. Mysterious objects stood about him in the grey twilight; electric batteries, old bicycles and typewriters, a machine for making cement fence-posts, a vulcanizer, a stereoptican with a broken lens. The mechanical toys Ralph could not operate successfully, as well as those he had got tired of, were stored away here. If they were left in the barn, Mr. Wheeler saw them too often, and sometimes, when they happened to be in his way, he made sarcastic comments. Claude had begged his mother to let him pile this lumber into a wagon and dump it into some washout hole along the creek; but Mrs. Wheeler said he must not think of such a thing, as it would hurt Ralph's feelings very much. Nearly every time Claude went into the cellar, he made a desperate resolve to clear the place out some day, reflecting bitterly that the money this wreckage cost would have put a boy through college decently.

While Claude was planing off the board he meant to suspend from the joists, Mahailey left her work and came down to watch him. She made some pretence of hunting for pickled onions, then seated herself upon a cracker box; close at hand there was a plush "spring-rocker" with one arm gone, but it wouldn't have been her idea of good manners to sit there. Her eyes had a kind of sleepy contentment in them as she followed Claude's motions. She watched him as if he were a baby playing. Her hands lay comfortably in her lap.

"Mr. Ernest ain't been over for a long time. He ain't mad about nothin', is he?"

"Oh, no! He's awful busy this summer. I saw him in town yesterday. We went to the circus together."

Mahailey smiled and nodded. "That's nice. I'm glad for you two boys to have a good time. Mr. Ernest's a nice boy; I always liked him first rate. He's a little feller, though. He ain't big like you, is he? I guess he ain't as tall as Mr. Ralph, even."

"Not quite," said Claude between strokes. "He's strong, though, and gets through a lot of work."

"Oh, I know! I know he is. I know he works hard. All them foreigners works hard, don't they, Mr. Claude? I reckon he liked the circus. Maybe they don't have circuses like our'n, over where he come from."

Claude began to tell her about the clown elephant and the trained dogs, and she sat listening to him with her pleased, foolish smile; there was something wise and far-seeing about her smile, too.

Mahailey had come to them long ago, when Claude was only a few months old. She had been brought West by a shiftless Virginia family which went to pieces and scattered under the rigours of pioneer farm-life. When the mother of the family died, there was nowhere for Mahailey to go, and Mrs. Wheeler took her in. Mahailey had no one to take care of her, and Mrs. Wheeler had no one to help her with the work; it had turned out very well.

Mahailey had had a hard life in her young days, married to a savage mountaineer who often abused her and never provided for her. She could remember times when she sat in the cabin, beside an empty meal-barrel and a cold iron pot, waiting for "him" to bring home a squirrel he had shot or a chicken he had stolen. Too often he brought nothing but a jug of mountain whiskey and a pair of brutal fists. She thought herself well off now, never to have to beg for food or go off into the woods to gather firing, to be sure of a warm bed and shoes and decent clothes. Mahailey was one of eighteen children; most of them grew up lawless or half-witted, and two of her brothers, like her husband, ended their lives in jail. She had never been sent to school, and could not read or write. Claude, when he was a little boy, tried to teach her to read, but what she learned one night she had forgotten by the next. She could count, and tell the time of day by the clock, and she was very proud of knowing the alphabet and of being able to spell out let-ters on the flour sacks and coffee packages. "That's a big A," she would murmur, "and that there's a little a."

Mahailey was shrewd in her estimate of people, and Claude thought her judgment sound in a good many things. He knew she sensed all the shades of personal feeling, the accords and antipathies in the household, as keenly as he did, and he would have hated to lose her good opinion. She consulted him in all her little difficulties. If the leg of the kitchen table got wobbly, she knew he would put in new screws for her. When she broke a handle off her rolling pin, he put on another, and he fitted a haft to her favourite butcher-knife after every one else said it must be thrown away. These objects, after they had been mended, acquired a new value in her eyes, and she liked to work with them. When Claude helped her lift or carry anything, he never avoided touching her,—this she felt deeply. She suspected that Ralph was a little ashamed of her, and would prefer to have some brisk young thing about the kitchen.

On days like this, when other people were not about, Mahailey liked to talk to Claude about the things they did together when he was little; the Sundays when they used to wander along the creek, hunting for wild grapes and watching the red squirrels; or trailed across the high pastures to a wild-plum thicket at the north end of the Wheeler farm. Claude could remember warm spring days when the plum bushes were all in blossom and Mahailey used to lie down under them and sing to herself, as if the honey-heavy sweetness made her drowsy; songs without words, for the most part, though he recalled one mountain dirge which said over and over, "And they laid Jesse James in his grave."

IV

THE time was approaching for Claude to go back to the strug-gling denominational college on the outskirts of the state capital, where he had already spent two dreary and unprofitable winters.

"Mother," he said one morning when he had an opportunity to speak to her alone, "I wish you would let me quit the Temple, and go to the State University."

She looked up from the mass of dough she was kneading.

"But why, Claude?"

"Well, I could learn more, for one thing. The professors at the Temple aren't much good. Most of them are just preachers who couldn't make a living at preaching."

The look of pain that always disarmed Claude came instantly into his mother's face. "Son, don't say such things. I can't believe but teachers are more interested in their students when they are concerned for their spiritual development, as well as the mental. Brother Weldon said many of the professors at the State University are not Christian men; they even boast of it, in some cases."

"Oh, I guess most of them are good men, all right; at any rate they know their subjects. These little pin-headed preachers like Weldon do a lot of harm, running about the country talking. He's sent around to pull in students for his own school. If he didn't get them he'd lose his job. I wish he'd never got me. Most of the fellows who flunk out at the State come to us, just as he did."

"But how can there be any serious study where they give so much time to athletics and frivolity? They pay their football coach a larger salary than their Chancellor. And those fraternity houses are places where boys learn all sorts of evil. I've heard that dreadful things go on in them sometimes. Besides, it would take more money, and you couldn't live as cheaply as you do at the Chapins'."

Claude made no reply. He stood before her frowning and pulling at a calloused spot on the inside of his palm. Mrs. Wheeler looked at him wistfully. "I'm sure you must be able to study better in a quiet, serious atmosphere," she said.

He sighed and turned away. If his mother had been the least bit unctuous, like Brother Weldon, he could have told her many enlightening facts. But she was so trusting and childlike, so faithful by nature and so ignorant of life as he knew it, that it was hopeless to argue with her. He could shock her and make her fear the world even more than she did, but he could never make her understand.

His mother was old-fashioned. She thought dancing and card-playing dangerous pastimes—only rough people did such things when she was a girl in Vermont—and "worldliness" only another word for wickedness. According to her conception of education, one should learn, not think; and above all, one must not enquire. The history of the human race, as it lay behind one, was already explained; and so was its destiny, which lay before. The mind should remain obediently within the theological concept of history.

Nat Wheeler didn't care where his son went to school, but he, too, took it for granted that the religious institution was cheaper than the State University; and that because the students there looked shabbier they were less likely to become too knowing, and to be offensively intelligent at home. However, he referred the matter to Bayliss one day when he was in town.

"Claude's got some notion he wants to go to the State University this winter."

Bayliss at once assumed that wise, better-be-prepared-for-the-worst expression which had made him seem shrewd and seasoned from boyhood. "I don't see any point in changing unless he's got good reasons."

"Well, he thinks that bunch of parsons at the Temple don't make first-rate teachers."

"I expect they can teach Claude quite a bit yet. If he gets in with that fast football crowd at the State, there'll be no holding him." For some reason Bayliss detested football. "This athletic business is a good deal over-done. If Claude wants exercise, he might put in the fall wheat."

That night Mr. Wheeler brought the subject up at supper, questioned Claude, and tried to get at the cause of his discontent. His manner was jocular, as usual, and Claude hated any public discussion of his personal affairs. He was afraid of his father's humour when it got too near him.

Claude might have enjoyed the large and somewhat gross cartoons with which Mr. Wheeler enlivened daily life, had they been of any other authorship. But he unreasonably wanted his father to be the most dignified, as he was certainly the handsomest and most intelligent, man in the community. Moreover, Claude couldn't bear ridicule very well. He squirmed before he was hit; saw it coming, invited it. Mr. Wheeler had observed this trait in him when he was a little chap, called it false pride, and often purposely outraged his feelings to harden him, as he had hardened Claude's mother, who was afraid of everything but schoolbooks and prayer-meetings when he first married her. She was still more or less bewildered, but she had long ago got over any fear of him and any dread of living with him. She accepted everything about her husband as part of his rugged masculinity, and of that she was proud, in her quiet way.

Claude had never quite forgiven his father for some of his practical jokes. One warm spring day, when he was a boisterous little boy of five, playing in and out of the house, he heard his mother entreating Mr. Wheeler to go down to the orchard and pick the cherries from a tree that hung loaded. Claude remembered that she persisted rather complainingly, saying that the cherries were too high for her to reach, and that even if she had a ladder it would hurt her back. Mr. Wheeler was always annoyed if his wife referred to any physical weakness, especially if she

25

complained about her back. He got up and went out. After a while he returned. "All right now, Evangeline," he called cheerily as he passed through the kitchen. "Cherries won't give you any trouble. You and Claude can run along and pick 'em as easy as can be."

Mrs. Wheeler trustfully put on her sunbonnet, gave Claude a little pail and took a big one herself, and they went down the pasture hill to the orchard, fenced in on the low land by the creek. The ground had been ploughed that spring to make it hold moisture, and Claude was running happily along in one of the furrows, when he looked up and beheld a sight he could never forget. The beautiful, round-topped cherry tree, full of green leaves and red fruit,—his father had sawed it through! It lay on the ground beside its bleeding stump. With one scream Claude became a little demon. He threw away his tin pail, jumped about howling and kicking the loose earth with his copper-toed shoes, until his mother was much more concerned for him than for the tree.

"Son, son," she cried, "it's your father's tree. He has a perfect right to cut it down if he wants to. He's often said the trees were too thick in here. Maybe it will be better for the others."

"'Tain't so! He's a damn fool, damn fool!" Claude bellowed, still hopping and kicking, almost choking with rage and hate.

His mother dropped on her knees beside him. "Claude, stop! I'd rather have the whole orchard cut down than hear you say such things."

After she got him quieted they picked the cherries and went back to the house. Claude had promised her that he would say nothing, but his father must have noticed the little boy's angry eyes fixed upon him all through dinner, and his expression of scorn. Even then his flexible lips were only too well adapted to hold the picture of that feeling. For days afterwards Claude went down to the orchard and watched the tree grow sicker, wilt and wither away. God would surely punish a man who could do that, he thought.

A violent temper and physical restlessness were the most conspicuous things about Claude when he was a little boy. Ralph was docile, and had a precocious sagacity for keeping out of trouble. Quiet in manner, he was fertile in devising mischief, and easily persuaded his older brother, who was always looking for something to do, to execute his plans. It was usually Claude who was caught red-handed. Sitting mild and contemplative on his quilt on the floor, Ralph would whisper to Claude that it might be amusing to climb up and take the clock from the shelf, or to operate the sewing-machine. When they were older, and played out of doors, he had only to insinuate that Claude was afraid, to make him try a frosted axe with his tongue, or jump from the shed roof.

The usual hardships of country boyhood were not enough for Claude; he imposed physical tests and penances upon himself. Whenever he burned his finger, he followed Mahailey's advice and held his hand close to the stove to "draw out the fire." One year he went to school all winter in his jacket, to make himself tough. His mother would button him up in his overcoat and put his dinner-pail in his hand and start him off. As soon as he got out of sight of the house, he pulled off his coat, rolled it under his arm, and scudded along the edge of the frozen fields, arriving at the frame schoolhouse panting and shivering, but very well pleased with himself.

V

CLAUDE waited for his elders to change their mind about where he should go to school; but no one seemed much concerned, not even his mother.

Two years ago, the young man whom Mrs. Wheeler called "Brother Weldon" had come out from Lincoln, preaching in little towns and country churches, and recruiting students for the institution at which he taught in the winter. He had convinced Mrs. Wheeler that his college was the safest possible place for a boy who was leaving home for the first time.

Claude's mother was not discriminating about preachers. She believed them all chosen and sanctified, and was never happier than when she had one in the house to cook for and wait upon. She made young Mr. Weldon so comfortable that he remained under her roof for several weeks, occupying the spare room, where he spent the mornings in study and meditation. He appeared regularly at mealtime to ask a blessing upon the food and to sit with devout, downcast eyes while the chicken was being dismembered. His top-shaped head hung a little to one side, the thin hair was parted precisely over his high forehead and brushed in little ripples. He was soft-spoken and apologetic in manner and took up as little room as possible. His meekness amused Mr. Wheeler, who liked to ply him with food and never failed to ask him gravely "what part of the chicken he would prefer," in order to hear him murmur, "A little of the white meat, if you please," while he drew his elbows close, as if he were adroitly sliding over a dangerous place. In the afternoon Brother Weldon usually put on a fresh lawn necktie and a hard, glistening straw hat which left a red streak across his forehead, tucked his Bible under his arm, and went out to make calls. If he went far, Ralph took him in the automobile.

Claude disliked this young man from the moment he first met him, and could scarcely answer him civilly. Mrs. Wheeler, always absent-minded, and now absorbed in her cherishing care of the visitor, did not notice Claude's scornful silences until Mahailey, whom such things never escaped, whispered to her over the stove one day: "Mr. Claude, he don't like the preacher. He just ain't got no use fur him, but don't you let on."

As a result of Brother Weldon's sojourn at the farm, Claude was sent to the Temple College. Claude had come to believe that the things and people he most disliked were the ones that were to shape his destiny.

When the second week of September came round, he threw a few clothes and books into his trunk and said good-bye to his mother and Mahailey. Ralph took him into Frankfort to catch the train for Lincoln. After settling himself in the dirty day-coach, Claude fell to meditating upon his prospects. There was a Pullman car on the train, but to take a Pullman for a daylight journey was one of the things a Wheeler did not do.

Claude knew that he was going back to the wrong school, that he was wasting both time and money. He sneered at himself for his lack of spirit. If he had to do with strangers, he told himself, he could take up his case and fight for it. He could not assert himself against his father or mother, but he could be bold enough with the rest of the world. Yet, if this were true, why did he continue to live with the tiresome Chapins?

The Chapin household consisted of a brother and sister. Edward Chapin was a man of twenty-six, with an old, wasted face,—and he was still going to school, studying for the ministry. His sister Annabelle kept house for him; that is to say, she did whatever housework was done. The brother supported himself and his sister by getting odd jobs from churches and religious societies; he "supplied" the pulpit when a minister was ill,

29

did secretarial work for the college and the Young Men's Christian Association. Claude's weekly payment for room and board, though a small sum, was very necessary to their comfort.

Chapin had been going to the Temple College for four years, and it would probably take him two years more to complete the course. He conned his book on trolley-cars, or while he waited by the track on windy corners, and studied far into the night. His natural stupidity must have been something quite out of the ordinary; after years of reverential study, he could not read the Greek Testament without a lexicon and grammar at his elbow. He gave a great deal of time to the practise of elocution and oratory. At certain hours their frail domicile—it had been thinly built for the academic poor and sat upon concrete blocks in lieu of a foundation—re-echoed with his hoarse, overstrained voice, declaiming his own orations or those of Wendell Phillips.

Annabelle Chapin was one of Claude's classmates. She was not as dull as her brother; she could learn a conjugation and recognize the forms when she met with them again. But she was a gushing, silly girl, who found almost everything in their grubby life too good to be true; and she was, unfortunately, sentimental about Claude. Annabelle chanted her lessons over and over to herself while she cooked and scrubbed. She was one of those people who can make the finest things seem tame and flat merely by alluding to them. Last winter she had recited the odes of Horace about the house—it was exactly her notion of the student-like thing to do— until Claude feared he would always associate that poet with the heaviness of hurriedly prepared luncheons.

Mrs. Wheeler liked to feel that Claude was assisting this worthy pair in their struggle for an education; but he had long ago decided that since neither of the Chapins got anything out of their efforts but a kind of messy inefficiency, the struggle might better have been relinquished in the beginning. He took care of his own room; kept it bare and habitable, free from Annabelle's attentions and decorations. But the flimsy pretences of light-housekeeping were very distasteful to him. He was born with a love of order, just as he was born with red hair. It was a personal attribute.

The boy felt bitterly about the way in which he had been brought up, and about his hair and his freckles and his awkwardness. When he went to the theatre in Lincoln, he took a seat in the gallery, because he knew that he looked like a green country boy. His clothes were never right. He bought collars that were too high and neckties that were too bright, and hid them away in his trunk. His one experiment with a tailor was unsuccessful. The tailor saw at once that his stammering client didn't know what he wanted, so he persuaded him that as the season was spring he needed light checked trousers and a blue serge coat and vest. When Claude wore his new clothes to St. Paul's church on Sunday morning, the eyes of every one he met followed his smart legs down the street. For the next week he observed the legs of old men and young, and decided there wasn't another pair of checked pants in Lincoln. He hung his new clothes up in his closet and never put them on again, though Annabelle Chapin watched for them wistfully.

Nevertheless, Claude thought he could recognize a well-dressed man when he saw one. He even thought he could recognize a well-dressed woman. If an attractive woman got into the street car when he was on his way to or from Temple Place, he was distracted between the desire to look at her and the wish to seem indifferent.

Claude is on his way back to Lincoln, with a fairly liberal allowance which does not contribute much to his comfort or pleasure. He has no friends or instructors whom he can regard with admiration, though the need to admire is just now uppermost in his nature. He is convinced that the people who might mean something to him will always misjudge him and pass him by. He is not so much afraid of loneliness as he is of accepting cheap substitutes; of making excuses to himself for a teacher who flatters him, of waking up some morning to find himself admiring a girl merely because she is accessible. He has a dread of easy compromises, and he is terribly afraid of being fooled.

VI

THREE months later, on a grey December day, Claude was seated in the passenger coach of an accommodation freight train, going home for the holidays. He had a pile of books on the seat beside him and was reading, when the train stopped with a jerk that sent the volumes tumbling to the floor. He picked them up and looked at his watch. It was noon. The freight would lie here for an hour or more, until the east-bound passenger went by. Claude left the car and walked slowly up the platform toward the station. A bundle of little spruce, trees had been flung off near the freight office, and sent a smell of Christmas into the cold air. A few drays stood about, the horses blanketed. The steam from the locomotive made a spreading, deep-violet stain as it curled up against the grey sky.

Claude went into a restaurant across the street and ordered an oyster stew. The proprietress, a plump little German woman with a frizzed bang, always remembered him from trip to trip. While he was eating his oysters she told him that she had just finished roasting a chicken with sweet potatoes, and if he liked he could have the first brown cut off the breast before the trainmen came in for dinner. Asking her to bring it along, he waited, sitting on a stool, his boots on the lead-pipe foot-rest, his elbows on the shiny brown counter, staring at a pyramid of tough looking bun-sandwiches under a glass globe.

"I been lookin' for you every day," said Mrs. Voigt when she brought his plate. "I put plenty good gravy on dem sweet pertaters, ja."

"Thank you. You must be popular with your boarders."

She giggled. "Ja, all de train men is friends mit me. Sometimes dey bring me a liddle *Sweitzerkase* from one of dem big saloons in Omaha what de Cherman beobles batronize. I ain't got no boys mein own self, so I got to fix up liddle tings for dem boys, eh?"

She stood nursing her stumpy hands under her apron, watching every mouthful he ate so eagerly that she might have been tasting it herself. The train crew trooped in, shouting to her and asking what there was for dinner, and she ran about like an excited little hen, chuckling and cackling. Claude wondered whether working-men were as nice as that to old women the world over. He didn't believe so. He liked to think that such geniality was common only in what he broadly called "the West." He bought a big cigar, and strolled up and down the platform, enjoying the fresh air until the passenger whistled in.

After his freight train got under steam he did not open his books again, but sat looking out at the grey homesteads as they unrolled before him, with their stripped, dry cornfields, and the great ploughed stretches where the winter wheat was asleep. A starry sprinkling of snow lay like hoar-frost along the crumbly ridges between the furrows.

Claude believed he knew almost every farm between Frankfort and Lincoln, he had made the journey so often, on fast trains and slow. He went home for all the holidays, and had been again and again called back on various pretexts; when his mother was sick, when Ralph overturned the car and broke his shoulder, when his father was kicked by a vicious stallion. It was not a Wheeler custom to employ a nurse; if any one in the household was ill, it was understood that some member of the family would act in that capacity.

Claude was reflecting upon the fact that he had never gone home before in such good spirits. Two fortunate things had happened to him since he went over this road three months ago.

As soon as he reached Lincoln in September, he had matriculated at the State University for special work in European History. The year before he had heard the head of the department lecture for some charity, and resolved that even if he were not allowed to change his college, he would manage to study under that man. The course Claude selected was one upon which a student could put as much time as he chose. It was based upon the reading of historical sources, and the Professor was notoriously greedy for full notebooks. Claude's were of the fullest. He worked early and late at the University Library, often got his supper in town and went back to read until closing hour. For the first time he was studying a subject which seemed to him vital, which had to do with events and ideas, instead of with lexicons and grammars. How often he had wished for Ernest during the lectures! He could see Ernest drinking them up, agreeing or dissenting in his independent way. The class was very large, and the Professor spoke without notes, — he talked rapidly, as if he were addressing his equals, with none of the coaxing persuasiveness to which Temple students were accustomed. His lectures were condensed like a legal brief, but there was a kind of dry fervour in his voice, and when he occasionally interrupted his exposition with purely personal comment, it seemed valuable and important.

Claude usually came out from these lectures with the feeling that the world was full of stimulating things, and that one was fortunate to be alive and to be able to find out about them. His reading that autumn actually made the future look brighter to him; seemed to promise him something. One of his chief difficulties had always been that he could not make himself believe in the importance of making money or spending it. If that were all, then life was not worth the trouble.

The second good thing that had befallen him was that he had got to know some people he liked. This came about accidentally, after a football game between the Temple eleven and the State University team—merely a practice game for the latter. Claude was playing half-back with the Temple. Toward the close of the first quarter, he followed his interference safely around the right end, dodged a tackle which threatened to end the play, and broke loose for a ninety-yard run down the field

for a touchdown. He brought his eleven off with a good showing. The State men congratulated him warmly, and their coach
went so far as to hint that if he ever wanted to make a change,
there would be a place for him on the University team.

Claude had a proud moment, but even while coach Ballinger
was talking to him, the Temple students rushed howling from
the grandstand, and Annabelle Chapin, ridiculous in a sport suit
of her own construction, bedecked with the Temple colours and
blowing a child's horn, positively threw herself upon his neck.
He disengaged himself, not very gently, and stalked grimly away
to the dressing shed. . . . What was the use, if you were always
with the wrong crowd?

Julius Erlich, who played quarter on the State team, took him
aside and said affably: "Come home to supper with me tonight,
Wheeler, and meet my mother. Come along with us and dress in
the Armory. You have your clothes in your suitcase, haven't you?"

"They're hardly clothes to go visiting in," Claude replied
doubtfully.

"Oh, that doesn't matter! We're all boys at home. Mother
wouldn't mind if you came in your track things."

Claude consented before he had time to frighten himself by
imagining difficulties. The Erlich boy often sat next him in the
history class, and they had several times talked together.
Hitherto Claude had felt that he "couldn't make Erlich out,"
but this afternoon, while they dressed after their shower, they
became good friends, all in a few minutes. Claude was perhaps
less tied-up in mind and body than usual. He was so astonished
at finding himself on easy, confidential terms with Erlich that
he scarcely gave a thought to his second-day shirt and his collar
with a broken edge, — wretched economies he had been
trained to observe.

They had not walked more than two blocks from the Armory
when Julius turned in at a rambling wooden house with an
unfenced, terraced lawn. He led Claude around to the wing, and
through a glass door into a big room that was all windows on
three sides, above the wainscoting. The room was full of boys

and young men, seated on long divans or perched on the arms of easy chairs, and they were all talking at once. On one of the couches a young man in a smoking jacket lay reading as composedly as if he were alone.

"Five of these are my brothers," said his host, "and the rest are friends."

The company recognized Claude and inducted him in their talk about the game. When the visitors had gone, Julius introduced his brothers. They were all nice boys, Claude thought, and had easy, agreeable manners. The three older ones were in business, but they too had been to the game that afternoon. Claude had never before seen brothers who were so outspoken and frank with one another. To him they were very cordial; the one who was lying down came forward to shake hands, keeping the place in his book with his finger.

On a table in the middle of the room were pipes and boxes of tobacco, cigars in a glass jar, and a big Chinese bowl full of cigarettes. This provisionment seemed the more remarkable to Claude because at home he had to smoke in the cowshed. The number of books astonished him almost as much; the wainscoting all around the room was built up in open bookcases, stuffed with volumes fat and thin, and they all looked interesting and hard-used. One of the brothers had been to a party the night before, and on coming home had put his dress-tie about the neck of a little plaster bust of Byron that stood on the mantel. This head, with the tie at a rakish angle, drew Claude's attention more than anything else in the room, and for some reason instantly made him wish he lived there.

Julius brought in his mother, and when they went to supper Claude was seated beside her at one end of the long table. Mrs. Erlich seemed to him very young to be the head of such a family. Her hair was still brown, and she wore it drawn over her ears and twisted in two little horns, like the ladies in old daguerreotypes. Her face, too, suggested a daguerreotype; there was something old-fashioned and picturesque about it. Her skin had the soft whiteness of white flowers that have been drenched by rain. She talked with quick gestures, and her decided little nod was quaint and very personal. Her hazel-coloured eyes peered expectantly over her nose-glasses, always watching to see things turn out wonderfully well; always looking for some good German fairy in the cupboard or the cake-box, or in the steaming vapor of wash-day.

The boys were discussing an engagement that had just been announced, and Mrs. Erlich began to tell Claude a long story about how this brilliant young man had come to Lincoln and met this beautiful young girl, who was already engaged to a cold and academic youth, and how after many heart-burnings the beautiful girl had broken with the wrong man and become betrothed to the right one, and now they were so happy,—and every one, she asked Claude to believe, was equally happy! In the middle of her narrative Julius reminded her smilingly that since Claude didn't know these people, he would hardly be interested in their romance, but she merely looked at him over her nose-glasses and said, "And is that so, Herr Julius!" One could see that she was a match for them.

The conversation went racing from one thing to another. The brothers began to argue hotly about a new girl who was visiting in town; whether she was pretty, how pretty she was, whether she was naive. To Claude this was like talk in a play. He had never heard a living person discussed and analysed thus before. He had never heard a family talk so much, or with anything like so much zest. Here there was none of the poisonous reticence he had always associated with family gatherings, nor the awkwardness of people sitting with their hands in their lap, facing each other, each one guarding his secret or his suspicion, while he hunted for a safe subject to talk about. Their fertility of phrase, too, astonished him; how could people find so much to say about one girl? To be sure, a good deal of it sounded far-fetched to him, but he sadly admitted that in such matters he was no judge.

When they went back to the living room Julius began to pick out airs on his guitar, and the bearded brother sat down to read. Otto, the youngest, seeing a group of students passing the house, ran out on to the lawn and called them in,—two boys, and a girl with red cheeks and a fur stole. Claude had made for a corner, and was perfectly content to be an on-looker, but Mrs. Erlich soon came and seated herself beside him. When the doors into the parlour were opened, she noticed his eyes straying to an engraving of Napoleon which hung over the piano, and made him go and look at it. She told him it was a rare engraving, and she showed him a portrait of her great-grandfather, who was an officer in Napoleon's army. To explain how this came about was a long story.

As she talked to Claude, Mrs. Erlich discovered that his eyes were not really pale, but only looked so because of his light lashes. They could say a great deal when they looked squarely into hers, and she liked what they said. She soon found out that he was discontented; how he hated the Temple school, and why his mother wished him to go there.

When the three who had been called in from the sidewalk took their leave, Claude rose also. They were evidently familiars of the house, and their careless exit, with a gay "Good-night, everybody!" gave him no practical suggestion as to what he ought to say or how he was to get out. Julius made things more difficult by telling him to sit down, as it wasn't time to go yet. But Mrs. Erlich said it was time; he would have a long ride out to Temple Place.

It was really very easy. She walked to the door with him and gave him his hat, patting his arm in a final way. "You will come often to see us. We are going to be friends." Her forehead, with its neat curtains of brown hair, came something below Claude's chin, and she peered up at him with that quaintly hopeful expression, as if—as if even he might turn out wonderfully well! Certainly, nobody had ever looked at him like that before.

"It's been lovely," he murmured to her, quite without embarrassment, and in happy unconsciousness he turned the knob and passed out through the glass door.

While the freight train was puffing slowly across the winter country, leaving a black trail suspended in the still air, Claude went over that experience minutely in his mind, as if he feared to lose something of it on approaching home. He could remember exactly how Mrs. Erlich and the boys had looked to him on that first night, could repeat almost word for word the conversation which had been so novel to him. Then he had supposed the Erlichs were rich people, but he found out afterwards that they were poor. The father was dead, and all the boys had to work, even those who were still in school. They merely knew how to live, he discovered, and spent their money on themselves, instead of on machines to do the work and machines to entertain people. Machines, Claude decided, could not make pleasure, whatever else they could do. They could not make agreeable people, either. In so far as he could see, the latter were made by judicious indulgence in almost everything he had been taught to shun.

Since that first visit, he had gone to the Erlichs', not as often as he wished, certainly, but as often as he dared. Some of the University boys seemed to drop in there whenever they felt like it, were almost members of the family; but they were better looking than he, and better company. To be sure, long Baumgartner was an intimate of the house, and he was a gawky boy with big red hands and patched shoes; but he could at least speak German to the mother, and he played the piano, and seemed to know a great deal about music.

Claude didn't wish to be a bore. Sometimes in the evening, when he left the Library to smoke a cigar, he walked slowly past the Erlichs' house, looking at the lighted windows of the sitting-room and wondering what was going on inside. Before he went there to call, he racked his brain for things to talk about. If there had been a football game, or a good play at the theatre, that helped, of course.

Almost without realizing what he was doing, he tried to think things out and to justify his opinions to himself, so that he would have something to say when the Erlich boys questioned him. He had grown up with the conviction that it was beneath his dignity to explain himself, just as it was to dress carefully, or to be caught taking pains about anything. Ernest was the only person he knew who tried to state clearly just why he believed this or that; and people at home thought him very conceited and foreign. It wasn't American to explain yourself; you didn't have to! On the farm you said you would or you wouldn't; that Roosevelt was all right, or that he was crazy. You weren't supposed to say more unless you were a stump speaker,—if you tried to say more, it was because you liked to hear yourself talk. Since you never said anything, you didn't form the habit of thinking. If you got too much bored, you went to town and bought something new.

But all the people he met at the Erlichs' talked. If they asked him about a play or a book and he said it was "no good," they at once demanded why. The Erlichs thought him a clam, but Claude sometimes thought himself amazing. Could it really be he, who was airing his opinions in this indelicate manner? He caught himself using words that had never crossed his lips before, that in his mind were associated only with the printed page. When he suddenly realized that he was using a word for the first time, and probably mispronouncing it, he would become as much confused as if he were trying to pass a lead dollar, would blush and stammer and let some one finish his sentence for him.

Claude couldn't resist occasionally dropping in at the Erlichs' in the afternoon; then the boys were away, and he could have Mrs. Erlich to himself for half-an-hour. When she talked to him she taught him so much about life. He loved to hear her sing sentimental German songs as she worked; *"Spinn, spinn, du Tochter mein."* He didn't know why, but he simply adored it! Every time he went away from her he felt happy and full of kindness, and thought about beechwoods and walled towns, or about Carl Schurz and the Romantic revolution.

He had been to see Mrs. Erlich just before starting home for the holidays, and found her making German Christmas cakes. She took him into the kitchen and explained the almost holy traditions that governed this complicated cookery. Her excitement and seriousness as she beat and stirred were very pretty, Claude thought. She told off on her fingers the many ingredients, but he believed there were things she did not name: the fragrance of old friendships, the glow of early memories, belief in wonder-working rhymes and songs. Surely these were fine things to put into little cakes! After Claude left her, he did something a Wheeler didn't do; he went down to O street and sent her a box of the reddest roses he could find. In his pocket was the little note she had written to thank him.

VII

It was beginning to grow dark when Claude reached the farm. While Ralph stopped to put away the car, he walked on alone to the house. He never came back without emotion,—try as he would to pass lightly over these departures and returns which were all in the day's work. When he came up the hill like this, toward the tall house with its lighted windows, something always clutched at his heart. He both loved and hated to come home. He was always disappointed, and yet he always felt the rightness of returning to his own place. Even when it broke his spirit and humbled his pride, he felt it was right that he should be thus humbled. He didn't question that the lowest state of mind was the truest, and that the less a man thought of himself, the more likely he was to be correct in his estimate.

Approaching the door, Claude stopped a moment and peered in at the kitchen window. The table was set for supper, and Mahailey was at the stove, stirring something in a big iron pot; cornmeal mush, probably,—she often made it for herself now that her teeth had begun to fail. She stood leaning over, embracing the pot with one arm, and with the other she beat the stiff contents, nodding her head in time to this rotary movement. Confused emotions surged up in Claude. He went in quickly and gave her a bearish hug.

Her face wrinkled up in the foolish grin he knew so well. "Lord, how you scared me, Mr. Claude! A little more'n I'd 'a' had my mush all over the floor. You lookin' fine, you nice boy, you!"

He knew Mahailey was gladder to see him come home than any one except his mother. Hearing Mrs. Wheeler's wandering, uncertain steps in the enclosed stairway, he opened the door and ran halfway up to meet her, putting his arm about her with the almost painful tenderness he always felt, but seldom was at liberty to show. She reached up both hands and stroked his hair for a moment, laughing as one does to a little boy, and telling him she believed it was redder every time he came back.

"Have we got all the corn in, Mother?"

"No, Claude, we haven't. You know we're always behind-hand. It's been fine, open weather for husking, too. But at least we've got rid of that miserable Jerry; so there's something to be thankful for. He had one of his fits of temper in town one day, when he was hitching up to come home, and Leonard Dawson saw him beat one of our horses with the neck-yoke. Leonard told your father, and spoke his mind, and your father discharged Jerry. If you or Ralph had told him, he most likely wouldn't have done anything about it. But I guess all fathers are the same." She chuckled confidingly, leaning on Claude's arm as they descended the stairs.

"I guess so. Did he hurt the horse much? Which one was it?"

"The little black, Pompey. I believe he is rather a mean horse. The men said one of the bones over the eye was broken, but he would probably come round all right."

"Pompey isn't mean; he's nervous. All the horses hated Jerry, and they had good reason to." Claude jerked his shoulders to shake off disgusting recollections of this mongrel man which flashed back into his mind. He had seen things happen in the barn that he positively couldn't tell his father.

Mr. Wheeler came into the kitchen and stopped on his way upstairs long enough to say, "Hello, Claude. You look pretty well."

"Yes, sir. I'm all right, thank you."

"Bayliss tells me you've been playing football a good deal."

"Not more than usual. We played half a dozen games; generally got licked. The State has a fine team, though."

"I ex-pect," Mr. Wheeler drawled as he strode upstairs.

Supper went as usual. Dan kept grinning and blinking at Claude, trying to discover whether he had already been informed of Jerry's fate. Ralph told him the neighbourhood gossip: Gus Yoeder, their German neighbour, was bringing suit against a farmer who had shot his dog. Leonard Dawson was going to marry Susie Grey. She was the girl on whose account Leonard had slapped Bayliss, Claude remembered.

After supper Ralph and Mr. Wheeler went off in the car to a Christmas entertainment at the country schoolhouse. Claude and his mother sat down for a quiet talk by the hard-coal burner in the living room upstairs. Claude liked this room, especially when his father was not there. The old carpet, the faded chairs, the secretary book-case, the spotty engraving with all the scenes from Pilgrim's Progress that hung over the sofa, — these things made him feel at home. Ralph was always proposing to refurnish the room in Mission oak, but so far Claude and his mother had saved it.

Claude drew up his favourite chair and began to tell Mrs. Wheeler about the Erlich boys and their mother. She listened, but he could see that she was much more interested in hearing about the Chapins, and whether Edward's throat had improved, and where he had preached this fall. That was one of the disappointing things about coming home; he could never interest his mother in new things or people unless they in some way had to do with the church. He knew, too, she was always hoping to hear that he at last felt the need of coming closer to the church. She did not harass him about these things, but she had told him once or twice that nothing could happen in the world which would give her so much pleasure as to see him reconciled to Christ. He realized, as he talked to her about the Erlichs, that she was wondering whether they weren't very "worldly" people, and was apprehensive about their influence on him. The evening was rather a failure, and he went to bed early.

Claude had gone through a painful time of doubt and fear when he thought a great deal about religion. For several years, from fourteen to eighteen, he believed that he would be lost if he did not repent and undergo that mysterious change called conversion. But there was something stubborn in him that would not let him avail himself of the pardon offered. He felt condemned, but he did not want to renounce a world he as yet knew nothing of. He would like to go into life with all his vigour, with all his faculties free. He didn't want to be like the young men who said in prayer-meeting that they leaned on their Saviour. He hated their way of meekly accepting permitted pleasures.

In those days Claude had a sharp physical fear of death. A funeral, the sight of a neighbour lying rigid in his black coffin, overwhelmed him with terror. He used to lie awake in the dark, plotting against death, trying to devise some plan of escaping it, angrily wishing he had never been born. Was there no way out of the world but this? When he thought of the millions of lonely creatures rotting away under ground, life seemed nothing but a trap that caught people for one horrible end. There had never been a man so strong or so good that he had escaped. And yet he sometimes felt sure that he, Claude Wheeler, would escape; that he would actually invent some clever shift to save himself from dissolution. When he found it, he would tell nobody; he would be crafty and secret. Putrefaction, decay. . . . He could not give his pleasant, warm body over to that filthiness! What did it mean, that verse in the Bible, "He shall not suffer His holy one to see corruption"?

If anything could cure an intelligent boy of morbid religious fears, it was a denominational school like that to which Claude had been sent. Now he dismissed all Christian theology as something too full of evasions and sophistries to be reasoned about. The men who made it, he felt sure, were like the men who taught it. The noblest could be damned, according to their theory, while almost any mean-spirited parasite could be saved by faith. "Faith," as he saw it exemplified in the faculty of the Temple school, was a substitute for most of the manly qualities he admired. Young men went into the ministry because they were timid or lazy and wanted society to take care of them; because they wanted to be pampered by kind, trusting women like his mother.

Though he wanted little to do with theology and theologians, Claude would have said that he was a Christian. He believed in God, and in the spirit of the four Gospels, and in the Sermon on the Mount. He used to halt and stumble at, "Blessed are the meek," until one day he happened to think that this verse was meant exactly for people like Mahailey; and surely she was blessed!

VIII

ON the Sunday after Christmas Claude and Ernest were walking along the banks of Lovely Creek. They had been as far as Mr. Wheeler's timber claim and back. It was like an autumn afternoon, so warm that they left their overcoats on the limb of a crooked elm by the pasture fence. The fields and the bare tree-tops seemed to be swimming in light. A few brown leaves still clung to the bushy trees along the creek. In the upper pasture, more than a mile from the house, the boys found a bittersweet vine that wound about a little dogwood and covered it with scarlet berries. It was like finding a Christmas tree growing wild out of doors. They had just been talking about some of the books Claude had brought home, and his history course. He was not able to tell Ernest as much about the lectures as he had meant to, and he felt that this was more Ernest's fault than his own; Ernest was such a literal-minded fellow. When they came upon the bittersweet, they forgot their discussion and scrambled down the bank to admire the red clusters on the woody, smoke-coloured vine, and its pale gold leaves, ready to fall at a touch. The vine and the little tree it honoured, hidden away in the cleft of a ravine, had escaped the stripping winds, and the eyes of schoolchildren who sometimes took a short cut home through the pasture. At its roots, the creek trickled thinly along, black between two jagged crusts of melting ice.

When they left the spot and climbed back to the level, Claude again felt an itching to prod Ernest out of his mild and reasonable mood.

"What are you going to do after a while, Ernest? Do you mean to farm all your life?"

"Naturally. If I were going to learn a trade, I'd be at it before now. What makes you ask that?"

"Oh, I don't know! I suppose people must think about the future sometime. And you're so practical."

"The future, eh?" Ernest shut one eye and smiled. "That's a big word. After I get a place of my own and have a good start, I'm going home to see my old folks some winter. Maybe I'll marry a nice girl and bring her back."

"Is that all?"

"That's enough, if it turns out right, isn't it?"

"Perhaps. It wouldn't be for me. I don't believe I can ever settle down to anything. Don't you feel that at this rate there isn't much in it?"

"In what?"

"In living at all, going on as we do. What do we get out of it? Take a day like this: you waken up in the morning and you're glad to be alive; it's a good enough day for anything, and you feel sure something will happen. Well, whether it's a workday or a holiday, it's all the same in the end. At night you go to bed — nothing has happened."

"But what do you expect? What can happen to you, except in your own mind? If I get through my work, and get an afternoon off to see my friends like this, it's enough for me."

"Is it? Well, if we've only got once to live, it seems like there ought to be something—well, something splendid about life, sometimes."

Ernest was sympathetic now. He drew nearer to Claude as they walked along and looked at him sidewise with concern. "You Americans are always looking for something outside yourselves to warm you up, and it is no way to do. In old countries, where not very much can happen to us, we know that,—and we learn to make the most of little things."

"The martyrs must have found something outside themselves. Otherwise they could have made themselves comfortable with little things."

"Why, I should say they were the ones who had nothing but their idea! It would be ridiculous to get burned at the stake for the sensation. Sometimes I think the martyrs had a good deal of vanity to help them along, too."

Claude thought Ernest had never been so tiresome. He squinted at a bright object across the fields and said cuttingly, "The fact is, Ernest, you think a man ought to be satisfied with his board and clothes and Sundays off, don't you?"

Ernest laughed rather mournfully. "It doesn't matter much what I think about it; things are as they are. Nothing is going to reach down from the sky and pick a man up, I guess."

Claude muttered something to himself, twisting his chin about over his collar as if, he had a bridle-bit in his mouth.

The sun had dropped low, and the two boys, as Mrs. Wheeler watched them from the kitchen window, seemed to be walking beside a prairie fire. She smiled as she saw their black figures moving along on the crest of the hill against the golden sky; even at that distance the one looked so adaptable, and the other so unyielding. They were arguing, probably, and probably Claude was on the wrong side.

IX

AFTER the vacation Claude again settled down to his reading in the University Library. He worked at a table next the alcove where the books on painting and sculpture were kept. The art students, all of whom were girls, read and whispered together in this enclosure, and he could enjoy their company without having to talk to them. They were lively and friendly; they often asked him to lift heavy books and portfolios from the shelves, and greeted him gaily when he met them in the street or on the campus, and talked to him with the easy cordiality usual between boys and girls in a co-educational school. One of these girls, Miss Peachy Millmore, was different from the others, — different from any girl Claude had ever known. She came from Georgia, and was spending the winter with her aunt on B street.

Although she was short and plump, Miss Millmore moved with what might be called a "carriage," and she had altogether more manner and more reserve than the Western girls. Her hair was yellow and curly, — the short ringlets about her ears were just the colour of a new chicken. Her vivid blue eyes were a trifle too prominent, and a generous blush of colour mantled her cheeks. It seemed to pulsate there, — one had a desire to touch her cheeks to see if they were hot. The Erlich brothers and their friends called her "the Georgia peach." She was considered very pretty, and the University boys had rushed her when she first came to town. Since then her vogue had somewhat declined.

Miss Millmore often lingered about the campus to walk down town with Claude. However he tried to adapt his long stride to her tripping gait, she was sure to get out of breath. She was always dropping her gloves or her sketchbook or her purse, and he liked to pick them up for her, and to pull on her rubbers, which kept slipping off at the heel. She was very kind to single him out and be so gracious to him, he thought. She even coaxed him to pose in his track clothes for the life class on Saturday morning, telling him that he had "a magnificent physique," a compliment which covered him with confusion. But he posed, of course.

Claude looked forward to seeing Peachy Millmore, missed her if she were not in the alcove, found it quite natural that she should explain her absences to him, — tell him how often she washed her hair and how long it was when she uncoiled it.

One Friday in February Julius Erlich overtook Claude on the campus and proposed that they should try the skating tomorrow.

"Yes, I'm going out," Claude replied. "I've promised to teach Miss Millmore to skate. Won't you come along and help me?"

Julius laughed indulgently. "Oh, no! Some other time. I don't want to break in on that."

"Nonsense! You could teach her better than I."

"Oh, I haven't the courage!"

"What do you mean?"

"You know what I mean."

"No, I don't. Why do you always laugh about that girl, anyhow?"

Julius made a little grimace. "She wrote some awfully slushy letters to Phil Bowen, and he read them aloud at the frat house one night."

"Didn't you slap him?" Claude demanded, turning red.

"Well, I would have thought I would," said Julius smiling, "but I didn't. They were too silly to make a fuss about. I've been wary of the Georgia peach ever since. If you touched that sort of peach ever so lightly, it might remain in your hand."

"I don't think so," replied Claude haughtily. "She's only kind-hearted."

"Perhaps you're right. But I'm terribly afraid of girls who are too kind-hearted," Julius confessed. He had wanted to drop Claude a word of warning for some time.

Claude kept his engagement with Miss Millmore. He took her out to the skating pond several times, indeed, though in the beginning he told her he feared her ankles were too weak. Their last excursion was made by moonlight, and after that evening Claude avoided Miss Millmore when he could do so without being rude. She was attractive to him no more. It was her way to subdue by clinging contact. One could scarcely call it design; it was a degree less subtle than that. She had already thus subdued a pale cousin in Atlanta, and it was on this account that she had been sent North. She had, Claude angrily admitted, no reserve, —though when one first met her she seemed to have so much. Her eager susceptibility presented not the slightest temptation to him. He was a boy with strong impulses, and he detested the idea of trifling with them. The talk of the disreputable men his father kept about the place at home, instead of corrupting him, had given him a sharp disgust for sensuality. He had an almost Hippolytean pride in candour.

X

THE Elrich family loved anniversaries, birthdays, occasions. That spring Mrs. Erlich's first cousin, Wilhelmina Schroeder-Schatz, who sang with the Chicago Opera Company, came to Lincoln as soloist for the May Festival. As the date of her engagement approached, her relatives began planning to entertain her. The Matinée Musical was to give a formal reception for the singer, so the Erlichs decided upon a dinner. Each member of the family invited one guest, and they had great difficulty in deciding which of their friends would be most appreciative of the honour. There were to be more men than women, because Mrs. Erlich remembered that cousin Wilhelmina had never been partial to the society of her own sex.

One evening when her sons were revising their list, Mrs. Erlich reminded them that she had not as yet named her guest. "For me," she said with decision, "you may put down Claude Wheeler."

This announcement was met with groans and laughter.

"You don't mean it, Mother," the oldest son protested. "Poor old Claude wouldn't know what it was all about,—and one stick can spoil a dinner party."

Mrs. Erlich shook her finger at him with conviction. "You will see; your cousin Wilhelmina will be more interested in that boy than in any of the others!"

Julius thought if she were not too strongly opposed she might still yield her point. "For one thing, Mother, Claude hasn't any dinner clothes," he murmured.

She nodded to him. "That has been attended to, Herr Julius. He is having some made. When I sounded him, he told me he could easily afford it."

The boys said if things had gone as far as that, they supposed they would have to make the best of it, and the eldest wrote down "Claude Wheeler" with a flourish.

If the Erlich boys were apprehensive, their anxiety was nothing to Claude's. He was to take Mrs. Erlich to Madame Schroeder-Schatz's recital, and on the evening of the concert, when he appeared at the door, the boys dragged him in to look him over. Otto turned on all the lights, and Mrs. Erlich, in her new black lace over white satin, fluttered into the parlour to see what figure her escort cut.

Claude pulled off his overcoat as he was bid, and presented himself in the sooty blackness of fresh broadcloth. Mrs. Erlich's eyes swept his long black legs, his smooth shoulders, and lastly his square red head, affectionately inclined toward her. She laughed and clapped her hands.

"Now all the girls will turn round in their seats to look, and wonder where I got him!"

Claude began to bestow her belongings in his overcoat pockets; opera glasses in one, fan in another. She put a lorgnette into her little bag, along with her powder-box, handkerchief and smelling salts,—there was even a little silver box of peppermint drops, in case she might begin to cough. She drew on her long gloves, arranged a lace scarf over her hair, and at last was ready to have the evening cloak which Claude held wound about her. When she reached up and took his arm, bowing to her sons, they laughed and liked Claude better. His steady, protecting air was a frame for the gay little picture she made.

The dinner party came off the next evening. The guest of honour, Madame Wilhelmina Schroeder-Schatz, was some years younger than her cousin, Augusta Erlich. She was short, stalwart, with an enormous chest, a fine head, and a commanding presence. Her great contralto voice, which she used without much discretion, was a really superb organ and gave people a pleasure as substantial as food and drink. At dinner she sat on the right of the oldest son. Claude, beside Mrs. Erlich at the other end of the table, watched attentively the lady attired in green velvet and blazing rhinestones.

After dinner, as Madame Schroeder-Schatz swept out of the dining room, she dropped her cousin's arm and stopped before Claude, who stood at attention behind his chair.

"If cousin Augusta can spare you, we must have a little talk together. We have been very far separated," she said.

She led Claude to one of the window seats in the living-room, at once complained of a draft, and sent him to hunt for her green scarf. He brought it and carefully put it about her shoulders; but after a few moments, she threw it off with a slightly annoyed air, as if she had never wanted it. Claude with solicitude reminded her about the draft.

"Draft?" she said lifting her chin, "there is no draft here."

She asked Claude where he lived, how much land his father owned, what crops they raised, and about their poultry and dairy. When she was a child she had lived on a farm in Bavaria, and she seemed to know a good deal about farming and live-stock. She was disapproving when Claude told her they rented half their land to other farmers. "If I were a young man, I would begin to acquire land, and I would not stop until I had a whole county," she declared. She said that when she met new people, she liked to find out the way they made their living; her own way was a hard one.

Later in the evening Madame Schroeder-Schatz graciously consented to sing for her cousins. When she sat down to the piano, she beckoned Claude and asked him to turn for her. He shook his head, smiling ruefully.

"I'm sorry I'm so stupid, but I don't know one note from another."

She tapped his sleeve. "Well, never mind. I may want the piano moved yet; you could do that for me, eh?"

When Madame Schroeder-Schatz was in Mrs. Erlich's bedroom, powdering her nose before she put on her wraps, she remarked, "What a pity, Augusta, that you have not a daughter now, to marry to Claude Melnotte. He would make you a perfect son-in-law."

"Ah, if I only had!" sighed Mrs. Erlich.

"Or," continued Madame Schroeder-Schatz, energetically pulling on her large carriage shoes, "if you were but a few years younger, it might not yet be too late. Oh, don't be a fool, Augusta! Such things have happened, and will happen again. However, better a widow than to be tied to a sick man—like a stone about my neck! What a husband to go home to! and I a woman in full vigour. *Das ist ein Kreuz ich trage!*" She smote her bosom, on the left side.

Having put on first a velvet coat, then a fur mantle, Madame Schroeder-Schatz moved like a galleon out into the living room and kissed all her cousins, and Claude Wheeler, good-night.

XI

ONE warm afternoon in May Claude sat in his upstairs room at the Chapins', copying his thesis, which was to take the place of an examination in history. It was a criticism of the testimony of Jeanne d'Arc in her nine private examinations and the trial in ordinary. The Professor had assigned him the subject with a flash of humour. Although this evidence had been pawed over by so many hands since the fifteenth century, by the phlegmatic and the fiery, by rhapsodists and cynics, he felt sure that Wheeler would not dismiss the case lightly.

Indeed, Claude put a great deal of time and thought upon the matter, and for the time being it seemed quite the most important thing in his life. He worked from an English translation of the Procès, but he kept the French text at his elbow, and some of her replies haunted him in the language in which they were spoken. It seemed to him that they were like the speech of her saints, of whom Jeanne said, *"the voice is beautiful, sweet and low, and it speaks in the French tongue."* Claude flattered himself that he had kept all personal feeling out of the paper; that it was a cold estimate of the girl's motives and character as indicated by the consistency and inconsistency of her replies; and of the change wrought in her by imprisonment and by "the fear of the fire."

When he had copied the last page of his manuscript and sat contemplating the pile of written sheets, he felt that after all his conscientious study he really knew very little more about the Maid of Orleans than when he first heard of her from his mother, one day when he was a little boy. He had been shut up in

57

the house with a cold, he remembered, and he found a picture of her in armour, in an old book, and took it down to the kitchen where his mother was making apple pies. She glanced at the picture, and while she went on rolling out the dough and fitting it to the pans, she told him the story. He had forgotten what she said,—it must have been very fragmentary,—but from that time on he knew the essential facts about Joan of Arc, and she was a living figure in his mind. She seemed to him then as clear as now, and now as miraculous as then.

It was a curious thing, he reflected, that a character could perpetuate itself thus; by a picture, a word, a phrase, it could renew itself in every generation and be born over and over again in the minds of children. At that time he had never seen a map of France, and had a very poor opinion of any place farther away than Chicago; yet he was perfectly prepared for the legend of Joan of Arc, and often thought about her when he was bringing in his cobs in the evening, or when he was sent to the windmill for water and stood shaking in the cold while the chilled pump brought it slowly up. He pictured her then very much as he did now; about her figure there gathered a luminous cloud, like dust, with soldiers in it . . . the banner with lilies . . . a great church . . . cities with walls.

On this balmy spring afternoon, Claude felt softened and reconciled to the world. Like Gibbon, he was sorry to have finished his labour,—and he could not see anything else as interesting ahead. He must soon be going home now. There would be a few examinations to sit through at the Temple, a few more evenings with the Erlichs, trips to the Library to carry back the books he had been using,—and then he would suddenly find himself with nothing to do but take the train for Frankfort.

He rose with a sigh and began to fasten his history papers between covers. Glancing out of the window, he decided that he would walk into town and carry his thesis, which was due today; the weather was too fine to sit bumping in a street car. The truth was, he wished to prolong his relations with his manuscript as far as possible.

He struck off by the road,—it could scarcely be called a street, since it ran across raw prairie land where the buffalo-peas were in blossom. Claude walked slower than was his custom, his straw hat pushed back on his head and the blaze of the sun full in his face. His body felt light in the scented wind, and he listened drowsily to the larks, singing on dried weeds and sunflower stalks. At this season their song is almost painful to hear, it is so sweet. He sometimes thought of this walk long afterward; it was memorable to him, though he could not say why.

On reaching the University, he went directly to the Department of European History, where he was to leave his thesis on a long table, with a pile of others. He rather dreaded this, and was glad when, just as he entered, the Professor came out from his private office and took the bound manuscript into his own hands, nodding cordially.

"Your thesis? Oh yes, Jeanne d'Arc. The Procès. I had forgotten. Interesting material, isn't it?" He opened the cover and ran over the pages. "I suppose you acquitted her on the evidence?"

Claude blushed. "Yes, sir."

"Well, now you might read what Michelet has to say about her. There's an old translation in the Library. Did you enjoy working on it?"

"I did, very much." Claude wished to heaven he could think of something to say.

"You've got a good deal out of your course, altogether, haven't you? I'll be interested to see what you do next year. Your work has been very satisfactory to me." The Professor went back into his study, and Claude was pleased to see that he carried the manuscript with him and did not leave it on the table with the others.

XII

BETWEEN haying and harvest that summer Ralph and Mr. Wheeler drove to Denver in the big car, leaving Claude and Dan to cultivate the corn. When they returned Mr. Wheeler announced that he had a secret. After several days of reticence, during which he shut himself up in the sitting-room writing letters, and passed mysterious words and winks with Ralph at table, he disclosed a project which swept away all Claude's plans and purposes.

On the return trip from Denver Mr. Wheeler had made a detour down into Yucca county, Colorado, to visit an old friend who was in difficulties. Tom Wested was a Maine man, from Wheeler's own neighbourhood. Several years ago he had lost his wife. Now his health had broken down, and the Denver doctors said he must retire from business and get into a low altitude. He wanted to go back to Maine and live among his own people, but was too much discouraged and frightened about his condition even to undertake the sale of his ranch and live stock. Mr. Wheeler had been able to help his friend, and at the same time did a good stroke of business for himself. He owned a farm in Maine, his share of his father's estate, which for years he had rented for little more than the up-keep. By making over this property, and assuming certain mortgages, he got Wested's fine, well-watered ranch in exchange. He paid him a good price for his cattle, and promised to take the sick man back to Maine and see him comfortably settled there.

All this Mr. Wheeler explained to his family when he called them up to the living room one hot, breathless night after supper. Mrs. Wheeler, who seldom concerned herself with her husband's business affairs, asked absently why they bought more land, when they already had so much they could not farm half of it.

"Just like a woman, Evangeline, just like a woman!" Mr. Wheeler replied indulgently. He was sitting in the full glare of the acetyline lamp, his neck-band open, his collar and tie on the table beside him, fanning himself with a palm-leaf fan. "You might as well ask me why I want to make more money, when I haven't spent all I've got."

He intended, he said, to put Ralph on the Colorado ranch and "give the boy some responsibility." Ralph would have the help of Wested's foreman, an old hand in the cattle business, who had agreed to stay on under the new management. Mr. Wheeler assured his wife that he wasn't taking advantage of poor Wested; the timber on the Maine place was really worth a good deal of money; but because his father had always been so proud of his great pine woods, he had never, he said, just felt like turning a sawmill loose in them. Now he was trading a pleasant old farm that didn't bring in anything for a grammar-grass ranch which ought to turn over a profit of ten or twelve thousand dollars in good cattle years, and wouldn't lose much in bad ones. He expected to spend about half his time out there with Ralph. "When I'm away," he remarked genially, "you and Mahailey won't have so much to do. You can devote yourselves to embroidery, so to speak."

"If Ralph is to live in Colorado, and you are to be away from home half of the time, I don't see what is to become of this place," murmured Mrs. Wheeler, still in the dark.

"Not necessary for you to see, Evangeline," her husband replied, stretching his big frame until the rocking chair creaked under him. "It will be Claude's business to look after that."

"Claude?" Mrs. Wheeler brushed a lock of hair back from her damp forehead in vague alarm.

"Of course." He looked with twinkling eyes at his son's straight, silent figure in the corner. "You've had about enough theology, I presume? No ambition to be a preacher? This winter I mean to turn the farm over to you and give you a chance to straighten things out. You've been dissatisfied with the way the place is run for some time, haven't you? Go ahead and put new blood into it. New ideas, if you want to; I've no objection. They're expensive, but let it go. You can fire Dan if you want, and get what help you need."

Claude felt as if a trap had been sprung on him. He shaded his eyes with his hand. "I don't think I'm competent to run the place right," he said unsteadily.

"Well, you don't think I am either, Claude, so we're up against it. It's always been my notion that the land was made for man, just as it's old Dawson's that man was created to work the land. I don't mind your siding with the Dawsons in this difference of opinion, if you can get their results."

Mrs. Wheeler rose and slipped quickly from the room, feeling her way down the dark staircase to the kitchen. It was dusky and quiet there. Mahailey sat in a corner, hemming dish-towels by the light of a smoky old brass lamp which was her own cherished luminary. Mrs. Wheeler walked up and down the long room in soft, silent agitation, both hands pressed tightly to her breast, where there was a physical ache of sympathy for Claude.

She remembered kind Tom Wested. He had stayed overnight with them several times, and had come to them for consolation after his wife died. It seemed to her that his decline in health and loss of courage, Mr. Wheeler's fortuitous trip to Denver, the old pine-wood farm in Maine, were all things that fitted together and made a net to envelop her unfortunate son. She knew that he had been waiting impatiently for the autumn, and that for the first time he looked forward eagerly to going back to school. He was homesick for his friends, the Erlichs, and his mind was all the time upon the history course he meant to take.

Yet all this would weigh nothing in the family councils—probably he would not even speak of it—and he had not one substantial objection to offer to his father's wishes. His disappointment would be bitter. "Why, it will almost break his heart," she murmured aloud. Mahailey was a little deaf and heard nothing. She sat holding her work up to the light, driving her needle with a big brass thimble, nodding with sleepiness between stitches. Though Mrs. Wheeler was scarcely conscious of it, the old woman's presence was a comfort to her, as she walked up and down with her drifting, uncertain step.

She had left the sitting-room because she was afraid Claude might get angry and say something hard to his father, and because she couldn't bear to see him hectored. Claude had always found life hard to live; he suffered so much over little things,—and she suffered with him. For herself, she never felt disappointments. Her husband's careless decisions did not disconcert her. If he declared that he would not plant a garden at all this year, she made no protest. It was Mahailey who grumbled. If he felt like eating roast beef and went out and killed a steer, she did the best she could to take care of the meat, and if some of it spoiled she tried not to worry. When she was not lost in religious meditation, she was likely to be thinking about some one of the old books she read over and over. Her personal life was so far removed from the scene of her daily activities that rash and violent men could not break in upon it. But where Claude was concerned, she lived on another plane,—dropped into the lower air, tainted with human breath and pulsating with poor, blind, passionate human feelings.

It had always been so. And now, as she grew older, and her flesh had almost ceased to be concerned with pain or pleasure, like the wasted wax images in old churches, it still vibrated with his feelings and became quick again for him. His chagrins shrivelled her. When he was hurt and suffered silently, something ached in her. On the other hand, when he was happy, a wave of physical contentment went through her. If she wakened in the night and happened to think that he had been happy lately, she would lie softly and gratefully in her warm place.

"Rest, rest perturbéd spirit," she sometimes whispered to him in her mind, when she wakened thus and thought of him. There was a singular light in his eyes when he smiled at her on one of his good days, as if to tell her that all was well in his inner kingdom. She had seen that same look again and again, and she could always remember it in the dark,—a quick blue flash, tender and a little wild, as if he had seen a vision or glimpsed bright uncertainties.

XIII

THE next few weeks were busy ones on the farm. Before the
wheat harvest was over, Nat Wheeler packed his leather trunk,
put on his "store clothes," and set off to take Tom Wested back
to Maine. During his absence Ralph began to outfit for life in
Yucca county. Ralph liked being a great man with the
Frankfort merchants, and he had never before had such an
opportunity as this. He bought a new shot gun, saddles, bri-
dles, boots, long and short storm coats, a set of furniture for
his own room, a fireless cooker, another music machine, and
had them shipped to Colorado. His mother, who did not like
phonograph music, and detested phonograph monologues,
begged him to take the machine at home, but he assured her
that she would be dull without it on winter evenings. He
wanted one of the latest make, put out under the name of a
great American inventor.

Some of the ranches near Wested's were owned by New
York men who brought their families out there in the summer. Ralph had heard about the dances they gave, and he
was counting on being one of the guests. He asked Claude to
give him his dress suit, since Claude wouldn't be needing
it any more.

"You can have it if you want it," said Claude indifferently. "But
it won't fit you."

"I'll take it in to Fritz and have the pants cut off a little, and
the shoulders taken in," his brother replied lightly.

Claude was impassive. "Go ahead. But if that old Dutchman takes a whack at it, it will look like the devil."

"I think I'll let him try. Father won't say anything about what I've ordered for the house, but he isn't much for glad rags, you know." Without more ado he threw Claude's black clothes into the back seat of the Ford and ran into town to enlist the services of the German tailor.

Mr. Wheeler, when he returned, thought Ralph had been rather free in expenditures, but Ralph told him it wouldn't do to take over the new place too modestly. "The ranchers out there are all high-fliers. If we go to squeezing nickels, they won't think we mean business."

The country neighbours, who were always amused at the Wheelers' doings, got almost as much pleasure out of Ralph's lavishness as he did himself. One said Ralph had shipped a new piano out to Yucca county, another heard he had ordered a billiard table. August Yoeder, their prosperous German neighbour, asked grimly whether he could, maybe, get a place as hired man with Ralph. Leonard Dawson, who was to be married in October, hailed Claude in town one day and shouted;

"My God, Claude, there's nothing left in the furniture store for me and Susie! Ralph's bought everything but the coffins. He must be going to live like a prince out there."

"I don't know anything about it," Claude answered coolly. "It's not my enterprise."

"No, you've got to stay on the old place and make it pay the debts, I understand." Leonard jumped into his car, so that Claude wouldn't have a chance to reply.

Mrs. Wheeler, too, when she observed the magnitude of these preparations, began to feel that the new arrangement was not fair to Claude, since he was the older boy and much the steadier. Claude had always worked hard when he was at home, and made a good field hand, while Ralph had never done much but tinker with machinery and run errands in his car. She couldn't understand why he was selected to manage an undertaking in which so much money was invested.

"Why, Claude," she said dreamily one day, "if your father were an older man, I would almost think his judgment had begun to fail. Won't we get dreadfully into debt at this rate?"

"Don't say anything, Mother. It's Father's money. He shan't think I want any of it."

"I wish I could talk to Bayliss. Has he said anything?"

"Not to me, he hasn't."

Ralph and Mr. Wheeler took another flying trip to Colorado, and when they came back Ralph began coaxing his mother to give him bedding and table linen. He said he wasn't going to live like a savage, even in the sand hills. Mahailey was outraged to see the linen she had washed and ironed and taken care of for so many years packed into boxes. She was out of temper most of the time now, and went about muttering to herself.

The only possessions Mahailey brought with her when she came to live with the Wheelers, were a feather bed and three patchwork quilts, interlined with wool off the backs of Virginia sheep, washed and carded by hand. The quilts had been made by her old mother, and given to her for a marriage portion. The patchwork on each was done in a different design; one was the popular "log-cabin" pattern, another the "laurel-leaf," the third the "blazing star." This quilt Mahailey thought too good for use, and she had told Mrs. Wheeler that she was saving it "to give Mr. Claude when he got married."

She slept on her feather bed in winter, and in summer she put it away in the attic. The attic was reached by a ladder, which, because of her weak back, Mrs. Wheeler very seldom climbed. Up there Mahailey had things her own way, and thither she often retired to air the bedding stored away there, or to look at the pictures in the piles of old magazines. Ralph facetiously called the attic "Mahailey's library."

One day, while things were being packed for the western ranch, Mrs. Wheeler, going to the foot of the ladder to call Mahailey, narrowly escaped being knocked down by a large feather bed which came plumping through the trap door. A moment later Mahailey herself descended backwards, holding to the rungs with one hand, and in the other arm carrying her quilts.

"Why, Mahailey," gasped Mrs. Wheeler. "It's not winter yet; whatever are you getting your bed for?"

"I'm just a-goin' to lay on my fedder bed," she broke out, "or direc'ly I won't have none. I ain't a-goin' to have Mr. Ralph carryin' off my quilts my mudder pieced fur me."

Mrs. Wheeler tried to reason with her, but the old woman took up her bed in her arms and staggered down the hall with it, muttering and tossing her head like a horse in fly-time.

That afternoon Ralph brought a barrel and a bundle of straw into the kitchen and told Mahailey to carry up preserves and canned fruit, and he would pack them. She went obediently to the cellar, and Ralph took off his coat and began to line the barrel with straw. He was some time in doing this, but still Mahailey had not returned. He went to the head of the stairs and whistled.

"I'm a-comin', Mr. Ralph, I'm a-comin'! Don't hurry me, I don't want to break nothin'."

Ralph waited a few minutes. "What are you doing down there, Mahailey?" he fumed. "I could have emptied the whole cellar by this time. I suppose I'll have to do it myself."

"I'm a-comin'. You'd git yourself all dusty down here." She came breathlessly up the stairs, carrying a hamper basket full of jars, her hands and face streaked with black.

"Well, I should say it is dusty!" Ralph snorted. "You might clean your fruit closet once in awhile, you know, Mahailey. You ought to see how Mrs. Dawson keeps hers. Now, let's see." He sorted the jars on the table. "Take back the grape jelly. If there's anything I hate, it's grape jelly. I know you have lots of it, but you can't work it off on me. And when you come up, don't forget the pickled peaches. I told you particularly, the pickled peaches!"

"We ain't got no pickled peaches." Mahailey stood by the cellar door, holding a corner of her apron up to her chin, with a queer, animal look of stubbornness in her face.

"No pickled peaches? What nonsense, Mahailey! I saw you making them here, only a few weeks ago."

"I know you did, Mr. Ralph, but they ain't none now. I didn't have no luck with my peaches this year. I must 'a' let the air git at 'em. They all worked on me, an' I had to throw 'em out."

Ralph was thoroughly annoyed. "I never heard of such a thing, Mahailey! You get more careless every year. Think of wasting all that fruit and sugar! Does mother know?"

Mahailey's low brow clouded. "I reckon she does. I don't wase your mudder's sugar. I never did wase nothin'," she muttered. Her speech became queerer than ever when she was angry.

Ralph dashed down the cellar stairs, lit a lantern, and searched the fruit closet. Sure enough, there were no pickled peaches. When he came back and began packing his fruit, Mahailey stood watching him with a furtive expression, very much like the look that is in a chained coyote's eyes when a boy is showing him off to visitors and saying he wouldn't run away if he could.

"Go on with your work," Ralph snapped. "Don't stand there watching me!"

That evening Claude was sitting on the windmill platform, down by the barn, after a hard day's work ploughing for winter wheat. He was solacing himself with his pipe. No matter how much she loved him, or how sorry she felt for him, his mother could never bring herself to tell him he might smoke in the house. Lights were shining from the upstairs rooms on the hill, and through the open windows sounded the singing snarl of a phonograph. A figure came stealing down the path. He knew by her low, padding step that it was Mahailey, with her apron thrown over her head. She came up to him and touched him on the shoulder in a way which meant that what she had to say was confidential.

"Mr. Claude, Mr. Ralph's done packed up a barr'l of your mudder's jelly an' pickles to take out there."

"That's all right, Mahailey. Mr. Wested was a widower, and I guess there wasn't anything of that sort put up at his place."

She hesitated and bent lower. "He asked me fur them pickled peaches I made fur you, but I didn't give him none. I hid 'em all in my old cook-stove we done put down cellar when Mr. Ralph

bought the new one. I didn't give him your mudder's new preserves, nudder. I give him the old last year's stuff we had left over,
and now you an' your mudder'll have plenty."

Claude laughed. "Oh, I don't care if Ralph takes all the fruit
on the place, Mahailey!"

She shrank back a little, saying confusedly, "No, I know you
don't, Mr. Claude. I know you don't."

"I surely ought not to take it out on her," Claude thought,
when he saw her disappointment. He rose and patted her on
the back. "That's all right, Mahailey. Thank you for saving
the peaches, anyhow."

She shook her finger at him. "Don't you let on!"

He promised, and watched her slipping back over the zigzag
path up the hill.

XIV

RALPH and his father moved to the new ranch the last of August, and Mr. Wheeler wrote back that late in the fall he meant to ship a carload of grass steers to the home farm to be fattened during the winter. This, Claude saw, would mean a need for fodder. There was a fifty-acre corn field west of the creek,—just on the sky-line when one looked out from the west windows of the house. Claude decided to put this field into winter wheat, and early in September he began to cut and bind the corn that stood upon it for fodder. As soon as the corn was gathered, he would plough up the ground, and drill in the wheat when he planted the other wheat fields.

This was Claude's first innovation, and it did not meet with approval. When Bayliss came out to spend Sunday with his mother, he asked her what Claude thought he was doing, anyhow. If he wanted to change the crop on that field, why didn't he plant oats in the spring, and then get into wheat next fall? Cutting fodder and preparing the ground now, would only hold him back in his work. When Mr. Wheeler came home for a short visit, he jocosely referred to that quarter as "Claude's wheat field."

Claude went ahead with what he had undertaken to do, but all through September he was nervous and apprehensive about the weather. Heavy rains, if they came, would make him late with his wheat-planting, and then there would certainly be criticism. In reality, nobody cared much whether the planting was late or not, but Claude thought they did, and sometimes in the morning he awoke in a state of panic because he wasn't getting ahead faster. He had Dan and one of August Yoeder's four sons to help him, and he worked early and late. The new field he ploughed and drilled himself. He put a great deal of young energy into it, and buried a great deal of discontent in its dark furrows. Day after day he flung himself upon the land and planted it with what was fermenting in him, glad to be so tired at night that he could not think.

Ralph came home for Leonard Dawson's wedding, on the first of October. All the Wheelers went to the wedding, even Mahailey, and there was a great gathering of the country folk and townsmen.

After Ralph left, Claude had the place to himself again, and the work went on as usual. The stock did well, and there were no vexatious interruptions. The fine weather held, and every morning when Claude got up, another gold day stretched before him like a glittering carpet, leading . . . ? When the question where the days were leading struck him on the edge of his bed, he hurried to dress and get down-stairs in time to fetch wood and coal for Mahailey. They often reached the kitchen at the same moment, and she would shake her finger at him and say, "You come down to help me, you nice boy, you!" At least he was of some use to Mahailey. His father could hire one of the Yoeder boys to look after the place, but Mahailey wouldn't let any one else save her old back.

Mrs. Wheeler, as well as Mahailey, enjoyed that fall. She slept late in the morning, and read and rested in the afternoon. She made herself some new house-dresses out of a grey material Claude chose. "It's almost like being a bride, keeping house for just you, Claude," she sometimes said.

Soon Claude had the satisfaction of seeing a blush of green come up over his brown wheat fields, visible first in the dimples and little hollows, then flickering over the knobs and levels like a fugitive smile. He watched the green blades coming every day, when he and Dan went afield with their wagons to gather corn. Claude sent Dan to shuck on the north quarter, and he worked on the south. He always brought in one more load a day than

Dan did,—that was to be expected. Dan explained this very reasonably, Claude thought, one afternoon when they were hooking up their teams.

"It's all right for you to jump at that corn like you was a-beating carpets, Claude; it's your corn, or anyways it's your Paw's. Them fields will always lay betwixt you and trouble. But a hired man's got no property but his back, and he has to save it. I figure that I've only got about so many jumps left in me, and I ain't a-going to jump too hard at no man's corn."

"What's the matter? I haven't been hinting that you ought to jump any harder, have I?"

"No, you ain't, but I just want you to know that there's reason in all things." With this Dan got into his wagon and drove off. He had probably been meditating upon this declaration for some time.

That afternoon Claude suddenly stopped flinging white ears into the wagon beside him. It was about five o'clock, the yellowest hour of the autumn day. He stood lost in a forest of light, dry, rustling corn leaves, quite hidden away from the world. Taking off his husking-gloves, he wiped the sweat from his face, climbed up to the wagon box, and lay down on the ivory-coloured corn. The horses cautiously advanced a step or two, and munched with great content at ears they tore from the stalks with their teeth.

Claude lay still, his arms under his head, looking up at the hard, polished blue sky, watching the flocks of crows go over from the fields where they fed on shattered grain, to their nests in the trees along Lovely Creek. He was thinking about what Dan had said while they were hitching up. There was a great deal of truth in it, certainly. Yet, as for him, he often felt that he would rather go out into the world and earn his bread among strangers than sweat under this half-responsibility for acres and crops that were not his own. He knew that his father was sometimes called a "land hog" by the country people, and he himself had begun to feel that it was not right they should have so much land,—to farm, or to rent, or to leave idle, as they chose. It was strange that in all the centuries the world had been going, the question of property had not been better adjusted. The people who had it were slaves to it, and the people who didn't have it were slaves to them.

He sprang down into the gold light to finish his load. Warm silence nestled over the cornfield. Sometimes a light breeze rose for a moment and rattled the stiff, dry leaves, and he himself made a great rustling and crackling as he tore the husks from the ears.

Greedy crows were still cawing about before they flapped homeward. When he drove out to the highway, the sun was going down, and from his seat on the load he could see far and near. Yonder was Dan's wagon, coming in from the north quarter; over there was the roof of Leonard Dawson's new house, and his windmill, standing up black in the declining day. Before him were the bluffs of the pasture, and the little trees, almost bare, huddled in violet shadow along the creek, and the Wheeler farm-house on the hill, its windows all aflame with the last red fire of the sun.

XV

CLAUDE dreaded the inactivity of the winter, to which the farmer usually looks forward with pleasure. He made the Thanksgiving football game a pretext for going up to Lincoln, — went intending to stay three days and stayed ten. The first night, when he knocked at the glass door of the Erlichs' sitting-room and took them by surprise, he thought he could never go back to the farm. Approaching the house on that clear, frosty autumn evening, crossing the lawn strewn with crackling dry leaves, he told himself that he must not hope to find things the same. But they were the same. The boys were loung-ing and smoking about the square table with the lamp on it, and Mrs. Erlich was at the piano, playing one of Mendelssohn's "Songs Without Words." When he knocked, Otto opened the door and called:

"A surprise for you, Mother! Guess who's here."

What a welcome she gave him, and how much she had to tell him! While they were all talking at once, Henry, the old-est son, came downstairs dressed for a Colonial ball, with satin breeches and stockings and a sword. His brothers began to point out the inaccuracies of his costume, telling him that he couldn't possibly call himself a French *émigré* unless he wore a powdered wig. Henry took a book of mem-oirs from the shelf to prove to them that at the time when the French *émigrés* were coming to Philadelphia, powder was going out of fashion.

During this discussion, Mrs. Erlich drew Claude aside and told him in excited whispers that her cousin Wilhelmina, the singer, had at last been relieved of the invalid husband whom she had supported for so many years, and now was going to marry her accompanist, a man much younger than herself.

After the French *émigré* had gone off to his party, two young instructors from the University dropped in, and Mrs. Erlich introduced Claude as her "landed proprietor" who managed a big ranch out in one of the western counties. The instructors took their leave early, but Claude stayed on. What was it that made life seem so much more interesting and attractive here than elsewhere? There was nothing wonderful about this room; a lot of books, a lamp . . . comfortable, hard-used furniture, some people whose lives were in no way remarkable—and yet he had the sense of being in a warm and gracious atmosphere, charged with generous enthusiasms and ennobled by romantic friendships. He was glad to see the same pictures on the wall; to find the Swiss wood-cutter on the mantel, still bending under his load of faggots; to handle again the heavy brass paper-knife that in its time had cut so many interesting pages. He picked it up from the cover of a red book lying there,—one of Trevelyan's volumes on Garibaldi, which Julius told him he must read before he was another week older.

The next afternoon Claude took Mrs. Erlich to the football game and came home with the family for dinner. He lingered on day after day, but after the first few evenings his heart was growing a little heavier all the time. The Erlich boys had so many new interests he couldn't keep up with them; they had been going on, and he had been standing still. He wasn't conceited enough to mind that. The thing that hurt was the feeling of being out of it, of being lost in another kind of life in which ideas played but little part. He was a stranger who walked in and sat down here; but he belonged out in the big, lonely country, where people worked hard with their backs and got tired like the horses, and were too sleepy at night to think of anything to say. If Mrs. Erlich and her Hungarian woman made lentil soup and potato dumplings and Wiener-Schnitzel for him, it only made the plain fare on the farm seem the heavier.

When the second Friday came round, he went to bid his friends good-bye and explained that he must be going home tomorrow. On leaving the house that night, he looked back at the ruddy windows and told himself that it was good-bye indeed, and not, as Mrs. Erlich had fondly said, *auf wiedersehen.* Coming here only made him more discontented with his lot; his frail claim on this kind of life existed no longer. He must settle down into something that was his own, take hold of it with both hands, no matter how grim it was. The next day, during his journey out through the bleak winter country, he felt that he was going deeper and deeper into reality.

Claude had not written when he would be home, but on Saturday there were always some of the neighbours in town. He rode out with one of the Yoeder boys, and from their place walked on the rest of the way. He told his mother he was glad to be back again. He sometimes felt as if it were disloyal to her for him to be so happy with Mrs. Erlich. His mother had been shut away from the world on a farm for so many years; and even before that, Vermont was no very stimulating place to grow up in, he guessed. She had not had a chance, any more than he had, at those things which make the mind more supple and keep the feeling young.

The next morning it was snowing outside, and they had a long, pleasant Sunday breakfast. Mrs. Wheeler said they wouldn't try to go to church, as Claude must be tired. He worked about the place until noon, making the stock comfortable and looking after things that Dan had neglected in his absence. After dinner he sat down at the secretary and wrote a long letter to his friends in Lincoln. Whenever he lifted his eyes for a moment, he saw the pasture bluffs and the softly falling snow. There was something beautiful about the submissive way in which the country met winter. It made one contented,—sad, too. He sealed his letter and lay down on the couch to read the paper, but was soon asleep.

When he awoke the afternoon was already far gone. The clock on the shelf ticked loudly in the still room, the coal stove sent out a warm glow. The blooming plants in the south bow-window looked brighter and fresher than usual in the soft white light that came up from the snow. Mrs. Wheeler was reading by the west window, looking away from her book now and then to gaze off at the grey sky and the muffled fields. The creek made a winding violet chasm down through the pasture, and the trees followed it in a black thicket, curiously tufted with snow. Claude lay for some time without speaking, watching his mother's profile against the glass, and thinking how good this soft, clinging snow-fall would be for his wheat fields.

"What are you reading, Mother?" he asked presently.

She turned her head toward him. "Nothing very new. I was just beginning 'Paradise Lost' again. I haven't read it for a long while."

"Read aloud, won't you? Just wherever you happen to be. I like the sound of it."

Mrs. Wheeler always read deliberately, giving each syllable its full value. Her voice, naturally soft and rather wistful, trailed over the long measures and the threatening Biblical names, all familiar to her and full of meaning.

> "A dungeon horrible, on all sides round
> As one great furnace flamed; yet from the flames
> No light, but rather darkness visible
> Served only to discover sights of woe."

Her voice groped as if she were trying to realize something. The room was growing greyer as she read on through the turgid catalogue of the heathen gods, so packed with stories and pictures, so unaccountably glorious. At last the light failed, and Mrs. Wheeler closed the book.

"That's fine," Claude commented from the couch. "But Milton couldn't have got along without the wicked, could he?"

Mrs. Wheeler looked up. "Is that a joke?" she asked slyly.

"Oh no, not at all! It just struck me that this part is so much more interesting than the books about perfect innocence in Eden."

"And yet I suppose it shouldn't be so," Mrs. Wheeler said slowly, as if in doubt.

Her son laughed and sat up, smoothing his rumpled hair. "The fact remains that it is, dear Mother. And if you took all the great sinners out of the Bible, you'd take out all the interesting characters, wouldn't you?"

"Except Christ," she murmured.

"Yes, except Christ. But I suppose the Jews were honest when they thought him the most dangerous kind of criminal."

"Are you trying to tangle me up?" his mother inquired, with both reproach and amusement in her voice.

Claude went to the window where she was sitting, and looked out at the snowy fields, now becoming blue and desolate as the shadows deepened. "I only mean that even in the Bible the people who were merely free from blame didn't amount to much."

"Ah, I see!" Mrs. Wheeler chuckled softly. "You are trying to get me back to Faith and Works. There's where you always balked when you were a little fellow. Well, Claude, I don't know as much about it as I did then. As I get older, I leave a good deal more to God. I believe He wants to save whatever is noble in this world, and that He knows more ways of doing it than I." She rose like a gentle shadow and rubbed her cheek against his flannel shirt-sleeve, murmuring, "I believe He is sometimes where we would least expect to find Him,—even in proud, rebellious hearts."

For a moment they clung together in the pale, clear square of the west window, as the two natures in one person sometimes meet and cling in a fated hour.

XVI

RALPH and his father came home to spend the holidays, and on Christmas day Bayliss drove out from town for dinner. He arrived early, and after greeting his mother in the kitchen, went up to the sitting-room, which shone with a holiday neatness, and, for once, was warm enough for Bayliss,—having a low circulation, he felt the cold acutely. He walked up and down, jingling the keys in his pockets and admiring his mother's winter chrysanthemums, which were still blooming. Several times he paused before the old-fashioned secretary, looking through the glass doors at the volumes within. The sight of some of those books awoke disagreeable memories. When he was a boy of fourteen or fifteen, it used to make him bitterly jealous to hear his mother coaxing Claude to read aloud to her. Bayliss had never been bookish. Even before he could read, when his mother told him stories, he at once began to prove to her how they could not possibly be true. Later he found arithmetic and geography more interesting than "Robinson Crusoe." If he sat down with a book, he wanted to feel that he was learning something. His mother and Claude were always talking over his head about the people in books and stories.

Though Bayliss had a sentimental feeling about coming home, he considered that he had had a lonely boyhood. At the country school he had not been happy; he was the boy who always got the answers to the test problems when the others didn't, and he kept his arithmetic papers buttoned up in the inside pocket of his little jacket until he modestly handed them to the teacher, never giving a neighbour the benefit of his cleverness.

Leonard Dawson and other lusty lads of his own age made life as terrifying for him as they could. In winter they used to throw him into a snow-drift, and then run away and leave him. In summer they made him eat live grasshoppers behind the schoolhouse, and put big bull-snakes in his dinner pail to surprise him. To this day, Bayliss liked to see one of those fellows get into difficulties that his big fists couldn't get him out of.

It was because Bayliss was quick at figures and undersized for a farmer that his father sent him to town to learn the implement business. From the day he went to work, he managed to live on his small salary. He kept in his vest pocket a little day-book wherein he noted down all his expenditures, — like the millionaire about whom the Baptist preachers were never tired of talking, — and his offering to the contribution box stood out conspicuous in his weekly account.

In Bayliss' voice, even when he used his insinuating drawl and said disagreeable things, there was something a little plaintive; the expression of a deep-seated sense of injury. He felt that he had always been misunderstood and underestimated. Later after he went into business for himself, the young men of Frankfort had never urged him to take part in their pleasures. He had not been asked to join the tennis club or the whist club. He envied Claude his fine physique and his unreckoning, impulsive vitality, as if they had been given to his brother by unfair means and should rightly have been his.

Bayliss and his father were talking together before dinner when Claude came in and was so inconsiderate as to put up a window, though he knew his brother hated a draft. In a moment Bayliss addressed him without looking at him:

"I see your friends, the Erlichs, have bought out the Jenkinson company, in Lincoln; at least, they've given their notes."

Claude had promised his mother to keep his temper today. "Yes, I saw it in the paper. I hope they'll succeed."

"I doubt it." Bayliss shook his head with his wisest look. "I understand they've put a mortgage on their home. That old woman will find herself without a roof one of these days."

"I don't think so. The boys have wanted to go into business together for a long while. They are all intelligent and industrious; why shouldn't they get on?" Claude flattered himself that he spoke in an easy, confidential way.

Bayliss screwed up his eyes. "I expect they're too fond of good living. They'll pay their interest, and spend whatever's left entertaining their friends. I didn't see the young fellow's name in the notice of incorporation,—Julius, do they call him?"

"Julius is going abroad to study this fall. He intends to be a professor."

"What's the matter with him? Does he have poor health?"

At this moment the dinner bell sounded, Ralph ran down from his room where he had been dressing, and they all descended to the kitchen to greet the turkey. The dinner progressed pleasantly. Bayliss and his father talked politics, and Ralph told stories about his neighbours in Yucca county. Bayliss was pleased that his mother had remembered he liked oyster stuffing, and he complimented her upon her mince pies. When he saw her pour a second cup of coffee for herself and for Claude at the end of dinner, he said, in a gentle, grieved tone, "I'm sorry to see you taking two, Mother."

Mrs. Wheeler looked at him over the coffee-pot with a droll, guilty smile. "I don't believe coffee hurts me a particle, Bayliss."

"Of course it does; it's a stimulant." What worse could it be, his tone implied! When you said anything was a "stimulant," you had sufficiently condemned it; there was no more noxious word.

Claude was in the upper hall, putting on his coat to go down to the barn and smoke a cigar, when Bayliss came out from the sitting-room and detained him by an indefinite remark.

"I believe there's to be a musical show in Hastings Saturday night."

Claude said he had heard something of the sort.

"I was thinking," Bayliss affected a careless tone, as if he thought of such things every day, "that we might make a party and take Gladys and Enid. The roads are pretty good."

"It's a hard drive home, so late at night," Claude objected. Bayliss meant, of course, that Claude should drive the party up and back in Mr. Wheeler's big car. Bayliss never used his glistening Cadillac for long, rough drives.

"I guess Mother would put us up overnight, and we needn't take the girls home till Sunday morning. I'll get the tickets."

"You'd better arrange it with the girls, then. I'll drive you, of course, if you want to go."

Claude escaped and went out, wishing that Bayliss would do his own courting and not drag him into it. Bayliss, who didn't know one tune from another, certainly didn't want to go to this concert, and it was doubtful whether Enid Royce would care much about going. Gladys Farmer was the best musician in Frankfort, and she would probably like to hear it.

Claude and Gladys were old friends, from their High School days, though they hadn't seen much of each other while he was going to college. Several times this fall Bayliss had asked Claude to go somewhere with him on a Sunday, and then stopped to "pick Gladys up," as he said. Claude didn't like it. He was disgusted, anyhow, when he saw that Bayliss had made up his mind to marry Gladys. She and her mother were so poor that he would probably succeed in the end, though so far Gladys didn't seem to give him much encouragement. Marrying Bayliss, he thought, would be no joke for any woman, but Gladys was the one girl in town whom he particularly ought not to marry. She was as extravagant as she was poor. Though she taught in the Frankfort High School for twelve hundred a year, she had prettier clothes than any of the other girls, except Enid Royce, whose father was a rich man. Her new hats and suède shoes were discussed and criticized year in and year out. People said if she married Bayliss Wheeler, he would soon bring her down to hard facts. Some hoped she would, and some hoped she wouldn't. As for Claude, he had kept away from Mrs. Farmer's cheerful parlour ever since Bayliss had begun to drop in there. He was disappointed in Gladys. When he was offended, he seldom stopped to reason about his state of feeling. He avoided the person and the thought of the person, as if it were a sore spot in his mind.

XVII

IT had been Mr. Wheeler's intention to stay at home until spring, but Ralph wrote that he was having trouble with his foreman, so his father went out to the ranch in February. A few days after his departure there was a storm which gave people something to talk about for a year to come.

The snow began to fall about noon on St. Valentine's day, a soft, thick, wet snow that came down in billows and stuck to everything. Later in the afternoon the wind rose, and wherever there was a shed, a tree, a hedge, or even a clump of tall weeds, drifts began to pile up. Mrs. Wheeler, looking anxiously out from the sitting-room windows, could see nothing but driving waves of soft white, which cut the tall house off from the rest of the world.

Claude and Dan, down in the corral, where they were provisioning the cattle against bad weather, found the air so thick that they could scarcely breathe; their ears and mouths and nostrils were full of snow, their faces plastered with it. It melted constantly upon their clothing, and yet they were white from their boots to their caps as they worked, — there was no shaking it off. The air was not cold, only a little below freezing. When they came in for supper, the drifts had piled against the house until they covered the lower sashes of the kitchen windows, and as they opened the door, a frail wall of snow fell in behind them. Mahailey came running with her broom and pail to sweep it up.

"Ain't it a tumble storm, Mr. Claude? I reckon poor Mr. Ernest won't git over tonight, will he? You never mind, honey; I'll wipe up that water. Run along and git dry clothes on you, an' take a bath, or you'll ketch cold. Th' ole tank's full of hot water for you." Exceptional weather of any kind always delighted Mahailey.

Mrs. Wheeler met Claude at the head of the stairs. "There's no danger of the steers getting snowed under along the creek, is there?" she asked anxiously.

"No, I thought of that. We've driven them all into the little corral on the level, and shut the gates. It's over my head down in the creek bottom now. I haven't a dry stitch on me. I guess I'll follow Mahailey's advice and get in the tub, if you can wait supper for me."

"Put your clothes outside the bathroom door, and I'll see to drying them for you."

"Yes, please. I'll need them tomorrow. I don't want to spoil my new corduroys. And, Mother, see if you can make Dan change. He's too wet and steamy to sit at the table with. Tell him if anybody has to go out after supper, I'll go."

Mrs. Wheeler hurried down stairs. Dan, she knew, would rather sit all evening in wet clothes than take the trouble to put on dry ones. He tried to sneak past her to his own quarters behind the wash-room, and looked aggrieved when he heard her message.

"I ain't got no other outside clothes, except my Sunday ones," he objected.

"Well, Claude says he'll go out if anybody has to. I guess you'll have to change for once, Dan, or go to bed without your supper." She laughed quietly at his dejected expression as he slunk away.

"Mrs. Wheeler," Mahailey whispered, "can't I run down to the cellar an' git some of them nice strawberry preserves? Mr. Claude, he loves 'em on his hot biscuit. He don't eat the honey no more; he's got tired of it."

"Very well. I'll make the coffee good and strong; that will please him more than anything."

Claude came down feeling clean and warm and hungry. As he opened the stair door he sniffed the coffee and frying ham, and when Mahailey bent over the oven the warm smell of browning biscuit rushed out with the heat. These combined odours somewhat dispersed Dan's gloom when he came back in squeaky Sunday shoes and a bunglesome cut-away coat. The latter was not required of him, but he wore it for revenge.

During supper Mrs. Wheeler told them once again how, long ago when she was first married, there were no roads or fences west of Frankfort. One winter night she sat on the roof of their first dugout nearly all night, holding up a lantern tied to a pole to guide Mr. Wheeler home through a snowstorm like this.

Mahailey, moving about the stove, watched over the group at the table. She liked to see the men fill themselves with food — though she did not count Dan a man, by any means, — and she looked out to see that Mrs. Wheeler did not forget to eat altogether, as she was apt to do when she fell to remembering things that had happened long ago. Mahailey was in a happy frame of mind because her weather predictions had come true; only yesterday she had told Mrs. Wheeler there would be snow, because she had seen snowbirds. She regarded supper as more than usually important when Claude put on his "velvet close," as she called his brown corduroys.

After supper Claude lay on the couch in the sitting room, while his mother read aloud to him from "Bleak House," — one of the few novels she loved. Poor Jo was drawing toward his end when Claude suddenly sat up. "Mother, I believe I'm too sleepy. I'll have to turn in. Do you suppose it's still snowing?"

He rose and went to look out, but the west windows were so plastered with snow that they were opaque. Even from the one on the south he could see nothing for a moment; then Mahailey must have carried her lamp to the kitchen window beneath, for all at once a broad yellow beam shone out into the choked air, and down it millions of snowflakes hurried like armies, an unceasing progression, moving as close as they could without forming a solid mass. Claude struck the frozen window-frame with his fist, lifted the lower sash, and thrusting out his head tried to look abroad into the engulfed night. There was a solemnity about a storm of such magnitude; it gave one a feeling of infinity. The myriads of white particles that crossed the rays of lamplight seemed to have a quiet purpose, to be hurrying toward a definite end. A faint purity, like a fragrance almost too fine for human senses, exhaled from them as they clustered about his head and shoulders. His mother, looking under his lifted arm, strained her eyes to see out into that swarming movement, and murmured softly in her quavering voice:

> "Ever thicker, thicker, thicker,
> Froze the ice on lake and river;
> Ever deeper, deeper, deeper,
> Fell the snow o'er all the landscape."

XVIII

CLAUDE'S bedroom faced the east. The next morning, when he looked out of his windows, only the tops of the cedars in the front yard were visible. Hurriedly putting on his clothes he ran to the west window at the end of the hall; Lovely Creek, and the deep ravine in which it flowed, had disappeared as if they had never been. The rough pasture was like a smooth field, except for humps and mounds like haycocks, where the snow had drifted over a post or a bush.

At the kitchen stairs Mahailey met him in gleeful excitement. "Lord 'a' mercy, Mr. Claude, I can't git the storm door open. We're snowed in fas'." She looked like a tramp woman, in a jacket patched with many colours, her head tied up in an old black "fascinator," with ravelled yarn hanging down over her face like wild locks of hair. She kept this costume for calamitous occasions; appeared in it when the water-pipes were frozen and burst, or when spring storms flooded the coops and drowned her young chickens.

The storm door opened outward. Claude put his shoulder to it and pushed it a little way. Then, with Mahailey's fire-shovel he dislodged enough snow to enable him to force back the door. Dan came tramping in his stocking-feet across the kitchen to his boots, which were still drying behind the stove. "She's sure a bad one, Claude," he remarked, blinking.

"Yes. I guess we won't try to go out till after breakfast. We'll have to dig our way to the barn, and I never thought to bring the shovels up last night."

"Th' ole snow shovels is in the cellar. I'll git 'em."

"Not now, Mahailey. Give us our breakfast before you do anything else."

Mrs. Wheeler came down, pinning on her little shawl, her shoulders more bent than usual. "Claude," she said fearfully, "the cedars in the front yard are all but covered. Do you suppose our cattle could be buried?"

He laughed. "No, Mother. The cattle have been moving around all night, I expect."

When the two men started out with the wooden snow shovels, Mrs. Wheeler and Mahailey stood in the doorway, watching them. For a short distance from the house the path they dug was like a tunnel, and the white walls on either side were higher than their heads. On the breast of the hill the snow was not so deep, and they made better headway. They had to fight through a second heavy drift before they reached the barn, where they went in and warmed themselves among the horses and cows. Dan was for getting next a warm cow and beginning to milk.

"Not yet," said Claude. "I want to have a look at the hogs before we do anything here."

The hog-house was built down in a draw behind the barn. When Claude reached the edge of the gully, blown almost bare, he could look about him. The draw was full of snow, smooth . . . except in the middle, where there was a rumpled depression, resembling a great heap of tumbled bed-linen.

Dan gasped. "God a' mighty, Claude, the roof's fell in! Them hogs'll be smothered."

"They will if we don't get at them pretty quick. Run to the house and tell Mother Mahailey will have to milk this morning, and get back here as fast as you can."

The roof was a flat thatch, and the weight of the snow had been too much for it. Claude wondered if he should have put on a new thatch that fall; but the old one wasn't leaky, and had seemed strong enough.

When Dan got back they took turns, one going ahead and throwing out as much snow as he could, the other handling the snow that fell back. After an hour or so of this work, Dan leaned on his shovel.

"We'll never do it, Claude. Two men couldn't throw all that snow out in a week. I'm about all in."

"Well, you can go back to the house and sit by the fire," Claude called fiercely. He had taken off his coat and was working in his shirt and sweater. The sweat was rolling from his face, his back and arms ached, and his hands, which he couldn't keep dry, were blistered. There were thirty-seven hogs in the hog-house.

Dan sat down in the hole. "Maybe if I could git a drink of water, I could hold on a-ways," he said dejectedly.

It was past noon when they got into the shed; a cloud of steam rose, and they heard grunts. They found the pigs all lying in a heap at one end, and pulled the top ones off alive and squealing. Twelve hogs, at the bottom of the pile, had been suffocated. They lay there wet and black in the snow, their bodies warm and smoking, but they were dead; there was no mistaking that.

Mrs. Wheeler, in her husband's rubber boots and an old overcoat, came down with Mahailey to view the scene of disaster.

"You ought to git right at them hawgs an' butcher 'em today," Mahailey called down to the men. She was standing on the edge of the draw, in her patched jacket and ravelled hood.

Claude, down in the hole, brushed the sleeve of his sweater across his streaming face. "Butcher them?" he cried indignantly. "I wouldn't butcher them if I never saw meat again."

"You ain't a-goin' to let all that good hawg-meat go to wase, air you, Mr. Claude?" Mahailey pleaded. "They didn't have no sickness nor nuthin'. Only you'll have to git right at 'em, or the meat won't be healthy."

"It wouldn't be healthy for me, anyhow. I don't know what I will do with them, but I'm mighty sure I won't butcher them."

"Don't bother him, Mahailey," Mrs. Wheeler cautioned her. "He's tired, and he has to fix some place for the live hogs."

BOOK ONE: ON LOVELY CREEK

"I know he is, mam, but I could easy cut up one of them hawgs myself. I butchered my own little pig onct, in Virginia. I could save the hams, anyways, and the spare-ribs. We ain't had no spare-ribs for ever so long."

What with the ache in his back and his chagrin at losing the pigs, Claude was feeling desperate. "Mother," he shouted, "if you don't take Mahailey into the house, I'll go crazy!"

That evening Mrs. Wheeler asked him how much the twelve hogs would have been worth in money. He looked a little startled.

"Oh, I don't know exactly; three hundred dollars, anyway."

"Would it really be as much as that? I don't see how we could have prevented it, do you?" Her face looked troubled.

Claude went to bed immediately after supper, but he had no sooner stretched his aching body between the sheets than he began to feel wakeful. He was humiliated at losing the pigs, because they had been left in his charge; but for the loss in money, about which even his mother was grieved, he didn't seem to care. He wondered whether all that winter he hadn't been working himself up into a childish contempt for money-values.

When Ralph was home at Christmas time, he wore on his little finger a heavy gold ring, with a diamond as big as a pea, surrounded by showy grooves in the metal. He admitted to Claude that he had won it in a poker game. Ralph's hands were never free from automobile grease—they were the red, stumpy kind that couldn't be kept clean. Claude remembered him milking in the barn by lantern light, his jewel throwing off jabbing sparkles of colour, and his fingers looking very much like the teats of the cow. That picture rose before him now, as a symbol of what successful farming led to.

The farmer raised and took to market things with an intrinsic value; wheat and corn as good as could be grown anywhere in the world, hogs and cattle that were the best of their kind. In return he got manufactured articles of poor quality; showy furniture that went to pieces, carpets and draperies that faded, clothes that made a handsome man look like a clown. Most of his money was paid out for machinery,—and that, too, went to pieces. A steam thrasher didn't last long; a horse outlived three automobiles.

Claude felt sure that when he was a little boy and all the neighbours were poor, they and their houses and farms had more individuality. The farmers took time then to plant fine cottonwood groves on their places, and to set osage orange hedges along the borders of their fields. Now these trees were all being cut down and grubbed up. Just why, nobody knew; they impoverished the land . . . they made the snow drift . . . nobody had them any more. With prosperity came a kind of callousness; everybody wanted to destroy the old things they used to take pride in. The orchards, which had been nursed and tended so carefully twenty years ago, were now left to die of neglect. It was less trouble to run into town in an automobile and buy fruit than it was to raise it.

The people themselves had changed. He could remember when all the farmers in this community were friendly toward each other; now they were continually having lawsuits. Their sons were either stingy and grasping, or extravagant and lazy, and they were always stirring up trouble. Evidently, it took more intelligence to spend money than to make it.

When he pondered upon this conclusion, Claude thought of the Erlichs. Julius could go abroad and study for his doctor's degree, and live on less than Ralph wasted every year. Ralph would never have a profession or a trade, would never do or make anything the world needed.

Nor did Claude find his own outlook much better. He was twenty-one years old, and he had no skill, no training,—no ability that would ever take him among the kind of people he admired. He was a clumsy, awkward farmer boy, and even Mrs. Erlich seemed to think the farm the best place for him. Probably it was; but all the same he didn't find this kind of life worth the trouble of getting up every morning. He could not see the use of working for money, when money brought nothing one wanted. Mrs. Erlich said it brought security. Sometimes he thought this security was what was the matter with everybody; that only perfect safety was required to kill all the best qualities in people and develop the mean ones.

Ernest, too, said "it's the best life in the world, Claude." But if you went to bed defeated every night, and dreaded to wake in the morning, then clearly it was too good a life for you. To be assured, at his age, of three meals a day and plenty of sleep, was like being assured of a decent burial. Safety, security; if you followed that reasoning out, then the unborn, those who would never be born, were the safest of all; nothing could happen to them.

Claude knew, and everybody else knew, seemingly, that there was something wrong with him. He had been unable to conceal his discontent. Mr. Wheeler was afraid he was one of those visionary fellows who make unnecessary difficulties for themselves and other people. Mrs. Wheeler thought the trouble with her son was that he had not yet found his Saviour. Bayliss was convinced that his brother was a moral rebel, that behind his reticence and his guarded manner he concealed the most dangerous opinions. The neighbours liked Claude, but they laughed at him, and said it was a good thing his father was well fixed. Claude was aware that his energy, instead of accomplishing something, was spent in resisting unalterable conditions, and in unavailing efforts to subdue his own nature. When he thought he had at last got himself in hand, a moment would undo the work of days; in a flash he would be transformed from a wooden post into a living boy. He would spring to his feet, turn over quickly in bed, or stop short in his walk, because the old belief flashed up in him with an intense kind of hope, an intense kind of pain, — the conviction that there was something splendid about life, if he could but find it!

IX

THE weather, after the big storm, behaved capriciously. There was a partial thaw which threatened to flood everything, — then a hard freeze. The whole country glittered with an icy crust, and people went about on a platform of frozen snow, quite above the level of ordinary life. Claude got out Mr. Wheeler's old double sleigh from the mass of heterogenous objects that had for years lain on top of it, and brought the rusty sleighbells up to the house for Mahailey to scour with brick dust. Now that they had automobiles, most of the farmers had let their old sleighs go to pieces. But the Wheelers always kept everything.

Claude told his mother he meant to take Enid Royce for a sleigh-ride. Enid was the daughter of Jason Royce, the grain merchant, one of the early settlers, who for many years had run the only grist mill in Frankfort county. She and Claude were old playmates; he made a formal call at the mill-house, as it was called, every summer during his vacation, and often dropped in to see Mr. Royce at his town office.

Immediately after supper, Claude put the two wiry little blacks, Pompey and Satan, to the sleigh. The moon had been up since long before the sun went down, had been hanging pale in the sky most of the afternoon, and now it flooded the snow-terraced land with silver. It was one of those sparkling winter nights when a boy feels that though the world is very big, he himself is bigger; that under the whole crystalline blue sky there is no one quite so warm and sentient as himself, and that all this magnificence is for him. The sleighbells rang out with a kind of musical lightheartedness, as if they were glad to sing again, after the many winters they had hung rusty and dust-choked in the barn.

The mill road, that led off the highway and down to the river, had pleasant associations for Claude. When he was a youngster, every time his father went to mill, he begged to go along. He liked the mill and the miller and the miller's little girl. He had never liked the miller's house, however, and he was afraid of Enid's mother. Even now, as he tied his horses to the long hitch-bar down by the engine room, he resolved that he would not be persuaded to enter that formal parlour, full of new-looking, expensive furniture, where his energy always deserted him and he could never think of anything to talk about. If he moved, his shoes squeaked in the silence, and Mrs. Royce sat and blinked her sharp little eyes at him, and the longer he stayed, the harder it was to go.

Enid herself came to the door.

"Why, it's Claude!" she exclaimed. "Won't you come in?"

"No, I want you to go riding. I've got the old sleigh out. Come on, it's a fine night!"

"I thought I heard bells. Won't you come in and see Mother while I get my things on?"

Claude said he must stay with his horses, and ran back to the hitch-bar. Enid didn't keep him waiting long; she wasn't that kind. She came swiftly down the path and through the front gate in the Maine seal motor-coat she wore when she drove her electric coupe in cold weather.

"Now, which way?" Claude asked as the horses sprang forward and the bells began to jingle.

"Almost any way. What a beautiful night! And I love your bells, Claude. I haven't heard sleighbells since you used to bring me and Gladys home from school in stormy weather. Why don't we stop for her tonight? She has furs now, you know!" Here Enid laughed. "All the old ladies are so terribly puzzled about them; they can't find out whether your brother really gave them to her for Christmas or not. If they were sure she bought them for herself, I believe they'd hold a public meeting."

Claude cracked his whip over his eager little blacks. "Doesn't it make you tired, the way they are always nagging at Gladys?"

"It would, if she minded. But she's just as serene! They must have something to fuss about, and of course poor Mrs. Farmer's back taxes are piling up. I certainly suspect Bayliss of the furs."

Claude did not feel as eager to stop for Gladys as he had been a few moments before. They were approaching the town now, and lighted windows shone softly across the blue whiteness of the snow. Even in progressive Frankfort, the street lights were turned off on a night so glorious as this. Mrs. Farmer and her daughter had a little white cottage down in the south part of the town, where only people of modest means lived. "We must stop to see Gladys' mother, if only for a minute," Enid said as they drew up before the fence. "She is so fond of company." He tied his team to a tree, and they went up to the narrow, sloping porch, hung with vines that were full of frozen snow.

Mrs. Farmer met them; a large, rosy woman of fifty, with a pleasant Kentucky voice. She took Enid's arm affectionately, and Claude followed them into the long, low sitting-room, which had an uneven floor and a lamp at either end, and was scantily furnished in rickety mahogany. There, close beside the hard-coal burner, sat Bayliss Wheeler. He did not rise when they entered, but said, "Hello, folks," in a rather sheepish voice. On a little table, beside Mrs. Farmer's workbasket, was the box of candy he had lately taken out of his overcoat pocket, still tied up with its gold cord. A tall lamp stood beside the piano, where Gladys had evidently been practising. Claude wondered whether Bayliss actually pretended to an interest in music! At this moment Gladys was in the kitchen, Mrs. Farmer explained, looking for her mother's glasses, — mislaid when she was copying a recipe for a cheese soufflé.

"Are you still getting new recipes, Mrs. Farmer?" Enid asked her. "I thought you could make every dish in the world already."

"Oh, not quite!" Mrs. Farmer laughed modestly and showed that she liked compliments. "Do sit down, Claude," she besought of the stiff image by the door. "Daughter will be here directly."

At that moment Gladys Farmer appeared.

"Why, I didn't know you had company, Mother," she said, coming in to greet them.

This meant, Claude supposed, that Bayliss was not company. He scarcely glanced at Gladys as he took the hand she held out to him.

One of Gladys' grandfathers had come from Antwerp, and she had the settled composure, the full red lips, brown eyes, and dimpled white hands which occur so often in Flemish portraits of young women. Some people thought her a trifle heavy, too mature and positive to be called pretty, even though they admired her rich, tulip-like complexion. Gladys never seemed aware that her looks and her poverty and her extravagance were the subject of perpetual argument, but went to and from school every day with the air of one whose position is assured. Her musicianship gave her a kind of authority in Frankfort.

Enid explained the purpose of their call. "Claude has got out his old sleigh, and we've come to take you for a ride. Perhaps Bayliss will go, too?"

Bayliss said he guessed he would, though Claude knew there was nothing he hated so much as being out in the cold. Gladys ran upstairs to put on a warm dress, and Enid accompanied her, leaving Mrs. Farmer to make agreeable conversation between her two incompatible guests.

"Bayliss was just telling us how you lost your hogs in the storm, Claude. What a pity!" she said sympathetically.

Yes, Claude thought, Bayliss wouldn't be at all reticent about that incident!

"I suppose there was really no way to save them," Mrs. Farmer went on in her polite way; her voice was low and round, like her daughter's, different from the high, tight Western voice. "So I hope you don't let yourself worry about it."

"No, I don't worry about anything as dead as those hogs were. What's the use?" Claude asked boldly.

"That's right," murmured Mrs. Farmer, rocking a little in her chair. "Such things will happen sometimes, and we ought not to take them too hard. It isn't as if a person had been hurt, is it?"

Claude shook himself and tried to respond to her cordiality, and to the shabby comfort of her long parlour, so evidently doing its best to be attractive to her friends. There weren't four steady legs on any of the stuffed chairs or little folding tables she had brought up from the South, and the heavy gold moulding was half broken away from the oil portrait of her father, the Judge. But she carried her poverty lightly, as Southern people did after the Civil War, and she didn't fret half so much about her back taxes as her neighbours did. Claude tried to talk agreeably to her, but he was distracted by the sound of stifled laughter upstairs. Probably Gladys and Enid were joking about Bayliss' being there. How shameless girls were, anyhow!

People came to their front windows to look out as the sleigh dashed jingling up and down the village streets. When they left town, Bayliss suggested that they drive out past the Trevor place. The girls began to talk about the two young New Englanders, Trevor and Brewster, who had lived there when Frankfort was still a tough little frontier settlement. Every one was talking about them now, for a few days ago word had come that one of the partners, Amos Brewster, had dropped dead in his law office in Hartford. It was thirty years since he and his friend, Bruce Trevor, had tried to be great cattle men in Frankfort county, and had built the house on the round hill east of the town, where they wasted a great deal of money very joyously. Claude's father always declared that the amount they squandered in carousing was negligible compared to their losses in commendable industrial endeavour. The country, Mr. Wheeler said, had never been the same since those boys left it. He delighted to tell about the time when Trevor and Brewster went into sheep. They imported a breeding ram from Scotland at a great expense, and when he arrived were so impatient to get the good of him that they turned him in with the ewes as soon as he was out of his crate. Consequently all the lambs were born at the wrong season; came at the beginning of March, in a blinding blizzard, and the mothers died from exposure. The gallant Trevor took horse and spurred all over the county, from one little settlement to another, buying up nursing bottles and nipples to feed the orphan lambs.

The rich bottom land about the Trevor place had been rented out to a truck gardener for years now; the comfortable house with its billiard-room annex—a wonder for that part of the country in its day—remained closed, its windows boarded up. It sat on the top of a round knoll, a fine cottonwood grove behind it. Tonight, as Claude drove toward it, the hill with its tall straight trees looked like a big fur cap put down on the snow.

"Why hasn't some one bought that house long ago and fixed it up?" Enid remarked. "There is no building site around here to compare with it. It looks like the place where the leading citizen of the town ought to live."

"I'm glad you like it, Enid," said Bayliss in a guarded voice. "I've always had a sneaking fancy for the place myself. Those fellows back there never wanted to sell it. But now the estate's got to be settled up. I bought it yesterday. The deed is on its way to Hartford for signature."

Enid turned round in her seat. "Why Bayliss, are you in earnest? Think of just buying the Trevor place off-hand, as if it were any ordinary piece of real estate! Will you make over the house, and live there some day?"

"I don't know about living there. It's too far to walk to my business, and the road across this bottom gets pretty muddy for a car in the spring."

"But it's not far, less than a mile. If I once owned that spot, I'd surely never let anybody else live there. Even Carrie remembers it. She often asks in her letters whether any one has bought the Trevor place yet."

Carrie Royce, Enid's older sister, was a missionary in China.

"Well," Bayliss admitted, "I didn't buy it for an investment, exactly. I paid all it was worth."

Enid turned to Gladys, who was apparently not listening. "You'd be the one who could plan a mansion for Trevor Hill, Gladys. You always have such original ideas about houses."

"Yes, people who have no houses of their own often seem to have ideas about building," said Gladys quietly. "But I like the Trevor place as it is. I hate to think that one of them is dead. People say they did have such good times up there."

Bayliss grunted. "Call it good times if you like. The kids were still grubbing whiskey bottles out of the cellar when I first came to town. Of course, if I decide to live there, I'll pull down that old trap and put up something modern." He often took this gruff tone with Gladys in public.

Enid tried to draw the driver into the conversation. "There seems to be a difference of opinion here, Claude."

"Oh," said Gladys carelessly, "it's Bayliss' property, or soon will be. He will build what he likes. I've always known somebody would get that place away from me, so I'm prepared."

"Get it away from you?" muttered Bayliss, amazed.

"Yes. As long as no one bought it and spoiled it, it was mine as much as it was anybody's."

"Claude," said Enid banteringly, "now both your brothers have houses. Where are you going to have yours?"

"I don't know that I'll ever have one. I think I'll run about the world a little before I draw my plans," he replied sarcastically.

"Take me with you, Claude!" said Gladys in a tone of sudden weariness. From that spiritless murmur Enid suspected that Bayliss had captured Gladys' hand under the buffalo robe.

Grimness had settled down over the sleighing party. Even Enid, who was not highly sensitive to unuttered feelings, saw that there was an uncomfortable constraint. A sharp wind had come up. Bayliss twice suggested turning back, but his brother answered, "Pretty soon," and drove on. He meant that Bayliss should have enough of it. Not until Enid whispered reproachfully, "I really think you ought to turn; we're all getting cold," did he realize that he had made his sleighing party into a punishment! There was certainly nothing to punish Enid for; she had done her best, and had tried to make his own bad manners less conspicuous. He muttered a blundering apology to her when he lifted her from the sleigh at the mill house. On his long drive home he had bitter thoughts for company.

He was so angry with Gladys that he hadn't been able to bid her good-night. Everything she said on the ride had nettled him. If she meant to marry Bayliss, then she ought to throw off this affectation of freedom and independence. If she did not mean to, why did she accept favours from him and let him get into the habit of walking into her house and putting his box of candy on the table, as all Frankfort fellows did when they were courting? Certainly she couldn't make herself believe that she liked his society!

When they were classmates at the Frankfort High School, Gladys was Claude's aesthetic proxy. It wasn't the proper thing for a boy to be too clean, or too careful about his dress and manners. But if he selected a girl who was irreproachable in these respects, got his Latin and did his laboratory work with her, then all her personal attractions redounded to his credit. Gladys had seemed to appreciate the honour Claude did her, and it was not all on her own account that she wore such beatifully ironed muslin dresses when they went on botanical expeditions.

Driving home after that miserable sleigh-ride, Claude told himself that in so far as Gladys was concerned he could make up his mind to the fact that he had been "stung" all along. He had believed in her fine feelings; believed implicitly. Now he knew she had none so fine that she couldn't pocket them when there was enough to be gained by it. Even while he said these things over and over, his old conception of Gladys, down at the bottom of his mind, remained persistently unchanged. But that only made his state of feeling the more painful. He was deeply hurt,—and for some reason, youth, when it is hurt, likes to feel itself betrayed.

BOOK TWO

ENID

I

ONE afternoon that spring Claude was sitting on the long flight of granite steps that leads up to the State House in Denver. He had been looking at the collection of Cliff Dweller remains in the Capitol, and when he came out into the sunlight the faint smell of fresh-cut grass struck his nostrils and persuaded him to linger. The gardeners were giving the grounds their first light mowing. All the lawns on the hill were bright with daffodils and hyacinths. A sweet, warm wind blew over the grass, drying the water-drops. There had been showers in the afternoon, and the sky was still a tender, rainy blue, where it showed through the masses of swiftly moving clouds.

Claude had been away from home for nearly a month. His father had sent him out to see Ralph and the new ranch, and from there he went on to Colorado Springs and Trinidad. He had enjoyed travelling, but now that he was back in Denver he had that feeling of loneliness which often overtakes country boys in a city; the feeling of being unrelated to anything, of not mattering to anybody. He had wandered about Colorado Springs wishing he knew some of the people who were going in and out of the houses; wishing that he could talk to some of those pretty girls he saw driving their own cars about the streets, if only to say a few words. One morning when he was walking out in the hills a girl passed him, then slowed her car to ask if she could give him a lift. Claude would have said that she was just the sort who would never stop to pick him up,—yet she did, and she talked to him pleasantly all the way back to town. It was only twenty minutes or so, but it was worth everything else that happened on his trip. When she asked him where she should put him down, he said at the Antlers, and blushed so furiously that she must have known at once he wasn't staying there.

He wondered this afternoon how many discouraged young men had sat here on the State House steps and watched the sun go down behind the mountains. Every one was always saying it was a fine thing to be young; but it was a painful thing, too. He didn't believe older people were ever so wretched. Over there, in the golden light, the mass of mountains was splitting up into four distinct ranges, and as the sun dropped lower the peaks emerged in perspective, one behind the other. It was a lonely splendour that only made the ache in his breast the stronger. What *was* the matter with him, he asked himself entreatingly. He must answer that question before he went home again.

The statue of Kit Carson on horseback, down in the Square, pointed Westward; but there was no West, in that sense, any more. There was still South America; perhaps he could find something below the Isthmus. Here the sky was like a lid shut down over the world; his mother could see saints and martyrs behind it.

Well, in time he would get over all this, he supposed. Even his father had been restless as a young man, and had run away into a new country. It was a storm that died down at last,—but what a pity not to do anything with it! A waste of power—for it was a kind of power; he sprang to his feet and stood frowning against the ruddy light, so deep in his own struggling thoughts that he did not notice a man, mounting from the lower terraces, who stopped to look at him.

The stranger scrutinized Claude with interest. He saw a young man standing bareheaded on the long flight of steps, his fists clenched in an attitude of arrested action,—his sandy hair, his tanned face, his tense figure copper-coloured in the oblique rays. Claude would have been astonished if he could have known how he seemed to this stranger.

II

THE next morning Claude stepped off the train at Frankfort and had his breakfast at the station before the town was awake. His family were not expecting him, so he thought he would walk home and stop at the mill to see Enid Royce. After all, old friends were best.

He left town by the low road that wound along the creek. The willows were all out in new yellow leaves, and the sticky cottonwood buds were on the point of bursting. Birds were calling everywhere, and now and then, through the studded willow wands, flashed the dazzling wing of a cardinal.

All over the dusty, tan-coloured wheatfields there was a tender mist of green, — millions of little fingers reaching up and waving lightly in the sun. To the north and south Claude could see the corn-planters, moving in straight lines over the brown acres where the earth had been harrowed so fine that it blew off in clouds of dust to the roadside. When a gust of wind rose, gay little twisters came across the open fields, corkscrews of powdered earth that whirled through the air and suddenly fell again. It seemed as if there were a lark on every fence post, singing for everything that was dumb; for the great ploughed lands, and the heavy horses in the rows, and the men guiding the horses.

Along the roadsides, from under the dead weeds and wisps of dried bluestem, the dandelions thrust up their clean, bright faces. If Claude happened to step on one, the acrid smell made him think of Mahailey, who had probably been out this very morning, gouging the sod with her broken butcher-knife and stuffing dandelion greens into her apron. She always went for greens with an air of secrecy, very early, and sneaked along the roadsides stooping close to the ground, as if she might be detected and driven away, or as if the dandelions were wild things and had to be caught sleeping.

Claude was thinking, as he walked, of how he used to like to come to mill with his father. The whole process of milling was mysterious to him then; and the mill house and the miller's wife were mysterious; even Enid was, a little,—until he got her down in the bright sun among the cat-tails. They used to play in the bins of clean wheat, watch the flour coming out of the hopper and get themselves covered with white dust.

Best of all he liked going in where the water-wheel hung dripping in its dark cave, and quivering streaks of sunlight came in through the cracks to play on the green slime and the spotted jewel-weed growing in the shale. The mill was a place of sharp contrasts; bright sun and deep shade, roaring sound and heavy, dripping silence. He remembered how astonished he was one day, when he found Mr. Royce in gloves and goggles, cleaning the millstones, and discovered what harmless looking things they were. The miller picked away at them with a sharp hammer until the sparks flew, and Claude still had on his hand a blue spot where a chip of flint went under the skin when he got too near.

Jason Royce must have kept his mill going out of sentiment, for there was not much money in it now. But milling had been his first business, and he had not found many things in life to be sentimental about. Sometimes one still came upon him in dusty miller's clothes, giving his man a day off. He had long ago ceased to depend on the risings and fallings of Lovely Creek for his power, and had put in a gasoline engine. The old dam now lay "like a holler tooth," as one of his men said, grown up with weeds and willow-brush.

Mr. Royce's family affairs had never gone as well as his business. He had not been blessed with a son, and out of five daughters he had succeeded in bringing up only two. People thought the mill house damp and unwholesome. Until he built a tenant's cottage and got a married man to take charge of the mill, Mr. Royce was never able to keep his millers long. They complained of the gloom of the house, and said they could not get enough to eat. Mrs. Royce went every summer to a vegetarian sanatorium in Michigan, where she learned to live on nuts and toasted cereals. She gave her family nourishment, to be sure, but there was never during the day a meal that a man could look forward to with pleasure, or sit down to with satisfaction. Mr. Royce usually dined at the hotel in town. Nevertheless, his wife was distinguished for certain brilliant culinary accomplishments. Her bread was faultless. When a church supper was toward, she was always called upon for her wonderful mayonnaise dressing, or her angel-food cake,—sure to be the lightest and spongiest in any assemblage of cakes.

A deep preoccupation about her health made Mrs. Royce like a woman who has a hidden grief, or is preyed upon by a consuming regret. It wrapped her in a kind of insensibility. She lived differently from other people, and that fact made her distrustful and reserved. Only when she was at the sanatorium, under the care of her idolized doctors, did she feel that she was understood and surrounded by sympathy. Her distrust had communicated itself to her daughters and in countless little ways had coloured their feelings about life. They grew up under the shadow of being "different," and formed no close friendships. Gladys Farmer was the only Frankfort girl who had ever gone much to the mill house. Nobody was surprised when Caroline Royce, the older daughter, went out to China to be a missionary, or that her mother let her go without a protest. The Royce women were strange, anyhow, people said; with Carrie gone, they hoped Enid would grow up to be more like other folk. She dressed well, came to town often in her electric car, and was always ready to work for the church or the public library.

Besides, in Frankfort, Enid was thought very pretty,—in itself a humanizing attribute. She was slender, with a small, well-shaped head, a smooth, pale skin, and large, dark, opaque eyes with heavy lashes. The long line from the lobe of her ear to the tip of her chin gave her face a certain rigidity, but to the old ladies, who are the best critics in such matters, this meant firmness and dignity. She moved quickly and gracefully, just brushing things rather than touching them, so that there was a suggestion of flight about her slim figure, of gliding away from her surroundings. When the Sunday School gave *tableaux vivantes,* Enid was chosen for Lydia, the blind girl of Pompeii, and for the martyr in "Christ or Diana." The pallor of her skin, the submissive inclination of her forehead, and her dark, unchanging eyes, made one think of something "early Christian."

On this May morning when Claude Wheeler came striding up the mill road, Enid was in the yard, standing by a trellis for vines built near the fence, out from under the heavy shade of the trees. She was raking the earth that had been spaded up the day before, and making furrows in which to drop seeds. From the turn of the road, by the knotty old willows, Claude saw her pink starched dress and little white sunbonnet. He hurried forward.

"Hello, are you farming?" he called as he came up to the fence.

Enid, who was bending over at that moment, rose quickly, but without a start. "Why, Claude! I thought you were out West somewhere. This *is* a surprise!" She brushed the earth from her hands and gave him her limp white fingers. Her arms, bare below the elbow, were thin, and looked cold, as if she had put on a summer dress too early.

"I just got back this morning. I'm walking out home. What are you planting?"

"Sweet peas."

"You always have the finest ones in the country. When I see a bunch of yours at church or anywhere, I always know them."

"Yes, I'm quite successful with my sweet peas," she admitted. "The ground is rich down here, and they get plenty of sun."

"It isn't only your sweet peas. Nobody else has such lilacs or rambler roses, and I expect you have the only wistaria vine in Frankfort county."

"Mother planted that a long while ago, when she first moved here. She is very partial to wistaria. I'm afraid we'll lose it, one of these hard winters."

"Oh, that would be a shame! Take good care of it. You must put in a lot of time looking after these things, anyway." He spoke admiringly.

Enid leaned against the fence and pushed back her little bonnet. "Perhaps I take more interest in flowers than I do in people. I often envy you, Claude; you have so many interests."

He coloured. "I? Good gracious, I don't have many! I'm an awfully discontented sort of fellow. I didn't care about going to school until I had to stop, and then I was sore because I couldn't go back. I guess I've been sulking about it all winter."

She looked at him with quiet astonishment. "I don't see why you should be discontented; you're so free."

"Well, aren't you free, too?"

"Not to do what I want to. The only thing I really want to do is to go out to China and help Carrie in her work. Mother thinks I'm not strong enough. But Carrie was never very strong here. She is better in China, and I think I might be."

Claude felt concern. He had not seen Enid since the sleigh-ride, when she had been gayer than usual. Now she seemed sunk in lassitude. "You must get over such notions, Enid. You don't want to go wandering off alone like that. It makes people queer. Isn't there plenty of missionary work to be done right here?"

She sighed. "That's what everybody says. But we all of us have a chance, if we'll take it. Out there they haven't. It's terrible to think of all those millions that live and die in darkness."

Claude glanced up at the sombre mill house, hidden in cedars,—then off at the bright, dusty fields. He felt as if he were a little to blame for Enid's melancholy. He hadn't been very neighbourly this last year. "People can live in darkness here, too, unless they fight it. Look at me. I told you I've been moping all winter. We all feel friendly enough, but we go plodding on and never get together. You and I are old friends, and yet we hardly ever see each other. Mother says you've been promising for two years to run up and have a visit with her. Why don't you come? It would please her."

"Then I will. I've always been fond of your mother." She paused a moment, absently twisting the strings of her bonnet, then twitched it from her head with a quick movement and looked at him squarely in the bright light. "Claude, you haven't really become a free-thinker, have you?"

He laughed outright. "Why, what made you think I had?"

"Everybody knows Ernest Havel is, and people say you and he read that kind of books together."

"Has that got anything to do with our being friends?"

"Yes, it has. I couldn't feel the same confidence in you. I've worried about it a good deal."

"Well, you just cut it out. For one thing, I'm not worth it," he said quickly.

"Oh, yes, you are! If worrying would do any good —" she shook her head at him reproachfully.

Claude took hold of the fence pickets between them with both hands. "It will do good! Didn't I tell you there was missionary work to be done right here? Is that why you've been so stand-offish with me the last few years, because you thought I was an atheist?"

"I never, you know, liked Ernest Havel," she murmured.

When Claude left the mill and started homeward he felt that he had found something which would help him through the summer. How fortunate he had been to come upon Enid alone and talk to her without interruption, — without once seeing Mrs. Royce's face, always masked in powder, peering at him from behind a drawn blind. Mrs. Royce had always looked old, even long ago when she used to come into church with her little girls, — a tiny woman in tiny high-heeled shoes and a big hat with nodding plumes, her black dress covered with bugles and jet that glittered and rattled and made her seem hard on the outside, like an insect.

Yes, he must see to it that Enid went about and saw more of other people. She was too much with her mother, and with her own thoughts. Flowers and foreign missions — her garden and the great kingdom of China; there was something unusual and touching about her preoccupations. Something quite charming, too. Women ought to be religious; faith was the natural fragrance of their minds. The more incredible the things they believed, the more lovely was the act of belief. To him the story of "Paradise Lost" was as mythical as the "Odyssey"; yet when his mother read it aloud to him, it was not only beautiful but true. A woman who didn't have holy thoughts about mysterious things far away would be prosaic and commonplace, like a man.

III

During the next few weeks Claude often ran his car down to the mill house on a pleasant evening and coaxed Enid to go into Frankfort with him and sit through a moving picture show, or to drive to a neighbouring town. The advantage of this form of companionship was that it did not put too great a strain upon one's conversational powers. Enid could be admirably silent, and she was never embarrassed by either silence or speech. She was cool and sure of herself under any circumstances, and that was one reason why she drove a car so well,—much better than Claude, indeed.

One Sunday, when they met after church, she told Claude that she wanted to go to Hastings to do some shopping, and they arranged that he should take her on Tuesday in his father's big car. The town was about seventy miles to the northeast and, from Frankfort, it was an inconvenient trip by rail.

On Tuesday morning Claude reached the mill house just as the sun was rising over the damp fields. Enid was on the front porch waiting for him, wearing a blanket coat over her spring suit. She ran down to the gate and slipped into the seat beside him.

"Good morning, Claude. Nobody else is up. It's going to be a glorious day, isn't it?"

"Splendid. A little warm for this time of year. You won't need that coat long."

For the first hour they found the roads empty. All the fields were grey with dew, and the early sunlight burned over everything with the transparent brightness of a fire that has just been kindled. As the machine noiselessly wound off the miles, the sky grew deeper and bluer, and the flowers along the roadside opened in the wet grass. There were men and horses abroad on every hill now. Soon they began to pass children on the way to school, who stopped and waved their bright dinner pails at the two travellers. By ten o'clock they were in Hastings.

While Enid was shopping, Claude bought some white shoes and duck trousers. He felt more interest than usual in his summer clothes. They met at the hotel for lunch, both very hungry and both satisfied with their morning's work. Seated in the dining room, with Enid opposite him, Claude thought they did not look at all like a country boy and girl come to town, but like experienced people touring in their car.

"Will you make a call with me after dinner?" she asked while they were waiting for their dessert.

"Is it any one I know?"

"Certainly. Brother Weldon is in town. His meetings are over, and I was afraid he might be gone, but he is staying on a few days with Mrs. Gleason. I brought some of Carrie's letters along for him to read."

Claude made a wry face. "He won't be delighted to see me. We never got on well at school. He's a regular muff of a teacher, if you want to know," he added resolutely.

Enid studied him judicially. "I'm surprised to hear that; he's such a good speaker. You'd better come along. It's so foolish to have a coolness with your old teachers."

An hour later the Reverend Arthur Weldon received the two young people in Mrs. Gleason's half-darkened parlour, where he seemed quite as much at home as that lady herself. The hostess, after chatting cordially with the visitors for a few moments, excused herself to go to a P. E. O. meeting. Every one rose at her departure, and Mr. Weldon approached Enid, took her hand, and stood looking at her with his head inclined and his oblique smile. "This is an unexpected pleasure, to see you again, Miss Enid. And you, too, Claude," turning a little toward the latter. "You've come up from Frankfort together this beautiful day?" His tone seemed to say, "How lovely for you!"

He directed most of his remarks to Enid and, as always, avoided looking at Claude except when he definitely addressed him.

"You are farming this year, Claude? I presume that is a great satisfaction to your father. And Mrs. Wheeler is quite well?"

Mr. Weldon certainly bore no malice, but he always pronounced Claude's name exactly like the word "Clod," which annoyed him. To be sure, Enid pronounced his name in the same way, but either Claude did not notice this, or did not mind it from her. He sank into a deep, dark sofa, and sat with his driving cap on his knee while Brother Weldon drew a chair up to the one open window of the dusky room and began to read Carrie Royce's letters. Without being asked to do so, he read them aloud, and stopped to comment from time to time. Claude observed with disappointment that Enid drank in all his platitudes just as Mrs. Wheeler did. He had never looked at Weldon so long before. The light fell full on the young man's pear-shaped head and his thin, rippled hair. What in the world could sensible women like his mother and Enid Royce find to admire in this purring, whitenecktied fellow? Enid's dark eyes rested upon him with an expression of profound respect. She both looked at him and spoke to him with more feeling than she ever showed toward Claude.

"You see, Brother Weldon," she said earnestly, "I am not naturally much drawn to people. I find it hard to take the proper interest in the church work at home. It seems as if I had always been holding myself in reserve for the foreign field, — by not making personal ties, I mean. If Gladys Farmer went to China, everybody would miss her. She could never be replaced in the High School. She has the kind of magnetism that draws people to her. But I have always been keeping myself free to do what Carrie is doing. There I know I could be of use."

Claude saw it was not easy for Enid to talk like this. Her face looked troubled, and her dark eyebrows came together in a sharp angle as she tried to tell the young preacher exactly what was going on in her mind. He listened with his habitual, smiling attention, smoothing the paper of the folded letter pages and murmuring, "Yes, I understand. Indeed, Miss Enid?"

When she pressed him for advice, he said it was not always easy to know in what field one could be most useful; perhaps this very restraint was giving her some spiritual discipline that she particularly needed. He was careful not to commit himself, not to advise anything unconditionally, except prayer.

"I believe that all things are made clear to us in prayer, Miss Enid."

Enid clasped her hands; her perplexity made her features look sharper. "But it is when I pray that I feel this call the strongest. It seems as if a finger were pointing me over there. Sometimes when I ask for guidance in little things, I get none, and only get the feeling that my work lies far away, and that for it, strength would be given me. Until I take that road, Christ withholds himself."

Mr. Weldon answered her in a tone of relief, as if something obscure had been made clear. "If that is the case, Miss Enid, I think we need have no anxiety. If the call recurs to you in prayer, and it is your Saviour's will, then we can be sure that the way and the means will be revealed. A passage from one of the Prophets occurs to me at this moment; *'And behold a way shall be opened up before thy feet; walk thou in it.'* We might say that this promise was originally meant for Enid Royce! I believe God likes us to appropriate passages of His word personally." This last remark was made playfully, as if it were a kind of Christian Endeavour jest. He rose and handed Enid back the letters. Clearly, the interview was over.

As Enid drew on her gloves she told him that it had been a great help to talk to him, and that he always seemed to give her what she needed. Claude wondered what it was. He hadn't seen Weldon do anything but retreat before her eager questions. He, an "atheist," could have given her stronger reinforcement.

Claude's car stood under the maple trees in front of Mrs. Gleason's house. Before they got into it, he called Enid's attention to a mass of thunderheads in the west.

"That looks to me like a storm. It might be a wise thing to stay at the hotel tonight."

"Oh, no! I don't want to do that. I haven't come prepared."

He reminded her that it wouldn't be impossible to buy whatever she might need for the night.

"I don't like to stay in a strange place without my own things," she said decidedly.

"I'm afraid we'll be going straight into it. We may be in for something pretty rough,—but it's as you say." He still hesitated, with his hand on the door.

"I think we'd better try it," she said with quiet determination. Claude had not yet learned that Enid always opposed the unexpected, and could not bear to have her plans changed by people or circumstances.

For an hour he drove at his best speed, watching the clouds anxiously. The table-land, from horizon to horizon, was glowing in sunlight, and the sky itself seemed only the more brilliant for the mass of purple vapours rolling in the west, with bright edges, like new-cut lead. He had made fifty odd miles when the air suddenly grew cold, and in ten minutes the whole shining sky was blotted out. He sprang to the ground and began to jack up his wheels. As soon as a wheel left the earth, Enid adjusted the chain. Claude told her he had never got the chains on so quickly before. He covered the packages in the back seat with an oilcloth and drove forward to meet the storm.

The rain swept over them in waves, seemed to rise from the sod as well as to fall from the clouds. They made another five miles, ploughing through puddles and sliding over liquefied roads. Suddenly the heavy car, chains and all, bounded up a two-foot bank, shot over the sod a dozen yards before the brake caught it, then swung a half-circle and stood still. Enid sat calm and motionless.

Claude drew a long breath. "If that had happened on a culvert, we'd be in the ditch with the car on top of us. I simply can't control the thing. The whole top soil is loose, and there's nothing to hold to. That's Tommy Rice's place over there. We'd better get him to take us in for the night."

"But that would be worse than the hotel," Enid objected. "They are not very clean people, and there are a lot of children."

"Better be crowded than dead," he murmured. "From here on, it would be a matter of luck. We might land anywhere."

"We are only about ten miles from your place. I can stay with your mother tonight."

"It's too dangerous, Enid. I don't like the responsibility. Your father would blame me for taking such a chance."

"I know, it's on my account you're nervous." Enid spoke reasonably enough. "Do you mind letting me drive for awhile? There are only three bad hills left, and I think I can slide down them sideways; I've often tried it."

Claude got out and let her slip into his seat, but after she took the wheel he put his hand on her arm. "Don't do anything so foolish," he pleaded.

Enid smiled and shook her head. She was amiable, but inflexible.

He folded his arms. "Go on."

He was chafed by her stubbornness, but he had to admire her resourcefulness in handling the car. At the bottom of one of the worst hills was a new cement culvert, overlaid with liquid mud, where there was nothing for the chains to grip. The car slid to the edge of the culvert and stopped on the very brink. While they were ploughing up the other side of the hill, Enid remarked; "It's a good thing your starter works well; a little jar would have thrown us over."

They pulled up at the Wheeler farm just before dark, and Mrs. Wheeler came running out to meet them with a rubber coat over her head.

"You poor drowned children!" she cried, taking Enid in her arms. "How did you ever get home? I so hoped you had stayed in Hastings."

"It was Enid who got us home," Claude told her. "She's a dreadfully foolhardy girl, and somebody ought to shake her, but she's a fine driver."

Enid laughed as she brushed a wet lock back from her forehead. "You were right, of course; the sensible thing would have been to turn in at the Rice place; only I didn't want to."

Later in the evening Claude was glad they hadn't. It was pleasant to be at home and to see Enid at the supper table, sitting on his father's right and wearing one of his mother's new grey housedresses. They would have had a dismal time at the Rices', with no beds to sleep in except such as were already occupied by Rice children. Enid had never slept in his mother's guest room before, and it pleased him to think how comfortable she would be there.

At an early hour Mrs. Wheeler took a candle to light her guest to bed; Enid passed near Claude's chair as she was leaving the room. "Have you forgiven me?" she asked teasingly.

"What made you so pig-headed? Did you want to frighten me? or to show me how well you could drive?"

"Neither. I wanted to get home. Good-night."

Claude settled back in his chair and shaded his eyes. She did feel that this was home, then. She had not been afraid of his father's jokes, or disconcerted by Mahailey's knowing grin. Her ease in the household gave him unaccountable pleasure. He picked up a book, but did not read. It was lying open on his knee when his mother came back half an hour later.

"Move quietly when you go upstairs, Claude. She is so tired that she may be asleep already."

He took off his shoes and made his ascent with the utmost caution.

IV

ERNEST Havel was cultivating his bright, glistening young cornfield one summer morning, whistling to himself an old German song which was somehow connected with a picture that rose in his memory. It was a picture of the earliest ploughing he could remember.

He saw a half-circle of green hills, with snow still lingering in the clefts of the higher ridges; behind the hills rose a wall of sharp mountains, covered with dark pine forests. In the meadows at the foot of that sweep of hills there was a winding creek, with polled willows in their first yellow-green, and brown fields. He himself was a little boy, playing by the creek and watching his father and mother plough with two great oxen, that had rope traces fastened to their heads and their long horns. His mother walked barefoot beside the oxen and led them; his father walked behind, guiding the plough. His father always looked down. His mother's face was almost as brown and furrowed as the fields, and her eyes were pale blue, like the skies of early spring. The two would go up and down thus all morning without speaking, except to the oxen. Ernest was the last of a long family, and as he played by the creek he used to wonder why his parents looked so old.

Leonard Dawson drove his car up to the fence and shouted, waking Ernest from his revery. He told his team to stand, and ran out to the edge of the field.

"Hello, Ernest," Leonard called. "Have you heard Claude Wheeler got hurt day before yesterday?"

"You don't say so! It can't be anything bad, or they'd let me know."

"Oh, it's nothing very bad, I guess, but he got his face scratched up in the wire quite a little. It was the queerest thing I ever saw. He was out with the team of mules and a heavy plough, working the road in that deep cut between their place and mine. The gasoline motor-truck came along, making more noise than usual, maybe. But those mules know a motor truck, and what they did was pure cussedness. They begun to rear and plunge in that deep cut. I was working my corn over in the field and shouted to the gasoline man to stop, but he didn't hear me. Claude jumped for the critters' heads and got 'em by the bits, but by that time he was all tangled up in the lines. Those damned mules lifted him off his feet and started to run. Down the draw and up the bank and across the fields they went, with that big plough-blade jumping three or four feet in the air every clip. I was sure it would cut one of the mules open, or go clean through Claude. It would have got him, too, if he hadn't kept his hold on the bits. They carried him right along, swinging in the air, and finally ran him into the barb-wire fence and cut his face and neck up."

"My goodness! Did he get cut bad?"

"No, not very, but yesterday morning he was out cultivating corn, all stuck up with court plaster. I knew that was a fool thing to do; a wire cut's nasty if you get overheated out in the dust. But you can't tell a Wheeler anything. Now they say his face has swelled and is hurting him terrible, and he's gone to town to see the doctor. You'd better go over there tonight, and see if you can make him take care of himself."

Leonard drove on, and Ernest went back to his team. "It's queer about that boy," he was thinking. "He's big and strong, and he's got an education and all that fine land, but he don't seem to fit in right." Sometimes Ernest thought his friend was unlucky. When that idea occurred to him, he sighed and shook it off. For Ernest believed there was no help for that; it was something rationalism did not explain.

The next afternoon Enid Royce's coupé drove up to the Wheeler farmyard. Mrs. Wheeler saw Enid get out of her car and came down the hill to meet her, breathless and distressed. "Oh, Enid! You've heard of Claude's accident? He wouldn't take care of himself, and now he's got erysipelas. He's in such pain, poor boy!"

Enid took her arm, and they started up the hill toward the house. "Can I see Claude, Mrs. Wheeler? I want to give him these flowers."

Mrs. Wheeler hesitated. "I don't know if he will let you come in, dear. I had hard work persuading him to see Ernest for a few moments last night. He seems so low-spirited, and he's sensitive about the way he's bandaged up. I'll go to his room and ask him."

"No, just let me go up with you, please. If I walk in with you, he won't have time to fret about it. I won't stay if he doesn't wish it, but I want to see him."

Mrs. Wheeler was alarmed at this suggestion, but Enid ignored her uncertainty. They went up to the third floor together, and Enid herself tapped at the door.

"It's I, Claude. May I come in for a moment?"

A muffled, reluctant voice answered. "No. They say this is catching, Enid. And anyhow, I'd rather you didn't see me like this."

Without waiting she pushed open the door. The dark blinds were down, and the room was full of a strong, bitter odor. Claude lay flat in bed, his head and face so smothered in surgical cotton that only his eyes and the tip of his nose were visible. The brown paste with which his features were smeared oozed out at the edges of the gauze and made his dressings look untidy. Enid took in these details at a glance.

"Does the light hurt your eyes? Let me put up one of the blinds for a moment, because I want you to see these flowers. I've brought you my first sweet peas."

Claude blinked at the bunch of bright colours she held out before him. She put them up to his face and asked him if he could smell them through his medicines. In a moment he ceased to feel embarrassed. His mother brought a glass bowl, and Enid arranged the flowers on the little table beside him.

"Now, do you want me to darken the room again?"

"Not yet. Sit down for a minute and talk to me. I can't say much because my face is stiff."

"I should think it would be! I met Leonard Dawson on the road yesterday, and he told me how you worked in the field after you were cut. I would like to scold you hard, Claude."

"Do. It might make me feel better." He took her hand and kept her beside him a moment. "Are those the sweet peas you were planting that day when I came back from the West?"

"Yes. Haven't they done well to blossom so early?"

"Less than two months. That's strange," he sighed.

"Strange? What?"

"Oh, that a handful of seeds can make anything so pretty in a few weeks, and it takes a man so long to do anything—and then it's not much account."

"That's not the way to look at things," she said reprovingly.

Enid sat prim and straight on a chair at the foot of his bed. Her flowered organdie dress was very much like the bouquet she had brought, and her floppy straw hat had a big lilac bow. She began to tell Claude about her father's several attacks of erysipelas. He listened but absently. He would never have believed that Enid, with her severe notions of decorum, would come into his room and sit with him like this. He noticed that his mother was quite as much astonished as he. She hovered about the visitor for a few moments, and then, seeing that Enid was quite at her ease, went downstairs to her work. Claude wished that Enid would not talk at all, but would sit there and let him look at her. The sunshine she had let into the room, and her tranquil, fragrant presence, soothed him. Presently he realized that she was asking him something.

"What is it, Enid? The medicine they give me makes me stupid. I don't catch things."

"I was asking whether you play chess."

"Very badly."

"Father says I play passably well. When you are better you must let me bring up my ivory chessmen that Carrie sent me from China. They are beautifully carved. And now it's time for me to go."

She rose and patted his hand, telling him he must not be foolish about seeing people. "I didn't know you were so vain. Bandages are as becoming to you as they are to anybody. Shall I pull the dark blind again for you?"

"Yes, please. There won't be anything to look at now."

"Why, Claude, you are getting to be quite a ladies' man!"

Something in the way Enid said this made him wince a little. He felt his burning face grow a shade warmer. Even after she went downstairs he kept wishing she had not said that.

His mother came to give him his medicine. She stood beside him while he swallowed it. "Enid Royce is a real sensible girl —" she said as she took the glass. Her upward inflection expressed not conviction but bewilderment.

Enid came every afternoon, and Claude looked forward to her visits restlessly; they were the only pleasant things that happened to him, and made him forget the humiliation of his poisoned and disfigured face. He was disgusting to himself; when he touched the welts on his forehead and under his hair, he felt unclean and abject. At night, when his fever ran high, and the pain began to tighten in his head and neck, it wrought him to a distressing pitch of excitement. He fought with it as one bulldog fights with another. His mind prowled about among dark legends of torture,—everything he had ever read about the Inquisition, the rack and the wheel.

When Enid entered his room, cool and fresh in her pretty summer clothes, his mind leaped to meet her. He could not talk much, but he lay looking at her and breathing in a sweet contentment. After awhile he was well enough to sit up half-dressed in a steamer chair and play chess with her.

One afternoon they were by the west window in the sitting-room with the chess board between them, and Claude had to admit that he was beaten again.

"It must be dull for you, playing with me," he murmured, brushing the beads of sweat from his forehead. His face was clean now, so white that even his freckles had disappeared, and his hands were the soft, languid hands of a sick man.

"You will play better when you are stronger and can fix your mind on it," Enid assured him. She was puzzled because Claude, who had a good head for some things, had none at all for chess, and it was clear that he would never play well.

"Yes," he sighed, dropping back into his chair, "my wits do wander. Look at my wheatfield, over there on the skyline. Isn't it lovely? And now I won't be able to harvest it. Sometimes I wonder whether I'll ever finish anything I begin."

Enid put the chessmen back into their box. "Now that you are better, you must stop feeling blue. Father says that with your trouble people are always depressed."

Claude shook his head slowly, as it lay against the back of the chair. "No, it's not that. It's having so much time to think that makes me blue. You see, Enid, I've never yet done anything that gave me any satisfaction. I must be good for something. When I lie still and think, I wonder whether my life has been happening to me or to somebody else. It doesn't seem to have much connection with me. I haven't made much of a start."

"But you are not twenty-two yet. You have plenty of time to start. Is that what you are thinking about all the time!" She shook her finger at him.

"I think about two things all the time. That is one of them." Mrs. Wheeler came in with Claude's four o'clock milk; it was his first day downstairs.

When they were children, playing by the mill-dam, Claude had seen the future as a luminous vagueness in which he and Enid would always do things together. Then there came a time when he wanted to do everything with Ernest, when girls were disturbing and a bother, and he pushed all that into the distance, knowing that some day he must reckon with it again.

Now he told himself he had always known Enid would come back; and she had come on that afternoon when she entered his drug-smelling room and let in the sunlight. She would have done that for nobody but him. She was not a girl who would depart lightly from conventions that she recognized as authoritative. He remembered her as she used to march up to the platform for Children's Day exercises with the other little girls of the infant class; in her stiff white dress, never a curl awry or a wrinkle in her stocking, keeping her little comrades in order by the acquiescent gravity of her face, which seemed to say, "How pleasant it is to do thus and to do Right!"

Old Mr. Smith was the minister in those days,—a good man who had been much tossed about by a stormy and temperamental wife—and his eyes used to rest yearningly upon little Enid Royce, seeing in her the promise of "virtuous and comely Christian, womanhood," to use one of his own phrases. Claude, in the boys' class across the aisle, used to tease her and try to distract her, but he respected her seriousness.

When they played together she was fair-minded, didn't whine if she got hurt, and never claimed a girl's exemption from anything unpleasant. She was calm, even on the day when she fell into the mill-dam and he fished her out; as soon as she stopped choking and coughing up muddy water, she wiped her face with her little drenched petticoats, and sat shivering and saying over and over, "Oh, Claude, Claude!" Incidents like that one now seemed to him significant and fateful.

When Claude's strength began to return to him, it came overwhelmingly. His blood seemed to grow strong while his body was still weak, so that the in-rush of vitality shook him. The desire to live again sang in his veins while his frame was unsteady. Waves of youth swept over him and left him exhausted. When Enid was with him these feelings were never so strong; her actual presence restored his equilibrium— almost. This fact did not perplex him; he fondly attributed it to something beautiful in the girl's nature,—a quality so lovely and subtle that there is no name for it.

During the first days of his recovery he did nothing but enjoy the creeping stir of life. Respiration was a soft physical pleasure. In the nights, so long he could not sleep them through, it was delightful to lie upon a cloud that floated lazily down the sky. In the depths of this lassitude the thought of Enid would start up like a sweet, burning pain, and he would drift out into the darkness upon sensations he could neither prevent nor control. So long as he could plough, pitch hay, or break his back in the wheatfield, he had been master; but now he was overtaken by himself. Enid was meant for him and she had come for him; he would never let her go. She should never know how much he longed for her. She would be slow to feel even a little of what he was feeling; he knew that. It would take a long while. But he would be infinitely patient, infinitely tender of her. It should be he who suffered, not she. Even in his dreams he never wakened her, but loved her while she was still and unconscious like a statue. He would shed love upon her until she warmed and changed without knowing why.

Sometimes when Enid sat unsuspecting beside him, a quick blush swept across his face and he felt guilty toward her,—meek and humble, as if he must beg her forgiveness for something. Often he was glad when she went away and left him alone to think about her. Her presence brought him sanity, and for that he ought to be grateful. When he was with her, he thought how she was to be the one who would put him right with the world and make him fit into the life about him. He had troubled his mother and disappointed his father. His marriage would be the first natural, dutiful, expected thing he had ever done. It would be the beginning of usefulness and content; as his mother's oft-repeated Psalm said, it would restore his soul. Enid's willingness to listen to him he could scarcely doubt. Her devotion to him during his illness was probably regarded by her friends as equivalent to an engagement.

V

CLAUDE's first trip to Frankfort was to get his hair cut. After leaving the barber-shop he presented himself, glistening with bayrum, at Jason Royce's office. Mr. Royce, in the act of closing his safe, turned and took the young man by the hand.

"Hello, Claude, glad to see you around again! Sickness can't do much to a husky young farmer like you. With old fellows, it's another story. I'm just starting off to have a look at my alfalfa, south of the river. Get in and go along with me."

They went out to the open car that stood by the sidewalk, and when they were spinning along between fields of ripening grain Claude broke the silence. "I expect you know what I want to see you about, Mr. Royce?"

The older man shook his head. He had been preoccupied and grim ever since they started.

"Well," Claude went on modestly, "it oughtn't to surprise you to hear that I've set my heart on Enid. I haven't said anything to her yet, but if you're not against me, I'm going to try to persuade her to marry me."

"Marriage is a final sort of thing, Claude," said Mr. Royce. He sat slumping in his seat, watching the road ahead of him with intense abstraction, looking more gloomy and grizzled than usual. "Enid is a vegetarian, you know," he remarked unexpectedly.

Claude smiled. "That could hardly make any difference to me, Mr. Royce."

The other nodded slightly. "I know. At your age you think it doesn't. Such things do make a difference, however." His lips closed over his half-dead cigar, and for some time he did not open them.

"Enid is a good girl," he said at last. "Strictly speaking, she has more brains than a girl needs. If Mrs. Royce had another daughter at home, I'd take Enid into my office. She has good judgment. I don't know but she'd run a business better than a house." Having got this out, Mr. Royce relaxed his frown, took his cigar from his mouth, looked at it, and put it back between his teeth without relighting it.

Claude was watching him with surprise. "There's no question about Enid, Mr. Royce. I didn't come to ask you about her," he exclaimed. "I came to ask if you'd be willing to have me for a son-in-law. I know, and you know, that Enid could do a great deal better than to marry me. I surely haven't made much of a showing, so far."

"Here we are," announced Mr. Royce. "I'll leave the car under this elm, and we'll go up to the north end of the field and have a look."

They crawled under the wire fence and started across the rough ground through a field of purple blossoms. Clouds of yellow butterflies darted up before them. They walked jerkily, breaking through the sun-baked crust into the soft soil beneath. Mr. Royce lit a fresh cigar, and as he threw away the match let his hand drop on the young man's shoulder. "I always envied your father. You took my fancy when you were a little shaver, and I used to let you in to see the water-wheel. When I gave up water power and put in an engine, I said to myself; 'There's just one fellow in the country will be sorry to see the old wheel go, and that's Claude Wheeler.'"

"I hope you don't think I'm too young to marry," Claude said as they tramped on.

"No, it's right and proper a young man should marry. I don't say anything against marriage," Mr. Royce protested doggedly. "You may find some opposition in Enid's missionary motives. I don't know how she feels about that now. I don't enquire. I'd be pleased to see her get rid of such notions. They don't do a woman any good."

"I want to help her get rid of them. If it's all right with you, I hope I can persuade Enid to marry me this fall."

Jason Royce turned his head quickly toward his companion, studied his artless, hopeful countenance for a moment, and then looked away with a frown.

The alfalfa field sloped upward at one corner, lay like a bright green-and-purple handkerchief thrown down on the hillside. At the uppermost angle grew a slender young cotton-wood, with leaves as light and agitated as the swarms of little butterflies that hovered above the clover. Mr. Royce made for this tree, took off his black coat, rolled it up, and sat down on it in the flickering shade. His shirt showed big blotches of moisture, and the sweat was rolling in clear drops along the creases in his brown neck. He sat with his hands clasped over his knees, his heels braced in the soft soil, and looked blankly off across the field. He found himself absolutely unable to touch upon the vast body of experience he wished to communicate to Claude. It lay in his chest like a physical misery, and the desire to speak struggled there. But he had no words, no way to make himself understood. He had no argument to present. What he wanted to do was to hold up life as he had found it, like a picture, to his young friend; to warn him, without explanation, against certain heart-breaking disappointments. It could not be done, he saw. The dead might as well try to speak to the living as the old to the young. The only way that Claude could ever come to share his secret, was to live. His strong yellow teeth closed tighter and tighter on the cigar, which had gone out like the first. He did not look at Claude, but while he watched the wind plough soft, flowery roads in the field, the boy's face was clearly before him, with its expression of reticent pride melting into the desire to please, and the slight stiffness of his shoulders, set in a kind of stubborn loyalty. Claude lay on the sod beside him, rather tired after his walk in the sun, a little melancholy, though he did not know why.

After a long while Mr. Royce unclasped his broad, thick-fingered miller's hands, and for a moment took out the macerated cigar. "Well, Claude," he said with determined cheerfulness, "we'll always be better friends than is common between father and son-in-law. You'll find out that pretty nearly everything you believe about life—about marriage, especially—is lies. I don't know why people prefer to live in that sort of a world, but they do."

VI

AFTER his interview with Mr. Royce, Claude drove directly to the mill house. As he came up the shady road, he saw with disappointment the flash of two white dresses instead of one, moving about in the sunny flower garden. The visitor was Gladys Farmer. This was her vacation time. She had walked out to the mill in the cool of the morning to spend the day with Enid. Now they were starting off to gather water-cresses, and had stopped in the garden to smell the heliotrope. On this scorching afternoon the purple sprays gave out a fragrance that hung over the flower-bed and brushed their cheeks like a warm breath. The girls looked up at the same moment and recognized Claude. They waved to him and hurried down to the gate to congratulate him on his recovery. He took their little tin pails and followed them around the old dam-head and up a sandy gorge, along a clear thread of water that trickled into Lovely Creek just above the mill. They came to the gravelly hill where the stream took its source from a spring hollowed out under the exposed roots of two elm trees. All about the spring, and in the sandy bed of the shallow creek, the cresses grew cool and green.

Gladys had strong feelings about places. She looked around her with satisfaction. "Of all the places where we used to play, Enid, this was my favourite," she declared.

"You girls sit up there on the elm roots," Claude suggested. "Wherever you put your foot in this soft gravel, water gathers. You'll spoil your white shoes. I'll get the cress for you."

"Stuff my pail as full as you can, then," Gladys called as they sat down. "I wonder why the Spanish dagger grows so thick on this hill, Enid? These plants were old and tough when we were little. I love it here."

She leaned back upon the hot, glistening hill-side. The sun came down in red rays through the elm-tops, and all the pebbles and bits of quartz glittered dazzlingly. Down in the stream bed the water, where it caught the light, twinkled like tarnished gold. Claude's sandy head and stooping shoulders were mottled with sunshine as they moved about over the green patches, and his duck trousers looked much whiter than they were. Gladys was too poor to travel, but she had the good fortune to be able to see a great deal within a few miles of Frankfort, and a warm imagination helped her to find life interesting. She did, as she confided to Enid, want to go to Colorado; she was ashamed of never having seen a mountain.

Presently Claude came up the bank with two shining, dripping pails. "Now may I sit down with you for a few minutes?"

Moving to make room for him beside her, Enid noticed that his thin face was heavily beaded with perspiration. His pocket handkerchief was wet and sandy, so she gave him her own, with a proprietary air. "Why, Claude, you look quite tired! Have you been over-doing? Where were you before you came here?"

"I was out in the country with your father, looking at his alfalfa."

"And he walked you all over the field in the hot sun, I suppose?"

Claude laughed. "He did."

"Well, I'll scold him tonight. You stay here and rest. I am going to drive Gladys home."

Gladys protested, but at last consented that they should both drive her home in Claude's car. They lingered awhile, however, listening to the soft, amiable bubbling of the spring; a wise, unobtrusive voice, murmuring night and day, continually telling the truth to people who could not understand it.

When they went back to the house Enid stopped long enough to cut a bunch of heliotrope for Mrs. Farmer,—though with the sinking of the sun its rich perfume had already vanished. They left Gladys and her flowers and cresses at the gate of the white cottage, now half hidden by gaudy trumpet vines.

Claude turned his car and went back along the dim, twilight road with Enid. "I usually like to see Gladys, but when I found her with you this afternoon, I was terribly disappointed for a minute. I'd just been talking with your father, and I wanted to come straight to you. Do you think you could marry me, Enid?"

"I don't believe it would be for the best, Claude." She spoke sadly.

He took her passive hand. "Why not?"

"My mind is full of other plans. Marriage is for most girls, but not for all."

Enid had taken off her hat. In the low evening light Claude studied her pale face under her brown hair. There was something graceful and charming about the way she held her head, something that suggested both submissiveness and great firmness. "I've had those far-away dreams, too, Enid; but now my thoughts don't get any further than you. If you could care ever so little for me to start on, I'd be willing to risk the rest."

She sighed. "You know I care for you. I've never made any secret of it. But we're happy as we are, aren't we?"

"No, I'm not. I've got to have some life of my own, or I'll go to pieces. If you won't have me, I'll try South America,—and I won't come back until I am an old man and you are an old woman."

Enid looked at him, and they both smiled.

The mill house was black except for a light in one upstairs window. Claude sprang out of his car and lifted Enid gently to the ground. She let him kiss her soft cool mouth, and her long lashes. In the pale, dusty dusk, lit only by a few white stars, and with the chill of the creek already in the air, she seemed to Claude like a shivering little ghost come up from the rushes where the old mill-dam used to be. A terrible melancholy clutched at the boy's heart. He hadn't thought it would be like

this. He drove home feeling weak and broken. Was there nothing in the world outside to answer to his own feelings, and was
every turn to be fresh disappointment? Why was life so mysteri-
ously hard? This country itself was sad, he thought, looking
about him, — and you could no more change that than you
could change the story in an unhappy human face. He wished
to God he were sick again; the world was too rough a place to
get about in.

There was one person in the world who felt sorry for Claude
that night. Gladys Farmer sat at her bedroom window for a long
while, watching the stars and thinking about what she had seen
plainly enough that afternoon. She had liked Enid ever since
they were little girls, — and knew all there was to know about her.
Claude would become one of those dead people that moved
about the streets of Frankfort; everything that was Claude would
perish, and the shell of him would come and go and eat and
sleep for fifty years. Gladys had taught the children of many such
dead men. She had worked out a misty philosophy for herself,
full of strong convictions and confused figures. She believed that
all things which might make the world beautiful—love and kindness, leisure and art—were shut up in prison, and that successful
men like Bayliss Wheeler held the keys. The generous ones, who
would let these things out to make people happy, were somehow
weak, and could not break the bars. Even her own little life was
squeezed into an unnatural shape by the domination of people
like Bayliss. She had not dared, for instance, to go to Omaha that
spring for the three performances of the Chicago Opera
Company. Such an extravagance would have aroused a corrective spirit in all her friends, and in the schoolboard as well; they
would probably have decided not to give her the little increase in
salary she counted upon having next year.

There were people, even in Frankfort, who had imagination
and generous impulses, but they were all, she had to admit,
inefficient—failures. There was Miss Livingstone, the fiery,
emotional old maid who couldn't tell the truth; old Mr. Smith, a

lawyer without clients, who read Shakespeare and Dryden all day long in his dusty office; Bobbie Jones, the effeminate drug clerk, who wrote free verse and "movie" scenarios, and tended the sodawater fountain.

Claude was her one hope. Ever since they graduated from High School, all through the four years she had been teaching, she had waited to see him emerge and prove himself. She wanted him to be more successful than Bayliss *and still be Claude.* She would have made any sacrifice to help him on. If a strong boy like Claude, so well endowed and so fearless, must fail, simply because he had that finer strain in his nature,—then life was not worth the chagrin it held for a passionate heart like hers.

At last Gladys threw herself upon the bed. If he married Enid, that would be the end. He would go about strong and heavy, like Mr. Royce; a big machine with the springs broken inside.

VII

CLAUDE was well enough to go into the fields before the harvest was over. The middle of July came, and the farmers were still cutting grain. The yield of wheat and oats was so heavy that there were not machines enough to thrash it within the usual time. Men had to await their turn, letting their grain stand in shock until a belching black engine lumbered into the field. Rains would have been disastrous; but this was one of those "good years" which farmers tell about, when everything goes well. At the time they needed rain, there was plenty of it; and now the days were miracles of dry, glittering heat.

Every morning the sun came up a red ball, quickly drank the dew, and started a quivering excitement in all living things. In great harvest seasons like that one, the heat, the intense light, and the important work in hand draw people together and make them friendly. Neighbours helped each other to cope with the burdensome abundance of man-nourishing grain; women and children and old men fell to and did what they could to save and house it. Even the horses had a more varied and sociable existence than usual, going about from one farm to another to help neighbour horses drag wagons and binders and headers. They nosed the colts of old friends, ate out of strange mangers, and drank, or refused to drink, out of strange water-troughs. Decrepit horses that lived on a pension, like the Wheelers' stiff-legged Molly and Leonard Dawson's Billy with the heaves—his asthmatic cough could be heard for a quarter of a mile—were pressed into service now. It was wonderful, too, how well these invalided beasts managed to keep up with the strong young mares and geldings; they bent their willing heads and pulled as if the chafing of the collar on their necks was sweet to them.

The sun was like a great visiting presence that stimulated and took its due from all animal energy. When it flung wide its cloak and stepped down over the edge of the fields at evening, it left behind it a spent and exhausted world. Horses and men and women grew thin, seethed all day in their own sweat. After supper they dropped over and slept anywhere at all, until the red dawn broke clear in the east again, like the fanfare of trumpets, and nerves and muscles began to quiver with the solar heat.

For several weeks Claude did not have time to read the newspapers; they lay about the house in bundles, unopened, for Nat Wheeler was in the field now, working like a giant. Almost every evening Claude ran down to the mill to see Enid for a few minutes; he did not get out of his car, and she sat on the old stile, left over from horse-back days, while she chatted with him. She said frankly that she didn't like men who had just come out of the harvest field, and Claude did not blame her. He didn't like himself very well after his clothes began to dry on him. But the hour or two between supper and bed was the only time he had to see anybody. He slept like the heroes of old; sank upon his bed as the thing he desired most on earth, and for a blissful moment felt the sweetness of sleep before it overpowered him. In the morning, he seemed to hear the shriek of his alarm clock for hours before he could come up from the deep places into which he had plunged. All sorts of incongruous adventures happened to him between the first buzz of the alarm and the moment when he was enough awake to put out his hand and stop it. He dreamed, for instance, that it was evening, and he had gone to see Enid as usual. While she was coming down the path from the house, he discovered that he had no clothes on at all! Then, with wonderful agility, he jumped over the picket fence into a clump of castor beans, and stood in the dusk, trying to cover himself with the leaves, like Adam in the garden, talking commonplaces to Enid through chattering teeth, afraid lest at any moment she might discover his plight.

Mrs. Wheeler and Mahailey always lost weight in thrashing-time, just as the horses did; this year Nat Wheeler had six hundred acres of winter wheat that would run close upon thirty bushels to the acre. Such a harvest was as hard on the women as it was on the men. Leonard Dawson's wife, Susie, came over to help Mrs. Wheeler, but she was expecting a baby in the fall, and the heat proved too much for her. Then one of the Yoeder daughters came; but the methodical German girl was so distracted by Mahailey's queer ways that Mrs. Wheeler said it was easier to do the work herself than to keep explaining Mahailey's psychology. Day after day ten ravenous men sat down at the long dinner table in the kitchen. Mrs. Wheeler baked pies and cakes and bread loaves as fast as the oven would hold them, and from morning till night the range was stoked like the fire-box of a locomotive. Mahailey wrung the necks of chickens until her wrist swelled up, as she said, "like a puff-adder."

By the end of July the excitement quieted down. The extra leaves were taken out of the dining table, the Wheeler horses had their barn to themselves again, and the reign of terror in the henhouse was over.

One evening Mr. Wheeler came down to supper with a bundle of newspapers under his arm. "Claude, I see this war scare in Europe has hit the market. Wheat's taken a jump. They're paying eighty-eight cents in Chicago. We might as well get rid of a few hundred bushel before it drops again. We'd better begin hauling tomorrow. You and I can make two trips a day over to Vicount, by changing teams,—there's no grade to speak of."

Mrs. Wheeler, arrested in the act of pouring coffee, sat holding the coffee-pot in the air, forgetting she had it. "If this is only a newspaper scare, as we think, I don't see why it should affect the market," she murmured mildly. "Surely those big bankers in New York and Boston have some way of knowing rumour from fact."

"Give me some coffee, please," said her husband testily. "I don't have to explain the market, I've only got to take advantage of it."

"But unless there's some reason, why are we dragging our wheat over to Vicount? Do you suppose it's some scheme the grain men are hiding under a war rumour? Have the financiers and the press ever deceived the public like this before?"

"I don't know a thing in the world about it, Evangeline, and I don't suppose. I telephoned the elevator at Vicount an hour ago, and they said they'd pay me seventy cents, subject to change in the morning quotations. Claude," with a twinkle in his eye, "you'd better not go to mill tonight. Turn in early. If we are on the road by six tomorrow, we'll be in town before the heat of the day."

"All right, sir. I want to look at the papers after supper. I haven't read anything but the headlines since before thrashing. Ernest was stirred up about the murder of that Grand Duke and said the Austrians would make trouble. But I never thought there was anything in it."

"There's seventy cents a bushel in it, anyway," said his father, reaching for a hot biscuit.

"If there's that much, I'm somehow afraid there will be more," said Mrs. Wheeler thoughtfully. She had picked up the paper fly-brush and sat waving it irregularly, as if she were trying to brush away a swarm of confusing ideas.

"You might call up Ernest, and ask him what the Bohemian papers say about it," Mr. Wheeler suggested.

Claude went to the telephone, but was unable to get any answer from the Havels. They had probably gone to a barndance down in the Bohemian township. He went upstairs and sat down before an armchair full of newspapers; he could make nothing reasonable out of the smeary telegrams in big type on the front page of the Omaha *World Herald*. The German army was entering Luxembourg; he didn't know where Luxembourg was, whether it was a city or a country; he seemed to have some vague idea that it was a palace! His mother had gone up to "Mahailey's library," the attic, to hunt for a map of Europe,—a thing for which Nebraska farmers had never had much need. But that night, on many prairie homesteads, the women, American and foreign-born, were hunting for a map.

Claude was so sleepy that he did not wait for his mother's return. He stumbled upstairs and undressed in the dark. The night was sultry, with thunder clouds in the sky and an unceasing play of sheet-lightning all along the western horizon. Mosquitoes had got into his room during the day, and after he threw himself upon the bed they began sailing over him with their high, excruciating note. He turned from side to side and tried to muffle his ears with the pillow. The disquieting sound became merged, in his sleepy brain, with the big type on the front page of the paper; those black letters seemed to be flying about his head with a soft, high, sing-song whizz.

VIII

LATE in the afternoon of the sixth of August, Claude and his empty wagon were bumping along the level road over the flat country between Vicount and the Lovely Creek valley. He had made two trips to town that day. Though he had kept his heaviest team for the hot afternoon pull, his horses were too tired to be urged off a walk. Their necks were marbled with sweat stains, and their flanks were plastered with the white dust that rose at every step. Their heads hung down, and their breathing was deep and slow. The wood of the green-painted wagon seat was blistering hot to the touch. Claude sat at one end of it, his head bared to catch the faint stir of air that sometimes dried his neck and chin and saved him the trouble of pulling out a handkerchief. On every side the wheat stubble stretched for miles and miles. Lonely straw stacks stood up yellow in the sun and cast long shadows. Claude peered anxiously along the distant locust hedges which told where the road ran. Ernest Havel had promised to meet him somewhere on the way home. He had not seen Ernest for a week: since then Time had brought prodigies to birth.

At last he recognized the Havel's team a long way off, and he stopped and waited for Ernest beside a thorny hedge, looking thoughtfully about him. The sun was already low. It hung above the stubble, all milky and rosy with the heat, like the image of a sun reflected in grey water. In the east the full moon had just risen, and its thin silver surface was flushed with pink until it looked exactly like the setting sun. Except for the place each occupied in the heavens, Claude could not have told which was which. They rested upon opposite rims of the world, two bright shields, and regarded each other,—as if they, too, had met by appointment.

Claude and Ernest sprang to the ground at the same instant and shook hands, feeling that they had not seen each other for a long while.

"Well, what do you make of it, Ernest?"

The young man shook his head cautiously, but replied no further. He patted his horses and eased the collars on their necks.

"I waited in town for the Hastings paper," Claude went on impatiently. "England declared war last night."

"The Germans," said Ernest, "are at Liège. I know where that is. I sailed from Antwerp when I came over here."

"Yes, I saw that. Can the Belgians do anything?"

"Nothing." Ernest leaned against the wagon wheel and drawing his pipe from his pocket slowly filled it. "Nobody can do anything. The German army will go where it pleases."

"If it's as bad as that, why are the Belgians putting up a fight?"

"I don't know. It's fine, but it will come to nothing in the end. Let me tell you something about the German army, Claude."

Pacing up and down beside the locust hedge, Ernest rehearsed the great argument; preparation, organization, concentration, inexhaustible resources, inexhaustible men. While he talked the sun disappeared, the moon contracted, solidified, and slowly climbed the pale sky. The fields were still glimmering with the bland reflection left over from daylight, and the distance grew shadowy,—not dark, but seemingly full of sleep.

"If I were at home," Ernest concluded, "I would be in the Austrian army this minute. I guess all my cousins and nephews are fighting the Russians or the Belgians already. How would you like it yourself, to be marched into a peaceful country like this, in the middle of harvest, and begin to destroy it?"

"I wouldn't do it, of course. I'd desert and be shot."

"Then your family would be persecuted. Your brothers, maybe even your father, would be made orderlies to Austrian officers and be kicked in the mouth."

"I wouldn't bother about that. I'd let my male relatives decide for themselves how often they would be kicked."

Ernest shrugged his shoulders. "You Americans brag like little boys; you would and you wouldn't! I tell you, nobody's will has anything to do with this. It is the harvest of all that has been planted. I never thought it would come in my life-time, but I knew it would come."

The boys lingered a little while, looking up at the soft radiance of the sky. There was not a cloud anywhere, and the low glimmer in the fields had imperceptibly changed to full, pure moonlight. Presently the two wagons began to creep along the white road, and on the backless seat of each the driver sat drooping forward, lost in thought. When they reached the corner where Ernest turned south, they said goodnight without raising their voices. Claude's horses went on as if they were walking in their sleep. They did not even sneeze at the low cloud of dust beaten up by their heavy foot-falls,—the only sounds in the vast quiet of the night.

Why was Ernest so impatient with him, Claude wondered? He could not pretend to feel as Ernest did. He had nothing behind him to shape his opinions or colour his feelings about what was going on in Europe; he could only sense it day by day. He had always been taught that the German people were pre-eminent in the virtues Americans most admire; a month ago he would have said they had all the ideals a decent American boy would fight for. The invasion of Belgium was contradictory to the German character as he knew it in his friends and neighbours. He still cherished the hope that there had been some great mistake; that this splendid people would apologize and right itself with the world.

Mr. Wheeler came down the hill, bareheaded and coatless, as Claude drove into the barnyard. "I expect you're tired. I'll put your team away. Any news?"

"England has declared war."

Mr. Wheeler stood still a moment and scratched his head. "I guess you needn't get up early tomorrow. If this is to be a sure enough war, wheat will go higher. I've thought it was a bluff until now. You take the papers up to your mother."

IX

ENID and Mrs. Royce had gone away to the Michigan sanatorium where they spent part of every summer, and would not be back until October. Claude and his mother gave all their attention to the war despatches. Day after day, through the first two weeks of August, the bewildering news trickled from the little towns out into the farming country.

About the middle of the month came the story of the fall of the forts at Liège, battered at for nine days and finally reduced in a few hours by siege guns brought up from the rear,—guns which evidently could destroy any fortifications that ever had been, or ever could be constructed. Even to these quiet wheatgrowing people, the siege guns before Liège were a menace; not to their safety or their goods, but to their comfortable, established way of thinking. They introduced the greater-than-man force which afterward repeatedly brought into this war the effect of unforseeable natural disaster, like tidal waves, earthquakes, or the eruption of volcanoes.

On the twenty-third came the news of the fall of the forts at Namur; again giving warning that an unprecedented power of destruction had broken loose in the world. A few days later the story of the wiping out of the ancient and peaceful seat of learning at Louvain made it clear that this force was being directed toward incredible ends. By this time, too, the papers were full of accounts of the destruction of civilian populations. Something new, and certainly evil, was at work among mankind. Nobody was ready with a name for it. None of the well-worn words descriptive of human behaviour seemed adequate. The epithets grouped about the name of "Attila" were too personal, too dramatic, too full of old, familiar human passion.

One afternoon in the first week of September Mrs. Wheeler was in the kitchen making cucumber pickles, when she heard Claude's car coming back from Frankfort. In a moment he entered, letting the screen door slam behind him, and threw a bundle of mail on the table.

"What do you think, Mother? The French have moved the seat of government to Bordeaux! Evidently, they don't think they can hold Paris."

Mrs. Wheeler wiped her pale, perspiring face with the hem of her apron and sat down in the nearest chair. "You mean that Paris is not the capital of France any more? Can that be true?"

"That's what it looks like. Though the papers say it's only a precautionary measure."

She rose. "Let's go up to the map. I don't remember exactly where Bordeaux is. Mahailey, you won't let my vinegar burn, will you?"

Claude followed her to the sitting-room, where her new map hung on the wall above the carpet lounge. Leaning against the back of a willow rocking-chair, she began to move her hand about over the brightly coloured, shiny surface, murmuring, "Yes, there is Bordeaux, so far to the south; and there is Paris."

Claude, behind her, looked over her shoulder. "Do you suppose they are going to hand their city over to the Germans, like a Christmas present? I should think they'd burn it first, the way the Russians did Moscow. They can do better than that now, they can dynamite it!"

"Don't say such things." Mrs. Wheeler dropped into the deep willow chair, realizing that she was very tired, now that she had left the stove and the heat of the kitchen. She began weakly to wave the palm leaf fan before her face. "It's said to be such a beautiful city. Perhaps the Germans will spare it, as they did Brussels. They must be sick of destruction by now. Get the encyclopaedia and see what it says. I've left my glasses downstairs."

Claude brought a volume from the bookcase and sat down on the lounge. He began: *"Paris, the capital city of France and the Department of the Seine,*—Shall I skip the history?"

"No. Read it all."

He cleared his throat and began again: *"At its first appearance in history, there was nothing to foreshadow the important part which Paris was to play in Europe and in the world,"* etc.

Mrs. Wheeler rocked and fanned, forgetting the kitchen and the cucumbers as if they had never been. Her tired body was resting, and her mind, which was never tired, was occupied with the account of early religious foundations under the Merovingian kings. Her eyes were always agreeably employed when they rested upon the sunburned neck and catapult shoulders of her red-headed son.

Claude read faster and faster until he stopped with a gasp.

"Mother, there are pages of kings! We'll read that some other time. I want to find out what it's like now, and whether it's going to have any more history." He ran his finger up and down the columns. "Here, this looks like business. *Defences: Paris, in a recent German account of the greatest fortresses of the world, possesses three distinct rings of defences"*—here he broke off. "Now what do you think of that? A German account, and this is an English book! The world simply made a mistake about the Germans all along. It's as if we invited a neighbour over here and showed him our cattle and barns, and all the time he was planning how he would come at night and club us in our beds."

Mrs. Wheeler passed her hand over her brow. "Yet we have had so many German neighbours, and never one that wasn't kind and helpful."

"I know it. Everything Mrs. Erlich ever told me about Germany made me want to go there. And the people that sing all those beautiful songs about women and children went into Belgian villages and—"

"Don't, Claude!" his mother put out her hands as if to push his words back. "Read about the defences of Paris; that's what we must think about now. I can't but believe there is one fort the

Germans didn't put down in their book, and that it will stand.
We know Paris is a wicked city, but there must be many God-
fearing people there, and God has preserved it all these years.
You saw in the paper how the churches are full all day of women
praying." She leaned forward and smiled at him indulgently.
"And you believe those prayers will accomplish nothing, son?"

Claude squirmed, as he always did when his mother touched
upon certain subjects. "Well, you see, I can't forget that the
Germans are praying, too. And I guess they are just naturally
more pious than the French." Taking up the book he began
once more: *"In the low ground again, at the narrowest part of the great
loop of the Marne,"* etc.

Claude and his mother had grown familiar with the name of
that river, and with the idea of its strategic importance, before it
began to stand out in black headlines a few days later.

The fall ploughing had begun as usual. Mr. Wheeler had
decided to put in six hundred acres of wheat again. Whatever
happened on the other side of the world, they would need
bread. He took a third team himself and went into the field every
morning to help Dan and Claude. The neighbours said that
nobody but the Kaiser had ever been able to get Nat Wheeler
down to regular work.

Since the men were all afield, Mrs. Wheeler now went every
morning to the mailbox at the crossroads, a quarter of a mile
away, to get yesterday's Omaha and Kansas City papers which the
carrier left. In her eagerness she opened and began to read
them as she turned homeward, and her feet, never too sure, took
a wandering way among sunflowers and buffalo-burrs. One
morning, indeed, she sat down on a red grass bank beside the
road and read all the war news through before she stirred, while
the grasshoppers played leap-frog over her skirts, and the
gophers came out of their holes and blinked at her. That noon,
when she saw Claude leading his team to the water tank, she hurried down to him without stopping to find her bonnet, and
reached the windmill breathless.

149

"The French have stopped falling back, Claude. They are standing at the Marne. There is a great battle going on. The papers say it may decide the war. It is so near Paris that some of the army went out in taxi-cabs."

Claude drew himself up. "Well, it will decide about Paris, anyway, won't it? How many divisions?"

"I can't make out. The accounts are so confusing. But only a few of the English are there, and the French are terribly outnumbered. Your father got in before you, and he has the papers upstairs."

"They are twenty-four hours old. I'll go to Vicount tonight after I'm done work, and get the Hastings paper."

In the evening, when he came back from town, he found his father and mother waiting up for him. He stopped a moment in the sitting-room. "There is not much news, except that the battle is on, and practically the whole French army is engaged. The Germans outnumber them five to three in men, and nobody knows how much in artillery. General Joffre says the French will fall back no farther." He did not sit down, but went straight upstairs to his room.

Mrs. Wheeler put out the lamp, undressed, and lay down, but not to sleep. Long afterward, Claude heard her gently closing a window, and he smiled to himself in the dark. His mother, he knew, had always thought of Paris as the wickedest of cities, the capital of a frivolous, wine-drinking, Catholic people, who were responsible for the massacre of St. Bartholomew and for the grinning atheist, Voltaire. For the last two weeks, ever since the French began to fall back in Lorraine, he had noticed with amusement her growing solicitude for Paris.

It was curious, he reflected, lying wide awake in the dark: four days ago the seat of government had been moved to Bordeaux,— with the effect that Paris seemed suddenly to have become the capital, not of France, but of the world! He knew he was not the only farmer boy who wished himself tonight beside the Marne. The fact that the river had a pronounceable name, with a hard Western "r" standing like a keystone in the middle of it, somehow

gave one's imagination a firmer hold on the situation. Lying still
and thinking fast, Claude felt that even he could clear the bar of
French "politeness" — so much more terrifying than German
bullets — and slip unnoticed into that outnumbered army. One's
manners wouldn't matter on the Marne tonight, the night of the
eighth of September, 1914. There was nothing on earth he
would so gladly be as an atom in that wall of flesh and blood that
rose and melted and rose again before the city which had meant
so much through all the centuries — but had never meant so
much before. Its name had come to have the purity of an
abstract idea. In great sleepy continents, in land-locked harvest
towns, in the little islands of the sea, for four days men watched
that name as they might stand out at night to watch a comet, or
to see a star fall.

X

IT was Sunday afternoon and Claude had gone down to the mill house, as Enid and her mother had returned from Michigan the day before. Mrs. Wheeler, propped back in a rocking chair, was reading, and Mr. Wheeler, in his shirt sleeves, his Sunday collar unbuttoned, was sitting at his walnut secretary, amusing himself with columns of figures. Presently he rose and yawned, stretching his arms above his head.

"Claude thinks he wants to begin building right away, up on the quarter next the timber claim. I've been figuring on the lumber. Building materials are cheap just now, so I suppose I'd better let him go ahead."

Mrs. Wheeler looked up absently from the page. "Why, I suppose so."

Her husband sat down astride a chair, and leaning his arms on the back of it, looked at her. "What do you think of this match, anyway? I don't know as I've heard you say."

"Enid is a good, Christian girl. . ." Mrs. Wheeler began resolutely, but her sentence hung in the air like a question.

He moved impatiently. "Yes, I know. But what does a husky boy like Claude want to pick out a girl like that for? Why, Evangeline, she'll be the old woman over again!"

Apparently these misgivings were not new to Mrs. Wheeler, for she put out her hand to stop him and whispered in solemn agitation, "Don't say anything! Don't breathe!"

"Oh, I won't interfere! I never do. I'd rather have her for a daughter-in-law than a wife, by a long shot. Claude's more of a fool than I thought him." He picked up his hat and strolled down to the barn, but his wife did not recover her composure so easily. She left the chair where she had hopefully settled herself for comfort, took up a feather duster and began moving distractedly about the room, brushing the surface of the furniture. When the war news was bad, or when she felt troubled about Claude, she set to cleaning house or overhauling the closets, thankful to be able to put some little thing to rights in such a disordered world.

As soon as the fall planting was done, Claude got the well-borers out from town to drill his new well, and while they were at work he began digging his cellar. He was building his house on the level stretch beside his father's timber claim because, when he was a little boy, he had thought that grove of trees the most beautiful spot in the world. It was a square of about thirty acres, set out in ash and box-elder and cotton-woods, with a thick mulberry hedge on the south side. The trees had been neglected of late years, but if he lived up there he could manage to trim them and care for them at odd moments.

Every morning now he ran up in the Ford and worked at his cellar. He had heard that the deeper a cellar was, the better it was; and he meant that this one should be deep enough. One day Leonard Dawson stopped to see what progress he was making. Standing on the edge of the hole, he shouted to the lad who was sweating below.

"My God, Claude, what do you want of a cellar as deep as that? When your wife takes a notion to go to China, you can open a trap-door and drop her through!"

Claude flung down his pick and ran up the ladder. "Enid's not going to have notions of that sort," he said wrathfully.

"Well, you needn't get mad. I'm glad to hear it. I was sorry when the other girl went. It always looked to me like Enid had her face set for China, but I haven't seen her for a good while, — not since before she went off to Michigan with the old lady."

After Leonard was gone, Claude returned to his work, still out of humour. He was not altogether happy in his mind about Enid. When he went down to the mill it was usually Mr. Royce, not Enid, who sought to detain him, followed him down the path to the gate and seemed sorry to see him go. He could not blame Enid with any lack of interest in what he was doing. She talked and thought of nothing but the new house, and most of her suggestions were good. He often wished she would ask for something unreasonable and extravagant. But she had no selfish whims, and even insisted that the comfortable upstairs sleeping room he had planned with such care should be reserved for a guest chamber.

As the house began to take shape, Enid came up often in her car, to watch its growth, to show Claude samples of wallpapers and draperies, or a design for a window-seat she had cut from some magazine. There could be no question of her pride in every detail. The disappointing thing was that she seemed more interested in the house than in him. These months when they could be together as much as they pleased, she treated merely as a period of time in which they were building a house.

Everything would be all right when they were married, Claude told himself. He believed in the transforming power of marriage, as his mother believed in the miraculous effects of conversion. Marriage reduced all women to a common denominator; changed a cool, self-satisfied girl into a loving and generous one. It was quite right that Enid should be unconscious now of everything that she was to be when she was his wife. He told himself he wouldn't want it otherwise.

But he was lonely, all the same. He lavished upon the little house the solicitude and cherishing care that Enid seemed not to need. He stood over the carpenters urging the greatest nicety in the finish of closets and cupboards, the convenient placing of shelves, the exact joining of sills and casings. Often he stayed late in the evening, after the workmen with their noisy boots had gone home to supper. He sat down on a rafter or on the skeleton of the upper porch and quite lost himself in brooding, in anticipation of things that seemed as far away as ever. The dying light, the quiet stars coming out, were friendly and sympathetic. One night a bird flew in and fluttered wildly about among the partitions, shrieking with fright before it darted out into the dusk through one of the upper windows and found its way to freedom.

When the carpenters were ready to put in the staircase, Claude telephoned Enid and asked her to come and show them just what height she wanted the steps made. His mother had always had to climb stairs that were too steep. Enid stopped her car at the Frankfort High School at four o'clock and persuaded Gladys Farmer to drive out with her.

When they arrived they found Claude working on the lattice enclosure of the back porch. "Claude is like Jonah," Enid laughed. "He wants to plant gourd vines here, so they will run over the lattice and make shade. I can think of other vines that might be more ornamental."

Claude put down his hammer and said coaxingly: "Have you ever seen a gourd vine when it had something to climb on, Enid? You wouldn't believe how pretty they are; big green leaves, and gourds and yellow blossoms hanging all over them at the same time. An old German woman who keeps a lunch counter at one of those stations on the road to Lincoln has them running up her back porch, and I've wanted to plant some ever since I first saw hers."

Enid smiled indulgently. "Well, I suppose you'll let me have clematis for the front porch, anyway? The men are getting ready to leave, so we'd better see about the steps."

After the workmen had gone, Claude took the girls upstairs by the ladder. They emerged from a little entry into a large room which extended over both the front and back parlours. The carpenters called it "the pool hall." There were two long windows, like doors, opening upon the porch roof, and in the sloping ceiling were two dormer windows, one looking north to the timber claim and the other south toward Lovely Creek. Gladys at once felt a singular pleasantness about this chamber, empty and unplastered as it was. "What a lovely room!" she exclaimed.

Claude took her up eagerly. "Don't you think so? You see it's my idea to have the second floor for ourselves, instead of cutting it up into little boxes as people usually do. We can come up here and forget the farm and the kitchen and all our troubles. I've made a big closet for each of us, and got everything just right. And now Enid wants to keep this room for preachers!"

Enid laughed. "Not only for preachers, Claude. For Gladys, when she comes to visit us—you see she likes it—and for your mother when she comes to spend a week and rest. I don't think we ought to take the best room for ourselves."

"Why not?" Claude argued hotly. "I'm building the whole house for ourselves. Come out on the porch roof, Gladys. Isn't this fine for hot nights? I want to put a railing round and make this into a balcony, where we can have chairs and a hammock."

Gladys sat down on the low window-sill. "Enid, you'd be foolish to keep this for a guest room. Nobody would ever enjoy it as much as you would. You can see the whole country from here."

Enid smiled, but showed no sign of relenting. "Let's wait and watch the sun go down. Be careful, Claude. It makes me nervous to see you lying there."

He was stretched out on the edge of the roof, one leg hanging over, and his head pillowed on his arm. The flat fields turned red, the distant windmills flashed white, and little rosy clouds appeared in the sky above them.

"If I make this into a balcony," Claude murmured, "the peak of the roof will always throw a shadow over it in the afternoon, and at night the stars will be right overhead. It will be a fine place to sleep in harvest time."

"Oh, you could always come up here to sleep on a hot night," Enid said quickly.

"It wouldn't be the same."

They sat watching the light die out of the sky, and Enid and Gladys drew close together as the coolness of the autumn evening came on. The three friends were thinking about the same thing; and yet, if by some sorcery each had begun to speak his thoughts aloud, amazement and bitterness would have fallen upon all. Enid's reflections were the most blameless. The discussion about the guest room had reminded her of Brother Weldon. In September, on her way to Michigan with Mrs. Royce, she had stopped for a day in Lincoln to take counsel with Arthur Weldon as to whether she ought to marry one whom she described to him as "an unsaved man." Young Mr. Weldon approached this subject with a cautious tread, but when he learned that the man in question was Claude Wheeler, he became more partisan than was his wont. He seemed to think that her marrying Claude was the one way to reclaim him, and did not hesitate to say that the most important service devout girls could perform for the church was to bring promising young men to its support. Enid had been almost certain that Mr. Weldon would approve her course before she consulted him, but his concurrence always gratified her pride. She told him that when she had a home of her own she would expect him to spend a part of his summer vacation there, and he blushingly expressed his willingness to do so.

Gladys, too, was lost in her own thoughts, sitting with that ease which made her seem rather indolent, her head resting against the empty window frame, facing the setting sun. The rosy light made her brown eyes gleam like old copper, and there was a moody look in them, as if in her mind she were defying something. When he happened to glance at her, it occurred to Claude that it was a hard destiny to be the exceptional person in a community, to be more gifted or more intelligent than the rest. For a girl it must be doubly hard. He sat up suddenly and broke the long silence.

"I forgot, Enid, I have a secret to tell you. Over in the timber claim the other day I started up a flock of quail. They must be the only ones left in all this neighbourhood, and I doubt if they ever come out of the timber. The bluegrass hasn't been mowed in there for years, — not since I first went away to school, — and maybe they live on the grass seeds. In summer, of course, there are mulberries."

Enid wondered whether the birds could have learned enough about the world to stay hidden in the timber lot. Claude was sure they had.

"Nobody ever goes near the place except Father; he stops there sometimes. Maybe he has seen them and never said a word. It would be just like him." He told them he had scattered shelled corn in the grass, so that the birds would not be tempted to fly over into Leonard Dawson's cornfield. "If Leonard saw them, he'd likely take a shot at them."

"Why don't you ask him not to?" Enid suggested.

Claude laughed. "That would be asking a good deal.

When a bunch of quail rise out of a cornfield they're a mighty tempting sight, if a man likes hunting. We'll have a picnic for you when you come out next summer, Gladys. There are some pretty places over there in the timber."

Gladys started up. "Why, it's night already! It's lovely here, but you must get me home, Enid."

They found it dark inside. Claude took Enid down the ladder and out to her car, and then went back for Gladys. She was sitting on the floor at the top of the ladder. Giving her his hand he helped her to rise.

"So you like my little house," he said gratefully.

"Yes. Oh, yes!" Her voice was full of feeling, but she did not exert herself to say more. Claude descended in front of her to keep her from slipping. She hung back while he led her through confusing doorways and helped her over the piles of laths that littered the floors. At the edge of the gaping cellar entrance she stopped and leaned wearily on his arm for a moment. She did not speak, but he understood that his new house made her sad; that she, too, had come to the place where she must turn out of the old path. He longed to whisper to her and beg her not to marry his brother. He lingered and hesitated, fumbling in the dark. She had his own cursed kind of sensibility; she would expect too much from life and be disappointed. He was reluctant to lead her out into the chilly evening without some word of entreaty. He would willingly have prolonged their passage,—through many rooms and corridors. Perhaps, had that been possible, the strength in him would have found what it was seeking; even in this short interval it had stirred and made itself felt, had uttered a confused appeal. Claude was greatly surprised at himself.

XI

ENID decided that she would be married in the first week of June. Early in May the plasterers and painters began to be busy in the new house. The walls began to shine, and Claude went about all day, oiling and polishing the hard-pine floors and wainscoting. He hated to have anybody step on his floors. He planted gourd vines about the back porch, set out clematis and lilac bushes, and put in a kitchen garden. He and Enid were going to Denver and Colorado Springs for their wedding trip, but Ralph would be at home then, and he had promised to come over and water the flowers and shrubs if the weather was dry.

Enid often brought her work and sat sewing on the front porch while Claude was rubbing the woodwork inside the house, or digging and planting outside. This was the best part of his courtship. It seemed to him that he had never spent such happy days before. If Enid did not come, he kept looking down the road and listening, went from one thing to another and made no progress. He felt full of energy, so long as she sat there on the porch, with lace and ribbons and muslin in her lap. When he passed by, going in or out, and stopped to be near her for a moment, she seemed glad to have him tarry. She liked him to admire her needlework, and did not hesitate to show him the featherstitching and embroidery she was putting on her new underclothes. He could see, from the glances they exchanged, that the painters thought this very bold behaviour in one so soon to be a bride. He thought it very charming behaviour himself, though he would never have expected it of Enid. His heart beat hard when he realized how far she confided in him, how little she was afraid of him! She would let him linger there, standing over her and looking down at her quick fingers, or sitting on the ground at her feet, gazing at the muslin pinned to her knee, until his own sense of propriety told him to get about his work and spare the feelings of the painters.

"When are you going over to the timber claim with me?" he asked, dropping on the ground beside her one warm, windy afternoon. Enid was sitting on the porch floor, her back against a pillar, and her feet on one of those round mats of pursley that grow over hard-beaten earth. "I've found my flock of quail again. They live in the deep grass, over by a ditch that holds water most of the year. I'm going to plant a few rows of peas in there, so they'll have a feeding ground at home. I consider Leonard's cornfield a great danger. I don't know whether to take him into my confidence or not."

"You've told Ernest Havel, I suppose?"

"Oh, yes!" Claude replied, trying not to be aware of the little note of acrimony in her voice. "He's perfectly safe. That place is a paradise for birds. The trees are full of nests. You can stand over there in the morning and hear the young robins squawking for their breakfast. Come up early tomorrow morning and go over with me, won't you? But wear heavy shoes; it's wet in the long grass."

While they were talking a sudden whirlwind swept round the corner of the house, caught up the little mound of folded lace corset-covers and strewed them over the dusty yard. Claude ran after them with Enid's flowered workbag and thrust them into it as he came upon one after another, fluttering in the weeds. When he returned, Enid had folded her needle-case and was putting on her hat. "Thank you," she said with a smile. "Did you find everything?"

"I think so." He hurried toward the car to hide his guilty face. One little lace thing he had not put into the bag, but had thrust into his pocket.

The next morning Enid came up early to hear the birds in the timber.

XII

On the night before his wedding Claude went to bed early. He had been dashing about with Ralph all day in the car, making final preparations, and was worn out. He fell asleep almost at once. The women of the household could not so easily forget the great event of tomorrow. After the supper dishes were washed, Mahailey clambered up to the attic to get the quilt she had so long been saving for a wedding present for Claude. She took it out of the chest, unfolded it, and counted the stars in the pattern—counting was an accomplishment she was proud of— before she wrapped it up. It was to go down to the mill house with the other presents tomorrow. Mrs. Wheeler went to bed many times that night. She kept thinking of things that ought to be looked after; getting up and going to make sure that Claude's heavy underwear had been put into his trunk, against the chance of cold in the mountains; or creeping downstairs to see that the six roasted chickens which were to help out at the wedding supper were securely covered from the cats. As she went about these tasks, she prayed constantly. She had not prayed so long and fervently since the battle of the Marne.

Early the next morning Ralph loaded the big car with the presents and baskets of food and ran down to the Royces'. Two motors from town were already standing in the mill yard; they had brought a company of girls who came with all the June roses in Frankfort to trim the house for the wedding. When Ralph tooted his horn, half-a-dozen of them ran out to greet him, reproaching him because he had not brought his brother along.

Ralph was immediately pressed into service. He carried the step-ladder wherever he was told, drove nails, and wound thorny sprays of rambler roses around the pillars between the front and back parlours, making the arch under which the ceremony was to take place.

Gladys Farmer had not been able to leave her classes at the High School to help in this friendly work, but at eleven o'clock a livery automobile drove up, laden with white and pink peonies from her front yard, and bringing a box of hothouse flowers she had ordered for Enid from Hastings. The girls admired them, but declared that Gladys was extravagant, as usual; the flowers from her own yard would really have been enough. The car was driven by a lank, ragged boy who worked about the town garage, and who was called "Silent Irv," because nobody could ever get a word out of him. He had almost no voice at all,—a thin little squeak in the top of his throat, like the gasping whisper of a medium in her trance state. When he came to the front door, both arms full of peonies, he managed to wheeze out:

"These are from Miss Farmer. There are some more down there."

The girls went back to his car with him, and he took out a square box, tied up with white ribbons and little silver bells, containing the bridal bouquet.

"How did you happen to get these?" Ralph asked the thin boy. "I was to go to town for them."

The messenger swallowed. "Miss Farmer told me if there were any other flowers at the station marked for here, I should bring them along."

"That was nice of her." Ralph thrust his hand into his trousers pocket. "How much? I'll settle with you before I forget."

A pink flush swept over the boy's pale face,—a delicate face under ragged hair, contracted by a kind of shrinking unhappiness. His eyes were always half-closed, as if he did not want to see the world around him, or to be seen by it. He went about like somebody in a dream. "Miss Farmer," he whispered, "has paid me."

"Well, she thinks of everything!" exclaimed one of the girls. "You used to go to school to Gladys, didn't you, Irv?"

"Yes, mam." He got into his car without opening the door, slipping like an eel round the steering-rod, and drove off.

The girls followed Ralph up the gravel walk toward the house. One whispered to the others: "Do you suppose Gladys will come out tonight with Bayliss Wheeler? I always thought she had a pretty warm spot in her heart for Claude, myself."

Some one changed the subject. "I can't get over hearing Irv talk so much. Gladys must have put a spell on him."

"She was always kind to him in school," said the girl who had questioned the silent boy. "She said he was good in his studies, but he was so frightened he could never recite. She let him write out the answers at his desk."

Ralph stayed for lunch, playing about with the girls until his mother telephoned for him. "Now I'll have to go home and look after my brother, or he'll turn up tonight in a striped shirt."

"Give him our love," the girls called after him, "and tell him not to be late."

As he drove toward the farm, Ralph met Dan, taking Claude's trunk into town. He slowed his car. "Any message?" he called.

Dan grinned. "Naw. I left him doin' as well as could be expected."

Mrs. Wheeler met Ralph on the stairs. "He's up in his room. He complains his new shoes are too tight. I think it's nervousness. Perhaps he'll let you shave him; I'm sure he'll cut himself. And I wish the barber hadn't cut his hair so short, Ralph. I hate this new fashion of shearing men behind the ears. The back of his neck is the ugliest part of a man." She spoke with such resentment that Ralph broke into a laugh.

"Why, Mother, I thought all men looked alike to you! Anyhow, Claude's no beauty."

"When will you want your bath? I'll have to manage so that everybody won't be calling for hot water at once." She turned to Mr. Wheeler who sat writing a check at the secretary. "Father, could you take your bath now, and be out of the way?"

"Bath?" Mr. Wheeler shouted, "I don't want any bath! I'm not going to be married tonight. I guess we don't have to boil the whole house for Enid."

Ralph snickered and shot upstairs. He found Claude sitting on the bed, with one shoe off and one shoe on. A pile of socks lay scattered on the rug. A suitcase stood open on one chair and a black travelling bag on another.

"Are you sure they're too small?" Ralph asked.

"About four sizes."

"Well, why didn't you get them big enough?"

"I did. That shark in Hastings worked off another pair on me when I wasn't looking. That's all right," snatching away the shoe his brother had picked up to examine. "I don't care, so long as I can stand in them. You'd better go telephone the depot and ask if the train's on time."

"They won't know yet. It's seven hours till it's due."

"Then telephone later. But find out, somehow. I don't want to stand around that station, waiting for the train."

Ralph whistled. Clearly, his young man was going to be hard to manage. He proposed a bath as a soothing measure. No, Claude had had his bath. Had he, then, packed his suitcase?

"How the devil can I pack it when I don't know what I'm going to put on?"

"You'll put on one shirt and one pair of socks. I'm going to get some of this stuff out of the way for you." Ralph caught up a handful of socks and fell to sorting them. Several had bright red spots on the toe. He began to laugh.

"I know why your shoe hurts, you've cut your foot!"

Claude sprang up as if a hornet had stung him. "Will you get out of here," he shouted, "and let me alone?"

Ralph vanished. He told his mother he would dress at once, as they might have to use force with Claude at the last moment.

The wedding ceremony was to be at eight, supper was to follow, and Claude and Enid were to leave Frankfort at 10:25, on the Denver express. At six o'clock, when Ralph knocked at his brother's door, he found him shaved and brushed, and dressed, except for his coat. His tucked shirt was not rumpled, and his tie was properly knotted. Whatever pain they concealed, his patent leather shoes were smooth and glistening and resolutely pointed.

"Are you packed?" Ralph asked in astonishment.

"Nearly. I wish you'd go over things and make them look a little neater, if you can. I'd hate to have a girl see the inside of that suitcase, the way it is. Where shall I put my cigars? They'll make everything smell, wherever I put them. All my clothes seem to smell of cooking, or starch, or something. I don't know what Mahailey does to them," he ended bitterly.

Ralph looked outraged. "Well, of all ingratitude! Mahailey's been ironing your damned old shirts for a week!"

"Yes, yes, I know. Don't rattle me. I forgot to put any handkerchiefs in my trunk, so you'll have to get the whole bunch in somewhere."

Mr. Wheeler appeared in the doorway, his Sunday black trousers gallowsed up high over a white shirt, wafting a rich odor of bayrum from his tumbled hair. He held a thin folded paper delicately between his thick fingers.

"Where is your bill-book, son?"

Claude caught up his discarded trousers and extracted a square of leather from the pocket. His father took it and placed the bit of paper inside with the bank notes. "You may want to pick up some trifle your wife fancies," he said. "Have you got your railroad tickets in here? Here is your trunk check Dan brought back. Don't forget, I've put it in with your tickets and marked it C. W., so you'll know which is your check and which is Enid's."

"Yes, sir. Thank you, sir."

Claude had already drawn from the bank all the money he would need. This additional bank check was Mr. Wheeler's admission that he was sorry for some sarcastic remarks he had made a few days ago, when he discovered that Claude had reserved a stateroom on the Denver express. Claude had answered curtly that when Enid and her mother went to Michigan they always had a stateroom, and he wasn't going to ask her to travel less comfortably with him.

At seven o'clock the Wheeler family set out in the two cars that stood waiting by the windmill. Mr. Wheeler drove the big Cadillac, and Ralph took Mahailey and Dan in the Ford. When they reached the mill house the outer yard was already black with motors, and the porch and parlours were full of people talking and moving about.

Claude went directly upstairs. Ralph began to seat the guests, arranging the folding chairs in such a way as to leave a passage from the foot of the stairs to the floral arch he had constructed that morning. The preacher had his Bible in his hand and was standing under the light, hunting for his chapter. Enid would have preferred to have Mr. Weldon come down from Lincoln to marry her, but that would have wounded Mr. Snowberry deeply. After all, he was her minister, though he was not eloquent and persuasive like Arthur Weldon. He had fewer English words at his command than most human beings, and even those did not come to him readily. In his pulpit he sought for them and struggled with them until drops of perspiration rolled from his forehead and fell upon his coarse, matted brown beard. But he believed what he said, and language was so little an accomplishment with him that he was not tempted to say more than he believed. He had been a drummer boy in the Civil War, on the losing side, and he was a simple, courageous man.

Ralph was to be both usher and best man. Gladys Farmer could not be one of the bridesmaids because she was to play the wedding march. At eight o'clock Enid and Claude came downstairs together, conducted by Ralph and followed by four girls dressed in white, like the bride. They took their places under the arch before the preacher. He began with the chapter from Genesis about the creation of man, and Adam's rib, reading in a laboured manner, as if he did not quite know why he had selected that passage and were looking for something he did not find. His nose-glasses kept falling off and dropping upon the open book. Throughout this prolonged fumbling Enid stood calm, looking at him respectfully, very pretty in her short veil. Claude was so pale that he looked unnatural,—nobody had ever seen him like that before. His face, between his very black clothes and his smooth, sandy hair, was white and severe, and he uttered his responses in a hollow voice. Mahailey, at the back of the room, in a black hat with green gooseberries on it, was standing, in order to miss nothing. She watched Mr. Snowberry as if she hoped to catch some visible sign of the miracle he was performing. She always wondered just what it was the preacher did to make the wrongest thing in the world the rightest thing in the world.

When it was over, Enid went upstairs to put on her travelling dress, and Ralph and Gladys began seating the guests for supper. Just twenty minutes later Enid came down and took her place beside Claude at the head of the long table. The company rose and drank the bride's health in grape-juice punch. Mr. Royce, however, while the guests were being seated, had taken Mr. Wheeler down to the fruit cellar, where the two old friends drank off a glass of well-seasoned Kentucky whiskey, and shook hands. When they came back to the table, looking younger than when they withdrew, the preacher smelled the tang of spirits and felt slighted. He looked disconsolately into his ruddy goblet and thought about the marriage at Cana. He tried to apply his Bible literally to life and, though he didn't dare breathe it aloud in these days, he could never see why he was better than his Lord.

Ralph, as master of ceremonies, kept his head and forgot nothing. When it was time to start, he tapped Claude on the shoulder, cutting his father short in one of his best stories. Contrary to custom, the bridal couple were to go to the station unaccompanied, and they vanished from the head of the table with only a nod and a smile to the guests. Ralph hurried them into the light car, where he had already stowed Enid's hand luggage. Only wizened little Mrs. Royce slipped out from the kitchen to bid them good-bye.

That evening some bad boys had come out from town and strewn the road near the mill with dozens of broken glass bottles, after which they hid in the wild plum bushes to wait for the fun. Ralph's was the first car out, and though his lights glittered on this bed of jagged glass, there was no time to stop; the road was ditched on either side, so he had to drive straight ahead, and got into Frankfort on flat tires. The express whistled just as he pulled up at the station. He and Claude caught up the four pieces of hand luggage and put them in the stateroom. Leaving Enid there with the bags, the two boys went to the rear platform of the observation car to talk until the last moment. Ralph checked off on his fingers the list of things he had promised Claude to attend to. Claude thanked him feelingly. He felt that without Ralph he could never have got married at all. They had never been such good friends as during the last fortnight.

The wheels began to turn. Ralph gripped Claude's hand, ran to the front of the car and stepped off. As Claude passed him, he stood waving his handkerchief, — a rather funny figure under the station lights, in his black clothes and his stiff straw hat, his short legs well apart, wearing his incurably jaunty air.

The train glided quietly out through the summer darkness, along the timbered river valley. Claude was alone on the back platform, smoking a nervous cigar. As they passed the deep cut where Lovely Creek flowed into the river, he saw the lights of the mill house flash for a moment in the distance. The night air was still; heavy with the smell of sweet clover that grew high along the tracks, and of wild grapevines wet with dew. The conductor came to ask for the tickets, saying with a wise smile that he had been hunting for him, as he didn't like to trouble the lady.

After he was gone, Claude looked at his watch, threw away the end of his cigar, and went back through the Pullman cars. The passengers had gone to bed; the overhead lights were always turned low when the train left Frankfort. He made his way through the aisles of swaying green curtains, and tapped at the door of his state room. It opened a little way, and Enid stood there in a white silk dressing-gown with many ruffles, her hair in two smooth braids over her shoulders.

"Claude," she said in a low voice, "would you mind getting a berth somewhere out in the car tonight? The porter says they are not all taken. I'm not feeling very well. I think the dressing on the chicken salad must have been too rich."

He answered mechanically. "Yes, certainly. Can't I get you something?"

"No, thank you. Sleep will do me more good than anything else. Good-night."

She closed the door, and he heard the lock slip. He stood looking at the highly polished wood of the panel for a moment, then turned irresolutely and went back along the slightly swaying aisle of green curtains. In the observation car he stretched himself out upon two wicker chairs and lit another cigar. At twelve o'clock the porter came in.

"This car is closed for the night, sah. Is you the gen'leman from the stateroom in fourteen? Do you want a lower?"

"No, thank you. Is there a smoking car?"

"They is the day-coach smokah, but it ain't likely very clean at this time o' night."

"That's all right. It's forward?" Claude absently handed him a coin, and the porter conducted him to a very dirty car where the floor was littered with newspapers and cigar stumps, and the leather cushions were grey with dust. A few desperate looking men lay about with their shoes off and their suspenders hanging down their back. The sight of them reminded Claude that his left foot was very sore, and that his shoes must have been hurting him for some time. He pulled them off, and thrust his feet, in their silk socks, on the opposite seat.

On that long, dirty, uncomfortable ride Claude felt many things, but the paramount feeling was homesickness. His hurt was of a kind that made him turn with a sort of aching cowardice to the old, familiar things that were as sure as the sunrise. If only the sagebrush plain, over which the stars were shining, could suddenly break up and resolve itself into the windings of Lovely Creek, with his father's house on the hill, dark and silent in the summer night! When he closed his eyes he could see the light in his mother's window; and, lower down, the glow of Mahailey's lamp, where she sat nodding and mending his old shirts. Human love was a wonderful thing, he told himself, and it was most wonderful where it had least to gain.

By morning the storm of anger, disappointment, and humiliation that was boiling in him when he first sat down in the observation car, had died out. One thing lingered; the peculiarly casual, indifferent, uninterested tone of his wife's voice when she sent him away. It was the flat tone in which people make commonplace remarks about common things.

Day broke with silvery brightness on the summer sage. The sky grew pink, the sand grew gold. The dawn-wind brought through the windows the acrid smell of the sagebrush: an odour that is peculiarly stimulating in the early morning, when it always seems to promise freedom . . . large spaces, new beginnings, better days.

The train was due in Denver at eight o'clock. Exactly at seven thirty Claude knocked at Enid's door,—this time firmly. She was dressed, and greeted him with a fresh, smiling face, holding her hat in her hand.

"Are you feeling better?" he asked.

"Oh, yes! I am perfectly all right this morning. I've put out all your things for you, there on the seat."

He glanced at them. "Thank you. But I won't have time to change, I'm afraid."

"Oh, won't you? I'm so sorry I forgot to give you your bag last night. But you must put on another necktie, at least. You look too much like a groom."

"Do I?" he asked, with a scarcely perceptible curl of his lip.

Everything he needed was neatly arranged on the plush seat; shirt, collar, tie, brushes, even a handkerchief. Those in his pockets were black from dusting off the cinders that blew in all night, and he threw them down and took up the clean one. There was a damp spot on it, and as he unfolded it he recognized the scent of a cologne Enid often used. For some reason this attention unmanned him. He felt the smart of tears in his eyes, and to hide them bent over the metal basin and began to scrub his face. Enid stood behind him, adjusting her hat in the mirror.

"How terribly smoky you are, Claude. I hope you don't smoke before breakfast?"

"No. I was in the smoking car awhile. I suppose my clothes got full of it."

"You are covered with dust and cinders, too!" She took the clothes broom from the rack and began to brush him.

Claude caught her hand. "Don't, please!" he said sharply. "The porter can do that for me."

Enid watched him furtively as he closed and strapped his suitcase. She had often heard that men were cross before breakfast.

"Sure you've forgotten nothing?" he asked before he closed her bag.

"Yes. I never lose things on the train,—do you?"

"Sometimes," he replied guardedly, not looking up as he snapped the catch.

BOOK THREE

SUNRISE ON THE PRAIRIE

CLAUDE was to continue farming with his father, and after he returned from his wedding journey, he fell at once to work. The harvest was almost as abundant as that of the summer before, and he was busy in the fields six days a week.

One afternoon in August he came home with his team, watered and fed the horses in a leisurely way, and then entered his house by the back door. Enid, he knew, would not be there. She had gone to Frankfort to a meeting of the Anti-Saloon League. The Prohibition party was bestirring itself in Nebraska that summer, confident of voting the State dry the following year, which purpose it triumphantly accomplished.

Enid's kitchen, full of the afternoon sun, glittered with new paint, spotless linoleum, and blue-and-white cooking vessels. In the dining-room the cloth was laid, and the table was neatly set for one. Claude opened the icebox, where his supper was arranged for him; a dish of canned salmon with a white sauce; hardboiled eggs, peeled and lying in a nest of lettuce leaves; a bowl of ripe tomatoes, a bit of cold rice pudding; cream and butter. He placed these things on the table, cut some bread, and after carelessly washing his face and hands, sat down to eat in his working shirt. He propped the newspaper against a red glass water pitcher and read the war news while he had his supper. He was annoyed when he heard heavy footsteps coming around the house. Leonard Dawson stuck his head in at the kitchen door, and Claude rose quickly and reached for his hat; but Leonard came in, uninvited, and sat down. His brown shirt was wet where his suspenders gripped his shoulders, and his face, under a wide straw hat which he did not remove, was unshaven and streaked with dust.

"Go ahead and finish your supper," he cried. "Having a wife with an electric is next thing to having no wife at all. How they do like to roll around! I've been mighty blamed careful to see that Susie never learned to drive a car. See here, Claude, how soon do you figure you'll be able to let me have the thrasher? My wheat will begin to sprout in the shock pretty soon. Do you guess your father would be willing to work on Sunday, if I helped you, to let the machine off a day earlier?"

"I'm afraid not. Mother wouldn't like it. We never have done that, even when we were crowded."

"Well, I think I'll go over and have a talk with your mother. If she could look inside my wheat shocks, maybe I could convince her it's pretty near a case of your neighbour's ox falling into a pit on the Sabbath day."

"That's a good idea. She's always reasonable."

Leonard rose. "What's the news?"

"The Germans have torpedoed an English passenger ship, the *Arabic;* coming this way, too."

"That's all right," Leonard declared. "Maybe Americans will stay at home now, and mind their own business. I don't care how they chew each other up over there, not a bit! I'd as soon one got wiped off the map as another."

"Your grandparents were English people, weren't they?"

"That's a long while ago. Yes, my grandmother wore a cap and little white curls, and I tell Susie I wouldn't mind if the baby turned out to have my grandmother's skin. She had the finest complexion I ever saw."

As they stepped out of the back door, a troop of white chickens with red combs ran squawking toward them. It was the hour at which the poultry was usually fed. Leonard stopped to admire them. "You've got a fine lot of hens. I always did like white leghorns. Where are all your roosters?"

"We've only got one. He's shut up in the coop. The brood hens are setting. Enid is going to try raising winter frys."

"Only one rooster? And may I ask what these hens do?"

Claude laughed. "They lay eggs, just the same,—better. It's the fertile eggs that spoil in warm weather."

This information seemed to make Leonard angry. "I never heard of such damned nonsense," he blustered. "I raise chickens on a natural basis, or I don't raise 'em at all." He jumped into his car for fear he would say more.

When he got home his wife was lifting supper, and the baby sat near her in its buggy, playing with a rattle. Dirty and sweaty as he was, Leonard picked up the clean baby and began to kiss it and smell it, rubbing his stubbly chin in the soft creases of its neck. The little girl was beside herself with delight.

"Go and wash up for supper, Len," Susie called from the stove. He put down the baby and began splashing in the tin basin, talking with his eyes shut.

"Susie, I'm in an awful temper. I can't stand that damned wife of Claude's!"

She was spearing roasting ears out of a big iron pot and looked up through the steam. "Why, have you seen her? I was listening on the telephone this morning and heard her tell Bayliss she would be in town until late."

"Oh, yes! She went to town all right, and he's over there eating a cold supper by himself. That woman's a fanatic. She ain't content with practising prohibition on humankind; she's begun now on the hens." While he placed the chairs and wheeled the baby up to the table, he explained Enid's method of raising poultry to his wife. She said she really didn't see any harm in it.

"Now be honest, Susie; did you ever know hens would keep on laying without a rooster?"

"No, I didn't, but I was brought up the old-fashioned way. Enid has poultry books and garden books, and all such things. I don't doubt she gets good ideas from them. But anyhow, you be careful. She's our nearest neighbour, and I don't want to have trouble with her."

"I'll have to keep out of her way, then. If she tries to do any missionary work among my chickens, I'll tell her a few home truths her husband's too bashful to tell her. It's my opinion she's got that boy cowed already."

"Now, Len, you know she won't bother your chickens. You keep quiet. But Claude does seem to sort of avoid people," Susie admitted, filling her husband's plate again. "Mrs. Joe Havel says Ernest don't go to Claude's any more. It seems Enid went over there and wanted Ernest to paste some Prohibition posters about fifteen million drunkards on their barn, for an example to the Bohemians. Ernest wouldn't do it, and told her he was going to vote for saloons, and Enid was quite spiteful, Mrs. Havel said. It's too bad, when those boys were such chums. I used to like to see them together." Susie spoke so kindly that her husband shot her a quick glance of shy affection.

"Do you suppose Claude relished having that preacher visiting them, when they hadn't been married two months? Sitting on the front porch in a white necktie every day, while Claude was out cutting wheat?"

"Well, anyhow, I guess Claude had more to eat when Brother Weldon was staying there. Preachers won't be fed on calories, or whatever it is Enid calls 'em," said Susie, who was given to looking on the bright side of things. "Claude's wife keeps a wonderful kitchen; but so could I, if I never cooked any more than she does."

Leonard gave her a meaning look. "I don't believe you would live with the sort of man you could feed out of a tin can."

"No, I don't believe I would." She pushed the buggy toward him. "Take her up, Daddy. She wants to play with you."

Leonard sat the baby on his shoulder and carried her off to show her the pigs. Susie kept laughing to herself as she cleared the table and washed the dishes; she was much amused by what her husband had told her.

Late that evening, when Leonard was starting for the barn to see that all was well before he went to bed, he observed a discreet black object rolling along the highroad in the moonlight, a red spark winking in the rear. He called Susie to the door.

"See, there she goes; going home to report the success of the meeting to Claude. Wouldn't that be a nice way to have your wife coming in?"

"Now, Leonard, if Claude likes it—"

"Likes it?" Big Leonard drew himself up. "What can he do, poor kid? He's stung!"

II

AFTER Leonard left him, Claude cleared away the remains of
his supper and watered the gourd vine before he went to milk.
It was not really a gourd vine at all, but a summer-squash, of the
crook-necked, warty, orange-coloured variety, and it was now
full of ripe squashes, hanging by strong stems among the rough
green leaves and prickly tendrils. Claude had watched its rapid
growth and the opening of its splotchy yellow blossoms, feeling
grateful to a thing that did so lustily what it was put there to do.
He had the same feeling for his little Jersey cow, which came
home every night with full udders and gave down her milk willingly, keeping her tail out of his face, as only a well-disposed
cow will do.

His milking done, he sat down on the front porch and lit a
cigar. While he smoked, he did not think about anything but
the quiet and the slow cooling of the atmosphere, and how
good it was to sit still. The moon swam up over the bare wheat
fields, big and magical, like a great flower. Presently he got
some bath towels, went across the yard to the windmill, took off
his clothes, and stepped into the tin horse tank. The water had
been warmed by the sun all afternoon, and was not much
cooler than his body. He stretched himself out in it, and resting
his head on the metal rim, lay on his back, looking up at the
moon. The sky was a midnight-blue, like warm, deep, blue
water, and the moon seemed to lie on it like a water-lily, floating forward with an invisible current. One expected to see its
great petals open.

For some reason, Claude began to think about the far-off times and countries it had shone upon. He never thought of the sun as coming from distant lands, or as having taken part in human life in other ages. To him, the sun rotated about the wheatfields. But the moon, somehow, came out of the historic past, and made him think of Egypt and the Pharaohs, Babylon and the hanging gardens. She seemed particularly to have looked down upon the follies and disappointments of men; into the slaves' quarters of old times, into prison windows, and into fortresses where captives languished.

Inside of living people, too, captives languished. Yes, inside of people who walked and worked in the broad sun, there were captives dwelling in darkness,—never seen from birth to death. Into those prisons the moon shone, and the prisoners crept to the windows and looked out with mournful eyes at the white globe which betrayed no secrets and comprehended all. Perhaps even in people like Mrs. Royce and his brother Bayliss there was something of this sort—but that was a shuddery thought. He dismissed it with a quick movement of his hand through the water, which, disturbed, caught the light and played black and gold, like something alive, over his chest. In his own mother the imprisoned spirit was almost more present to people than her corporeal self. He had so often felt it when he sat with her on summer nights like this. Mahailey, too, had one, though the walls of her prison were so thick—and Gladys Farmer. Oh, yes, how much Gladys must have to tell this perfect confidant! The people whose hearts were set high needed such intercourse— whose wish was so beautiful that there were no experiences in this world to satisfy it. And these children of the moon, with their unappeased longings and futile dreams, were a finer race than the children of the sun. This conception flooded the boy's heart like a second moonrise, flowed through him indefinite and strong, while he lay deathly still for fear of losing it.

At last the black cubical object which had caught Leonard Dawson's wrathful eye, came rolling along the highroad. Claude snatched up his clothes and towels, and without waiting to make use of either, he ran, a white man across a bare white yard. Gaining the shelter of the house, he found his bathrobe, and fled to the upper porch, where he lay down in the hammock. Presently he heard his name called, pronounced as if it were spelled "Clod." His wife came up the stairs and looked out at him. He lay motionless, with his eyes closed. She went away. When all was quiet again he looked off at the still country, and the moon in the dark indigo sky. His revelation still possessed him, making his whole body sensitive, like a tightly strung bow. In the morning he had forgotten, or was ashamed of what had seemed so true and so entirely his own the night before. He agreed, for the most part, that it was better not to think about such things, and when he could he avoided thinking.

III

AFTER the heavy work of harvest was over, Mrs. Wheeler often persuaded her husband, when he was starting off in his buckboard, to take her as far as Claude's new house. She was glad Enid didn't keep her parlour dark, as Mrs. Royce kept hers. The doors and windows were always open, the vines and the long petunias in the window-boxes waved in the breeze, and the rooms were full of sunlight and in perfect order. Enid wore white dresses about her work, and white shoes and stockings. She managed a house easily and systematically. On Monday morning Claude turned the washing machine before he went to work, and by nine o'clock the clothes were on the line. Enid liked to iron, and Claude had never before in his life worn so many clean shirts, or worn them with such satisfaction. She told him he need not economize in working shirts; it was as easy to iron six as three.

Although within a few months Enid's car travelled more than two thousand miles for the Prohibition cause, it could not be said that she neglected her house for reform. Whether she neglected her husband depended upon one's conception of what was his due. When Mrs. Wheeler saw how well their little establishment was conducted, how cheerful and attractive Enid looked when one happened to drop in there, she wondered that Claude was not happy. And Claude himself wondered. If his marriage disappointed him in some respects, he ought to be a man, he told himself, and make the best of what was good in it. If his wife didn't love him, it was because love meant one thing to him and quite another thing to her. She was proud of him, was glad to see him when he came in from the fields, and was solicitous for his comfort. Everything about a man's embrace was distasteful to Enid; something inflicted upon women, like the pain of childbirth, — for Eve's transgression, perhaps.

This repugnance was more than physical; she disliked ardour of any kind, even religious ardour. She had been fonder of Claude before she married him than she was now; but she hoped for a readjustment. Perhaps sometime she could like him again in exactly the same way. Even Brother Weldon had hinted to her that for the sake of their future tranquillity she must be lenient with the boy. And she thought she had been lenient. She could not understand his moods of desperate silence, the bitter, biting remarks he sometimes dropped, his evident annoyance if she went over to join him in the timber claim when he lay there idle in the deep grass on a Sunday afternoon.

Claude used to lie there and watch the clouds, saying to himself, "It's the end of everything for me." Other men than he must have been disappointed, and he wondered how they bore it through a lifetime. Claude had been a well-behaved boy because he was an idealist; he had looked forward to being wonderfully happy in love, and to deserving his happiness. He had never dreamed that it might be otherwise.

Sometimes now, when he went out into the fields on a bright summer morning, it seemed to him that Nature not only smiled, but broadly laughed at him. He suffered in his pride, but even more in his ideals, in his vague sense of what was beautiful. Enid could make his life hideous to him without ever knowing it. At such times he hated himself for accepting at all her grudging hospitality. He was wronging something in himself.

In her person Enid was still attractive to him. He wondered why she had no shades of feeling to correspond to her natural grace and lightness of movement, to the gentle, almost wistful attitudes of body in which he sometimes surprised her. When he came in from work and found her sitting on the porch, leaning against a pillar, her hands clasped about her knees, her head drooping a little, he could scarcely believe in the rigidity which met him at every turn. Was there something repellent in him? Was it, after all, his fault?

Enid was rather more indulgent with his father than with any one else, he noticed. Mr. Wheeler stopped to see her almost every day, and even took her driving in his old buckboard. Bayliss came out from town to spend the evening occasionally. Enid's vegetarian suppers suited him, and as she worked with him in the Prohibition campaign, they always had business to discuss. Bayliss had a social as well as a hygienic prejudice against alcohol, and he hated it less for the harm it did than for the pleasure it gave. Claude consistently refused to take any part in the activities of the Anti-Saloon League, or to distribute what Bayliss and Enid called "our literature."

In the farming towns the term "literature" was applied only to a special kind of printed matter; there was Prohibition literature, Sex-Hygiene literature, and, during a scourge of cattle disease, there was Hoof-and-Mouth literature. This special application of the word didn't bother Claude, but his mother, being an old-fashioned school-teacher, complained about it.

Enid did not understand her husband's indifference to a burning question, and could only attribute it to the influence of Ernest Havel. She sometimes asked Claude to go with her to one of her committee meetings. If it was a Sunday, he said he was tired and wanted to read the paper. If it was a week-day, he had something to do at the barn, or meant to clear out the timber claim. He did, indeed, saw off a few dead limbs, and cut down a tree the lightning had blasted. Further than that he wouldn't have let anybody clear the timber lot; he would have died defending it.

The timber claim was his refuge. In the open, grassy spots, shut in by the bushy walls of yellowing ash trees, he felt unmarried and free; free to smoke as much as he liked, and to read and dream. Some of his dreams would have frozen his young wife's blood with horror—and some would have melted his mother's heart with pity. To lie in the hot sun and look up at the stainless blue of the autumn sky, to hear the dry rustle of the leaves as they fell, and the sound of the bold squirrels leaping from branch to branch; to lie thus and let his imagination play with life—that was the best he could do. His thoughts, he told himself, were his own. He was no longer a boy. He went off into the timber claim to meet a young man more experienced and interesting than himself, who had not tied himself up with compromises.

IV

FROM her upstairs window Mrs. Wheeler could see Claude moving back and forth in the west field, drilling wheat. She felt lonely for him. He didn't come home as often as he might. She had begun to wonder whether he was one of those people who are always discontented; but whatever his disappointments were, he kept them locked in his own breast. One had to learn the lessons of life. Nevertheless, it made her a little sad to see him so settled and indifferent at twenty-three.

After watching from the window for a few moments, she turned to the telephone and called up Claude's house, asking Enid whether she would mind if he came there for dinner. "Mahailey and I get lonesome with Mr. Wheeler away so much," she added.

"Why, no, Mother Wheeler, of course not." Enid spoke cheerfully, as she always did. "Have you any one there you can send over to tell him?"

"I thought I would walk over myself, Enid. It's not far, if I take my time."

Mrs. Wheeler left the house a little before noon and stopped at the creek to rest before she climbed the long hill. At the edge of the field she sat down against a grassy bank and waited until the horses came tramping up the long rows. Claude saw her and pulled them in.

"Anything wrong, Mother?" he called.

"Oh, no! I'm going to take you home for dinner with me, that's all. I telephoned Enid."

He unhooked his team, and he and his mother started down the hill together, walking behind the horses. Though they had not been alone like this for a long while, she felt it best to talk about impersonal things.

"Don't let me forget to give you an article about the execution of that English nurse."

"Edith Cavell? I've read about it," he answered listlessly. "It's nothing to be surprised at. If they could sink the Lusitania, they could shoot an English nurse, certainly."

"Someway I feel as if this were different," his mother murmured. "It's like the hanging of John Brown. I wonder they could find soldiers to execute the sentence."

"Oh, I guess they have plenty of such soldiers!"

Mrs. Wheeler looked up at him. "I don't see how we can stay out of it much longer, do you? I suppose our army wouldn't be a drop in the bucket, even if we could get it over. They tell us we can be more useful in our agriculture and manufactories than we could by going into the war. I only hope it isn't campaign talk. I do distrust the Democrats."

Claude laughed. "Why, Mother, I guess there's no party politics in this."

She shook her head. "I've never yet found a public question in which there wasn't party politics. Well, we can only do our duty as it comes to us, and have faith. This field finishes your fall work?"

"Yes. I'll have time to do some things about the place, now. I'm going to make a good ice-house and put up my own ice this winter."

"Were you thinking of going up to Lincoln, for a little?"

"I guess not."

Mrs. Wheeler sighed. His tone meant that he had turned his back on old pleasures and old friends.

"Have you and Enid taken tickets for the lecture course in Frankfort?"

"I think so, Mother," he answered a little impatiently. "I told her she could attend to it when she was in town some day."

"Of course," his mother persevered, "some of the programs are not very good, but we ought to patronize them and make the best of what we have."

He knew, and his mother knew, that he was not very good at that. His horses stopped at the water tank. "Don't wait for me. I'll be along in a minute." Seeing her crestfallen face, he smiled. "Never mind, Mother, I can always catch you when you try to give me a pill in a raisin. One of us has to be pretty smart to fool the other."

She blinked up at him with that smile in which her eyes almost disappeared. "I thought I was smart that time!"

It was a comfort, she reflected, as she hurried up the hill, to get hold of him again, to get his attention, even.

While Claude was washing for dinner, Mahailey came to him with a page of newspaper cartoons, illustrating German brutality. To her they were all photographs,—she knew no other way of making a picture.

"Mr. Claude," she asked, "how comes it all them Germans is such ugly lookin' people? The Yoeders and the German folks round here ain't ugly lookin'."

Claude put her off indulgently. "Maybe it's the ugly ones that are doing the fighting, and the ones at home are nice, like our neighbours."

"Then why don't they make their soldiers stay home, an' not go breakin' other people's things, an' turnin' 'em out of their houses," she muttered indignantly. "They say little babies was born out in the snow last winter, an' no fires for their mudders nor nothin'. 'Deed, Mr. Claude, it wasn't like that in our war; the soldiers didn't do nothin' to the women an' chillun. Many a time our house was full of Northern soldiers, an' they never so much as broke a piece of my mudder's chiney."

"You'll have to tell me about it again sometime, Mahailey. I must have my dinner and get back to work. If we don't get our wheat in, those people over there won't have anything to eat, you know."

The picture papers meant a great deal to Mahailey, because she could faintly remember the Civil War. While she pored over photographs of camps and battlefields and devastated villages, things came back to her; the companies of dusty Union infantry that used to stop to drink at her mother's cold mountain spring. She had seen them take off their boots and wash their bleeding feet in the run. Her mother had given one louse-bitten boy a clean shirt, and she had never forgotten the sight of his back, "as raw as beef where he'd scratched it." Five of her brothers were in the Rebel army. When one was wounded in the second battle of Bull's Run, her mother had borrowed a wagon and horses, gone a three days' journey to the field hospital, and brought the boy home to the mountain. Mahailey could remember how her older sisters took turns pouring cold spring water on his gangrenous leg all day and all night. There were no doctors left in the neighbourhood, and as nobody could amputate the boy's leg, he died by inches. Mahailey was the only person in the Wheeler household who had ever seen war with her own eyes, and she felt that this fact gave her a definite superiority.

V

CLAUDE had been married a year and a half. One December morning he got a telephone message from his father-in-law, asking him to come in to Frankfort at once. He found Mr. Royce sunk in his desk-chair, smoking as usual, with several foreign-looking letters on the table before him. As he took these out of their envelopes and sorted the pages, Claude noticed how unsteady his hands had become.

One letter, from the chief of the medical staff in the mission school where Caroline Royce taught, informed Mr. Royce that his daughter was seriously ill in the mission hospital. She would have to be sent to a more salubrious part of the country for rest and treatment, and would not be strong enough to return to her duties for a year or more. If some member of her family could come out to take care of her, it would relieve the school authorities of great anxiety. There was also a letter from a fellow teacher, and a rather incoherent one from Caroline herself. After Claude finished reading them, Mr. Royce pushed a box of cigars toward him and began to talk despondently about missionaries.

"I could go to her," he complained, "but what good would that do? I'm not in sympathy with her ideas, and it would only fret her. You can see she's made her mind up not to come home. I don't believe in one people trying to force their ways or their religion on another. I'm not that kind of man." He sat looking at his cigar. After a long pause he broke out suddenly, "China has been drummed into my ears . . . It seems like a long way to go to hunt for trouble, don't it? A man hasn't got much control over his own life, Claude. If it ain't poverty or disease that torments him, it's a name on the map. I could have made out pretty well, if it hadn't been for China, and some other things. . . . If Carrie'd had to teach for her clothes and help pay off my notes, like old man Harrison's daughters, like enough she'd have stayed at home. There's always something. I don't know what to say about showing these letters to Enid."

"Oh, she will have to know about it, Mr. Royce. If she feels that she ought to go to Carrie, it wouldn't be right for me to interfere."

Mr. Royce shook his head. "I don't know. It don't seem fair that China should hang over you, too."

When Claude got home he remarked as he handed Enid the letters, "Your father has been a good deal upset by this. I never saw him look so old as he did today."

Enid studied their contents, sitting at her orderly little desk, while Claude pretended to read the paper.

"It seems clear that I am the one to go," she said when she had finished.

"You think it's necessary for some one to go? I don't see it."

"It would look very strange if none of us went," Enid replied with spirit.

"How, look strange?"

"Why, it would look to her associates as if her family had no feeling."

"Oh, if that's all!" Claude smiled perversely and took up his paper again. "I wonder how it will look to people here if you go off and leave your husband?"

"What a mean thing to say, Claude!" She rose sharply, then hesitated, perplexed. "People here know me better than that. It isn't as if you couldn't be perfectly comfortable at your mother's." As he did not glance up from his paper, she went into the kitchen.

Claude sat still, listening to Enid's quick movements as she opened up the range to get supper. The light in the room grew greyer. Outside the fields melted into one another as evening came on. The young trees in the yard bent and whipped about under a bitter north wind. He had often thought with pride that winter died at his front doorstep; within, no draughty halls, no chilly corners. This was their second year here. When he was driving home, the thought that he might be free of this house for a long while had stirred a pleasant excitement in him; but now, he didn't want to leave it. Something grew soft in him. He wondered whether they couldn't try again, and make things go better. Enid was singing in the kitchen in a subdued, rather lonely voice. He rose and went out for his milking coat and pail. As he passed his wife by the window, he stopped and put his arm about her questioningly.

She looked up. "That's right. You're feeling better about it, aren't you? I thought you would. Gracious, what a smelly coat, Claude! I must find another for you."

Claude knew that tone. Enid never questioned the rightness of her own decisions. When she made up her mind, there was no turning her. He went down the path to the barn with his hands stuffed in his trousers pockets, his bright pail hanging on his arm. Try again—what was there to try? Platitudes, littleness, falseness. . . . His life was choking him, and he hadn't the courage to break with it. Let her go! Let her go when she would! . . . What a hideous world to be born into! Or was it hideous only for him? Everything he touched went wrong under his hand—always had.

When they sat down at the supper table in the back parlour an hour later, Enid looked worn, as if this time her decision had cost her something. "I should think you might have a restful winter at your mother's," she began cheerfully. "You won't have nearly so much to look after as you do here. We needn't disturb things in this house. I will take the silver down to Mother, and we can leave everything else just as it is. Would there be room for my car in your father's garage? You might find it a convenience."

"Oh, no! I won't need it. I'll put it up at the mill house," he answered with an effort at carelessness.

All the familiar objects that stood about them in the lamplight seemed stiller and more solemn than usual, as if they were holding their breath.

"I suppose you had better take the chickens over to your mother's," Enid continued evenly. "But I shouldn't like them to get mixed with her Plymouth Rocks; there's not a dark feather among them now. Do ask Mother Wheeler to use all the eggs, and not to let my hens set in the spring."

"In the spring?" Claude looked up from his plate.

"Of course, Claude. I could hardly get back before next fall, if I'm to be of any help to poor Carrie. I might try to be home for harvest, if that would make it more convenient for you." She rose to bring in the dessert.

"Oh, don't hurry on my account!" he muttered, staring after her disappearing figure.

Enid came back with the hot pudding and the after-dinner coffee things. "This has come on us so suddenly that we must make our plans at once," she explained. "I should think your mother would be glad to keep Rose for us; she is such a good cow. And then you can have all the cream you want."

He took the little gold-rimmed cup she held out to him. "If you are going to be gone until next fall, I shall sell Rose," he announced gruffly.

"But why? You might look a long time before you found another like her."

"I shall sell her, anyhow. The horses, of course, are Father's; he paid for them. If you clear out, he may want to rent this place. You may find a tenant in here when you get back from China." Claude swallowed his coffee, put down the cup, and went into the front parlour, where he lit a cigar. He walked up and down, keeping his eyes fixed upon his wife, who still sat at the table in the circle of light from the hanging lamp. Her head, bent forward a little, showed the neat part of her brown hair. When she was perplexed, her face always looked sharper, her chin longer.

"If you've no feeling for the place," said Claude from the other room, "you can hardly expect me to hang around and take care of it. All the time you were campaigning, I played housekeeper here."

Enid's eyes narrowed, but she did not flush. Claude had never seen a wave of colour come over his wife's pale, smooth cheeks.

"Don't be childish. You know I care for this place; it's our home. But no feeling would be right that kept me from doing my duty. You are well, and you have your mother's house to go to. Carrie is ill and among strangers."

She began to gather up the dishes. Claude stepped quickly out into the light and confronted her. "It's not only your going. You know what's the matter with me. It's because you want to go. You are glad of a chance to get away among all those preachers, with their smooth talk and make-believe."

Enid took up the tray. "If I am glad, it's because you are not willing to govern our lives by Christian ideals. There is something in you that rebels all the time. So many important questions have come up since our marriage, and you have been indifferent or sarcastic about every one of them. You want to lead a purely selfish life."

She walked resolutely out of the room and shut the door behind her. Later, when she came back, Claude was not there. His hat and coat were gone from the hatrack; he must have let himself out quietly by the front door. Enid sat up until eleven and then went to bed.

In the morning, on coming out from her bedroom, she found Claude asleep on the lounge, dressed, with his overcoat on. She had a moment of terror and bent over him, but she could not detect any smell of spirits. She began preparations for breakfast, moving quietly.

Having once made up her mind to go out to her sister, Enid lost no time. She engaged passage and cabled the mission school. She left Frankfort the week before Christmas. Claude and Ralph took her as far as Denver and put her on a transcontinental express. When Claude came home, he moved over to his mother's, and sold his cow and chickens to Leonard Dawson. Except when he went to see Mr. Royce, he seldom left the farm now, and he avoided the neighbours. He felt that they were discussing his domestic affairs,—as, of course, they were. The Royces and the Wheelers, they said, couldn't behave like anybody else, and it was no use their trying. If Claude built the best house in the neighbourhood, he just naturally wouldn't live in it. And if he had a wife at all, it was like him to have a wife in China!

One snowy day, when nobody was about, Claude took the big car and went over to his own place to close the house for the winter and bring away the canned fruit and vegetables left in the cellar. Enid had packed her best linen in her cedar chest and had put the kitchen and china closets in scrupulous order before she went away. He began covering the upholstered chairs and the mattresses with sheets, rolled up the rugs, and fastened the windows securely. As he worked, his hands grew more and more numb and listless, and his heart was like a lump of ice. All these things that he had selected with care and in which he had taken such pride, were no more to him now than the lumber piled in the shop of any second-hand dealer.

How inherently mournful and ugly such objects were, when the feeling that had made them precious no longer existed! The débris of human life was more worthless and ugly than the dead and decaying things in nature. Rubbish . . . junk . . . his mind could not picture anything that so exposed and condemned all the dreary, weary, ever-repeated actions by which life is continued from day to day. Actions without meaning. . . . As he looked out and saw the grey landscape through the gently falling snow, he could not help thinking how much better it would be if people could go to sleep like the fields; could be blanketed down under the snow, to wake with their hurts healed and their defeats forgotten. He wondered how he was to go on through the years ahead of him, unless he could get rid of this sick feeling in his soul.

At last he locked the door, put the key in his pocket, and went over to the timber claim to smoke a cigar and say good-bye to the place. There he soberly walked about for more than an hour, under the crooked trees with empty birds' nests in their forks. Every time he came to a break in the hedge, he could see the little house, giving itself up so meekly to solitude. He did not believe that he would ever live there again. Well, at any rate, the money his father had put into the place would not be lost; he could always get a better tenant for having a comfortable house there. Several of the boys in the neighbourhood were planning to be married within the year. The future of the house was safe. And he? He stopped short in his walk; his feet had made an uncertain, purposeless trail all over the white ground. It vexed him to see his own footsteps. What was it—what *was* the matter with him? Why, at least, could he not stop feeling things, and hoping? What was there to hope for now?

He heard a sound of distress, and looking back, saw the barn cat, that had been left behind to pick up her living. She was standing inside the hedge, her jet black fur ruffled against the wet flakes, one paw lifted, mewing miserably. Claude went over and picked her up.

"What's the matter, Blackie? Mice getting scarce in the barn? Mahailey will say you are bad luck. Maybe you are, but you can't help it, can you?" He slipped her into his overcoat pocket. Later, when he was getting into his car, he tried to dislodge her and put her in a basket, but she clung to her nest in his pocket and dug her claws into the lining. He laughed. "Well, if you are bad luck, I guess you are going to stay right with me!"

She looked up at him with startled yellow eyes and did not even mew.

MRS. Wheeler was afraid that Claude might not find the old place comfortable, after having had a house of his own. She put her best rocking chair and a reading lamp in his bedroom. He often sat there all evening, shading his eyes with his hand, pretending to read. When he stayed downstairs after supper, his, mother and Mahailey were grateful. Besides collecting war pictures, Mahailey now hunted through the old magazines in the attic for pictures of China. She had marked on her big kitchen calendar the day when Enid would arrive in Hong-Kong.

"Mr. Claude," she would say as she stood at the sink washing the supper dishes, "it's broad daylight over where Miss Enid is, ain't it? Cause the world's round, an' the old sun, he's a-shinin' over there for the yaller people."

From time to time, when they were working together, Mrs. Wheeler told Mahailey what she knew about the customs of the Chinese. The old woman had never had two impersonal interests at the same time before, and she scarcely knew what to do with them. She would murmur on, half to Claude and half to herself: "They ain't fightin' over there where Miss Enid is, is they? An' she won't have to wear their kind of clothes, cause she's a white woman. She won't let 'em kill their girl babies nor do such awful things like they always have, an' she won't let 'em pray to them stone iboles, cause they can't help 'em none. I 'spect Miss Enid'll do a heap of good, all the time."

Behind her diplomatic monologues, however, Mahailey had her own ideas, and she was greatly scandalized at Enid's departure. She was afraid people would say that Claude's wife had "run off an' lef' him," and in the Virginia mountains, where her social standards had been formed, a husband or wife thus deserted was the object of boisterous ridicule. She once stopped Mrs. Wheeler in a dark corner of the cellar to whisper, "Mr. Claude's wife ain't goin' to stay off there, like her sister, is she?"

If one of the Yoeder boys or Susie Dawson happened to be at the Wheelers' for dinner, Mahailey never failed to refer to Enid in a loud voice. "Mr. Claude's wife, she cuts her potatoes up raw in the pan an' fries 'em. She don't boil 'em first like I do. I know she's an awful good cook, I know she is." She felt that easy references to the absent wife made things look better.

Ernest Havel came to see Claude now, but not often. They both felt it would be indelicate to renew their former intimacy. Ernest still felt aggrieved about his beer, as if Enid had snatched the tankard from his lips with her own corrective hand. Like Leonard, he believed that Claude had made a bad bargain in matrimony; but instead of feeling sorry for him, Ernest wanted to see him convinced and punished. When he married Enid, Claude had been false to liberal principles, and it was only right that he should pay for his apostacy. The very first time he came to spend an evening at the Wheelers' after Claude came home to live, Ernest undertook to explain his objections to Prohibition. Claude shrugged his shoulders.

"Why not drop it? It's a matter that doesn't interest me, one way or the other."

Ernest was offended and did not come back for nearly a month — not, indeed, until the announcement that Germany would resume unrestricted submarine warfare made every one look questioningly at his neighbour.

He walked into the Wheelers' kitchen the night after this news reached the farming country, and found Claude and his mother sitting at the table, reading the papers aloud to each other in snatches. Ernest had scarcely taken a seat when the telephone bell rang. Claude answered the call.

"It's the telegraph operator at Frankfort," he said, as he hung up the receiver. "He repeated a message from Father, sent from Wray: *Will be home day after tomorrow. Read the papers.* What does he mean? What does he suppose we are doing?"

"It means he considers our situation very serious. It's not like him to telegraph except in case of illness." Mrs. Wheeler rose and walked distractedly to the telephone box, as if it might further disclose her husband's state of mind.

"But what a queer message! It was addressed to you, too, Mother, not to me."

"He would know how I feel about it. Some of your father's people were sea-going men, out of Portsmouth. He knows what it means when our shipping is told where it can go on the ocean, and where it cannot. It isn't possible that Washington can take such an affront for us. To think that at this time, of all times, we should have a Democratic administration!"

Claude laughed. "Sit down, Mother. Wait a day or two. Give them time."

"The war will be over before Washington can do anything, Mrs. Wheeler," Ernest declared gloomily, "England will be starved out, and France will be beaten to a standstill. The whole German army will be on the Western front now. What could this country do? How long do you suppose it takes to make an army?"

Mrs. Wheeler stopped short in her restless pacing and met his moody glance. "I don't know anything, Ernest, but I believe the Bible. I believe that in the twinkling of an eye we shall be changed!"

Ernest looked at the floor. He respected faith. As he said, you must respect it or despise it, for there was nothing else to do.

Claude sat leaning his elbows on the table. "It always comes back to the same thing, Mother. Even if a raw army could do anything, how would we get it over there? Here's one naval authority who says the Germans are turning out submarines at the rate of three a day. They probably didn't spring this on us until they had enough built to keep the ocean clean."

"I don't pretend to say what we could accomplish, son. But we must stand somewhere, morally. They have told us all along that we could be more helpful to the Allies out of the war than in it, because we could send munitions and supplies. If we agree to withdraw that aid, where are we? Helping Germany, all the time we are pretending to mind our own business! If our only alternative is to be at the bottom of the sea, we had better be there!"

"Mother, do sit down! We can't settle it tonight. I never saw you so worked up."

"Your father is worked up, too, or he would never have sent that telegram." Mrs. Wheeler reluctantly took up her workbasket, and the boys talked with their old, easy friendliness.

When Ernest left, Claude walked as far as the Yoeders' place with him, and came back across the snow-drifted fields, under the frosty brilliance of the winter stars. As he looked up at them, he felt more than ever that they must have something to do with the fate of nations, and with the incomprehensible things that were happening in the world. In the ordered universe there must be some mind that read the riddle of this one unhappy planet, that knew what was forming in the dark eclipse of this hour. A question hung in the air; over all this quiet land about him, over him, over his mother, even. He was afraid for his country, as he had been that night on the State House steps in Denver, when this war was undreamed of, hidden in the womb of time.

Claude and his mother had not long to wait. Three days later they knew that the German ambassador had been dismissed, and the American ambassador recalled from Berlin. To older men these events were subjects to think and converse about; but to boys like Claude they were life and death, predestination.

VII

ONE stormy morning Claude was driving the big wagon to town to get a load of lumber. The roads were beginning to thaw out, and the country was black and dirty looking. Here and there on the dark mud, grey snow crusts lingered, perforated like honey-comb, with wet weed-stalks sticking up through them. As the wagon creaked over the high ground just above Frankfort, Claude noticed a brilliant new flag flying from the schoolhouse cupola. He had never seen the flag before when it meant any-thing but the Fourth of July, or a political rally. Today it was as if he saw it for the first time; no bands, no noise, no orators; a spot of restless colour against the sodden March sky.

He turned out of his way in order to pass the High School, drew up his team, and waited a few minutes until the noon bell rang. The older boys and girls came out first, with a flurry of raincoats and umbrellas. Presently he saw Gladys Farmer, in a yellow "slicker" and an oilskin hat, and waved to her. She came up to the wagon.

"I like your decoration," he said, glancing toward the cupola.

"It's a silk one the Senior boys bought with their athletic money. I advised them not to run it up in this rain, but the class president told me they bought that flag for storms."

"Get in, and I'll take you home."

She took his extended hand, put her foot on the hub of the wheel, and climbed to the seat beside him. He clucked to his team.

"So your High School boys are feeling war-like these days?"

"Very. What do you think?"

"I think they'll have a chance to express their feelings."

"Do you, Claude? It seems awfully unreal."

"Nothing else seems very real, either. I'm going to haul out a load of lumber, but I never expect to drive a nail in it. These things don't matter now. There is only one thing we ought to do, and only one thing that matters; we all know it."

"You feel it's coming nearer every day?"

"Every day."

Gladys made no reply. She only looked at him gravely with her calm, generous brown eyes. They stopped before the low house where the windows were full of flowers. She took his hand and swung herself to the ground, holding it for a moment while she said good-bye. Claude drove back to the lumber yard. In a place like Frankfort, a boy whose wife was in China could hardly go to see Gladys without making talk.

VIII

DURING the bleak month of March Mr. Wheeler went to town in his blackboard almost every day. For the first time in his life he had a secret anxiety. The one member of his family who had never given him the slightest trouble, his son Bayliss, was just now under a cloud.

Bayliss was a Pacifist, and kept telling people that if only the United States would stay out of this war, and gather up what Europe was wasting, she would soon be in actual possession of the capital of the world. There was a kind of logic in Bayliss' utterances that shook Nat Wheeler's imperturbable assumption that one point of view was as good as another. When Bayliss fought the dram and the cigarette, Wheeler only laughed. That a son of his should turn out a Prohibitionist, was a joke he could appreciate. But Bayliss' attitude in the present crisis disturbed him. Day after day he sat about his son's place of business, interrupting his arguments with funny stories. Bayliss did not go home at all that month. He said to his father, "No, Mother's too violent. I'd better not."

Claude and his mother read the papers in the evening, but they talked so little about what they read that Mahailey inquired anxiously whether they weren't still fighting over yonder. When she could get Claude alone for a moment, she pulled out Sunday supplement pictures of the devastated countries and asked him to tell her what was to become of this family, photographed among the ruins of their home; of this old woman, who sat by the roadside with her bundles. "Where's she goin' to, anyways? See, Mr. Claude, she's got her iron cook-pot, pore old thing, carryin' it all the way!"

Pictures of soldiers in gas-masks puzzled her; gas was something she hadn't learned about in the Civil War, so she worked it out for herself that these masks were worn by the army cooks, to protect their eyes when they were cutting up onions! "All them onions they have to cut up, it would put their eyes out if they didn't wear somethin'," she argued.

On the morning of the eighth of April Claude came downstairs early and began to clean his boots, which were caked with dry mud. Mahailey was squatting down beside her stove, blowing and puffing into it. The fire was always slow to start in heavy weather. Claude got an old knife and a brush, and putting his foot on a chair over by the west window, began to scrape his shoe. He had said good-morning to Mahailey, nothing more. He hadn't slept well, and was pale.

"Mr. Claude," Mahailey grumbled, "this stove ain't never drawed good like my old one Mr. Ralph took away from me. I can't do nothin' with it. Maybe you'll clean it out for me next Sunday."

"I'll clean it today, if you say so. I won't be here next Sunday. I'm going away."

Something in his tone made Mahailey get up, her eyes still blinking with the smoke, and look at him sharply. "You ain't goin' off there where Miss Enid is?" she asked anxiously.

"No, Mahailey." He had dropped the shoebrush and stood with one foot on the chair, his elbow on his knee, looking out of the window as if he had forgotten himself. "No, I'm not going to China. I'm going over to help fight the Germans."

He was still staring out at the wet fields. Before he could stop her, before he knew what she was doing, she had caught and kissed his unworthy hand.

"I knowed you would," she sobbed. "I always knowed you would, you nice boy, you! Old Mahail' knowed!"

Her upturned face was working all over; her mouth, her eyebrows, even the wrinkles on her low forehead were working and twitching. Claude felt a tightening in his throat as he tenderly regarded that face; behind the pale eyes, under the low brow where there was not room for many thoughts, an idea was struggling and tormenting her. The same idea that had been tormenting him.

"You're all right, Mahailey," he muttered, patting her back and turning away. "Now hurry breakfast."

"You ain't told your mudder yit?" she whispered.

"No, not yet. But she'll be all right, too." He caught up his cap and went down to the barn to look after the horses.

When Claude returned, the family were already at the breakfast table. He slipped into his seat and watched his mother while she drank her first cup of coffee. Then he addressed his father.

"Father, I don't see any use of waiting for the draft. If you can spare me, I'd like to get into a training camp somewhere. I believe I'd stand a chance of getting a commission."

"I shouldn't wonder." Mr. Wheeler poured maple syrup on his pancakes with a liberal hand. "How do you feel about it, Evangeline?"

Mrs. Wheeler had quietly put down her knife and fork. She looked at her husband in vague alarm, while her fingers moved restlessly about over the tablecloth.

"I thought," Claude went on hastily, "that maybe I would go up to Omaha tomorrow and find out where the training camps are to be located, and have a talk with the men in charge of the enlistment station. Of course," he added lightly, "they may not want me. I haven't an idea what the requirements are."

"No, I don't understand much about it either." Mr. Wheeler rolled his top pancake and conveyed it to his mouth. After a moment of mastication he said, "You figure on going tomorrow?"

"I'd like to. I won't bother with baggage — some shirts and underclothes in my suitcase. If the Government wants me, it will clothe me."

Mr. Wheeler pushed back his plate. "Well, now I guess you'd better come out with me and look at the wheat. I don't know but I'd best plough up that south quarter and put it in corn. I don't believe it will make anything much."

When Claude and his father went out of the door, Dan sprang up with more alacrity than usual and plunged after them. He did not want to be left alone with Mrs. Wheeler. She remained sitting at the foot of the deserted breakfast table. She was not crying. Her eyes were utterly sightless. Her back was so stooped that she seemed to be bending under a burden. Mahailey cleared the dishes away quietly.

Out in the muddy fields Claude finished his talk with his father. He explained that he wanted to slip away without saying good-bye to any one. "I have a way, you know," he said, flushing, "of beginning things and not getting very far with them. I don't want anything said about this until I'm sure. I may be rejected for one reason or another."

Mr. Wheeler smiled. "I guess not. However, I'll tell Dan to keep his mouth shut. Will you just go over to Leonard Dawson's and get that wrench he borrowed? It's about noon, and he'll likely be at home."

Claude found big Leonard watering his team at the windmill. When Leonard asked him what he thought of the President's message, he blurted out at once that he was going to Omaha to enlist. Leonard reached up and pulled the lever that controlled the almost motionless wheel.

"Better wait a few weeks and I'll go with you. I'm going to try for the Marines. They take my eye."

Claude, standing on the edge of the tank, almost fell backward. "Why, what—what for?"

Leonard looked him over. "Good Lord, Claude, you ain't the only fellow around here that wears pants! What for? Well, I'll tell you what for," he held up three large red fingers threateningly; "Belgium, the Lusitania, Edith Cavell. That dirt's got under my skin. I'll get my corn planted, and then Father'll look after Susie till I come back."

Claude took a long breath. "Well, Leonard, you fooled me. I believed all this chaff you've been giving me about not caring who chewed up who."

207

"And no more do I care," Leonard protested, "not a damn! But there's a limit. I've been ready to go since the Lusitania. I don't get any satisfaction out of my place any more. Susie feels the same way."

Claude looked at his big neighbour. "Well, I'm off tomorrow, Leonard. Don't mention it to my folks, but if I can't get into the army, I'm going to enlist in the navy. They'll always take an able-bodied man. I'm not coming back here." He held out his hand and Leonard took it with a smack.

"Good luck, Claude. Maybe we'll meet in foreign parts. Wouldn't that be a joke! Give my love to Enid when you write. I always did think she was a fine girl, though I disagreed with her on Prohibition." Claude crossed the fields mechanically, without looking where he went. His power of vision was turned inward upon scenes and events wholly imaginary as yet.

IX

ONE bright June day Mr. Wheeler parked his car in a line of motors before the new pressed-brick Court house in Frankfort. The Court house stood in an open square, surrounded by a grove of cotton-woods. The lawn was freshly cut, and the flower beds were blooming. When Mr. Wheeler entered the courtroom upstairs, it was already half-full of farmers and townspeople, talking in low tones while the summer flies buzzed in and out of the open windows. The Judge, a one-armed man, with white hair and side-whiskers, sat at his desk, writing with his left hand. He was an old settler in Frankfort county, but from his frock-coat and courtly manners you might have thought he had come from Kentucky yesterday instead of thirty years ago. He was to hear this morning a charge of disloyalty brought against two German farmers. One of the accused was August Yoeder, the Wheelers' nearest neighbour, and the other was Troilus Oberlies, a rich German from the northern part of the county.

Oberlies owned a beautiful farm and lived in a big white house set on a hill, with a fine orchard, rows of beehives, barns, granaries, and poultry yards. He raised turkeys and tumbler-pigeons, and many geese and ducks swam about on his cattle-ponds. He used to boast that he had six sons, "like our German Emperor." His neighbours were proud of his place, and pointed it out to strangers. They told how Oberlies had come to Frankfort county a poor man, and had made his fortune by his industry and intelligence. He had twice crossed the ocean to re-visit his fatherland, and when he returned to his home on the prairies he brought presents for every one; his lawyer, his banker, and the merchants with whom he dealt in Frankfort and Vicount. Each of his neighbours had in his parlour some piece of woodcarving or weaving, or some ingenious mechanical toy that Oberlies had picked up in Germany. He was an older man than Yoeder, wore a short beard that was white and curly, like his hair, and though he was low in stature, his puffy red face and full blue eyes, and a certain swagger about his carriage, gave him a look of importance. He was boastful and quick-tempered, but until the war broke out in Europe nobody had ever had any trouble with him. Since then he had constantly found fault and complained,—everything was better in the Old Country.

Mr. Wheeler had come to town prepared to lend Yoeder a hand if he needed one. They had worked adjoining fields for thirty years now. He was surprised that his neighbour had got into trouble. He was not a blusterer, like Oberlies, but a big, quiet man, with a serious, large-featured face, and a stern mouth that seldom opened. His countenance might have been cut out of red sandstone, it was so heavy and fixed. He and Oberlies sat on two wooden chairs outside the railing of the Judge's desk.

Presently the Judge stopped writing and said he would hear the charges against Troilus Oberlies. Several neighbours took the stand in succession; their complaints were confused and almost humorous. Oberlies had said the United States would be licked, and that would be a good thing; America was a great country, but it was run by fools, and to be governed by Germany was the best thing that could happen to it. The witness went on to say that since Oberlies had made his money in this country—

Here the Judge interrupted him. "Please confine yourself to statements which you consider disloyal, made in your presence by the defendant." While the witness proceeded, the Judge took off his glasses and laid them on the desk and began to polish the lenses with a silk handkerchief, trying them, and rubbing them again, as if he desired to see clearly.

A second witness had heard Oberlies say he hoped the German submarines would sink a few troopships; that would frighten the Americans and teach them to stay at home and mind their own business. A third complained that on Sunday afternoons the old man sat on his front porch and played *Die Wacht am Rhein* on a slide-trombone, to the great annoyance of his neighbours. Here Nat Wheeler slapped his knee with a loud guffaw, and a titter ran through the courtroom. The defendant's puffy red cheeks seemed fashioned by his Maker to give voice to that piercing instrument.

When asked if he had anything to say to these charges, the old man rose, threw back his shoulders, and cast a defiant glance at the courtroom. "You may take my property and imprison me, but I explain nothing, and I take back nothing," he declared in a loud voice.

The Judge regarded his inkwell with a smile. "You mistake the nature of this occasion, Mr. Oberlies. You are not asked to recant. You are merely asked to desist from further disloyal utterances, as much for your own protection and comfort as from consideration for the feelings of your neighbours. I will now hear the charges against Mr. Yoeder."

Mr. Yoeder, a witness declared, had said he hoped the United States would go to Hell, now that it had been bought over by England. When the witness had remarked to him that if the Kaiser were shot it would end the war, Yoeder replied that charity begins at home, and he wished somebody would put a bullet in the President.

When he was called upon, Yoeder rose and stood like a rock before the Judge. "I have nothing to say. The charges are true. I thought this was a country where a man could speak his mind."

"Yes, a man can speak his mind, but even here he must take the consequences. Sit down, please." The Judge leaned back in his chair, and looking at the two men in front of him, began with deliberation: "Mr. Oberlies, and Mr. Yoeder, you both know, and your friends and neighbours know, why you are here. You have not recognized the element of appropriateness, which must be regarded in nearly all the transactions of life; many of our civil laws are founded upon it. You have allowed a sentiment, noble in itself, to carry you away and lead you to make extravagant statements which I am confident neither of you mean. No man can demand that you cease from loving the country of your birth; but while you enjoy the benefits of this country, you should not defame its government to extol another. You both admit to utterances which I can only adjudge disloyal. I shall fine you each three hundred dollars; a very light fine under the circumstances. If I should have occasion to fix a penalty a second time, it will be much more severe."

After the case was concluded, Mr. Wheeler joined his neighbour at the door and they went downstairs together.

"Well, what do you hear from Claude?" Mr. Yoeder asked.

"He's still at Fort R——. He expects to get home on leave before he sails. Gus, you'll have to lend me one of your boys to cultivate my corn. The weeds are getting away from me."

"Yes, you can have any of my boys,—till the draft gets 'em," said Yoeder sourly.

"I wouldn't worry about it. A little military training is good for a boy. You fellows know that." Mr. Wheeler winked, and Yoeder's grim mouth twitched at one corner.

That evening at supper Mr. Wheeler gave his wife a full account of the court hearing, so that she could write it to Claude. Mrs. Wheeler, always more a school-teacher than a housekeeper, wrote a rapid, easy hand, and her long letters to Claude reported all the neighbourhood doings. Mr. Wheeler furnished much of the material for them. Like many long-married men he had fallen into the way of withholding neighbourhood news from his wife. But since Claude went away he reported to her everything in which he thought the boy would be interested. As she laconically said in one of her letters: "Your father talks a great deal more at home than formerly, and sometimes I think he is trying to take your place."

X

ON the first day of July Claude Wheeler found himself in the fast train from Omaha, going home for a week's leave. The uniform was still an unfamiliar sight in July, 1917. The first draft was not yet called, and the boys who had rushed off and enlisted were in training camps far away. Therefore a red-headed young man with long straight legs in puttees, and broad, energetic, responsible-looking shoulders in close-fitting khaki, made a conspicuous figure among the passengers. Little boys and young girls peered at him over the tops of seats, men stopped in the aisle to talk to him, old ladies put on their glasses and studied his clothes, his bulky canvas hold-all, and even the book he kept opening and forgetting to read.

The country that rushed by him on each side of the track was more interesting to his trained eye than the pages of any book. He was glad to be going through it at harvest,—the season when it is most itself. He noted that there was more corn than usual,— much of the winter wheat had been weather-killed, and the fields were ploughed up in the spring and replanted in maize. The pastures were already burned brown, the alfalfa was coming green again after its first cutting. Binders and harvesters were abroad in the wheat and oats, gathering the soft-breathing billows of grain into wide, subduing arms. When the train slowed down for a trestle in a wheat field, harvesters in blue shirts and overalls and wide straw hats stopped working to wave at the passengers.

Claude turned to the old man in the opposite seat. "When I see those fellows, I feel as if I'd wakened up in the wrong clothes."

His neighbour looked pleased and smiled. "That the kind of uniform you're accustomed to?"

"I surely never wore anything else in the month of July," Claude admitted. "When I find myself riding along in a train, in the middle of harvest, trying to learn French verbs, then I know the world is turned upside down, for a fact!"

The old man pressed a cigar upon him and began to question him. Like the hero of the Odyssey upon his homeward journey, Claude had often to tell what his country was, and who were the parents that begot him. He was constantly interrupted in his perusal of a French phrase-book (made up of sentences chosen for their usefulness to soldiers, — such as; "Non, jamais je ne regarde les femmes") by the questions of curious strangers. Presently he gathered up his luggage, shook hands with his neighbour, and put on his hat—the same old Stetson, with a gold cord and two hard tassels added to its conical severity. "I get off at this station and wait for the freight that goes down to Frankfort; the cotton-tail, we call it."

The old man wished him a pleasant visit home, and the best of luck in days to come. Every one in the car smiled at him as he stepped down to the platform with his suitcase in one hand and his canvas bag in the other. His old friend, Mrs. Voigt, the German woman, stood out in front of her restaurant, ringing her bell to announce that dinner was ready for travellers. A crowd of young boys stood about her on the sidewalk, laughing and shouting in disagreeable, jeering tones. As Claude approached, one of them snatched the bell from her hand, ran off across the tracks with it, and plunged into a cornfield. The other boys followed, and one of them shouted, "Don't go in there to eat, soldier. She's a German spy, and she'll put ground glass in your dinner!"

Claude went into the lunch room and threw his bags on the floor. "What's the matter, Mrs. Voigt? Can I do anything for you?"

She was sitting on one of her own stools, crying piteously, her false frizzes awry. Looking up, she gave a little screech of recognition. "Oh, I tank Gott it was you, and no more trouble coming!

You know I ain't no spy nor nodding, like what dem boys say. Dem young fellers is dreadful rough mit me. I sell dem candy since dey was babies, an' now dey turn on me like dis. Hindenburg, dey calls me, und Kaiser Bill!" She began to cry again, twisting her stumpy little fingers as if she would tear them off.

"Give me some dinner, ma'am, and then I'll go and settle with that gang. I've been away for a long time, and it seemed like getting home when I got off the train and saw your squash vines running over the porch like they used to."

"Ya? You remember dat?" she wiped her eyes. "I got a pot-pie today, und green peas, chust a few, out of my own garden."

"Bring them along, please. We don't get anything but canned stuff in camp."

Some railroad men came in for lunch. Mrs. Voigt beckoned Claude off to the end of the counter, where, after she had served her customers, she sat down and talked to him, in whispers.

"My, you look good in dem clothes," she said patting his sleeve. "I can remember some wars, too; when we got back dem provinces what Napoleon took away from us, Alsace und Lorraine. Dem boys is passed de word to come und put tar on me some night, und I am skeered to go in my bet. I chust wrap in a quilt und sit in my old chair."

"Don't pay any attention to them. You don't have trouble with the business people here, do you?"

"No-o, not troubles, exactly." She hesitated, then leaned impulsively across the counter and spoke in his ear. "But it ain't all so bad in de Old Country like what dey say. De poor people ain't slaves, und dey ain't ground down like what dey say here. Always de forester let de poor folks come into de wood und carry off de limbs dat fall, und de dead trees. Und if de rich farmer have maybe a liddle more manure dan he need, he let de poor man come und take some for his land. De poor folks don't git such wages like here, but dey lives chust as comfortable. Und dem wooden shoes, what dey makes such fun of, is cleaner dan what leather is, to go round in de mud und manure. Dey don't git so wet und dey don't stink so."

Claude could see that her heart was bursting with homesickness, full of tender memories of the far-away time and land of her youth. She had never talked to him of these things before, but now she poured out a flood of confidences about the big dairy farm on which she had worked as a girl; how she took care of nine cows, and how the cows, though small, were very strong,—drew a plough all day and yet gave as much milk at night as if they had been browsing in a pasture! The country people never had to spend money for doctors, but cured all diseases with roots and herbs, and when the old folks had the rheumatism they took "one of dem liddle jenny-pigs" to bed with them, and the guinea-pig drew out all the pain.

Claude would have liked to listen longer, but he wanted to find the old woman's tormentors before his train came in. Leaving his bags with her, he crossed the railroad tracks, guided by an occasional teasing tinkle of the bell in the cornfield. Presently he came upon the gang, a dozen or more, lying in a shallow draw that ran from the edge of the field out into an open pasture. He stood on the edge of the bank and looked down at them, while he slowly cut off the end of a cigar and lit it. The boys grinned at him, trying to appear indifferent and at ease.

"Looking for any one, soldier?" asked the one with the bell.

"Yes, I am. I'm looking for that bell. You'll have to take it back where it belongs. You every one of you know there's no harm in that old woman."

"She's a German, and we're fighting the Germans, ain't we?"

"I don't think you'll ever fight any. You'd last about ten minutes in the American army. You're not our kind. There's only one army in the world that wants men who'll bully old women. You might get a job with them."

The boys giggled. Claude beckoned impatiently. "Come along with that bell, kid."

The boy rose slowly and climbed the bank out of the gully. As they tramped back through the cornfield, Claude turned to him abruptly. "See here, aren't you ashamed of yourself?"

"Oh, I don't know about that!" the boy replied airily, tossing the bell up like a ball and catching it.

"Well, you ought to be. I didn't expect to see anything of this kind until I got to the front. I'll be back here in a week, and I'll make it hot for anybody that's been bothering her." Claude's train was pulling in, and he ran for his baggage.

Once seated in the "cotton-tail," he began going down into his own country, where he knew every farm he passed, — knew the land even when he did not know the owner, what sort of crops it yielded, and about how much it was worth. He did not recognize these farms with the pleasure he had anticipated, because he was so angry about the indignities Mrs. Voigt had suffered. He was still burning with the first ardour of the enlisted man. He believed that he was going abroad with an expeditionary force that would make war without rage, with uncompromising generosity and chivalry.

Most of his friends at camp shared his Quixotic ideas. They had come together from farms and shops and mills and mines, boys from college and boys from tough joints in big cities; sheep-herders, street car drivers, plumbers' assistants, billiard markers. Claude had seen hundreds of them when they first came in; "show men" in cheap, loud sport suits, ranch boys in knitted waistcoats, machinists with the grease still on their fingers, farm-hands like Dan, in their one Sunday coat. Some of them carried paper suitcases tied up with rope, some brought all they had in a blue handkerchief. But they all came to give and not to ask, and what they offered was just themselves; their big red hands, their strong backs, the steady, honest, modest look in their eyes. Sometimes, when he had helped the medical examiner, Claude had noticed the anxious expression in the faces of the long lines of waiting men. They seemed to say, "If I'm good enough, take me. I'll stay by." He found them like that to work with; servicea-ble, good-natured, and eager to learn. If they talked about the war, or the enemy they were getting ready to fight, it was usually in a facetious tone; they were going to "can the Kaiser," or to make the Crown Prince work for a living. Claude loved the men he trained with, — wouldn't choose to live in any better company.

The freight train swung into the river valley that meant home,—the place the mind always came back to, after its farthest quest. Rapidly the farms passed; the haystacks, the cornfields, the familiar red barns—then the long coal sheds and the water tank, and the train stopped.

On the platform he saw Ralph and Mr. Royce, waiting to welcome him. Over there, in the automobile, were his father and mother, Mr. Wheeler in the driver's seat. A line of motors stood along the siding. He was the first soldier who had come home, and some of the townspeople had driven down to see him arrive in his uniform. From one car Susie Dawson waved to him, and from another Gladys Farmer. While he stopped and spoke to them, Ralph took his bags.

"Come along, boys," Mr. Wheeler called, tooting his horn, and he hurried the soldier away, leaving only a cloud of dust behind.

Mr. Royce went over to old man Dawson's car and said rather childishly, "It can't be that Claude's grown taller? I suppose it's the way they learn to carry themselves. He always was a manly looking boy."

"I expect his mother's a proud woman," said Susie, very much excited. "It's too bad Enid can't be here to see him. She would never have gone away if she'd known all that was to happen."

Susie did not mean this as a thrust, but it took effect. Mr. Royce turned away and lit a cigar with some difficulty. His hands had grown very unsteady this last year, though he insisted that his general health was as good as ever. As he grew older, he was more depressed by the conviction that his women-folk had added little to the warmth and comfort of the world. Women ought to do that, whatever else they did. He felt apologetic toward the Wheelers and toward his old friends. It seemed as if his daughters had no heart.

XI

CAMP habits persisted. On his first morning at home Claude came downstairs before even Mahailey was stirring, and went out to have a look at the stock. The red sun came up just as he was going down the hill toward the cattle corral, and he had the pleasant feeling of being at home, on his father's land. Why was it so gratifying to be able to say "our hill," and "our creek down yonder"? to feel the crunch of this particular dried mud under his boots?

When he went into the barn to see the horses, the first creatures to meet his eye were the two big mules that had run away with him, standing in the stalls next the door. It flashed upon Claude that these muscular quadrupeds were the actual authors of his fate. If they had not bolted with him and thrown him into the wire fence that morning, Enid would not have felt sorry for him and come to see him every day, and his life might have turned out differently. Perhaps if older people were a little more honest, and a boy were not taught to idealize in women the very qualities which can make him utterly unhappy—But there, he had got away from those regrets. But wasn't it just like him to be dragged into matrimony by a pair of mules!

He laughed as he looked at them. "You old devils, you're strong enough to play such tricks on green fellows for years to come. You're chock full of meanness!"

One of the animals wagged an ear and cleared his throat threateningly. Mules are capable of strong affections, but they hate snobs, are the enemies of caste, and this pair had always

219

seemed to detect in Claude what his father used to call his "false pride." When he was a young lad they had been a source of humiliation to him, braying and balking in public places, trying to show off at the lumber yard or in front of the postoffice.

At the end manger Claude found old Molly, the grey mare with the stiff leg, who had grown a second hoof on her off forefoot, an achievement not many horses could boast of. He was sure she recognized him; she nosed his hand and arm and turned back her upper lip, showing her worn, yellow teeth.

"Mustn't do that, Molly," he said as he stroked her. "A dog can laugh, but it makes a horse look foolish. Seems to me Dan might curry you about once a week!" He took a comb from its niche behind a joist and gave her old coat a rubbing. Her white hair was flecked all over with little rust-coloured dashes, like India ink put on with a fine brush, and her mane and tail had turned a greenish yellow. She must be eighteen years old, Claude reckoned, as he polished off her round, heavy haunches. He and Ralph used to ride her over to the Yoeders' when they were barefoot youngsters, guiding her with a rope halter, and kicking at the leggy colt that was always running alongside.

When he entered the kitchen and asked Mahailey for warm water to wash his hands, she sniffed him disapprovingly.

"Why, Mr. Claude, you've been curryin' that old mare, and you've got white hairs all over your soldier-clothes. You're jist covered!"

If his uniform stirred feeling in people of sober judgment, over Mahailey it cast a spell. She was so dazzled by it that all the time Claude was at home she never once managed to examine it in detail. Before she got past his puttees, her powers of observation were befogged by excitement, and her wits began to jump about like monkeys in a cage. She had expected his uniform to be blue, like those she remembered, and when he walked into the kitchen last night she scarcely knew what to make of him. After Mrs. Wheeler explained to her that American soldiers didn't wear blue now, Mahailey repeated to herself that these brown clothes didn't show the dust, and that Claude would never look like the bedraggled men who used to stop to drink at her mother's spring.

"Them leather leggins is to keep the briars from scratchin' you, ain't they? I 'spect there's an awful lot of briars over there, like them long blackberry vines in the fields in Virginia. Your mudder says the soldiers git lice now, like they done in our war. You jist carry a little bottle of coal-oil in your pocket an' rub it on your head at night. It keeps the nits from hatchin'."

Over the flour barrel in the corner Mahailey had tacked a Red Cross poster; a charcoal drawing of an old woman poking with a stick in a pile of plaster and twisted timbers that had once been her home. Claude went over to look at it while he dried his hands.

"Where did you get your picture?"

"She's over there where you're goin', Mr. Claude. There she is, huntin' for somethin' to cook with; no stove nor no dishes nor nothin'—everything all broke up. I reckon she'll be mighty glad to see you comin'."

Heavy footsteps sounded on the stairs, and Mahailey whispered hastily, "Don't forgit about the coal-oil, and don't you be lousy if you can help it, honey." She considered lice in the same class with smutty jokes,—things to be whispered about.

After breakfast Mr. Wheeler took Claude out to the fields, where Ralph was directing the harvesters. They watched the binder for a while, then went over to look at the haystacks and alfalfa, and walked along the edge of the cornfield, where they examined the young ears. Mr. Wheeler explained and exhibited the farm to Claude as if he were a stranger; the boy had a curious feeling of being now formally introduced to these acres on which he had worked every summer since he was big enough to carry water to the harvesters. His father told him how much land they owned, and how much it was worth, and that it was unencumbered except for a trifling mortgage he had given on one quarter when he took over the Colorado ranch.

221

"When you come back," he said, "you and Ralph won't have to hunt around to get into business. You'll both be well fixed. Now you'd better go home by old man Dawson's and drop in to see Susie. Everybody about here was astonished when Leonard went." He walked with Claude to the corner where the Dawson land met his own. "By the way," he said as he turned back, "don't forget to go in to see the Yoeders sometime. Gus is pretty sore since they had him up in court. Ask for the old grandmother. You remember she never learned any English. And now they've told her it's dangerous to talk German, she don't talk at all and hides away from everybody. If I go by early in the morning, when she's out weeding the garden, she runs and squats down in the gooseberry bushes till I'm out of sight."

Claude decided he would go to the Yoeders' today, and to the Dawsons' tomorrow. He didn't like to think there might be hard feeling toward him in a house where he had had so many good times, and where he had often found a refuge when things were dull at home. The Yoeder boys had a music-box long before the days of Victrolas, and a magic lantern, and the old grandmother made wonderful shadow-pictures on a sheet, and told stories about them. She used to turn the map of Europe upside down on the kitchen table and showed the children how, in this position, it looked like a *Jungfrau;* and recited a long German rhyme which told how Spain was the maiden's head, the Pyrenees her lace ruff, Germany her heart and bosom, England and Italy were two arms, and Russia, though it looked so big, was only a hoopskirt. This rhyme would probably be condemned as dangerous propaganda now!

As he walked on alone, Claude was thinking how this country that had once seemed little and dull to him, now seemed large and rich in variety. During the months in camp he had been wholly absorbed in new work and new friendships, and now his own neighbourhood came to him with the freshness of things that have been forgotten for a long while, — came together before his eyes as a harmonious whole. He was going away, and he would carry the whole countryside in his mind, meaning more to him than it ever had before. There was Lovely Creek, gurgling on down there, where he and Ernest used to sit and lament that the book of History was finished; that the world had come to avaricious old age and noble enterprise was dead for ever. But he was going away. . . .

That afternoon Claude spent with his mother. It was the first time she had had him to herself. Ralph wanted terribly to stay and hear his brother talk, but understanding how his mother felt, he went back to the wheat field. There was no detail of Claude's life in camp so trivial that Mrs. Wheeler did not want to hear about it. She asked about the mess, the cooks, the laundry, as well as about his own duties. She made him describe the bayonet drill and explain the operation of machine guns and automatic rifles.

"I hardly see how we can bear the anxiety when our transports begin to sail," she said thoughtfully. "If they can once get you all over there, I am not afraid; I believe our boys are as good as any in the world. But with submarines reported off our own coast, I wonder how the Government can get our men across safely. The thought of transports going down with thousands of young men on board is something so terrible —" she put her hands quickly over her eyes.

Claude, sitting opposite his mother, wondered what it was about her hands that made them so different from any others he had ever seen. He had always known they were different, but now he must look closely and see why. They were slender, and always white, even when the nails were stained at preserving time. Her fingers arched back at the joints, as if they were shrinking from contacts. They were restless, and when she talked often brushed her hair or her dress lightly. When she was excited she sometimes put her hand to her throat, or felt about the neck of her gown, as if she were searching for a forgotten brooch. They were sensitive hands, and yet they seemed to have nothing to do with sense, to be almost like the groping fingers of a spirit.

"How do you boys feel about it?"

223

Claude started. "About what, Mother? Oh, the transportation! We don't worry about that. It's the Government's job to get us across. A soldier mustn't worry about anything except what he's directly responsible for. If the Germans should sink a few troop ships, it would be unfortunate, certainly,—but it wouldn't cut any figure in the long run. The British are perfecting an enormous dirigible, built to carry passengers. If our transports are sunk, it will only mean delay. In another year the Yankees will be flying over. They can't stop us."

Mrs. Wheeler bent forward. "That must be boys' talk, Claude. Surely you don't believe such a thing could be practicable?"

"Absolutely. The British are depending on their aircraft designers to do just that, if everything else fails. Of course, nobody knows yet how effective the submarines will be in our case."

Mrs. Wheeler again shaded her eyes with her hand. "When I was young, back in Vermont, I used to wish that I had lived in the old times when the world went ahead by leaps and bounds. And now, I feel as if my sight couldn't bear the glory that beats upon it. It seems as if we would have to be born with new faculties, to comprehend what is going on in the air and under the sea."

XII

THE afternoon sun was pouring in at the back windows of Mrs. Farmer's long, uneven parlour, making the dusky room look like a cavern with a fire at one end of it. The furniture was all in its cool, figured summer cretonnes. The glass flower vases that stood about on little tables caught the sunlight and twinkled like tiny lamps. Claude had been sitting there for a long while, and he knew he ought to go. Through the window at his elbow he could see rows of double hollyhocks, the flat leaves of the sprawling catalpa, and the spires of the tangled mint bed, all transparent in the gold-powdered light. They had talked about everything but the thing he had come to say. As he looked out into the garden he felt that he would never get it out. There was something in the way the mint bed burned and floated that made one a fatalist,— afraid to meddle. But after he was far away, he would regret; uncertainty would tease him like a splinter in his thumb.

He rose suddenly and said without apology: "Gladys, I wish I could feel sure you'd never marry my brother."

She did not reply, but sat in her easy chair, looking up at him with a strange kind of calmness.

"I know all the advantages," he went on hastily, "but they wouldn't make it up to you. That sort of a—compromise would make you awfully unhappy. I know."

"I don't think I shall ever marry Bayliss," Gladys spoke in her usual low, round voice, but her quick breathing showed he had touched something that hurt. "I suppose I have used him. It gives a school-teacher a certain prestige if people think she can marry the rich bachelor of the town whenever she wants to. But I am afraid I won't marry him,—because you are the member of the family I have always admired."

Claude turned away to the window. "A fine lot I've been to admire," he muttered.

"Well, it's true, anyway. It was like that when we went to High School, and it's kept up. Everything you do always seems exciting to me."

Claude felt a cold perspiration on his forehead. He wished now that he had never come. "But that's it, Gladys. What *have* I ever done, except make one blunder after another?"

She came over to the window and stood beside him. "I don't know; perhaps it's by their blunders that one gets to know people,—by what they can't do. If you'd been like all the rest, you could have got on in their way. That was the one thing I couldn't have stood."

Claude was frowning out into the flaming garden. He had not heard a word of her reply. "Why didn't you keep me from making a fool of myself?" he asked in a low voice.

"I think I tried—once. Anyhow, it's all turning out better than I thought. You didn't get stuck here. You've found your place. You're sailing away. You've just begun."

"And what about you?"

She laughed softly. "Oh, I shall teach in the High School!"

Claude took her hands and they stood looking searchingly at each other in the swimming golden light that made everything transparent. He never knew exactly how he found his hat and made his way out of the house. He was only sure that Gladys did not accompany him to the door. He glanced back once, and saw her head against the bright window.

She stood there, exactly where he left her, and watched the evening come on, not moving, scarcely breathing. She was thinking how often, when she came downstairs, she would see him standing here by the window, or moving about in the dusky room, looking at last as he ought to look,—like his convictions and the choice he had made. She would never let this house be sold for taxes now. She would save her salary and pay them off. She could never like any other room so well as this. It had always been a refuge from Frankfort; and now there would be this vivid, confident figure, an image as distinct to her as the portrait of her grandfather upon the wall.

XIII

SUNDAY was Claude's last day at home, and he took a long walk with Ernest and Ralph. Ernest would have preferred to lose Ralph, but when the boy was out of the harvest field he stuck to his brother like a burr. There was something about Claude's new clothes and new manner that fascinated him, and he went through one of those sudden changes of feeling that often occur in families. Although they had been better friends ever since Claude's wedding, until now Ralph had always felt a little ashamed of him. Why, he used to ask himself, wouldn't Claude "spruce up and be somebody?" Now, he was struck by the fact that he was somebody.

On Monday morning Mrs. Wheeler wakened early, with a faintness in her chest. This was the day on which she must acquit herself well. Breakfast would be Claude's last meal at home. At eleven o'clock his father and Ralph would take him to Frankfort to catch the train. She was longer than usual in dressing. When she got downstairs Claude and Mahailey were already talking. He was shaving in the washroom, and Mahailey stood watching him, a side of bacon in her hand.

"You tell 'em over there I'm awful sorry about them old women, with their dishes an' their stove all broke up."

"All right. I will." Claude scraped away at his chin.

She lingered. "Maybe you can help 'em mend their things, like you do mine fur me," she suggested hopefully.

"Maybe," he murmured absently.

Mrs. Wheeler opened the stair door, and Mahailey dodged back to the stove.

After breakfast Dan went out to the fields with the harvesters. Ralph and Claude and Mr. Wheeler were busy with the car all morning.

Mrs. Wheeler kept throwing her apron over her head and going down the hill to see what they were doing. Whether there was really something the matter with the engine, or whether the men merely made it a pretext for being together and keeping away from the house, she did not know. She felt that her presence was not much desired, and at last she went upstairs and resignedly watched them from the sitting-room window. Presently she heard Ralph run up to the third storey. When he came down with Claude's bags in his hands, he stuck his head in at the door and shouted cheerfully to his mother:

"No hurry. I'm just taking them down so they'll be ready."

Mrs. Wheeler ran after him, calling faintly, "Wait, Ralph! Are you sure he's got everything in? I didn't hear him packing."

"Everything ready. He says he won't have to go upstairs again. He'll be along pretty soon. There's lots of time." Ralph shot down through the basement.

Mrs. Wheeler sat down in her reading chair. They wanted to keep her away, and it was a little selfish of them. Why couldn't they spend these last hours quietly in the house, instead of dashing in and out to frighten her. Now she could hear the hot water running in the kitchen; probably Mr. Wheeler had come in to wash his hands. She felt really too weak to get up and go to the west window to see if he were still down at the garage. Waiting was now a matter of seconds, and her breath came short enough as it was.

She recognized a heavy, hob-nailed boot on the stairs, mounting quickly. When Claude entered, carrying his hat in his hand, she saw by his walk, his shoulders, and the way he held his head, that the moment had come, and that he meant to make it short. She rose, reaching toward him as he came up to her and caught her in his arms. She was smiling her little, curious intimate smile, with half-closed eyes.

"Well, is it good-bye?" she murmured. She passed her hands over his shoulders, down his strong back and the close-fitting sides of his coat, as if she were taking the mould and measure of his mortal frame. Her chin came just to his breast pocket, and she rubbed it against the heavy cloth. Claude stood looking down at her without speaking a word. Suddenly his arms tightened and he almost crushed her.

"Mother!" he whispered as he kissed her. He ran downstairs and out of the house without looking back.

She struggled up from the chair where she had sunk and crept to the window; he was vaulting down the hill as fast as he could go. He jumped into the car beside his father. Ralph was already at the wheel, and Claude had scarcely touched the cushions when they were off. They ran down the creek and over the bridge, then up the long hill on the other side. As they neared the crest of the hill, Claude stood up in the car and looked back at the house, waving his cone-shaped hat. She leaned out and strained her sight, but her tears blurred everything. The brown, upright figure seemed to float out of the car and across the fields, and before he was actually gone, she lost him. She fell back against the window-sill, clutching her temples with both hands, and broke into choking, passionate speech. "Old eyes," she cried, "why do you betray me? Why do you cheat me of my last sight of my splendid son!"

BOOK FOUR

THE VOYAGE OF THE ANCHISES

I

ALONG train of crowded cars, the passengers all of the same sex, almost of the same age, all dressed and hatted alike, was slowly steaming through the green sea-meadows late on a summer afternoon. In the cars, incessant stretching of cramped legs, shifting of shoulders, striking of matches, passing of cigarettes, groans of boredom; occasionally concerted laughter about nothing. Suddenly the train stops short. Clipped heads and tanned faces pop out at every window. The boys begin to moan and shout; what is the matter now?

The conductor goes through the cars, saying something about a freight wreck on ahead; he has orders to wait here for half an hour. Nobody pays any attention to him. A murmur of astonishment rises from one side of the train. The boys crowd over to the south windows. At last there is something to look at, —though what they see is so strangely quiet that their own exclamations are not very loud.

Their train is lying beside an arm of the sea that reaches far into the green shore. At the edge of the still water stand the hulls of four wooden ships, in the process of building. There is no town, there are no smoke-stacks—very few workmen. Piles of lumber lie about on the grass. A gasoline engine under a temporary shelter is operating a long crane that reaches down among the piles of boards and beams, lifts a load, silently and deliberately swings it over to one of the skeleton vessels, and lowers it somewhere into the body of the motionless thing. Along the sides of the clean hulls a few riveters are at work; they sit on suspended planks, lowering and raising themselves with pulleys, like house painters. Only by listening very closely can one hear the tap of their hammers. No orders are shouted, no thud of heavy machinery or scream of iron drills tears the air. These strange boats seem to be building themselves.

Some of the men got out of the cars and ran along the tracks, asking each other how boats could be built off in the grass like this. Lieutenant Claude Wheeler stretched his legs upon the opposite seat and sat still at his window, looking down on this strange scene. Shipbuilding, he had supposed, meant noise and forges and engines and hosts of men. This was like a dream. Nothing but green meadows, soft grey water, a floating haze of mist a little rosy from the sinking sun, spectre-like seagulls, flying slowly, with the red glow tinging their wings—and those four hulls lying in their braces, facing the sea, deliberating by the sea.

Claude knew nothing of ships or shipbuilding, but these craft did not seem to be nailed together,—they seemed all of a piece, like sculpture. They reminded him of the houses not made with hands; they were like simple and great thoughts, like purposes forming slowly here in the silence beside an unruffled arm of the Atlantic. He knew nothing about ships, but he didn't have to; the shape of those hulls—their strong, inevitable lines—told their story, *was* their story; told the whole adventure of man with the sea.

Wooden ships! When great passions and great aspirations stirred a country, shapes like these formed along its shores to be the sheath of its valour. Nothing Claude had ever seen or heard or read or thought had made it all so clear as these untried wooden bottoms. They were the very impulse, they were the potential act, they were the "going over," the drawn arrow, the great unuttered cry, they were Fate, they were tomorrow! . . .

The locomotive screeched to her scattered passengers, like an old turkey-hen calling her brood. The soldier boys came running back along the embankment and leaped aboard the train. The conductor shouted they would be in Hoboken in time for supper.

Hoboken? How many of them were already in France!

II

IT was midnight when the men had got their supper and began unrolling their blankets to sleep on the floor of the long dock waiting-rooms,—which in other days had been thronged by people who came to welcome home-coming friends, or to bid them God-speed to foreign shores. Claude and some of his men had tried to look about them; but there was little to be seen. The bow of a boat, painted in distracting patterns of black and white, rose at one end of the shed, but the water itself was not visible. Down in the cobble-paved street below they watched for awhile the long line of drays and motor trucks that bumped all night into a vast cavern lit by electricity, where crates and barrels and merchandise of all kinds were piled, marked American Expeditionary Forces; cases of electrical machinery from some factory in Ohio, parts of automobiles, gun-carriages, bath-tubs, hospital supplies bales of cotton, cases of canned food, grey metal tanks full of chemical fluids. Claude went back to the waiting room, lay down and fell asleep with the glare of an arc-light shining full in his face.

He was called at four in the morning and told where to report to headquarters. Captain Maxey, stationed at a desk on one of the landings, explained to his lieutenants that their company was to sail at eight o'clock on the *Anchises*. It was an English boat, an old liner pulled off the Australian trade, that could carry only twenty-five hundred men. The crew was English, but part of the stores,—the meat and fresh fruit and vegetables,—were furnished by the United States Government. The Captain had been over the boat during the night, and didn't like it very well. He had expected to be scheduled for one of the fine big Hamburg-American liners, with dining-rooms finished in rosewood, and ventilation plants and cooling plants, and elevators running from top to bottom like a New York office building. "However," he said, "we'll have to make the best of it. They're using everything that's got a bottom now."

The company formed for roll-call at one end of the shed, with their packs and rifles. Breakfast was served to them while they waited. After an hour's standing on the concrete, they saw encouraging signs. Two gangplanks were lowered from the vessel at the end of the slip, and up each of them began to stream a close brown line of men in smart service caps. They recognized a company of Kansas Infantry, and began to grumble because their own service caps hadn't yet been given to them; they would have to sail in their old Stetsons. Soon they were drawn into one of the brown lines that went continuously up the gangways, like belting running over machinery. On the deck one steward directed the men down to the hold, and another conducted the officers to their cabins. Claude was shown to a four-berth state-room. One of his cabin mates, Lieutenant Fanning, of his own company, was already there, putting his slender luggage in order. The steward told them the officers were breakfasting in the dining saloon.

By seven o'clock all the troops were aboard, and the men were allowed on deck. For the first time Claude saw the profile of New York City, rising thin and gray against an opal-coloured morning sky. The day had come on hot and misty. The sun, though it was now high, was a red ball, streaked across with purple clouds. The tall buildings, of which he had heard so much, looked unsubstantial and illusionary, — mere shadows of grey and pink and blue that might dissolve with the mist and fade away in it. The boys were disappointed. They were Western men, accustomed to the hard light of high altitudes, and they wanted to see the city clearly; they couldn't make anything of these uneven towers that rose dimly through the vapour. Everybody was asking questions. Which of those pale giants was the Singer Building? Which the Woolworth? What was the gold dome, dully glinting through the fog? Nobody knew. They agreed it was a shame they could not have had a day in New York before they sailed away from it, and that they would feel foolish in Paris when they had to admit they had never so much as walked up Broadway. Tugs and ferry boats and coal barges were moving up and down the oily river,—all novel sights to the men. Over in the Cunard and French docks they saw the first examples of the "camouflage" they had heard so much about; big vessels daubed over in crazy patterns that made the eyes ache, some in black and white, some in soft rainbow colours.

A tug steamed up alongside and fastened. A few moments later a man appeared on the bridge and began to talk to the captain. Young Fanning, who had stuck to Claude's side, told him this was the pilot, and that his arrival meant they were going to start. They could see the shiny instruments of a band assembling in the bow.

"Let's get on the other side, near the rail if we can," said Fanning. "The fellows are bunching up over here because they want to look at the Goddess of Liberty as we go out. They don't even know this boat turns around the minute she gets into the river. They think she's going over stern first!"

It was not easy to cross the deck; every inch was covered by a boot. The whole superstructure was coated with brown uniforms; they clung to the boat davits, the winches, the railings and ventilators, like bees in a swarm. Just as the vessel was backing out, a breeze sprang up and cleared the air. Blue sky broke overhead, and the pale silhouette of buildings on the long island grew sharp and hard. Windows flashed flame-coloured in their grey sides, the gold and bronze tops of towers began to gleam where the sunlight struggled through. The transport was sliding down toward the point, and to the left the eye was sliding down toward the point, and to the left the eye caught the silver cobweb of bridges, seen confusingly against each other.

"There she is!" "Hello, old girl!" "Good-bye, sweetheart!"

The swarm surged to starboard. They shouted and gesticulated to the image they were all looking for,—so much nearer than they had expected to see her, clad in green folds, with the mist streaming up like smoke behind. For nearly every one of those twenty-five hundred boys, as for Claude, it was their first glimpse of the Bartholdi statue. Though she was such a definite image in their minds, they had not imagined her in her setting of sea and sky, with the shipping of the world coming and going at her feet, and the moving cloud-masses behind her. Post-card pictures had given them no idea of the energy of her large gesture, or how her heaviness becomes light among the vapourish elements. "France gave her to us," they kept saying, as they saluted her. Before Claude had got over his first thrill, the Kansas band in the bow began playing "Over There." Two thousand voices took it up, booming out over the water the gay, indomitable resolution of that jaunty air.

A Staten Island ferry-boat passed close under the bow of the transport. The passengers were office-going people, on their way to work, and when they looked up and saw these hundreds of faces, all young, all bronzed and grinning, they began to shout and wave their handkerchiefs. One of the passengers was an old clergyman, a famous speaker in his day, now retired, who went over to the City every morning to write editorials for a church paper. He closed the book he was reading, stood by the rail, and taking off his hat began solemnly to quote from a poet who in his time was still popular. "Sail on," he quavered,

> "Thou, too, sail on, O Ship of State,
> Humanity, with all its fears,
> With all its hopes of future years,
> Is hanging breathless on thy fate."

As the troop ship glided down the sea lane, the old man still watched it from the turtle-back. That howling swarm of brown arms and hats and faces looked like nothing but a crowd of American boys going to a football game somewhere. But the scene was ageless; youths were sailing away to die for an idea, a sentiment, for the mere sound of a phrase . . . and on their departure they were making vows to a bronze image in the sea.

III

ALL the first morning Tod Fanning showed Claude over the boat,—not that Fanning had ever been on anything bigger than a Lake Michigan steamer, but he knew a good deal about machinery, and did not hesitate to ask the deck stewards to explain anything he didn't know. The stewards, indeed all the crew, struck the boys as an unusually good-natured and obliging set of men.

The fourth occupant of number 96, Claude's cabin, had not turned up by noon, nor had any of his belongings, so the three who had settled their few effects there began to hope they would have the place to themselves. It would be crowded enough, at that. The third bunk was assigned to an officer from the Kansas regiment, Lieutenant Bird, a Virginian, who had been working in his uncle's bank in Topeka when he enlisted. He and Claude sat together at mess. When they were at lunch, the Virginian said in his very gentle voice:

"Lieutenant, I wish you'd explain Lieutenant Fanning to me. He seems very immature. He's been telling me about a submarine destroyer he's invented, but it looks to me like foolishness."

Claude laughed. "Don't try to understand Fanning. Just let him sink in, and you'll come to like him. I used to wonder how he ever got a commission. You never can tell what crazy thing he'll do."

Fanning had, for instance, brought on board a pair of white flannel pants, his first and only tailor-made trousers, because he had a premonition that the boat would make an English port and

239

that he would be asked to a garden party! He had a way of using big words in the wrong place, not because he tried to show off, but because all words sounded alike to him. In the first days of their acquaintance in camp he told Claude that this was a failing he couldn't help, and that it was called "anaesthesia." Sometimes this failing was confusing; when Fanning sententiously declared that he would like to be on hand when the Crown Prince settled his little account with Plato, Claude was perplexed until subsequent witticisms revealed that the boy meant Pluto.

At three o'clock there was a band concert on deck. Claude fell into talk with the bandmaster, and was delighted to find that he came from Hillport, Kansas, a town where Claude had once been with his father to buy cattle, and that all his fourteen men came from Hillport. They were the town band, had enlisted in a body, had gone into training together, and had never been separated. One was a printer who helped to get out the Hillport *Argus* every week, another clerked in a grocery store, another was the son of a German watch repairer, one was still in High School, one worked in an automobile livery. After supper Claude found them all together, very much interested in their first evening at sea, and arguing as to whether the sunset on the water was as fine as those they saw every night in Hillport. They hung together in a quiet, determined way, and if you began to talk to one, you soon found that all the others were there.

When Claude and Fanning and Lieutenant Bird were undressing in their narrow quarters that night, the fourth berth was still unclaimed. They were in their bunks and almost asleep, when the missing man came in and unceremoniously turned on the light. They were astonished to see that he wore the uniform of the Royal Flying Corps and carried a cane. He seemed very young, but the three who peeped out at him felt that he must be a person of consequence. He took off his coat with the spread wings on the collar, wound his watch, and brushed his teeth with an air of special personal importance. Soon after he had turned out the light and climbed into the berth over Lieutenant Bird, a heavy smell of rum spread in the close air.

Fanning, who slept under Claude, kicked the sagging mattress above him and stuck his head out. "Hullo, Wheeler! What have you got up there?"

"Nothing."

"Nothing smells pretty good to me. I'll have some with anybody that asks me."

No response from any quarter. Bird, the Virginian, murmured, "Don't make a row," and they went to sleep.

In the morning, when the bath steward came, he edged his way into the narrow cabin and poked his head into the berth over Bird's. "I'm sorry, sir, I've made careful search for your luggage, and it's not to be found, sir."

"I tell you it must be found," fumed a petulant voice overhead. "I brought it over from the St. Regis myself in a taxi. I saw it standing on the pier with the officers' luggage,—a black cabin trunk with V.M. lettered on both ends. Get after it."

The steward smiled discreetly. He probably knew that the aviator had come on board in a state which precluded any very accurate observation on his part. "Very well, sir. Is there anything I can get you for the present?"

"You can take this shirt out and have it laundered and bring it back to me tonight. I've no linen in my bag."

"Yes, sir."

Claude and Fanning got on deck as quickly as possible and found scores of their comrades already there, pointing to dark smudges of smoke along the clear horizon. They knew that these vessels had come from unknown ports, some of them far away, steaming thither under orders known only to their commanders. They would all arrive within a few hours of each other at a given spot on the surface of the ocean. There they would fall into place, flanked by their destroyers, and would proceed in orderly formation, without changing their relative positions. Their escort would not leave them until they were joined by gunboats and destroyers off whatever coast they were bound for,—what that coast was, not even their own officers knew as yet.

Later in the morning this meeting was actually accomplished. There were ten troop ships, some of them very large boats, and six destroyers. The men stood about the whole morning, gazing spellbound at their sister transports, trying to find out their names, guessing at their capacity. Tanned as they already were, their lips and noses began to blister under the fiery sunlight. After long months of intensive training, the sudden drop into an idle, soothing existence was grateful to them. Though their pasts were neither long or varied, most of them, like Claude Wheeler, felt a sense of relief at being rid of all they had ever been before and facing something absolutely new. Said Tod Fanning, as he lounged against the rail, "Whoever likes it can run for a train every morning, and grind his days out in a Westinghouse works; but not for me any more!"

The Virginian joined them. "That Englishman ain't got out of bed yet. I reckon he's been liquouring up pretty steady. The place smells like a bar. The room steward was just coming out, and he winked at me. He was slipping something in his pocket, looked like a banknote."

Claude was curious, and went down to the cabin. As he entered, the air-man, lying half-dressed in his upper berth, raised himself on one elbow and looked down at him. His blue eyes were contracted and hard, his curly hair disordered, but his cheeks were as pink as a girl's, and the little yellow humming-bird moustache on his upper lip was twisted sharp.

"You're missing fine weather," said Claude affably.

"Oh, there'll be a great deal of weather before we get over, and damned little of anything else!" He drew a bottle from under his pillow. "Have a nip?"

"I don't mind if I do," Claude put out his hand.

The other laughed and sank back on his pillow, drawling lazily, "Brave boy! Go ahead; drink to the Kaiser."

"Why to him in particular?"

"It's not particular. Drink to Hindenburg, or the High Command, or anything else that got you out of the cornfield. That's where they did get you, didn't they?"

"Well, it's a good guess, anyhow. Where did they get you?"

"Crystal Lake, Iowa. I think that was the place." He yawned and folded his hands over his stomach.

"Why, we thought you were an Englishman."

"Not quite. I've served in His Majesty's army two years, though."

"Have you been flying in France?"

"Yes. I've been back and forth all the time, England and France. Now I've wasted two months at Fort Worth. Instructor. That's not my line. I may have been sent over as a reprimand. You can't tell about my Colonel, though; may have been his way of getting me out of danger."

Claude glanced up at him, shocked at such an idea.

The young man in the berth smiled with listless compassion. "Oh, I don't mean Bosch planes! There are dangers and dangers. You'll find you got bloody little information about this war, where they trained you. They don't communicate any details of importance. Going?"

Claude hadn't intended to, but at this suggestion he pulled back the door.

"One moment," called the aviator. "Can't you keep that long-legged ass who bunks under you quiet?"

"Fanning? He's a good kid. What's the matter with him?"

"His general ignorance and his insufferably familiar tone," snapped the other as he turned over.

Claude found Fanning and the Virginian playing checkers, and told them that the mysterious air-man was a fellow country-man. Both seemed disappointed.

"Pshaw!" exclaimed Lieutenant Bird.

"He can't put on airs with me, after that," Fanning declared. "Crystal Lake! Why it's no town at all!"

All the same, Claude wanted to find out how a youth from Crystal Lake ever became a member of the Royal Flying Corps. Already, from among the hundreds of strangers, half-a-dozen stood out as men he was determined to know better. Taking them altogether the men were a fine sight as they lounged about the decks in the sunlight, the petty rivalries and jealousies of camp days forgotten. Their youth seemed to flow together, like their brown uniforms. Seen in the mass like this, Claude thought, they were rather noble looking fellows. In so many of the faces there was a look of fine candour, an expression of cheerful expectancy and confident goodwill.

There was on board a solitary Marine, with the stripes of Border service on his coat. He had been sick in the Navy Hospital in Brooklyn when his regiment sailed, and was now going over to join it. He was a young fellow, rather pale from his recent illness, but he was exactly Claude's idea of what a soldier ought to look like. His eye followed the Marine about all day.

The young man's name was Albert Usher, and he came from a little town up in the Wind River mountains, in Wyoming, where he had worked in a logging camp. He told Claude these facts when they found themselves standing side by side that evening, watching the broad purple sun go down into a violet coloured sea.

It was the hour when the farmers at home drive their teams in after the day's work. Claude was thinking how his mother would be standing at the west window every evening now, watching the sun go down and following him in her mind. When the young Marine came up and joined him, he confessed to a pang of homesickness.

"That's a kind of sickness I don't have to wrastle with," said Albert Usher. "I was left an orphan on a lonesome ranch, when I was nine, and I've looked out for myself ever since."

Claude glanced sidewise at the boy's handsome head, that came up from his neck with clean, strong lines, and thought he had done a pretty good job for himself. He could not have said exactly what it was he liked about young Usher's face, but it seemed to him a face that had gone through things, — that had been trained down like his body, and had developed a definite character. What Claude thought due to a manly, adventurous life, was really due to well-shaped bones; Usher's face was more "modelled" than most of the healthy countenances about him.

When questioned, the Marine went on to say that though he had no home of his own, he had always happened to fall on his feet, among kind people. He could go back to any house in Pinedale or Du Bois and be welcomed like a son.

"I suppose there are kind women everywhere," he said, "but in that respect Wyoming's got the rest of the world beat. I never felt the lack of a home. Now the U. S. Marines are my family. Wherever they are, I'm at home."

"Were you at Vera Cruz?" Claude asked.

"I guess! We thought that was quite a little party at the time, but I suppose it will seem small potatoes when we get over there. I'm figuring on seeing some first-rate scrapping. How long have you been in the army?"

"Year ago last April. I've had hard luck about getting over. They kept me jumping about to train men."

"Then yours is all to come. Are you a college graduate?"

"No. I went away to school, but I didn't finish."

Usher frowned at the gilded path on the water where the sun lay half-submerged, like a big, watchful eye, closing. "I always wanted to go to college, but I never managed it. A man in Laramie offered to stake me to a course in the University there, but I was too restless. I guess I was ashamed of my handwriting." He paused as if he had run against some old regret. A moment later he said suddenly, "Can you parlez-vous?"

"No. I know a few words, but I can't put them together."

"Same here. I expect to pick up some. I pinched quite a little Spanish down on the Border."

By this time the sun had disappeared, and all over the west the yellow sky came down evenly, like a gold curtain, on the still sea that seemed to have solidified into a slab of dark blue stone, — not a twinkle on its immobile surface. Across its dusky smoothness were two long smears of pale green, like a robin's egg.

"Do you like the water?" Usher asked, in the tone of a polite host. "When I first shipped on a cruiser I was crazy about it. I still am. But, you know, I like them old bald mountains back in Wyoming, too. There's waterfalls you can see twenty miles off from the plains; they look like white sheets or something, hanging up there on the cliffs. And down in the pine woods, in the cold streams, there's trout as long as my fore-arm."

That evening Claude was on deck, almost alone; there was a concert down in the ward room. To the west heavy clouds had come up, moving so low that they flapped over the water like a black washing hanging on the line.

The music sounded well from below. Four Swedish boys from the Scandinavian settlement at Lindsborg, Kansas, were singing "Long, Long Ago." Claude listened from a sheltered spot in the stern. What were they, and what was he, doing here on the Atlantic? Two years ago he had seemed a fellow for whom life was over; driven into the ground like a post, or like those Chinese criminals who are planted upright in the earth, with only their heads left out for birds to peck at and insects to sting. All his comrades had been tucked away in prairie towns, with their little jobs and their little plans. Yet here they were, attended by unknown ships called in from the four quarters of the earth. How had they come to be worth the watchfulness and devotion of so many men and machines, this extravagant consumption of fuel and energy? Taken one by one, they were ordinary fellows like himself. Yet here they were. And in this massing and movement of men there was nothing mean or common; he was sure of that It was, from first to last, unforeseen, almost incredible. Four years ago, when the French were holding the Marne, the wisest men in the world had not conceived of this as possible; they had reckoned with every fortuity but this. *"Out of these stones can my Father raise up seed unto Abraham."*

Downstairs the men began singing "Annie Laurie." Where were those summer evenings when he used to sit dumb by the windmill, wondering what to do with his life?

IV

THE morning of the third day; Claude and the Virginian and the Marine were up very early, standing in the bow, watching the *Anchises* mount the fresh-blowing hills of water, her prow, as it rose and fell, always a dull triangle against the glitter. Their escorts looked like dream ships, soft and iridescent as shell in the pearl-coloured tints of the morning. Only the dark smudges of smoke told that they were mechanical realities with stokers and engines.

While the three stood there, a sergeant brought Claude word that two of his men would have to report at sick-call. Corporal Tannhauser had had such an attack of nose-bleed during the night that the sergeant thought he might die before they got it stopped. Tannhauser was up now, and in the breakfast line, but the sergeant was sure he ought not to be. This Fritz Tannhauser was the tallest man in the company, a German-American boy who, when asked his name, usually said that his name was Dennis and that he was of Irish descent. Even this morning he tried to joke, and pointing to his big red face told Claude he thought he had measles. "Only they ain't German measles, Lieutenant," he insisted.

Medical inspection took a long while that morning. There seemed to be an outbreak of sickness on board. When Claude brought his two men up to the Doctor, he told them to go below and get into bed. As they left he turned to Claude.

"Give them hot tea, and pile army blankets on them. Make them sweat if you can."

Claude remarked that the hold wasn't a very cheerful place for sick men.

"I know that, Lieutenant, but there are a number of sick men this morning, and the only other physician on board is the sickest of the lot. There's the ship's doctor, of course, but he's only responsible for the crew, and so far he doesn't seem interested. I've got to overhaul the hospital and the medical stores this morning."

"Is there an epidemic of some sort?"

"Well, I hope not. But I'll have plenty to do today, so I count on you to look after those two." The doctor was a New Englander who had joined them at Hoboken. He was a brisk, trim man, with piercing eyes, clean-cut features, and grey hair just the colour of his pale face. Claude felt at once that he knew his business, and he went below to carry out instructions as well as he could.

When he came up from the hold, he saw the aviator—whose name, he had learned, was Victor Morse—smoking by the rail. This cabin-mate still piqued his curiosity.

"First time you've been up, isn't it?"

The aviator was looking at the distant smoke plumes over the quivering, bright water. "Time enough. I wish I knew where we are heading for. It will be awfully awkward for me if we make a French port."

"I thought you said you were to report in France."

"I am. But I want to report in London first." He continued to gaze off at the painted ships. Claude noticed that in standing he held his chin very high. His eyes, now that he was quite sober, were brilliantly young and daring; they seemed scornful of things about him. He held himself conspicuously apart, as if he were not among his own kind. Claude had seen a captured crane, tied by its leg to a hencoop, behave exactly like that among Mahailey's chickens; hold its wings to its sides, and move its head about quickly and glare.

"I suppose you have friends in London?" he asked.

"Rather!" the aviator replied with feeling.

"Do you like it better than Paris?"

"I shouldn't imagine anything was much better than London. I've not been in Paris; always went home when I was on leave. They work us pretty hard. In the infantry and artillery our men get only a fortnight off in twelve months. I understand the Americans have leased the Riviera,—recuperated at Nice and Monte Carlo. The only Cook's tour we had was Gallipoli," he added grimly.

Victor had gone a good way toward acquiring an English accent, the boys thought. At least he said 'necess'ry' and 'dysent'ry' and called his suspenders 'braces.' He offered Claude a cigarette, remarking that his cigars were in his lost trunk.

"Take one of mine. My brother sent me two boxes just before we sailed. I'll put a box in your bunk next time I go down. They're good ones."

The young man turned and looked him over with surprise. "I say, that's very decent of you! Yes, thank you, I will."

Claude had tried yesterday, when he lent Victor some shirts, to make him talk about his aerial adventures, but upon that subject he was as close as a clam. He admitted that the long red scar on his upper arm had been drilled by a sharpshooter from a German Fokker, but added hurriedly that it was of no consequence, as he had made a good landing. Now, on the strength of the cigars, Claude thought he would probe a little further. He asked whether there was anything in the lost trunk that couldn't be replaced, anything "valuable."

"There's one thing that's positively invaluable; a Zeiss lens, in perfect condition. I've got several good photographic outfits from time to time, but the lenses are always cracked by heat,— the things usually come down on fire. This one I got out of a plane I brought down up at Bar-le-Duc, and there's not a scratch on it; simply a miracle."

"You get all the loot when you bring down a machine, do you?" Claude asked encouragingly.

"Of course. I've a good collection; alimeters and compasses and glasses. This lens I always carry with me, because I'm afraid to leave it anywhere."

"I suppose it makes a fellow feel pretty fine to bring down one of those German planes."

"Sometimes. I brought down one too many, though; it was very unpleasant." Victor paused, frowning. But Claude's open, credulous face was too much for his reserve. "I brought down a woman once. She was a plucky devil, flew a scouting machine and had bothered us a bit, going over our lines. Naturally, we didn't know it was a woman until she came down. She was crushed underneath things. She lived a few hours and dictated a letter to her people. I went out and dropped it inside their lines. It was nasty business. I was quite knocked out. I got a fortnight's leave in London, though. Wheeler," he broke out suddenly, "I wish I knew we were going there now!"

"I'd like it well enough if we were."

Victor shrugged. "I should hope so!" He turned his chin in Claude's direction. "See here, if you like, I'll show you London! It's a promise. Americans never see it, you know. They sit in a Y hut and write to their Pollyannas, or they go round hunting for the Tower. I'll show you a city that's alive; that is, unless you've a preference for museums."

His listener laughed. "No, I want to see life, as they say."

"Umph! I'd like to set you down in some places I can think of. Very well, I invite you to dine with me at the Savoy, the first night we're in London. The curtain will rise on this world for you. Nobody admitted who isn't in evening dress. The jewels will dazzle you. Actresses, duchesses, all the handsomest women in Europe."

"But I thought London was dark and gloomy since the war."

Victor smiled and teased his small straw-coloured moustache with his thumb and middle finger. "There are a few bright spots left, thank you!" He began to explain to a novice what life at the front was really like. Nobody who had seen service talked about the war, or thought about it; it was merely a condition under which they lived. Men talked about the particular regiment they were jealous of, or the favoured division that was put in for all the show fighting. Everybody thought about his own game, his personal life that he managed to keep going in spite of discipline;

his next leave, how to get champagne without paying for it, dodging the guard, getting into scrapes with women and getting out again. "Are you quick with your French?" he asked.

Claude grinned. "Not especially."

"You'd better brush up on it if you want to do anything with French girls. I hear your M. P.'s are very strict. You must be able to toss the word the minute you see a skirt, and make your date before the guard gets onto you."

"I suppose French girls haven't any scruples?" Claude remarked carelessly.

Victor shrugged his narrow shoulders. "I haven't found that girls have many, anywhere. When we Canadians were training in England, we all had our week-end wives. I believe the girls in Crystal Lake used to be more or less fussy,—but that's long ago and far away. You won't have any difficulty."

When Victor was in the middle of a tale of amorous adventure, a little different from any Claude had ever heard, Tod Fanning joined them. The aviator did not acknowledge the presence of a new listener, but when he had finished his story, walked away with his special swagger, his eyes fixed upon the distance.

Fanning looked after him with disgust. "Do you believe him? I don't think he's any such heart-smasher. I like his nerve, calling you 'Leftenant'! When he speaks to me he'll have to say Lootenant, or I'll spoil his beauty."

That day the men remembered long afterward, for it was the end of the fine weather, and of those first long, care-free days at sea. In the afternoon Claude and the young Marine, the Virginian and Fanning, sat together in the sun watching the water scoop itself out in hollows and pile itself up in blue, rolling hills. Usher was telling his companions a long story about the landing of the Marines at Vera Cruz.

"It's a great old town," he concluded. "One thing there I'll never forget. Some of the natives took a few of us out to the old prison that stands on a rock in the sea. We put in the whole day there, and it wasn't any tourist show, believe me! We went down into dungeons underneath the water, where they used to keep

State prisoners, kept them buried alive for years. We saw all the old instruments of torture; rusty iron cages where a man couldn't lie down or stand up, but had to sit bent over till he grew crooked. It made you feel queer when you came up, to think how people had been left to rot away down there, when there was so much sun and water outside. Seems like something used to be the matter with the world." He said no more, but Claude thought from his serious look that he believed he and his countrymen who were pouring over-seas would help to change all that; the old dungeons and cages would be broken open for ever. The image of a black prison, lying out in a blue Gulf, lingered in his mind, and he felt as if he had been there.

V

THAT night the Virginian, who berthed under Victor Morse, had an alarming attack of nose-bleed, and by morning he was so weak that he had to be carried to the hospital. The Doctor said they might as well face the facts; a scourge of influenza had broken out on board, of a peculiarly bloody and malignant type.[1] Everybody was a little frightened. Some of the officers shut themselves up in the smoking-room, and drank whiskey and soda and played poker all day, as if they could keep contagion out.

Lieutenant Bird died late in the afternoon and was buried at sunrise the next day, sewed up in a tarpaulin, with an eighteen pound shell at his feet. The morning broke brilliantly clear and bitter cold. The sea was rolling blue walls of water, and the boat was raked by a wind as sharp as ice. Excepting those who were sick, the boys turned out to a man. It was the first burial at sea they had ever witnessed, and they couldn't help finding it interesting. The Chaplain read the burial service while they stood with uncovered heads. The Kansas band played a solemn march, the Swedish quartette sang a hymn. Many a man turned his face away when that brown sack was lowered into the cold, leaping indigo ridges that seemed so destitute of anything friendly to human kind. In a moment it was done, and they steamed on without him.

The glittering walls of water kept rolling in, indigo, purple, more brilliant than on the days of mild weather. The blinding sunlight did not temper the cold, which cut the face and made the lungs ache. Landsmen began to have that miserable sense of being where they were never meant to be. The boys lay in heaps on the deck, trying to keep warm by hugging each other close. Everybody was seasick. Fanning went to bed with his clothes on, so sick he couldn't take off his boots. Claude lay in the crowded stern, too cold, too faint to move. The sun poured over them like flame, without any comfort in it. The strong, curling, foam-crested waves threw off the light like millions of mirrors, and their colour was almost more than the eye could bear. The water seemed denser than before, heavy like melted glass, and the foam on the edges of each blue ridge looked sharp as crystals. If a man should fall into them, he would be cut to pieces.

The whole ocean seemed suddenly to have come to life, the waves had a malignant, graceful, muscular energy, were animated by a kind of mocking cruelty. Only a few hours ago a gentle boy had been thrown into that freezing water and forgotten. Yes, already forgotten; every one had his own miseries to think about.

Late in the afternoon the wind fell, and there was a sinister sunset. Across the red west a small, ragged black cloud hurried, — then another, and another. They came up out of the sea, — wild, witchlike shapes that travelled fast and met in the west as if summoned for an evil conclave. They hung there against the after-glow, distinct black shapes, drawing together, devising something. The few men who were left on deck felt that no good could come out of a sky like that. They wished they were at home, in France, anywhere but here.

VI

THE next morning Doctor Trueman asked Claude to help him at sick call. "I've got a bunch of sergeants taking temperatures, but it's too much for one man to oversee. I don't want to ask anything of those dude officers who sit in there playing poker all the time. Either they've got no conscience, or they're not awake to the gravity of the situation."

The Doctor stood on deck in his raincoat, his foot on the rail to keep his equilibrium, writing on his knee as the long string of men came up to him. There were more than seventy in the line that morning, and some of them looked as if they ought to be in a drier place. Rain beat down on the sea like lead bullets. The old *Anchises* floundered from one grey ridge to another, quite alone. Fog cut off the cheering sight of the sister ships. The doctor had to leave his post from time to time, when seasickness got the better of his will. Claude, at his elbow, was noting down names and temperatures. In the middle of his work he told the sergeants to manage without him for a few minutes. Down near the end of the line he had seen one of his own men misconducting himself, snivelling and crying like a baby,—a fine husky boy of eighteen who had never given any trouble. Claude made a dash for him and clapped him on the shoulder.

"If you can't stop that, Bert Fuller, get where you won't be seen. I don't want all these English stewards standing around to watch an American soldier cry. I never heard of such a thing!"

"I can't help it, Lieutenant," the boy blubbered. "I've kept it back just as long as I can. I can't hold in any longer!"

"What's the matter with you? Come over here and sit down on this box and tell me."

Private Fuller willingly let himself be led, and dropped on the box. "I'm so sick, Lieutenant!"

"I'll see how sick you are." Claude stuck a thermometer into his mouth, and while he waited, sent the deck steward to bring a cup of tea. "Just as I thought, Fuller. You've not half a degree of fever. You're scared, and that's all. Now drink this tea. I expect you didn't eat any breakfast."

"No, sir. I can't eat the awful stuff on this boat."

"It is pretty bad. Where are you from?"

"I'm from P-P-Pleasantville, up on the P-P-Platte," the boy gulped, and his tears began to flow afresh.

"Well, now, what would they think of you, back there? I suppose they got the band out and made a fuss over you when you went away, and thought they were sending off a fine soldier. And I've always thought you'd be a first-rate soldier. I guess we'll forget about this. You feel better already, don't you?"

"Yes, sir. This tastes awful good. I've been so sick to my stomach, and last night I got pains in my chest. All my crowd is sick, and you took big Tannhauser, I mean Corporal, away to the hospital. It looks like we're all going to die out here."

"I know it's a little gloomy. But don't you shame me before these English stewards."

"I won't do it again, sir," he promised.

When the medical inspection was over, Claude took the Doctor down to see Fanning, who had been coughing and wheezing all night and hadn't got out of his berth. The examination was short. The Doctor knew what was the matter before he put the stethoscope on him. "It's pneumonia, both lungs," he said when they came out into the corridor. "I have one case in the hospital that will die before morning."

"What can you do for him, Doctor?"

"You see how I'm fixed; close onto two hundred men sick, and one doctor. The medical supplies are wholly inadequate. There's not castor oil enough on this boat to keep the men clean inside. I'm using my own drugs, but they won't last through an epidemic like this. I can't do much for Lieutenant Fanning. You can, though, if you'll give him the time. You can take better care of him right here than he could get in the hospital. We haven't an empty bed there."

Claude found Victor Morse and told him he had better get a berth in one of the other staterooms. When Victor left with his belongings, Fanning stared after him. "Is he going?"

"Yes. It's too crowded in here, if you've got to stay in bed."

"Glad of it. His stories are too raw for me. I'm no sissy, but that fellow's a regular Don Quixote."

Claude laughed. "You mustn't talk. It makes you cough."

"Where's the Virginian?"

"Who, Bird?" Claude asked in astonishment,—Fanning had stood beside him at Bird's funeral. "Oh, he's gone, too. You sleep if you can."

After dinner Doctor Trueman came in and showed Claude how to give his patient an alcohol bath. "It's simply a question of whether you can keep up his strength. Don't try any of this greasy food they serve here. Give him a raw egg beaten up in the juice of an orange every two hours, night and day. Waken him out of his sleep when it's time, don't miss a single two-hour period. I'll write an order to your table steward, and you can beat the eggs up here in your cabin. Now I must go to the hospital. It's wonderful what those band boys are doing there. I begin to take some pride in the place. That big German has been asking for you. He's in a very bad way."

As there were no nurses on board, the Kansas band had taken over the hospital. They had been trained for stretcher and first aid work, and when they realized what was happening on the *Anchises*, the bandmaster came to the Doctor and offered the services of his men. He chose nurses and orderlies, divided them into night and day shifts.

When Claude went to see his Corporal, big Tannhauser did not recognize him. He was quite out of his head and was conversing with his own family in the language of his early childhood. The Kansas boys had singled him out for special attention. The mere fact that he kept talking in a tongue forbidden on the surface of the seas, made him seem more friendless and alone than the others.

From the hospital Claude went down into the hold where half-a-dozen of his company were lying ill. The hold was damp and musty as an old cellar, so steeped in the smells and leakage of innumerable dirty cargoes that it could not be made or kept clean. There was almost no ventilation, and the air was fetid with sickness and sweat and vomit. Two of the band boys were working in the stench and dirt, helping the stewards. Claude stayed to lend a hand until it was time to give Fanning his nourishment. He began to see that the wrist watch, which he had hitherto despised as effeminate and had carried in his pocket, might be a very useful article. After he had made Fanning swallow his egg, he piled all the available blankets on him and opened the port to give the cabin an airing. While the fresh wind blew in, he sat down on the edge of his berth and tried to collect his wits. What had become of those first days of golden weather, leisure and good-comradeship? The band concerts, the Lindsborg Quartette, the first excitement and novelty of being at sea: all that had gone by like a dream.

That night when the Doctor came in to see Fanning, he threw his stethoscope on the bed and said wearily, "It's a wonder that instrument doesn't take root in my ears and grow there." He sat down and sucked his thermometer for a few minutes, then held it out for inspection. Claude looked at it and told him he ought to go to bed.

"Then who's to be up and around? No bed for me, tonight. But I will have a hot bath by and by."

Claude asked why the ship's doctor didn't do anything and added that he must be as little as he looked.

"Chessup? No, he's not half bad when you get to know him. He's given me a lot of help about preparing medicines, and it's a great assistance to talk the cases over with him. He'll do anything for me except directly handle the patients. He doesn't want to exceed his authority. It seems the English marine is very particular about such things. He's a Canadian, and he graduated first in his class at Edinburgh. I gather he was frozen out in private practice. You see, his appearance is against him. It's an awful handicap to look like a kid and be as shy as he is."

The Doctor rose, shored up his shoulders and took his bag. "You're looking fine yourself, Lieutenant," he remarked. "Parents both living? Were they quite young when you were born? Well, then their parents were, probably. I'm a crank about that. Yes, I'll get my bath pretty soon, and I will lie down for an hour or two. With those splendid band boys running the hospital, I get a little lee-way."

Claude wondered how the Doctor kept going. He knew he hadn't had more than four hours sleep out of the last forty-eight, and he was not a man of rugged constitution. His bath steward was, as he said, his comfort. Hawkins was an old fellow who had held better positions on better boats,—yes, in better times, too. He had first gone to sea as a bath steward, and now, through the fortunes of war, he had come back where he began,—not a good place for an old man. His back was bent meekly, and he shuffled along with broken arches. He looked after the comfort of all the officers, and attended the doctor like a valet; got out his clean linen, persuaded him to lie down and have a hot drink after his bath, stood on guard at his door to take messages for him in the short hours when he was resting. Hawkins had lost two sons in the war and he seemed to find a solemn consolation in being of service to soldiers. "Take it a bit easy now, sir. You'll 'ave it 'ard enough over there," he used to say to one and another.

At eleven o'clock one of the Kansas men came to tell Claude that his Corporal was going fast. Big Tannhauser's fever had left him, but so had everything else. He lay in a stupor. His congested eyeballs were rolled back in his head and only the yellowish whites were visible. His mouth was open and his tongue hung out at one side. From the end of the corridor Claude had heard the frightful sounds that came from his throat, sounds like violent vomiting, or the choking rattle of a man in strangulation,—and, indeed, he was being strangled. One of the band boys brought Claude a camp chair, and said kindly, "He doesn't suffer. It's mechanical now. He'd go easier if he hadn't so much vitality. The Doctor says he may have a few moments of consciousness just at the last, if you want to stay."

"I'll go down and give my private patient his egg, and then I'll come back." Claude went away and returned, and sat dozing by the bed. After three o'clock the noise of struggle ceased; instantly the huge figure on the bed became again his good-natured corporal. The mouth closed, the glassy jellies were once more seeing, intelligent human eyes. The face lost its swollen, brutish look and was again the face of a friend. It was almost unbelievable that anything so far gone could come back. He looked up wistfully at his Lieutenant as if to ask him something. His eyes filled with tears, and he turned his head away a little.

"Mein' arme Mutter!" he whispered distinctly.

A few moments later he died in perfect dignity, not struggling under torture, but consciously, it seemed to Claude, — like a brave boy giving back what was not his to keep.

Claude returned to his cabin, roused Fanning once more, and then threw himself upon his tipping bunk. The boat seemed to wallow and sprawl in the waves, as he had seen animals do on the farm when they gave birth to young. How helpless the old vessel was out here in the pounding seas, and how much misery she carried! He lay looking up at the rusty water pipes and unpainted joinings. This liner was in truth the "Old Anchises"; even the carpenters who made her over for the service had not thought her worth the trouble, and had done their worst by her. The new partitions were hung to the joists by a few nails.

Big Tannhauser had been one of those who were most anxious to sail. He used to grin and say, "France is the only climate that's healthy for a man with a name like mine." He had waved his good-bye to the image in the New York harbour with the rest, believed in her like the rest. He only wanted to serve. It seemed hard.

When Tannhauser first came to camp he was confused all the time, and couldn't remember instructions. Claude had once stepped him out in front of the line and reprimanded him for not knowing his right side from his left. When he looked into the case, he found that the fellow was not eating anything, that he was ill from homesickness. He was one of those farmer boys who are afraid of town. The giant baby of a long family, he had never slept away from home a night in his life before he enlisted.

Corporal Tannhauser, along with four others, was buried at sunrise. No band this time; the chaplain was ill, so one of the young captains read the service. Claude stood by watching until the sailors shot one sack, longer by half a foot than the other four, into a lead-coloured chasm in the sea. There was not even a splash. After breakfast one of the Kansas orderlies called him into a little cabin where they had prepared the dead men for burial. The Army regulations minutely defined what was to be done with a deceased soldier's effects. His uniform, shoes, blankets, arms, personal baggage, were all disposed of according to instructions. But in each case there was a residue; the dead man's toothbrushes, his razors, and the photographs he carried upon his person. There they were in five pathetic little heaps; what should be done with them?

Claude took up the photographs that had belonged to his corporal; one was a fat, foolish-looking girl in a white dress that was too tight for her, and a floppy hat, a little flag pinned on her plump bosom. The other was an old woman, seated, her hands crossed in her lap. Her thin hair was drawn back tight from a hard, angular face — unmistakably an Old-World face — and her eyes squinted at the camera. She looked honest and stubborn and unconvinced, he thought, as if she did not in the least understand.

"I'll take these," he said. "And the others — just pitch them over, don't you think?"

VII

B Company's first officer, Captain Maxey, was so seasick throughout the voyage that he was of no help to his men in the epidemic. It must have been a frightful blow to his pride, for nobody was ever more anxious to do an officer's whole duty.

Claude had known Harris Maxey slightly in Lincoln; had met him at the Erlichs' and afterward kept up a campus acquaintance with him. He hadn't liked Maxey then, and he didn't like him now, but he thought him a good officer. Maxey's family were poor folk from Mississippi, who had settled in Nemaha county, and he was very ambitious, not only to get on in the world, but, as he said, to "be somebody." His life at the University was a feverish pursuit of social advantages and useful acquaintances. His feeling for the "right people" amounted to veneration. After his graduation, Maxey served on the Mexican Border. He was a tireless drill master, and threw himself into his duties with all the energy of which his frail physique was capable. He was slight and fair-skinned; a rigid jaw threw his lower teeth out beyond the upper ones and made his face look stiff. His whole manner, tense and nervous, was the expression of a passionate desire to excel.

Claude seemed to himself to be leading a double life these days. When he was working over Fanning, or was down in the hold helping to take care of the sick soldiers, he had no time to think,—did mechanically the next thing that came to hand. But when he had an hour to himself on deck, the tingling sense of ever-widening freedom flashed up in him again. The weather was a continual adventure; he had never known any like it before. The fog, and rain, the grey sky and the lonely grey stretches of the ocean were like something he had imagined long ago—memories of old sea stories read in childhood, perhaps—and they kindled a warm spot in his heart. Here on the *Anchises* he seemed to begin where childhood had left off. The ugly hiatus between had closed up. Years of his life were blotted out in the fog. This fog which had been at first depressing had become a shelter; a tent moving through space, hiding one from all that had been before, giving one a chance to correct one's ideas about life and to plan the future. The past was physically shut off; that was his illusion. He had already travelled a great many more miles than were told off by the ship's log. When Bandmaster Fred Max asked him to play chess, he had to stop a moment and think why it was that game had such disagreeable associations for him. Enid's pale, deceptive face seldom rose before him unless some such accident brought it up. If he happened to come upon a group of boys talking about their sweethearts and war-brides, he listened a moment and then moved away with the happy feeling that he was the least married man on the boat.

There was plenty of deck room, now that so many men were ill either from sea-sickness or the epidemic, and sometimes he and Albert Usher had the stormy side of the boat almost to themselves. The Marine was the best sort of companion for these gloomy days; steady, quiet, self-reliant. And he, too, was always looking forward. As for Victor Morse, Claude was growing positively fond of him. Victor had tea in a special corner of the officers' smoking-room every afternoon—he would have perished without it—and the steward always produced some special garnishes of toast and jam or sweet biscuit for him. Claude usually managed to join him at that hour.

On the day of Tannhauser's funeral he went into the smoking-room at four. Victor beckoned the steward and told him to bring a couple of hot whiskeys with the tea. "You're very wet, you know, Wheeler, and you really should. There," he said as he put down his glass, "don't you feel better with a drink?"

"Very much. I think I'll have another. It's agreeable to be warm inside."

"Two more, steward, and bring me some fresh lemon." The occupants of the room were either reading or talking in low tones. One of the Swedish boys was playing softly on the old piano. Victor began to pour the tea. He had a neat way of doing it, and today he was especially solicitous. "This Scotch mist gets into one's bones, doesn't it? I thought you were looking rather seedy when I passed you on deck."

"I was up with Tannhauser last night. Didn't get more than an hour's sleep," Claude murmured, yawning.

"Yes, I heard you lost your big corporal. I'm sorry. I've had bad news, too. It's out now that we're to make a French port. That dashes all my plans. However, *c'est la guerre!*" He pushed back his cup with a shrug. "Take a turn outside?"

Claude had often wondered why Victor liked him, since he was so little Victor's kind. "If it isn't a secret," he said, "I'd like to know how you ever got into the British army, anyway."

As they walked up and down in the rain, Victor told his story briefly. When he had finished High School, he had gone into his father's bank at Crystal Lake as bookkeeper. After banking hours he skated, played tennis, or worked in the strawberry-bed, according to the season. He bought two pairs of white pants every summer and ordered his shirts from Chicago and thought he was a swell, he said. He got himself engaged to the preacher's daughter. Two years ago, the summer he was twenty, his father wanted him to see Niagara Falls; so he wrote a modest check, warned his son against saloons—Victor had never been inside one—against expensive hotels and women who came up to ask the time without an introduction, and sent him off, telling him it wasn't necessary to fee porters or waiters. At Niagara Falls, Victor fell in with some young Canadian officers who opened his eyes to a great many things. He went over to Toronto with them. Enlistment was going strong, and he saw an avenue of escape from the bank and the strawberry-bed. The air force seemed the most brilliant and attractive branch of the service. They accepted him, and here he was.

"You'll never go home again," Claude said with conviction. "I don't see you settling down in any little Iowa town."

"In the air service," said Victor carelessly, "we don't concern ourselves about the future. It's not worth while." He took out a dull gold cigarette case which Claude had noticed before.

"Let me see that a minute, will you? I've often admired it. A present from somebody you like, isn't it?"

A twitch of feeling, something quite genuine, passed over the air-man's boyish face, and his rather small red mouth compressed sharply. "Yes, a woman I want you to meet. Here," twitching his chin over his high collar, "I'll write Maisie's address on my card: 'Introducing Lieutenant Wheeler, A. E. F.' That's all you'll need. If you should get to London before I do, don't hesitate. Call on her at once. Present this card, and she'll receive you."

Claude thanked him and put the card in his pocketbook, while Victor lit a cigarette. "I haven't forgotten that you're dining with us at the Savoy, if we happen in London together. If I'm there, you can always find me. Her address is mine. It will really be a great thing for you to meet a woman like Maisie. She'll be nice to you, because you're my friend." He went on to say that she had done everything in the world for him; had left her husband and given up her friends on his account. She now had a studio flat in Chelsea, where she simply waited his coming and dreaded his going. It was an awful life for her. She entertained other officers, of course, old acquaintances; but it was all camouflage. He was the man.

Victor went so far as to produce her picture, and Claude gazed without knowing what to say at a large moon-shaped face with heavy-lidded, weary eyes,—the neck clasped by a pearl collar, the shoulders bare to the matronly swell of the bosom. There was not a line or wrinkle in that smooth expanse of flesh, but from the heavy mouth and chin, from the very shape of the face, it was easy to see that she was quite old enough to be Victor's mother. Across the photograph was written in a large splashy hand, À mon aigle! Had Victor been delicate enough to leave him in any doubt, Claude would have preferred to believe that his relations with this lady were wholly of a filial nature.

"Women like her simply don't exist in your part of the world," the aviator murmured, as he snapped the photograph case. "She's a linguist and musician and all that. With her, every-day living is a fine art. Life, as she says, is what one makes it. In itself, it's nothing. Where you came from it's nothing—a sleeping sickness."

Claude laughed. "I don't know that I agree with you, but I like to hear you talk."

"Well; in that part of France that's all shot to pieces, you'll find more life going on in the cellars than in your home town, wherever that is. I'd rather be a stevedore in the London docks than a banker-king in one of your prairie States. In London, if you're lucky enough to have a shilling, you can get something for it."

"Yes, things are pretty tame at home," the other admitted.

"Tame? My God, it's death in life! What's left of men if you take all the fire out of them? They're afraid of everything. I know them; Sunday-school sneaks, prowling around those little towns after dark!" Victor abruptly dismissed the subject. "By the way, you're pals with the doctor, aren't you? I'm needing some medicine that is somewhere in my lost trunk. Would you mind asking him if he can put up this prescription? I don't want to go to him myself. All these medicos blab, and he might report me. I've been lucky dodging medical inspections. You see, I don't want to get held up anywhere. Tell him it's not for you, of course."

When Claude presented the piece of blue paper to Doctor Trueman, he smiled contemptuously. "I see; this has been filled by a London chemist. No, we have nothing of this sort." He handed it back. "Those things are only palliatives. If your friend wants that, he needs treatment,—and he knows where he can get it."

Claude returned the slip of paper to Victor as they left the dining-room after supper, telling him he hadn't been able to get any.

"Sorry," said Victor, flushing haughtily. "Thank you so much!"

VIII

Tod Fanning held out better than many of the stronger men; his vitality surprised the doctors. The death list was steadily growing; and the worst of it was that patients died who were not very sick. Vigorous, clean-blooded young fellows of nineteen and twenty turned over and died because they had lost their courage, because other people were dying,—because death was in the air. The corridors of the vessel had the smell of death about them. Doctor Trueman said it was always so in an epidemic; patients died who, had they been isolated cases, would have recovered.

"Do you know, Wheeler," the doctor remarked one day when they came up from the hospital together to get a breath of air, "I sometimes wonder whether all these inoculations they've been having, against typhoid and smallpox and whatnot, haven't lowered their vitality. I'll go off my head if I keep losing men! What would you give to be out of it all, and safe back on the farm?" Hearing no reply, he turned his head, peered over his raincoat collar, and saw a startled, resisting look in the young man's blue eyes, followed by a quick flush.

"You don't want to be back on the farm, do you! Not a little bit! Well, well; that's what it is to be young!" He shook his head with a smile which might have been commiseration, might have been envy, and went back to his duties.

Claude stayed where he was, drawing the wet grey air into his lungs and feeling vexed and reprimanded. It was quite true, he realized; the doctor had caught him. He was enjoying himself all the while and didn't want to be safe anywhere. He was sorry about Tannhauser and the others, but he was not sorry for himself. The discomforts and misfortunes of this voyage had not spoiled it for him. He grumbled, of course, because others did. But life had never seemed so tempting as it did here and now. He could come up from heavy work in the hospital, or from poor Fanning and his everlasting eggs, and forget all that in ten minutes. Something inside him, as elastic as the grey ridges over which they were tipping, kept bounding up and saying; "I am all here. I've left everything behind me. I am going over."

Only on that one day, the cold day of the Virginian's funeral, when he was seasick, had he been really miserable. He must be heartless, certainly, not to be overwhelmed by the sufferings of his own men, his own friends—but he wasn't. He had them on his mind and did all he could for them, but it seemed to him just now that he took a sort of satisfaction in that, too, and was somewhat vain of his usefulness to Doctor Trueman. A nice attitude! He awoke every morning with that sense of freedom and going forward, as if the world were growing bigger each day and he were growing with it. Other fellows were sick and dying, and that was terrible,—but he and the boat went on, and always on.

Something was released that had been struggling for a long while, he told himself. He had been due in France since the first battle of the Marne; he had followed false leads and lost precious time and seen misery enough, but he was on the right road at last, and nothing could stop him. If he hadn't been so green, so bashful, so afraid of showing what he felt, and so stupid at finding his way about, he would have enlisted in Canada, like Victor, or run away to France and joined the Foreign Legion. All that seemed perfectly possible now. Why hadn't he?

Well, that was not "the Wheelers' way." The Wheelers were terribly afraid of poking themselves in where they weren't wanted, of pushing their way into a crowd where they didn't belong. And they were even more afraid of doing anything that might look affected or "romantic." They couldn't let themselves adopt a conspicuous, much less a picturesque course of action, unless it was all in the day's work. Well, History had condescended to such as he; this whole brilliant adventure had become the day's work. He had got into it after all, along with Victor and the Marine and other fellows who had more imagination and self-confidence in the first place. Three years ago he used to sit moping by the windmill because he didn't see how a Nebraska farmer boy had any "call," or, indeed, any way, to throw himself into the struggle in France. He used enviously to read about Alan Seeger and those fortunate American boys who had a right to fight for a civilization they knew.

But the miracle had happened; a miracle so wide in its amplitude that the Wheelers,—all the Wheelers and the rough-necks and the low-brows were caught up in it. Yes, it was the rough-necks' own miracle, all this; it was their golden chance. He was in on it, and nothing could hinder or discourage him unless he were put over the side himself—which was only a way of joking, for that was a possibility he never seriously considered. The feeling of purpose, of fateful purpose, was strong in his breast.

IX

"Look at this, Doctor!" Claude caught Dr. Trueman on his way from breakfast and handed him a written notice, signed D. T. Micks, Chief Steward. It stated that no more eggs or oranges could be furnished to patients, as the supply was exhausted.

The doctor squinted at the paper. "I'm afraid that's your patient's death warrant. You'll never be able to keep him going on anything else. Why don't you go and talk it over with Chessup? He's a resourceful fellow. I'll join you there in a few minutes."

Claude had often been to Dr. Chessup's cabin since the epidemic broke out, — rather liked to wait there when he went for medicines or advice. It was a comfortable, personal sort of place with cheerful chintz hangings. The walls were lined with books, held in place by sliding wooden slats, padlocked at the ends. There were a great many scientific works in German and English; the rest were French novels in paper covers. This morning he found Chessup weighing out white powders at his desk. In the rack over his bunk was the book with which he had read himself to sleep last night; the title, "Un Crime d'Amour," lettered in black on yellow, caught Claude's eye. The doctor put on his coat and pointed his visitor to the jointed chair in which patients were sometimes examined. Claude explained his predicament.

The ship's doctor was a strange fellow to come from Canada, the land of big men and rough. He looked like a schoolboy, with small hands and feet and a pink complexion. On his left cheek-bone was a large brown mole, covered with silky hair, and for some reason that seemed to make his face effeminate. It was easy to see why he had not been successful in private practice. He was like somebody trying to protect a raw surface from heat and cold; so cursed with diffidence, and so sensitive about his boyish appearance that he chose to shut himself up in an oscillating wooden coop on the sea. The long run to Australia had exactly suited him. A rough life and the pounding of bad weather had fewer terrors for him than an office in town, with constant exposure to human personalities.

"Have you tried him on malted milk?" he asked, when Claude had told him how Fanning's nourishment was threatened.

"Dr. Trueman hasn't a bottle left. How long do you figure we'll be at sea?"

"Four days; possibly five."

"Then Lieutenant Wheeler will lose his pal," said Dr. Trueman, who had just come in.

Chessup stood for a moment frowning and pulling nervously at the brass buttons on his coat. He slid the bolt on his door and turning to his colleague said resolutely: "I can give you some information, if you won't implicate me. You can do as you like, but keep my name out of it. For several hours last night cases of eggs and boxes of oranges were being carried into the Chief Steward's cabin by a flunky of his from the galley. Whatever port we make, he can get a shilling each for the fresh eggs, and perhaps sixpence for the oranges. They are your property, of course, furnished by your government; but this is his customary perquisite. I've been on this boat six years, and it's always been so. About a week before we make port, the choicest of the remaining stores are taken to his cabin, and he disposes of them after we dock. I can't say just how he manages it, but he does. The skipper may know of this custom, and there may be some reason why he permits it. It's not my business to see anything. The Chief Steward is a powerful man on an English vessel. If he has anything against me, sooner or later he can lose my berth for me. There you have the facts."

"Have I your permission to go to the Chief Steward?" Dr. Trueman asked.

"Certainly not. But you can go without my knowledge. He's an ugly man to cross, and he can make it uncomfortable for you and your patients."

"Well, we'll say no more about it. I appreciate your telling me, and I will see that you don't get mixed up in this. Will you go down with me to look at that new meningitis case?"

Claude waited impatiently in his stateroom for the doctor's return. He didn't see why the Chief Steward shouldn't be exposed and dealt with like any other grafter. He had hated the man ever since he heard him berating the old bath steward one morning. Hawkins had made no attempt to defend himself, but stood like a dog that has been terribly beaten, trembling all over, saying "Yes, sir. Yes, sir," while his chief gave him a cold cursing in a low, snarling voice. Claude had never heard a man or even an animal addressed with such contempt. The Steward had a cruel face,—white as cheese, with limp, moist hair combed back from a high forehead,—the peculiarly oily hair that seems to grow only on the heads of stewards and waiters. His eyes were exactly the shape of almonds, but the lids were so swollen that the dull pupil was visible only through a narrow slit. A long, pale moustache hung like a fringe over his loose lips.

When Dr. Trueman came back from the hospital, he declared he was now ready to call on Mr. Micks. "He's a nasty looking customer, but he can't do anything to me."

They went to the Chief Steward's cabin and knocked.

"What's wanted?" called a threatening voice.

The doctor made a grimace to his companion and walked in. The Steward was sitting at a big desk, covered with account books. He turned in his chair. "I beg your pardon," he said coldly, "I do not see any one here. I will be —"

The doctor held up his hand quickly. "That's all right, Steward. I'm sorry to intrude, but I've something I must say to you in private. I'll not detain you long." If he had hesitated for a moment, Claude believed the Steward would have thrown him out, but he went on rapidly. "This is Lieutenant Wheeler, Mr. Micks. His fellow officer lies very ill with pneumonia in stateroom 96. Lieutenant Wheeler has kept him alive by special nursing. He is not able to retain anything in his stomach but eggs and orange juice. If he has these, we may be able to keep up his strength till the fever breaks, and carry him to a hospital in France. If we can't get them for him, he will be dead within twenty-four hours. That's the situation."

The steward rose and turned out the drop-light on his desk. "Have you received notice that there are no more eggs and oranges on board? Then I am afraid there is nothing I can do for you. I did not provision this ship."

"No. I understand that. I believe the United States Government provided the fruit and eggs and meat. And I positively know that the articles I need for my patient are not exhausted. Without going into the matter further, I warn you that I'm not going to let a United States officer die when the means of saving him are procurable. I'll go to the skipper, I'll call a meeting of the army officers on board. I'll go any length to save this man."

"That is your own affair, but you will not interfere with me in the discharge of my duties. Will you leave my cabin?"

"In a moment, Steward. I know that last night a number of cases of eggs and oranges were carried into this room. They are here now, and they belong to the A. E. F. If you will agree to provision my man, what I know won't go any further. But if you refuse, I'll get this matter investigated. I won't stop till I do."

The Steward sat down, and took up a pen. His large, soft hand looked cheesy, like his face. "What is the number of the cabin?" he asked indifferently.

"Ninety-six."

"Exactly what do you require?"

"One dozen eggs and one dozen oranges every twenty-four hours, to be delivered at any time convenient to you."

"I will see what I can do."

The Steward did not look up from his writing pad, and his visitors left as abruptly as they had come.

At about four o'clock every morning, before even the bath stewards were on duty, there was a scratching at Claude's door, and a covered basket was left there by a messenger who was unwashed, half-naked, with a sacking apron tied round his middle and his hairy chest splashed with flour. He never spoke, had only one eye and an inflamed socket. Claude learned that he was a half-witted brother of the Chief Steward, a potato-peeler and dish-washer in the galley.

Four days after their interview with Mr. Micks, when they were at last nearing the end of the voyage, Doctor Trueman detained Claude after medical inspection to tell him that the Chief Steward had come down with the epidemic. "He sent for me last night and asked me to take his case,—won't have anything to do with Chessup. I had to get Chessup's permission. He seemed very glad to hand the case over to me."

"Is he very bad?"

"He hasn't a look-in, and he knows it. Complications; chronic Bright's disease. It seems he has nine children. I'll try to get him into a hospital when we make port, but he'll only live a few days at most. I wonder who'll get the shillings for all the eggs and oranges he hoarded away. Claude, my boy," the doctor spoke with sudden energy, "if I ever set foot on land again, I'm going to forget this voyage like a bad dream. When I'm in normal health, I'm a Presbyterian, but just now I feel that even the wicked get worse than they deserve."

A day came at last when Claude was wakened from sleep by a sense of stillness. He sprang up with a dazed fear that some one had died; but Fanning lay in his berth, breathing quietly.

Something caught his eye through the porthole,—a great grey shoulder of land standing up in the pink light of dawn, powerful and strangely still after the distressing instability of the sea. Pale trees and long, low fortifications . . . close grey buildings with red roofs . . . little sailboats bounding seaward . . . up on the cliff a gloomy fortress.

He had always thought of his destination as a country shattered and desolated, — "bleeding France"; but he had never seen anything that looked so strong, so self-sufficient, so fixed from the first foundation, as the coast that rose before him. It was like a pillar of eternity. The ocean lay submissive at its feet, and over it was the great meekness of early morning.

This grey wall, unshaken, mighty, was the end of the long preparation, as it was the end of the sea. It was the reason for everything that had happened in his life for the last fifteen months. It was the reason why Tannhauser and the gentle Virginian, and so many others who had set out with him, were never to have any life at all, or even a soldier's death. They were merely waste in a great enterprise, thrown overboard like rotten ropes. For them this kind release, — trees and a still shore and quiet water, — was never, never to be. How long would their bodies toss, he wondered, in that inhuman kingdom of darkness and unrest?

He was startled by a weak voice from behind.

"Claude, are we over?"

"Yes, Fanning. We're over."

BOOK FIVE

"BIDDING THE EAGLES OF
THE WEST FLY ON"

I

AT noon that day Claude found himself in a street of little shops, hot and perspiring, utterly confused and turned about. Truck drivers and boys on bell-less bicycles shouted at him indignantly, furiously. He got under the shade of a young plane tree and stood close to the trunk, as if it might protect him. His greatest care, at any rate, was off his hands. With the help of Victor Morse he had hired a taxi for forty francs, taken Fanning to the base hospital, and seen him into the arms of a big orderly from Texas. He came away from the hospital with no idea where he was going—except that he wanted to get to the heart of the city. It seemed, however, to have no heart; only long, stony arteries, full of heat and noise. He was still standing there, under his plane tree, when a group of uncertain, lost-looking brown figures, headed by Sergeant Hicks, came weaving up the street; nine men in nine different attitudes of dejection, each with a long loaf of bread under his arm. They hailed Claude with joy, straightened up, and looked as if now they had found their way! He saw that he must be a plane tree for somebody else.

Sergeant Hicks explained that they had been trudging about the town, looking for cheese. After sixteen days of heavy, taste-less food, cheese was what they all wanted. There was a grocery store up the street, where there seemed to be everything else. He had tried to make the old woman understand by signs.

"Don't these French people eat cheese, anyhow? What's their word for it, Lieutenant? I'm damned if I know, and I've lost my phrase book. Suppose you could make her understand?"

"Well, I'll try. Come along, boys."

Crowding close together, the ten men entered the shop. The proprietress ran forward with an exclamation of despair. Evidently she had thought she was done with them, and was not pleased to see them coming back. When she paused to take breath, Claude took off his hat respectfully, and performed the bravest act of his life; uttered the first phrase-book sentence he had ever spoken to a French person. His men were at his back; he had to say something or run, there was no other course. Looking the old woman in the eye, he steadily articulated:

"*Aves-vous du fromage, Madame?*" It was almost inspiration to add the last word, he thought; and when it worked, he was as much startled as if his revolver had gone off in his belt.

"*Du fromage?*" the shop woman screamed. Calling something to her daughter, who was at the desk, she caught Claude by the sleeve, pulled him out of the shop, and ran down the street with him. She dragged him into a doorway darkened by a long curtain, greeted the proprietress, and then pushed the men after their officer, as if they were stubborn burros.

They stood blinking in the gloom, inhaling a sour, damp, buttery, smear-kase smell, until their eyes penetrated the shadows and they saw that there was nothing but cheese and butter in the place. The shopkeeper was a fat woman, with black eyebrows that met above her nose; her sleeves were rolled up, her cotton dress was open over her white throat and bosom. She began at once to tell them that there was a restriction on milk products; every one must have cards; she could not sell them so much. But soon there was nothing left to dispute about. The boys fell upon her stock like wolves. The little white cheeses that lay on green leaves disappeared into big mouths. Before she could save it, Hicks had split a big round cheese through the middle and was carving it up like a melon. She told them they were dirty pigs and worse than the Boches, but she could not stop them.

"What's the matter with Mother, Lieutenant? What's she fussing about? Ain't she here to sell goods?"

Claude tried to look wiser than he was. "From what I can make out, there's some sort of restriction; you aren't allowed to buy all you want. We ought to have thought about that; this is a war country. I guess we've about cleaned her out."

"Oh, that's all right," said Hicks wiping his clasp-knife. "We'll bring her some sugar tomorrow. One of the fellows who helped us unload at the docks told me you can always quiet 'em if you give 'em sugar."

They surrounded her and held out their money for her to take her pay. "Come on, ma'm, don't be bashful. What's the matter, ain't this good money?"

She was distracted by the noise they made, by their bronzed faces with white teeth and pale eyes, crowding so close to her. Ten large, well-shaped hands with straight fingers, the open palms full of crumpled notes. . . . Holding the men off under the pretence of looking for a pencil, she made rapid calculations. The money that lay in their palms had no relation to these big, coaxing, boisterous fellows; it was a joke to them; they didn't know what it meant in the world. Behind them were shiploads of money, and behind the ships. . . .

The situation was unfair. Whether she took much or little out of their hands, couldn't possibly matter to the Americans,— couldn't even dash their good humour. But there was a strain on the cheesewoman, and the standards of a lifetime were in jeopardy. Her mind mechanically fixed upon two-and-a-half; she would charge them two-and-a-half times the market price of the cheese. With this moral plank to cling to, she made change with conscientious accuracy and did not keep a penny too much from anybody. Telling them what big stupids they were, and that it was necessary to learn to count in this world, she urged them out of her shop. She liked them well enough, but she did not like to do business with them. If she didn't take their money, the next one would. All the same, fictitious values were distasteful to her, and made everything seem flimsy and unsafe.

Standing in her doorway, she watched the brown band go ambling down the street; as they passed in front of the old church of St. Jacques, the two foremost stumbled on a sunken step that was scarcely above the level of the pavement. She laughed aloud. They looked back and waved to her. She replied with a smile that was both friendly and angry. She liked them, but not the legend of waste and prodigality that ran before them—and followed after. It was superfluous and disintegrating in a world of hard facts. An army in which the men had meat for breakfast, and ate more every day than the French soldiers at the front got in a week! Their moving kitchens and supply trains were the wonder of France. Down below Arles, where her husband's sister had married, on the desolate plain of the Crau, their tinned provisions were piled like mountain ranges, under sheds and canvas. Nobody had ever seen so much food before; coffee, milk, sugar, bacon, hams; everything the world was famished for. They brought shiploads of useless things, too. And useless people. Shiploads of women who were not nurses; some said they came to dance with the officers, so they would not be *ennuyés*.

All this was not war,—any more than having money thrust at you by grown men who could not count, was business. It was an invasion, like the other. The first destroyed material possessions, and this threatened everybody's integrity. Distaste of such methods, deep, recoiling distrust of them, clouded the cheese-woman's brow as she threw her money into the drawer and turned the key on it.

As for the doughboys, having once stubbed their toes on the sunken step, they examined it with interest, and went in to explore the church. It was in their minds that they must not let a church escape, any more than they would let a Boche escape. Within they came upon a bunch of their shipmates, including the Kansas band, to whom they boasted that their Lieutenant could "speak French like a native."

The Lieutenant himself thought he was getting on pretty well, but a few hours later his pride was humbled. He was sitting alone in a little triangular park beside another church, admiring the cropped locust trees and watching some old women who were doing their mending in the shade. A little boy in a black apron, with a close-shaved, bare head, came along, skipping rope. He hopped lightly up to Claude and said in a most persuasive and confiding voice:

"*Voules-vous me dire l'heure, si'l vous plait, M'sieu' l' soldat?*"

Claude looked down into his admiring eyes with a feeling of panic. He wouldn't mind being dumb to a man, or even to a pretty girl, but this was terrible. His tongue went dry, and his face grew scarlet. The child's expectant gaze changed to a look of doubt, and then of fear. He had spoken before to Americans who didn't understand, but they had not turned red and looked angry like this one; this soldier must be ill, or wrong in his head. The boy turned and ran away.

Many a serious mishap had distressed Claude less. He was disappointed, too. There was something friendly in the boy's face that he wanted . . . that he needed. As he rose he ground his heel into the gravel. "Unless I can learn to talk to the *children* of this country," he muttered, "I'll go home!"

II

CLAUDE set off to find the Grand Hotel, where he had promised to dine with Victor Morse. The porter there spoke English. He called a red-headed boy in a dirty uniform and told him to take the American to *vingt-quatre*. The boy also spoke English. "Plenty money in New York, I guess! In France, no money." He made their way, through musty corridors and up slippery staircases, as long as possible, shrewdly eyeing the visitor and rubbing his thumb nervously against his fingers all the while.

"*Vingt-quatre,* twen'y-four," he announced, rapping at a door with one hand and suggestively opening the other. Claude put something into it—anything to be rid of him.

Victor was standing before the fireplace. "Hello, Wheeler, come in. Our dinner will be served up here. It's big enough, isn't it? I could get nothing between a coop, and this at fifteen dollars a day."

The room was spacious enough for a banquet; with two huge beds, and great windows that swung in on hinges, like doors, and that had certainly not been washed since before the war. The heavy red cotton-brocade hangings and lace curtains were stiff with dust, the thick carpet was strewn with cigarette-ends and matches. Razor blades and "Khaki Comfort" boxes lay about on the dresser, and former occupants had left their autographs in the dust on the table. Officers slept there, and went away, and other officers arrived,—and the room remained the same, like a wood in which travellers camp for the night. The *valet de chambre* carried away only what he could use; discarded shirts and socks and old shoes. It seemed a rather dismal place to have a party.

When the waiter came, he dusted off the table with his apron and put on a clean cloth, napkins, and glasses. Victor and his guest sat down under an electric light bulb with a broken shade, around which a silent halo of flies moved unceasingly. They did not buzz, or dart aloft, or descend to try the soup, but hung there in the centre of the room as if they were a part of the lighting system. The constant attendance of the waiter embarrassed Claude; he felt as if he were being watched.

"By the way," said Victor while the soup plates were being removed, "what do you think of this wine? It cost me thirty francs the bottle."

"It tastes very good to me," Claude replied. "But then, it's the first champagne I've ever drunk."

"Really?" Victor drank off another glass and sighed. "I envy you. I wish I had it all to do over. Life's too short, you know."

"I should say you had made a good beginning. We're a long way from Crystal Lake."

"Not far enough." His host reached across the table and filled Claude's empty glass. "I sometimes waken up with the feeling I'm back there. Or I have bad dreams, and find myself sitting on that damned stool in the glass cage and can't make my books balance; I hear the old man coughing in his private room, the way he coughs when he's going to refuse a loan to some poor devil who needs it. I've had a narrow escape, Wheeler; *as a brand from the burning.* That's all the Scripture I remember."

The bright red spots on Victor's cheeks, his pale forehead and brilliant eyes and saucy little moustaches seemed to give his quotation a peculiar vividness. Claude envied him. It must be great fun to take up a part and play it to a finish; to believe you were making yourself over, and to admire the kind of fellow you made. He, too, in a way, admired Victor,—though he couldn't altogether believe in him.

"You'll never go back," he said, "I wouldn't worry about that."

"Take it from me, there are thousands who will never go back! I'm not speaking of the casualties. Some of you Americans are likely to discover the world this trip . . . and it'll make the hell of a lot of difference! You boys never had a fair chance. There's a conspiracy of Church and State to keep you down. I'm going off to play with some girls tonight, will you come along?"

Claude laughed. "I guess not."

"Why not? You won't be caught, I guarantee."

"I guess not." Claude spoke apologetically. "I'm going out to see Fanning after dinner."

Victor shrugged. "That ass!" He beckoned the waiter to open another bottle and bring the coffee. "Well, it's your last chance to go nutting with me." He looked intently at Claude and lifted his glass. "To the future, and our next meeting!" When he put down his empty goblet he remarked, "I got a wire through today; I'm leaving tomorrow."

"For London?"

"For Verdun."

Claude took a quick breath. Verdun . . . the very sound of the name was grim, like the hollow roll of drums. Victor was going there tomorrow. Here one could take a train for Verdun, or thereabouts, as at home one took a train for Omaha. He felt more "over" than he had done before, and a little crackle of excitement went all through him. He tried to be careless.

"Then you won't get to London soon?"

"God knows," Victor answered gloomily. He looked up at the ceiling and began to whistle softly an engaging air. "Do you know that? It's something Maisie often plays; 'Roses of Picardy.' You won't know what a woman can be till you meet her, Wheeler."

"I hope I'll have that pleasure. I was wondering if you'd forgotten her for the moment. She doesn't object to these—diversions?"

Victor lifted his eyebrows in the old haughty way. "Women don't require that sort of fidelity of the air service. Our engagements are too uncertain."

Half an hour later Victor had gone in quest of amorous adventure, and Claude was wandering alone in a brightly lighted street full of soldiers and sailors of all nations. There were black Senegalese, and Highlanders in kilts, and little lorry-drivers from

Siam,—all moving slowly along between rows of cabarets and cinema theatres. The wide-spreading branches of the plane trees met overhead, shutting out the sky and roofing in the orange glare. The sidewalks were crowded with chairs and little tables, at which marines and soldiers sat drinking sirrups and cognac and coffee. From every doorway music-machines poured out jazz tunes and strident Sousa marches. The noise was stupefying. Out in the middle of the street a band of bareheaded girls, hardy and tough looking, were following a string of awkward Americans, running into them, elbowing them, asking for treats, crying, "You dance me Fausse-trot, Sammie?"

Claude stationed himself before a movie theatre, where the sign in electric lights read, *"Amour, quand tu nous tiens!"* and stood watching the people. In the stream that passed him, his eye lit upon two walking arm-in-arm, their hands clasped, talking eagerly and unconscious of the crowd,—different, he saw at once, from all the other strolling, affectionate couples.

The man wore the American uniform; his left arm had been amputated at the elbow, and he carried his head awry, as if he had a stiff neck. His dark, lean face wore an expression of intense anxiety, his eyebrows twitched as if he were in constant pain. The girl, too, looked troubled. As they passed him, under the red light of the *Amour* sign, Claude could see that her eyes were full of tears. They were wide, blue eyes, innocent looking, and she had the prettiest face he had seen since he landed. From her silk shawl, and little bonnet with blue strings and a white frill, he thought she must be a country girl. As she listened to the soldier, with her mouth half-open, he saw a space between her two front teeth, as with children whose second teeth have just come. While they pushed along in the crowd she looked up intently at the man beside her, or off into the blur of light, where she evidently saw nothing. Her face, young and soft, seemed new to emotion, and her bewildered look made one feel that she did not know where to turn.

Without realizing what he did, Claude followed them out of the crowd into a quiet street, and on into another, even more deserted, where the houses looked as if they had been asleep a long while. Here there were no street lamps, not even a light in the windows, but natural darkness; with the moon high overhead throwing sharp shadows across the white cobble paving. The narrow street made a bend, and he came out upon the church he and his comrades had entered that afternoon. It looked larger by night, and but for the sunken step, he might not have been sure it was the same. The dark neighbouring houses seemed to lean toward it, the moonlight shone silver-grey upon its battered front.

The two walking before him ascended the steps and withdrew into the deep doorway, where they clung together in an embrace so long and still that it was like death. At last they drew shuddering apart. The girl sat down on the stone bench beside the door. The soldier threw himself upon the pavement at her feet, and rested his head on her knee, his one arm lying across her lap.

In the shadow of the houses opposite, Claude kept watch like a sentinel, ready to take their part if any alarm should startle them. The girl bent over her soldier, stroking his head so softly that she might have been putting him to sleep; took his one hand and held it against her bosom as if to stop the pain there. Just behind her, on the sculptured portal, some old bishop, with a pointed cap and a broken crozier, stood, holding up two fingers.

III

The next morning when Claude arrived at the hospital to see Fanning, he found every one too busy to take account of him. The courtyard was full of ambulances, and a long line of camions waited outside the gate. A train-load of wounded Americans had come in, sent back from evacuation hospitals to await transportation home.

As the men were carried past him, he thought they looked as if they had been sick a long while—looked, indeed, as if they could never get well. The boys who died on board the *Anchises* had never seemed as sick as these did. Their skin was yellow or purple, their eyes were sunken, their lips sore. Everything that belonged to health had left them, every attribute of youth was gone. One poor fellow, whose face and trunk were wrapped in cotton, never stopped moaning, and as he was carried up the corridor he smelled horribly. The Texas orderly remarked to Claude, "In the beginning that one only had a finger blown off; would you believe it?"

These were the first wounded men Claude had seen. To shed bright blood, to wear the red badge of courage,—that was one thing; but to be reduced to this was quite another. Surely, the sooner these boys died, the better.

The Texan, passing with his next load, asked Claude why he didn't go into the office and wait until the rush was over. Looking in through the glass door, Claude noticed a young man writing at a desk enclosed by a railing. Something about his figure, about the way he held his head, was familiar. When he lifted his left arm to prop open the page of his ledger, it was a stump below the

289

elbow. Yes, there could be no doubt about it; the pale, sharp face, the beak nose, the frowning, uneasy brow. Presently, as if he felt a curious eye upon him, the young man paused in his rapid writing, wriggled his shoulders, put an iron paperweight on the page of his book, took a case from his pocket and shook a cigarette out on the table. Going up to the railing, Claude offered him a cigar. "No, thank you. I don't use them any more. They seem too heavy for me." He struck a match, moved his shoulders again as if they were cramped, and sat down on the edge of his desk.

"Where do these wounded men come from?" Claude asked. "I just got in on the *Anchises* yesterday."

"They come from various evacuation hospitals. I believe most of them are the Belleau Wood lot."

"Where did you lose your arm?"

"Cantigny. I was in the First Division. I'd been over since last September, waiting for something to happen, and then got fixed in my first engagement."

"Can't you go home?"

"Yes, I could. But I don't want to. I've got used to things over here. I was attached to Headquarters in Paris for awhile."

Claude leaned across the rail. "We read about Cantigny at home, of course. We were a good deal excited; I suppose you were?"

"Yes, we were nervous. We hadn't been under fire, and we'd been fed up on all that stuff about it's taking fifty years to build a fighting machine. The Hun had a strong position; we looked up that long hill and wondered how we were going to behave." As he talked the boy's eyes seemed to be moving all the time, probably because he could not move his head at all. After blowing out deep clouds of smoke until his cigarette was gone, he sat down to his ledger and frowned at the page in a way which said he was too busy to talk.

Claude saw Dr. Trueman standing in the doorway, waiting for him. They made their morning call on Fanning, and left the hospital together. The Doctor turned to him as if he had something on his mind.

"I saw you talking to that wry-necked boy. How did he seem, all right?"

"Not exactly. That is, he seems very nervous. Do you know anything about him?"

"Oh, yes! He's a star patient here, a psychopathic case. I had just been talking to one of the doctors about him, when I came out and saw you with him. He was shot in the neck at Cantigny, where he lost his arm. The wound healed, but his memory is affected; some nerve cut, I suppose, that connects with that part of his brain. This psychopath, Phillips, takes a great interest in him and keeps him here to observe him. He's writing a book about him. He says the fellow has forgotten almost everything about his life before he came to France. The queer thing is, it's his recollection of women that is most affected. He can remember his father, but not his mother; doesn't know if he has sisters or not, — can remember seeing girls about the house, but thinks they may have been cousins. His photographs and belongings were lost when he was hurt, all except a bunch of letters he had in his pocket. They are from a girl he's engaged to, and he declares he can't remember her at all; doesn't know what she looks like or anything about her, and can't remember getting engaged. The doctor has the letters. They seem to be from a nice girl in his own town who is very ambitious for him to make the most of himself. He deserted soon after he was sent to this hospital, ran away. He was found on a farm out in the country here, where the sons had been killed and the people had sort of adopted him. He'd quit his uniform and was wearing the clothes of one of the dead sons. He'd probably have got away with it, if he hadn't had that wry neck. Some one saw him in the fields and recognized him and reported him. I guess nobody cared much but this psychopathic doctor; he wanted to get his pet patient back. They call him 'the lost American' here."

"He seems to be doing some sort of clerical work," Claude observed discreetly.

"Yes, they say he's very well educated. He remembers the books he has read better than his own life. He can't recall what his home town looks like, or his home. And the women are clear wiped out, even the girl he was going to marry."

Claude smiled. "Maybe he's fortunate in that."

The Doctor turned to him affectionately, "Now Claude, don't begin to talk like that the minute you land in this country."

Claude walked on past the church of St. Jacques. Last night already seemed like a dream, but it haunted him. He wished he could do something to help that boy; help him get away from the doctor who was writing a book about him, and the girl who wanted him to make the most of himself; get away and be lost altogether in what he had been lucky enough to find. All day, as Claude, came and went, he looked among the crowds for that young face, so compassionate and tender.

IV

DEEPER and deeper into flowery France! That was the sentence Claude kept saying over to himself to the jolt of the wheels, as the long troop train went southward, on the second day after he and his company had left the port of debarkation. Fields of wheat, fields of oats, fields of rye; all the low hills and rolling uplands clad with harvest. And everywhere, in the grass, in the yellowing grain, along the road-bed, the poppies spilling and streaming. On the second day the boys were still calling to each other about the poppies; nothing else had so entirely surpassed their expectations. They had supposed that poppies grew only on battle fields, or in the brains of war correspondents. Nobody knew what the cornflowers were, except Willy Katz, an Austrian boy from the Omaha packing-houses, and he knew only an objectionable name for them, so he offered no information. For a long time they thought the red clover blossoms were wild flowers, — they were as big as wild roses. When they passed the first alfalfa field, the whole train rang with laughter; alfalfa was one thing, they believed, that had never been heard of outside their own prairie states.

All the way down, Company B had been finding the old things instead of the new, — or, to their way of thinking, the new things instead of the old. The thatched roofs they had so counted upon seeing were few and far between. But American binders, of well-known makes, stood where the fields were beginning to ripen, — and they were being oiled and put in order, not by "peasants," but by wise-looking old farmers who seemed to

know their business. Pear trees, trained like vines against the
wall, did not astonish them half so much as the sight of the familiar cottonwood, growing everywhere. Claude thought he had
never before realized how beautiful this tree could be. In ver-
dant little valleys, along the clear rivers, the cottonwoods waved
and rustled; and on the little islands, of which there were so
many in these rivers, they stood in pointed masses, seemed to
grip deep into the soil and to rest easy, as if they had been there
for ever and would be there for ever more. At home, all about
Frankfort, the farmers were cutting down their cottonwoods
because they were "common," planting maples and ash trees to
struggle along in their stead. Never mind; the cottonwoods were
good enough for France, and they were good enough for him!
He felt they were a real bond between him and this people.

When B Company had first got their orders to go into a training camp in north-central France, all the men were disappointed. Troops much rawer than they were being rushed to the
front, so why fool around any longer? But now they were reconciled to the delay. There seemed to be a good deal of France that
wasn't the war, and they wouldn't mind travelling about a little in
a country like this. Was the harvest always a month later than at
home, as it seemed to be this year? Why did the farmers have
rows of trees growing along the edges of every field—didn't they
take the strength out of the soil? What did the farmers mean by
raising patches of mustard right along beside other crops?
Didn't they know that mustard got into wheat fields and strangled the grain?

The second night the boys were to spend in Rouen, and they
would have the following day to look about. Everybody knew
what had happened at Rouen—if any one didn't, his neighbours
were only too eager to inform him! It had happened in the market-
place, and the market-place was what they were going to find.

Tomorrow, when it came, proved to be black and cold, a day of
pouring rain. As they filed through the narrow, crowded streets,
that harsh Norman city presented no very cheering aspect. They
were glad, at last, to find the waterside, to go out on the bridge

and breathe the air in the great open space over the river, away from the clatter of cart-wheels and the hard voices and crafty faces of these townspeople, who seemed rough and unfriendly. From the bridge they looked up at the white chalk hills, the tops a blur of intense green under the low, lead-coloured sky. They watched the fleets of broad, deep-set river barges, coming and going under their feet, with tilted smoke-stacks. Only a little way up that river was Paris, the place where every doughboy meant to go; and as they leaned on the rail and looked down at the slow-flowing water, each one had in his mind a confused picture of what it would be like. The Seine, they felt sure, must be very much wider there, and it was spanned by many bridges, all longer than the bridge over the Missouri at Omaha. There would be spires and golden domes past counting, all the buildings higher than anything in Chicago, and brilliant—dazzlingly brilliant, nothing grey and shabby about it like this old Rouen. They attributed to the city of their desire incalculable immensity, bewildering vastness, Babylonian hugeness and heaviness—the only attributes they had been taught to admire.

Late in the morning Claude found himself alone before the Church of St. Ouen. He was hunting for the Cathedral, and this looked as, if it might be the right place. He shook the water from his raincoat and entered, removing his hat at the door. The day, so dark without, was darker still within; . . . far away, a few scattered candles, still little points of light . . . just before him, in the grey twilight, slender white columns in long rows, like the stems of silver poplars.

The entrance to the nave was closed by a cord, so he walked up the aisle on the right, treading softly, passing chapels where solitary women knelt in the light of a few tapers. Except for them, the church was empty . . . empty. His own breathing was audible in this silence. He moved with caution lest he should wake an echo.

When he reached the choir he turned, and saw, far behind him, the rose window, with its purple heart. As he stood staring, hat in hand, as still as the stone figures in the chapels, a great bell, up aloft, began to strike the hour in its deep, melodious throat; eleven beats, measured and far apart, as rich as the colours in the window, then silence . . . only in his memory the throbbing of an undreamed-of quality of sound. The revelations of the glass and the bell had come almost simultaneously, as if one produced the other; and both were superlatives toward which his mind had always been groping, — or so it seemed to him then.

In front of the choir the nave was open, with no rope to shut it off. Several straw chairs were huddled on a flag of the stone floor. After some hesitation he took one, turned it round, and sat down facing the window. If some one should come up to him and say anything, anything at all, he would rise and say, *"Pardon, Monsieur; je ne sais pas c'est defendu."* He repeated this to himself to be quite sure he had it ready. On the train, coming down, he had talked to the boys about the bad reputation Americans had acquired for slouching all over the place and butting in on things, and had urged them to tread lightly. "But Lieutenant," the kid from Pleasantville had piped up, "isn't this whole Expedition a butt-in? After all, it ain't our war." Claude laughed, but he told him he meant to make an example of the fellow who went to rough-housing.

He was well satisfied that he hadn't his restless companions on his mind now. He could sit here quietly until noon, and hear the bell strike again. In the meantime, he must try to think: This was, of course, Gothic architecture; he had read more or less about that, and ought to be able to remember something. Gothic . . . that was a mere word; to him it suggested something very peaked and pointed, — sharp arches, steep roofs. It had nothing to do with these slim white columns that rose so straight and far, — or with the window, burning up there in its vault of gloom. . . .

While he was vainly trying to think about architecture, some recollection of old astronomy lessons brushed across his brain, — something about stars whose light travels through space for hundreds of years before it reaches the earth and the human eye. The purple and crimson and peacock-green of this window had been shining quite as long as that before it got to him. . . . He felt distinctly that it went through him and farther still . . . as if his mother were looking over his shoulder. He sat solemnly through the hour until twelve, his elbows on his knees, his conical hat swinging between them in his hand, looking up through the twilight with candid, thoughtful eyes.

When Claude joined his company at the station, they had the laugh on him. They had found the Cathedral,—and a statue of Richard the Lion-hearted, over the spot where the lion-heart itself was buried; "the identical organ," fat Sergeant Hicks assured him. But they were all glad to leave Rouen.

V

B Company reached the training camp at S—— thirty-six men
short: twenty-five they had buried on the voyage over, and
eleven sick were left at the base hospital. The company was to be
attached to a battalion which had already seen service, commanded by Lieutenant Colonel Scott. Arriving early in the
morning, the officers reported at once to Headquarters.
Captain Maxey must have suffered a shock when the Colonel
rose from his desk to acknowledge his salute, then shook hands
with them all around and asked them about their journey. The
Colonel was not a very martial figure; short, fat, with slouching
shoulders, and a lumpy back like a sack of potatoes. Though he
wasn't much over forty, he was bald, and his collar would easily
slip over his head without being unbuttoned. His little twinkling
eyes and good-humoured face were without a particle of arro-
gance or official dignity.

Years ago, when General Pershing, then a handsome young
Lieutenant with a slender waist and yellow moustaches, was stationed as Commandant at the University of Nebraska, Walter
Scott was an officer in a company of cadets the Lieutenant took
about to military tournaments. The Pershing Rifles, they were
called, and they won prizes wherever they went. After his graduation, Scott settled down to running a hardware business in a
thriving Nebraska town, and sold gas ranges and garden hose for
twenty years. About the time Pershing was sent to the Mexican
border, Scott began to think there might eventually be something in the wind, and that he would better get into training. He

298

went down to Texas with the National Guard. He had come to France with the First Division, and had won his promotions by solid, soldierly qualities.

"I see you're an officer short, Captain Maxey," the Colonel remarked at their conference. "I think I've got a man here to take his place. Lieutenant Gerhardt is a New York man, came over in the band and got transferred to infantry. He has lately been given a commission for good service. He's had some experience and is a capable fellow." The Colonel sent his orderly out to bring in a young man whom he introduced to the officers as Lieutenant David Gerhardt.

Claude had been ashamed of Tod Fanning, who was always showing himself a sap-head, and who would never have got a commission if his uncle hadn't been a Congressman. But the moment he met Lieutenant Gerhardt's eye, something like jealously flamed up in him. He felt in a flash that he suffered by comparison with the new officer; that he must be on his guard and must not let himself be patronized.

As they were leaving the Colonel's office together, Gerhardt asked him whether he had got his billet. Claude replied that after the men were in their quarters, he would look out for something for himself.

The young man smiled. "I'm afraid you may have difficulty. The people about here have been overworked, keeping soldiers, and they are not willing as they once were. I'm with a nice old couple over in the village. I'm almost sure I can get you in there. If you'll come along, we'll speak to them, before some one else is put off on them."

Claude didn't want to go, didn't want to accept favours,— nevertheless he went. They walked together along a dusty road that ran between half-ripe wheatfields, bordered with poplar trees. The wild morning-glories and Queen Anne's lace that grew by the road-side were still shining with dew. A fresh breeze stirred the bearded grain, parting it in furrows and fanning out streaks of crimson poppies. The new officer was not intrusive, certainly. He walked along, whistling softly to himself, seeming quite lost in the freshness of the morning, or in his own thoughts. There had been nothing patronizing in his manner so far, and Claude began to wonder why he felt ill at ease with him. Perhaps it was because he did not look like the rest of them. Though he was young, he did not look boyish. He seemed experienced; a finished product, rather than something on the way. He was handsome, and his face, like his manner and his walk, had something distinguished about it. A broad white forehead under reddish brown hair, hazel eyes with no uncertainty in their look, an aquiline nose, finely cut, — a sensitive, scornful mouth, which somehow did not detract from the kindly, though slightly reserved, expression of his face.

Lieutenant Gerhardt must have been in this neighbourhood for some time; he seemed to know the people. On the road they passed several villagers; a rough-looking girl taking a cow out to graze, an old man with a basket on his arm, the postman on his bicycle; — they all spoke to Claude's companion as if they knew him well.

"What are these blue flowers that grow about everywhere?" Claude asked suddenly, pointing to a clump with his foot.

"Cornflowers," said the other. "The Germans call them *Kaiser-blumen.*"

They were approaching the village, which lay on the edge of a wood, — a wood so large one could not see the end of it; it met the horizon with a ridge of pines. The village was but a single street. On either side ran clay-coloured walls, with painted wooden doors here and there, and green shutters. Claude's guide opened one of these gates, and they walked into a little sanded garden; the house was built round it on three sides. Under a cherry tree sat a woman in a black dress, sewing, a work table beside her.

She was fifty, perhaps, but though her hair was grey she had a look of youthfulness; thin cheeks, delicately flushed with pink, and quiet, smiling, intelligent eyes. Claude thought she looked like a New England woman, — like the photographs of his mother's cousins and schoolmates. Lieutenant Gerhardt introduced him to Madame Joubert. He was quite disheartened by the colloquy that followed. Clearly his new fellow officer spoke Madame Joubert's perplexing language as readily as she herself did, and he felt irritated and grudging as he listened. He had been hoping that, wherever he stayed, he could learn to talk to the people a little; but with this accomplished young man about, he would never have the courage to try. He could see that Mme. Joubert liked Gerhardt, liked him very much; and all this, for some reason, discouraged him.

Gerhardt turned to Claude, speaking in a way which included Madame Joubert in the conversation, though she could not understand it: "Madame Joubert will let you come, although she has done her part and really doesn't have to take any one else in. But you will be so well off here that I'm glad she consents. You will have to share my room, but there are two beds. She will show you."

Gerhardt went out of the gate and left him alone with his hostess. Her mind seemed to read his thoughts. When he uttered a word, or any sound that resembled one, she quickly and smoothly made a sentence of it, as if she were quite accustomed to talking in this way and expected only monosyllables from strangers. She was kind, even a little playful with him; but he felt it was all good manners, and that underneath she was not thinking of him at all. When he was alone in the tile-floored sleeping room upstairs, unrolling his blankets and arranging his shaving things, he looked out of the window and watched her where she sat sewing under the cherry tree. She had a very sad face, he thought; it wasn't grief, nothing sharp and definite like sorrow. It was an old, quiet, impersonal sadness, — sweet in its expression, like the sadness of music.

As he came out of the house to start back to the barracks, he bowed to her and tried to say, *"Au revoir, Madame. Jusq' au ce soir."* He stopped near the kitchen door to look at a many-branched rose vine that ran all over the wall, full of cream-coloured, pink-tipped roses, just a shade stronger in colour than the clay wall behind them. Madame Joubert came over and stood beside him, looking at him and at the *rosier.* *"Oui, c'est joli, n'est-ce pas?"* She took the scissors that hung by a ribbon from her belt, cut one of the flowers and stuck it in his buttonhole. *"Voilà."* She made a little flourish with her thin hand.

Stepping into the street, he turned to shut the wooden door after him, and heard a soft stir in the dark tool-house at his elbow. From among the rakes and spades a child's frightened face was staring out at him. She was sitting on the ground with her lap full of baby kittens. He caught but a glimpse of her dull, pale face.

VI

THE next morning Claude awoke with such a sense of physical well-being as he had not had for a long time.

The sun was shining brightly on the white plaster walls and on the red tiles of the floor. Green jalousies, half-drawn, shaded the upper part of the two windows. Through their slats, he could see the forking branches of an old locust tree that grew by the gate. A flock of pigeons flew over it, dipping and mounting with a sharp twinkle of silver wings. It was good to lie again in a house that was cared for by women. He must have felt that even in his sleep, for when he opened his eyes he was thinking about Mahailey and breakfast and summer mornings on the farm. The early stillness was sweet, and the feeling of dry, clean linen against his body. There was a smell of lavender about his warm pillow. He lay still for fear of waking Lieutenant Gerhardt. This was the sort of peace one wanted to enjoy alone. When he rose cautiously on his elbow and looked at the other bed, it was empty. His companion must have dressed and slipped out when day first broke. Somebody else who liked to enjoy things alone; that looked hopeful. But now that he had the place to himself, he decided to get up.

While he was dressing he could see old M. Joubert down in the garden, watering the plants and vines, raking the sand fresh and smooth, clipping off dead leaves and withered flowers and throwing them into a wheelbarrow. These people had lost both their sons in the war, he had been told, and now they were taking care of the property for their grandchildren,—two daughters of the elder son. Claude saw Gerhardt come into the garden, and sit down at the table under the trees, where they had their dinner last night. He hurried down to join him. Gerhardt made room for him on the bench.

"Do you always sleep like that? It's an accomplishment. I made enough noise when I dressed,—kept dropping things, but it never reached you."

Madame Joubert came out of the kitchen in a purple flowered morning gown, her hair in curl-papers under a lace cap. She brought the coffee herself, and they sat down at the unpainted table without a cloth, and drank it out of big crockery bowls. They had fresh milk with it,—the first Claude had tasted in a long while, and sugar which Gerhardt produced from his pocket. The old cook had her coffee sitting in the kitchen door, and on the step, at her feet, sat the strange, pale little girl.

Madame Joubert amiably addressed herself to Claude; she knew that Americans were accustomed to a different sort of morning repast, and if he wished to bring bacon from the camp, she would gladly cook it for him. She had even made pancakes for officers who stayed there before. She seemed pleased, however, to learn that Claude had had enough of these things for awhile. She called David by his first name, pronouncing it the French way, and when Claude said he hoped she would do as much for him, she said, Oh, yes, that his was a very good French name, *"mais un peu, un peu . . . romanesque,"* at which he blushed, not quite knowing whether she were making fun of him or not.

"It is rather so in English, isn't it?" David asked.

"Well, it's a sissy name, if you mean that."

"Yes, it is, a little," David admitted candidly.

The day's work on the parade ground was hard, and Captain Maxey's men were soft, felt the heat,—didn't size up well with the Kansas boys who had been hardened by service. The Colonel wasn't pleased with B Company and detailed them to build new barracks and extend the sanitation system. Claude got out and worked with the men. Gerhardt followed his example, but it was easy to see that he had never handled lumber of tin-roofing before. A kind of rivalry seemed to have sprung up between him and Claude, neither of them knew why.

Claude could see that the sergeants and corporals were a little uncertain about Gerhardt. His laconic speech, never embroidered by the picturesque slang they relished, his gravity, and his rare, incredulous smile, alike puzzled them. Was the new officer a dude? Sergeant Hicks asked of his chum, Dell Able. No, he wasn't a dude. Was he a swell-head? No, not at all; but he wasn't a good mixer. He was "an Easterner"; what more he was would develop later. Claude sensed something unusual about him. He suspected that Gerhardt knew a good many things as well as he knew French, and that he tried to conceal it, as people sometimes do when they feel they are not among their equals; this idea nettled him. It was Claude who seized the opportunity to be patronizing, when Gerhardt betrayed that he was utterly unable to select lumber by given measurements.

The next afternoon, work on the new barracks was called off because of rain. Sergeant Hicks set about getting up a boxing match, but when he went to invite the lieutenants, they had both disappeared. Claude was tramping toward the village, determined to get into the big wood that had tempted him ever since his arrival.

The highroad became the village street, and then, at the edge of the wood, became a country road again. A little farther on, where the shade grew denser, it split up into three wagon trails, two of them faint and little used. One of these Claude followed. The rain had dwindled to a steady patter, but the tall brakes growing up in the path splashed him to the middle, and his feet sank in spongy, mossy earth. The light about him, the very air, was green. The trunks of the trees were overgrown with a soft green moss, like mould. He was wondering whether this forest was not always a damp, gloomy place, when suddenly the sun broke through and shattered the whole wood with gold. He had never seen anything like the quivering emerald of the moss, the silky green of the dripping beech-tops. Everything woke up; rabbits ran across the path, birds began to sing, and all at once the brakes were full of whirring insects.

The winding path turned again, and came out abruptly on a hillside, above an open glade piled with grey boulders. On the opposite rise of ground stood a grove of pines, with bare, red stems. The light, around and under them, was red like a rosy sunset. Nearly all the stems divided about half-way up into two great arms, which came together again at the top, like the pictures of old Grecian lyres.

Down in the grassy glade, among the piles of flint boulders, little white birches shook out their shining leaves in the lightly moving air. All about the rocks were patches of purple heath; it ran up into the crevices between them like fire. On one of these bald rocks sat Lieutenant Gerhardt, hatless, in an attitude of fatigue or of deep dejection, his hands clasped about his knees, his bronze hair ruddy in the sun. After watching him for a few minutes, Claude descended the slope, swishing the tall ferns.

"Will I be in the way?" he asked as he stopped at the foot of the rocks.

"Oh, no!" said the other, moving a little and unclasping his hands.

Claude sat down on a boulder. "Is this heather?" he asked. "I thought I recognized it, from 'Kidnapped.' This part of the world is not as new to you as it is to me."

"No. I lived in Paris for several years when I was a student."

"What were you studying?"

"The violin."

"You are a musician?" Claude looked at him wonderingly.

"I was," replied the other with a disdainful smile, languidly stretching out his legs in the heather.

"That seems too bad," Claude remarked gravely.

"What does?"

"Why, to take fellows with a special talent. There are enough of us who haven't any."

Gerhardt rolled over on his back and put his hands under his head. "Oh, this affair is too big for exceptions; it's universal. If you happened to be born twenty-six years ago, you couldn't escape. If this war didn't kill you in one way, it would in another." He told Claude he had trained at Camp Dix, and had come over eight months ago in a regimental band, but he hated the work he had to do and got transferred to the infantry.

When they retraced their steps, the wood was full of green twilight. Their relations had changed somewhat during the last half hour, and they strolled in confidential silence up the home-like street to the door of their own garden.

Since the rain was over, Madame Joubert had laid the cloth on the plank table under the cherry tree, as on the previous evenings. Monsieur was bringing the chairs, and the little girl was carrying out a pile of heavy plates. She rested them against her stomach and leaned back as she walked, to balance them. She wore shoes, but no stockings, and her faded cotton dress switched about her brown legs. She was a little Belgian refugee who had been sent there with her mother. The mother was dead now, and the child would not even go to visit her grave. She could not be coaxed from the court-yard into the quiet street. If the neighbour children came into the garden on an errand, she hid herself. She would have no playmates but the cat; and now she had the kittens in the tool house.

Dinner was very cheerful that evening. M. Joubert was pleased that the storm had not lasted long enough to hurt the wheat. The garden was fresh and bright after the rain. The cherry tree shook down bright drops on the tablecloth when the breeze stirred. The mother cat dozed on the red cushion in Madame Joubert's sewing chair, and the pigeons fluttered down to snap up earthworms that wriggled in the wet sand. The shadow of the house fell over the dinner-table, but the tree-tops stood up in full sunlight, and the yellow sun poured on the earth wall and the cream-coloured roses. Their petals, ruffled by the rain, gave out a wet, spicy smell.

M. Joubert must have been ten years older than his wife. There was a great contentment in his manner and a pleasant sparkle in his eye. He liked the young officers. Gerhardt had been there more than two weeks, and somewhat relieved the still-ness that had settled over the house since the second son died in hospital. The Jouberts had dropped out of things. They had done all they could do, given all they had, and now they had nothing to look forward to,—except the event to which all France looked forward. The father was talking to Gerhardt about the great sea-port the Americans were making of Bordeaux; he said he meant to go there after the war, to see it all for himself.

Madame Joubert was pleased to hear that they had been walk-ing in the wood. And was the heather in bloom? She wished they had brought her some. Next time they went, perhaps. She used to walk there often. Her eyes seemed to come nearer to them, Claude thought, when she spoke of it, and she evidently cared a great deal more about what was blooming in the wood than about what the Americans were doing on the Garonne. He wished he could talk to her as Gerhardt did. He admired the way she roused herself and tried to interest them, speaking her diffi-cult language with such spirit and precision. It was a language that couldn't be mumbled; that had to be spoken with energy and fire, or not spoken at all. Merely speaking that exacting tongue would help to rally a broken spirit, he thought.

The little maid who served them moved about noiselessly. Her dull eyes never seemed to look; yet she saw when it was time to bring the heavy soup tureen, and when it was time to take it away. Madame Joubert had found that Claude liked his potatoes with his meat—when there was meat—and not in a course by themselves. She had each time to tell the little girl to go and fetch them. This the child did with manifest reluctance,—sullenly, as if she were being forced to do something wrong. She was a very strange little creature, altogether. As the two soldiers left the table and started for the camp, Claude reached down into the tool house and took up one of the kittens, holding it out in the light to see it blink its eyes. The little girl, just coming out of the kitchen, uttered a shrill scream, a really terrible scream, and squatted down, covering her face with her hands. Madame Joubert came out to chide her.

"What is the matter with that child?" Claude asked as they hurried out of the gate. "Do you suppose she was hurt, or abused in some way?"

"Terrorized. She often screams like that at night. Haven't you heard her? They have to go and wake her, to stop it. She doesn't speak any French; only Walloon. And she can't of won't learn, so they can't tell what goes on in her poor little head."

In the two weeks of intensive training that followed, Claude marvelled at Gerhardt's spirit and endurance. The muscular strain of mimic trench operations was more of a tax on him than on any of the other officers. He was as tall as Claude, but he weighed only a hundred and forty-six pounds, and he had not been roughly bred like most of the others. When his fellow officers learned that he was a violinist by profession, that he could have had a soft job as interpreter or as an organizer of camp entertainments, they no longer resented his reserve or his occasional superciliousness. They respected a man who could have wriggled out and didn't.

VII

On the march at last; through a brilliant August day Colonel Scott's battalion was streaming along one of the dusty, well-worn roads east of the Somme, their railway base well behind them. The way led through rolling country; fields, hills, woods, little villages shattered but still habitable, where the people came out to watch the soldiers go by.

The Americans went through every village in march step, colours flying, the band playing, "to show that the morale was high," as the officers said. Claude trudged on the outside of the column,—now at the front of his company, now at the rear,— wearing a stoical countenance, afraid of betraying his satisfaction in the men, the weather, the country.

They were bound for the big show, and on every hand were reassuring signs: long lines of gaunt, dead trees, charred and torn; big holes gashed out in fields and hillsides, already half concealed by new undergrowth; winding depressions in the earth, bodies of wrecked motor-trucks and automobiles lying along the road, and everywhere endless straggling lines of rusty barbed-wire, that seemed to have been put there by chance,— with no purpose at all.

"Begins to look like we're getting in, Lieutenant," said Sergeant Hicks, smiling behind his salute.

Claude nodded and passed forward.

"Well, we can't arrive any too soon for us, boys?" The Sergeant looked over his shoulder, and they grinned, their teeth flashing white in their red, perspiring faces. Claude didn't wonder that everybody along the route, even the babies, came out to see them; he thought they were the finest sight in the world. This was the first day they had worn their tin hats; Gerhardt had shown them how to stuff grass and leaves inside to keep their heads cool. When they fell into fours, and the band struck up as they approached a town, Bert Fuller, the boy from Pleasantville on the Platte, who had blubbered on the voyage over, was guide right, and whenever Claude passed him his face seemed to say, "You won't get anything on me in a hurry, Lieutenant!"

They made camp early in the afternoon, on a hill covered with half-burned pines. Claude took Bert and Dell Able and Oscar the Swede, and set off to make a survey and report the terrain. Behind the hill, under the burned edge of the wood, they found an abandoned farmhouse and what seemed to be a clean well. It had a solid stone curb about it, and a wooden bucket hanging by a rusty wire. When the boys splashed the bucket about, the water sent up a pure, cool breath. But they were wise boys, and knew where dead Prussians most loved to hide. Even the straw in the stable they regarded with suspicion, and thought it would be just as well not to bed anybody there.

Swinging on to the right to make their circuit, they got into mud; a low field where the drain ditches had been neglected and had overflowed. There they came upon a pitiful group of humanity, bemired. A woman, ill and wretched looking, sat on a fallen log at the end of the marsh, a baby in her lap and three children hanging about her. She was far gone in consumption; one had only to listen to her breathing and to look at her white, perspiring face to feel how weak she was. Draggled, mud to the knees, she was trying to nurse her baby, half hidden under an old black shawl. She didn't look like a tramp woman, but like one who had once been able to take proper care of herself, and she was still young. The children were tired and discouraged. One little boy wore a clumsy blue jacket, made from a French army coat. The other wore a battered American Stetson that came down over his ears. He carried, in his two arms, a pink celluloid clock. They all looked up and waited for the soldiers to do something.

Claude approached the woman, and touching the rim of his helmet, began: *"Bon jour, Madame. Qu'est que c'est?"*

She tried to speak, but went off into a spasm of coughing, only able to gasp, "'Toinette, 'Toinette!"

'Toinette stepped quickly forward. She was about eleven, and seemed to be the captain of the party. A bold, hard little face with a long chin, straight black hair tied with rags, uneasy, crafty eyes; she looked much less gentle and more experienced than her mother. She began to explain, and she was very clever at making herself understood. She was used to talking to foreign soldiers,—spoke slowly, with emphasis and ingenious gestures.

She, too, had been reconnoitering. She had discovered the empty farmhouse and was trying to get her party there for the night. How did they come here? Oh, they were refugees. They had been staying with people thirty kilometers from here. They were trying to get back to their own village. Her mother was very sick, *presque morte,* and she wanted to go home to die. They had heard people were still living there; an old aunt was living in their own cellar,—and so could they if they once got there. The point was, and she made it over and over, that her mother wished to die *chez elle, comprenez-vous?* They had no papers, and the French soldiers would never let them pass, but now that the Americans were here they hoped to get through; the Americans were said to be *toujours gentils.*

While she talked in her shrill, clicking voice, the baby began to howl, dissatisfied with its nourishment. The little girl shrugged. *"Il est toujours en colère,"* she muttered. The woman turned it around with difficulty—it seemed a big, heavy baby, but white and sickly—and gave it the other breast. It began sucking her noisily, rooting and sputtering as if it were famished. It was too painful, it was almost indecent, to see this exhausted woman trying to feed her baby. Claude beckoned his men away to one side, and taking the little girl by the hand drew her after them.

"Il faut que votre mère se reposer," he told her, with the grave caesural pause which he always made in the middle of a French sentence. She understood him. No distortion of her native

tongue surprised or perplexed her. She was accustomed to being addressed in all persons, numbers, genders, tenses; by Germans, English, Americans. She only listened to hear whether the voice was kind, and with men in this uniform it usually was kind.

Had they anything to eat? *Vous aves quelque chose à manger?*

"Rien. Rien du tout."

Wasn't her mother *trop malade à marcher?*

She shrugged; Monsieur could see for himself.

And her father?

He was dead; *mort à la Marne, en quatorze.*

"At the Marne?" Claude repeated, glancing in perplexity at the nursing baby.

Her sharp eyes followed his, and she instantly divined his doubt. "The baby?" she said quickly. "Oh, the baby is not *my* brother, he is a Boche."

For a moment Claude did not understand. She repeated her explanation impatiently, something disdainful and sinister in her metallic little voice. A slow blush mounted to his forehead.

He pushed her toward her mother, *"Attendez là."*

"I guess we'll have to get them over to that farmhouse," he told the men. He repeated what he had got of the child's story. When he came to her laconic statement about the baby, they looked at each other. Bert Fuller was afraid he might cry again, so he kept muttering, "By God, if we'd a-got here sooner, by God if we had!" as they ran back along the ditch.

Dell and Oscar made a chair of their crossed hands and carried the woman,—she was no great weight. Bert picked up the little boy with the pink clock; "Come along, little frog, your legs ain't long enough."

Claude walked behind, holding the screaming baby stiffly in his arms. How was it possible for a baby to have such definite personality, he asked himself, and how was it possible to dislike a baby so much? He hated it for its square, tow-thatched head and bloodless ears, and carried it with loathing . . . no wonder it cried! When it got nothing by screaming and stiffening, however, it suddenly grew quiet; regarded him with pale blue eyes, and tried to make itself comfortable against his khaki coat. It put out a grimy little fist and took hold of one of his buttons. "Kamarad, eh?" he muttered, glaring at the infant. "Cut it out!"

Before they had their own supper that night, the boys carried hot food and blankets down to their family.

VIII

FOUR o'clock . . . a summer dawn . . . his first morning in the trenches.

Claude had just been along the line to see that the gun teams were in position. This hour, when the light was changing was a favourite time for attack. He had come in late last night, and had everything to learn. Mounting the fire-step, he peeped over the parapet between the sandbags, into the low, twisting mist. Just then he could see nothing but the wire entanglement, with birds hopping along the top wire, singing and chirping as they did on the wire fences at home. Clear and flute-like they sounded in the heavy air, — and they were the only sounds. A little breeze came up, slowly clearing the mist away. Streaks of green showed through the moving banks of vapour. The birds became more agitated.

That dull stretch of grey and green was No Man's Land. Those low, zigzag mounds, like giant molehills protected by wire hurdles, were the Hun trenches; five or six lines of them. He could easily follow the communication trenches without a glass. At one point their front line could not be more than eighty yards away, at another it must be all of three hundred. Here and there thin columns of smoke began to rise; the Hun was getting breakfast; everything was comfortable and natural. Behind the enemy's position the country rose gradually for several miles, with ravines and little woods, where, according to his map, they had masked artillery. Back on the hills were ruined farmhouses and broken trees, but nowhere a living

315

creature in sight. It was a dead, nerveless countryside, sunk in quiet and dejection. Yet everywhere the ground was full of men. Their own trenches, from the other side, must look quite as dead. Life was a secret, these days.

It was amazing how simply things could be done. His battalion had marched in quietly at midnight, and the line they came to relieve had set out as silently for the rear. It all took place in utter darkness. Just as B Company slid down an incline into the shallow rear trenches, the country was lit for a moment by two star shells, there was a rattling of machine guns, German Maxims,—a sporadic crackle that was not followed up. Filing along the communication trenches, they listened anxiously; artillery fire would have made it bad for the other men who were marching to the rear. But nothing happened. They had a quiet night, and this morning, here they were!

The sky flamed up saffron and silver. Claude looked at his watch, but he could not bear to go just yet. How long it took a Wheeler to get round to anything! Four years on the way; now that he was here, he would enjoy the scenery a bit, he guessed. He wished his mother could know how he felt this morning. But perhaps she did know. At any rate, she would not have him anywhere else. Five years ago, when he was sitting on the steps of the Denver State House and knew that nothing unexpected could ever happen to him . . . suppose he could have seen, in a flash, where he would be today? He cast a long look at the reddening, lengthening landscape, and dropped down on the duckboard.

Claude made his way back to the dugout into which he and Gerhardt had thrown their effects last night. The former occupants had left it clean. There were two bunks nailed against the side walls,—wooden frames with wire netting over them, covered with dry sandbags. Between the two bunks was a soap-box table, with a candle stuck in a green bottle, an alcohol stove, a *bain-marie,* and two tin cups. On the wall were coloured pictures from *Jugend,* taken out of some Hun trench.

He found Gerhardt still asleep on his bed, and shook him until he sat up.

"How long have you been out, Claude? Didn't you sleep?"

"A little. I wasn't very tired. I suppose we could heat shaving water on this stove; they've left us half a bottle of alcohol. It's quite a comfortable little hole, isn't it?"

"It will doubtless serve its purpose," David remarked dryly. "So sensitive to any criticism of this war! Why, it's not your affair; you've only just arrived."

"I know," Claude replied meekly, as he began to fold his blankets. "But it's likely the only one I'll ever be in, so I may as well take an interest."

. . . . . .

The next afternoon four young men, all more or less naked, were busy about a shellhole full of opaque brown water. Sergeant Hicks and his chum, Dell Able, had hunted through half the blazing hot morning to find a hole not too scummy, conveniently, and even picturesquely situated, and had reported it to the Lieutenants. Captain Maxey, Hicks said, could send his own orderly to find his own shellhole, and could take his bath in private. "He'd never wash himself with anybody else," the Sergeant added. "Afraid of exposing his dignity!"

Bruger and Hammond, the two second Lieutenants, were already out of their bath, and reclined on what might almost be termed a grassy slope, examining various portions of their body with interest. They hadn't had all their clothes off for some time, and four days of marching in hot weather made a man anxious to look at himself.

"You wait till winter," Gerhardt told them. He was still splashing in the hole, up to his armpits in muddy water. "You won't get a wash once in three months then. Some of the Tommies told me that when they got their first bath after Vimy, their skins peeled off like a snake's. What are you doing with my trousers, Bruger?"

"Hunting for your knife. I dropped mine yesterday, when that shell exploded in the cut-off. I darned near dropped my old nut!"

"Shucks, that wasn't anything. Don't keep blowing about it— shows you're a greenhorn."

Claude stripped off his shirt and slid into the pool beside
Gerhardt. "Gee, I hit something sharp down there! Why didn't
you fellows pull out the splinters?"

He shut his eyes, disappeared for a moment, and came up
sputtering, throwing on the ground a round metal object,
coated with rust and full of slime. "German helmet, isn't it?
Phew!" He wiped his face and looked about suspiciously.

"Phew is right!" Bruger turned the object over with a stick.
"Why in hell didn't you bring up the rest of him? You've spoiled
my bath. I hope you enjoy it."

Gerhardt scrambled up the side. "Get out, Wheeler! Look at
that," he pointed to big sleepy bubbles, bursting up through the
thick water. "You've stirred up trouble, all right! Something's
going very bad down there."

Claude got out after him, looking back at the activity in the
water. "I don't see how pulling out one helmet could stir the bottom up so. I should think the water would keep the smell down."

"Ever study chemistry?" Bruger asked scornfully. "You just
opened up a graveyard, and now we get the exhaust. If you swallowed any of that German cologne—Oh, you should worry!"

Lieutenant Hammond, still barelegged, with his shirt tied
over his shoulders, was scratching in his notebook. Before they
left he put up a placard on a split stick.

No Public Bathing! ! Private Beach

C. Wheeler, Co. B. 2-th Inf'ty.

.   .   .   .

The first letters from home! The supply wagons brought them
up, and every man in the Company got something except Ed Drier,
a farm-hand from the Nebraska sand hills, and Willy Katz, the tow-
headed Austrian boy from the South Omaha packing-houses.
Their comrades were sorry for them. Ed didn't have any "folks" of
his own, but he had expected letters all the same. Willy was sure his
mother must have written. When the last ragged envelope was
given out and he turned away empty-handed, he murmured, "She's
Bohunk, and she don't write so good. I guess the address wasn't
plain, and some fellow in another comp'ny has got my letter."

No second class matter was sent up,—the boys had hoped for newspapers from home to give them a little war news, since they never got any here. Dell Abie's sister, however, had enclosed a clipping from the Kansas City *Star;* a long account by one of the British war correspondents in Mesopotamia, describing the hardships the soldiers suffered there; dysentery, flies, mosquitoes, unimaginable heat. He read this article aloud to a group of his friends as they sat about a shell-hole pool where they had been washing their socks. He had just finished the story of how the Tommies had found a few mud huts at the place where the original Garden of Eden was said to have been,—a desolate spot full of stinging insects—when Oscar Petersen, a very religious Swedish boy who was often silent for days together, opened his mouth and said scornfully,

"That's a lie!"

Dell looked up at him, annoyed by the interruption. "How do you know it is?"

"Because; the Lord put four cherubims with swords to guard the Garden, and there ain't no man going to find it. It ain't intended they should. The Bible says so."

Hicks began to laugh. "Why, that was about six thousand years ago, you cheese! Do you suppose your cherubims are still there?"

"'Course they are. What's a thousand years to a cherubim? Nothin'!"

The Swede rose and sullenly gathered up his socks.

Dell Able looked at his chum. "Ain't he the complete bonehead? Solid ivory!"

Oscar wouldn't listen further to a "pack of lies" and walked off with his washing.

. . . .

Battalion Headquarters was nearly half a mile behind the front line, part dugout, part shed, with a plank roof sodded over. The Colonel's office was partitioned off at one end; the rest of the place he gave over to the officers for a kind of club room. One night Claude went back to make a report on the new placing of the gun teams. The young officers were sitting about on soap boxes, smoking and eating sweet crackers out of tin cases. Gerhardt was working at a plank table with paper and crayons, making a clean copy of a rough map they had drawn up together that morning, showing the limits of fire. Noise didn't fluster him; he could sit among a lot of men and write as calmly as if he were alone.

There was one officer who could talk all the others down, wherever he was; Captain Barclay Owens, attached from the Engineers. He was a little stumpy thumb of a man, only five feet four, and very broad,—a dynamo of energy. Before the war he was building a dam in Spain, "the largest dam in the world," and in his excavations he had discovered the ruins of one of Julius Caesar's fortified camps. This had been too much for his easily-inflamed imagination. He photographed and measured and brooded upon these ancient remains. He was an engineer by day and an archaeologist by night. He had crates of books sent down from Paris,—everything that had been written on Caesar, in French and German; he engaged a young priest to translate them aloud to him in the evening. The priest believed the American was mad.

When Owens was in college he had never shown the least interest in classical studies, but now it was as if he were giving birth to Caesar. The war came along, and stopped the work on his dam. It also drove other ideas into his exclusively engineering brains. He rushed home to Kansas to explain the war to his countrymen. He travelled about the West, demonstrating exactly what had happened at the first battle of the Marne, until he had a chance to enlist.

In the Battalion, Owens was called "Julius Caesar," and the men never knew whether he was explaining the Roman general's operations in Spain, or Joffre's at the Marne, he jumped so from one to the other. Everything was in the foreground with him; centuries made no difference. Nothing existed until Barclay Owens found out about it. The men liked to hear him talk. Tonight he was walking up and down, his yellow eyes rolling, a big black cigar in his hand, lecturing the young officers upon French characteristics, coaching and preparing them. It was his legs that made him so funny; his trunk was that of a big man, set on two short stumps.

"Now you fellows don't want to forget that the night-life of Paris is not a typical thing at all; that's a show got up for for-eigners. . . . The French peasant, he's a thrifty fellow. . . . This red wine's all right if you don't abuse it; take it two-thirds water and it keeps off dysentery. . . . You don't have to be rough with them, simply firm. Whenever one of them accosts me, I follow a regular plan; first, I give her twenty-five francs; then I look her in the eye and say, 'My girl, I've got three children, *three boys.*' She gets the point at once; never fails. She goes away ashamed of herself."

"But that's so expensive! It must keep you poor, Captain Owens," said young Lieutenant Hammond innocently. The others roared.

Claude knew that David particularly detested Captain Owens of the Engineers, and wondered that he could go on working with such concentration, when snatches of the Captain's lecture kept breaking through the confusion of casual talk and the noise of the phonograph. Owens, as he walked up and down, cast furtive glances at Gerhardt. He had got wind of the fact that there was something out of the ordinary about him.

The men kept the phonograph going; as soon as one record buzzed out, somebody put in another. Once, when a new tune began, Claude saw David look up from his paper with a curious expression. He listened for a moment with a half-contemptuous smile, then frowned and began sketching in his map again. Something about his momentary glance of recognition made Claude wonder whether he had particular associations with the air, — melancholy, but beautiful, Claude thought. He got up and went over to change the record him-self this time. He took out the disk, and holding it up to the light, read the inscription: "Meditation from Thaïs — Violin solo — David Gerhardt."

When they were going back along the communication trench in the rain, wading single file, Claude broke the silence abruptly. "That was one of your records they played tonight, that violin solo, wasn't it?"

"Sounded like it. Now we go to the right. I always get lost here."

"Are there many of your records?"

"Quite a number. Why do you ask?"

"I'd like to write my mother. She's fond of good music. She'll get your records, and it will sort of bring the whole thing closer to her, don't you see?"

"All right, Claude," said David good-naturedly. "She will find them in the catalogue, with my picture in uniform alongside. I had a lot made before I went out to Camp Dix. My own mother gets a little income from them. Here we are, at home." As he struck a match two black shadows jumped from the table and disappeared behind the blankets. "Plenty of them around these wet nights. Get one? Don't squash him in there. Here's the sack."

Gerhardt held open the mouth of a gunny sack, and Claude thrust the squirming corner of his blanket into it and vigorously trampled whatever fell to the bottom. "Where do you suppose the other is?"

"He'll join us later. I don't mind the rats half so much as I do Barclay Owens. What a sight he would be with his clothes off! Turn in; I'll go the rounds." Gerhardt splashed out along the submerged duckboard. Claude took off his shoes and cooled his feet in the muddy water. He wished he could ever get David to talk about his profession, and wondered what he looked like on a concert platform, playing his violin.

IX

THE following night, Claude was sent back to Division Headquarters at Q—— with information the Colonel did not care to
commit to paper. He set off at ten o'clock, with Sergeant Hicks
for escort. There had been two days of rain, and the communication trenches were almost knee-deep in water. About half a
mile back of the front line, the two men crawled out of the ditch
and went on above ground. There was very little shelling along
the front that night. When a flare went up, they dropped and lay
on their faces, trying, at the same time, to get a squint at what
was ahead of them.

The ground was rough, and the darkness thick; it was past
midnight when they reached the east-and-west road — usually
full of traffic, and not entirely deserted even on a night like
this. Trains of horses were splashing through the mud, with
shells on their backs, empty supply wagons were coming back
from the front. Claude and Hicks paused by the ditch, hoping
to get a ride. The rain began to fall with such violence that
they looked about for shelter. Stumbling this way and that,
they ran into a big artillery piece, the wheels sunk over the
hubs in a mud-hole.

"Who's there?" called a quick voice, unmistakably British.

"American infantrymen, two of us. Can we get onto one of
your trucks till this lets up?"

"Oh, certainly! We can make room for you in here, if you're
not too big. Speak quietly, or you'll waken the Major."

Giggles and smothered laughter; a flashlight winked for a moment and showed a line of five trucks, the front and rear ones covered with tarpaulin tents. The voices came from the shelter next the gun. The men inside drew up their legs and made room for the strangers; said they were sorry they hadn't anything dry to offer them except a little rum. The intruders accepted this gratefully.

The Britishers were a giggly lot, and Claude thought, from their voices, they must all be very young. They joked about their Major as if he were their schoolmaster. There wasn't room enough on the truck for anybody to lie down, so they sat with their knees under their chins and exchanged gossip. The gun team belonged to an independent battery that was sent about over the country, "wherever needed." The rest of the battery had got through, gone on to the east, but this big gun was always getting into trouble; now something had gone wrong with her tractor and they couldn't pull her out. They called her "Jenny," and said she was taken with fainting fits now and then, and had to be humoured. It was like going about with your grandmother, one of the invisible Tommies said, "she is such a pompous old thing!" The Major was asleep on the rear truck; he was going to get the V. C. for sleeping. More giggles.

No, they hadn't any idea where they were going; of course, the officers knew, but artillery officers never told anything. What was this country like, anyhow? They were new to this part, had just come down from Verdun.

Claude said he had a friend in the air service up there; did they happen to know anything about Victor Morse?

Morse, the American ace? Hadn't he heard? Why, that got into the London papers. Morse was shot down inside the Hun line three weeks ago. It was a brilliant affair. He was chased by eight Boche planes, brought down three of them, put the rest to flight, and was making for base, when they turned and got him. His machine came down in flames and he jumped, fell a thousand feet or more.

"Then I suppose he never got his leave?" Claude asked.

They didn't know. He got a fine citation.

The men settled down to wait for the weather to improve or the night to pass. Some of them fell into a doze, but Claude felt wide awake. He was wondering about the flat in Chelsea; whether the heavy-eyed beauty had been very sorry, or whether she was playing "Roses of Picardy" for other young officers. He thought mournfully that he would never go to London now. He had quite counted on meeting Victor there some day, after the Kaiser had been properly disposed of. He had really liked Victor. There was something about that fellow . . . a sort of debauched baby, he was, who went seeking his enemy in the clouds. What other age could have produced such a figure? That was one of the things about this war; it took a little fellow from a little town, gave him an air and a swagger, a life like a movie-film, — and then a death like the rebel angels.

A man like Gerhardt, for instance, had always lived in a more or less rose-coloured world; he belonged over here, really. How could he know what hard moulds and crusts the big guns had broken open on the other side of the sea? Who could ever make him understand how far it was from the strawberry bed and the glass cage in the bank, to the sky-roads over Verdun?

By three o'clock the rain had stopped. Claude and Hicks set off again, accompanied by one of the gun team who was going back to get help for their tractor. As it began to grow light, the two Americans wondered more and more at the extremely youthful appearance of their companion. When they stopped at a shellhole and washed the mud from their faces, the English boy, with his helmet off and the weather stains removed, showed a countenance of adolescent freshness, almost girlish; cheeks like pink apples, yellow curls above his forehead, long, soft lashes.

"You haven't been over very long, have you?" Claude asked in a fatherly tone, as they took the road again.

"I came out in 'sixteen. I was formerly in the infantry."

The Americans liked to hear him talk; he spoke very quickly, in a high, piping voice.

"How did you come to change?"

"Oh, I belonged to one of the Pal Battalions, and we got cut to pieces. When I came out of hospital, I thought I'd try another branch of the service, seeing my pals were gone."

"Now, just what is a Pal Battalion?" drawled Hicks. He hated all English words he didn't understand, though he didn't mind French ones in the least.

"Fellows who signed up together from school," the lad piped.

Hicks glanced at Claude. They both thought this boy ought to be in school for some time yet, and wondered what he looked like when he first came over.

"And you got cut up, you say?" he asked sympathetically.

"Yes, on the Somme. We had rotten luck. We were sent over to take a trench and couldn't. We didn't even get to the wire. The Hun was so well prepared that time, we couldn't manage it. We went over a thousand, and we came back seventeen."

"A hundred and seventeen?"

"No, seventeen."

Hicks whistled and again exchanged looks with Claude. They could neither of them doubt him. There was something very unpleasant about the idea of a thousand fresh-faced schoolboys being sent out against the guns. "It must have been a fool order," he commented. "Suppose there was some mistake at Headquarters?"

"Oh, no, Headquarters knew what it was about! We'd have taken it, if we'd had any sort of luck. But the Hun happened to be full of fight. His machine guns did for us."

"You were hit yourself?" Claude asked him.

"In the leg. He was popping away at me all the while, but I wriggled back on my tummy. When I came out of the hospital my leg wasn't strong, and there's less marching in the artillery."

"I should think you'd have had about enough."

"Oh, a fellow can't stay out after all his chums have been killed! He'd think about it all the time, you know," the boy replied in his clear treble.

Claude and Hicks got into Headquarters just as the cooks were turning out to build their fires. One of the Corporals took them to the officers' bath,—a shed with big tin tubs,—and carried away their uniforms to dry them in the kitchen. It would be an hour before the officers would be about, he said, and in the meantime he would manage to get clean shirts and socks for them.

"Say, Lieutenant," Hicks brought out as he was rubbing himself down with a real bath towel, "I don't want to hear any more about those Pal Battalions, do you? It gets my goat. So long as we were going to get into this, we might have been a little more previous. I hate to feel small."

"Guess we'll have to take our medicine," Claude said dryly. "There wasn't anywhere to duck, was there? I felt like it. Nice little kid. I don't believe American boys ever seem as young as that."

"Why, if you met him anywhere else, you'd be afraid of using bad words before him, he's so pretty! What's the use of sending an orphan asylum out to be slaughtered? I can't see it," grumbled the fat sergeant. "Well, it's their business. I'm not going to let it spoil my breakfast. Suppose we'll draw ham and eggs, Lieutenant?"

X

AFTER breakfast Claude reported to Headquarters and talked with one of the staff Majors. He was told he would have to wait until tomorrow to see Colonel James, who had been called to Paris for a general conference. He had left in his car at four that morning, in response to a telephone message.

"There's not much to do here, by way of amusement," said the Major. "A movie show tonight, and you can get anything you want at the *estaminet,*—the one on the square, opposite the English tank, is the best. There are a couple of nice Frenchwomen in the Red Cross barrack, up on the hill, in the old convent garden. They try to look out for the civilian population, and we're on good terms with them. We get their supplies through with our own, and the quartermaster has orders to help them when they run short. You might go up and call on them. They speak English perfectly."

Claude asked whether he could walk in on them without any kind of introduction.

"Oh, yes, they're used to us! I'll give you a card to Mlle. Olive, though. She's a particular friend of mine. There you are: *'Mlle. Olive de Courcy, introducing, etc.'* And, you understand," here he glanced up and looked Claude over from head to foot, "she's a perfect lady."

Even with an introduction, Claude felt some hesitancy about presenting himself to these ladies. Perhaps they didn't like Americans; he was always afraid of meeting French people who didn't. It was the same way with most of the fellows in his battalion, he had found; they were terribly afraid of being disliked.

And the moment they felt they were disliked, they hastened to behave as badly as possible, in order to deserve it; then they didn't feel that they had been taken in — the worst feeling a doughboy could possibly have!

Claude thought he would stroll about to look at the town a little. It had been taken by the Germans in the autumn of 1914, after their retreat from the Marne, and they had held it until about a year ago, when it was retaken by the English and the Chasseurs d'Alpins. They had been able to reduce it and to drive the Germans out, only by battering it down with artillery; not one building remained standing.

Ruin was ugly, and it was nothing more, Claude was thinking, as he followed the paths that ran over piles of brick and plaster. There was nothing picturesque about this, as there was in the war pictures one saw at home. A cyclone or a fire might have done just as good a job. The place was simply a great dump-heap; an exaggeration of those which disgrace the outskirts of American towns. It was the same thing over and over; mounds of burned brick and broken stone, heaps of rusty, twisted iron, splintered beams and rafters, stagnant pools, cellar holes full of muddy water. An American soldier had stepped into one of those holes a few nights before, and been drowned.

This had been a rich town of eighteen thousand inhabitants; now the civilian population was about four hundred. There were people there who had hung on all through the years of German occupation; others who, as soon as they heard that the enemy was driven out, came back from wherever they had found shelter. They were living in cellars, or in little wooden barracks made from old timbers and American goods boxes. As he walked along, Claude read familiar names and addresses, painted on boards built into the sides of these frail shelters: "From Emery Bird, Thayer Co. Kansas City, Mo." "Daniels and Fisher, Denver, Colo." These inscriptions cheered him so much that he began to feel like going up and calling on the French ladies.

The sun had come out hot after three days of rain. The stagnant pools and the weeds that grew in the ditches gave out a rank, heavy smell. Wild flowers grew triumphantly over the piles of rotting wood and rusty iron; cornflowers and Queen Anne's lace and poppies; blue and white and red, as if the French colours came up spontaneously out of the French soil, no matter what the Germans did to it.

Claude paused before a little shanty built against a half-demolished brick wall. A gilt cage hung in the doorway, with a canary, singing beautifully. An old woman was working in the garden patch, picking out bits of brick and plaster the rain had washed up, digging with her fingers around the pale carrot-tops and neat lettuce heads. Claude approached her, touched his helmet, and asked her how one could find the way to the Red Cross.

She wiped her hands on her apron and took him by the elbow. *"Vous saves le tank Anglais? Non? Marie, Marie!"*

(He learned afterward that every one was directed to go this way or that from a disabled British tank that had been left on the site of the old town hall.)

A little girl ran out of the barrack, and her grandmother told her to go at once and take the American to the Red Cross. Marie put her hand in Claude's and led him off along one of the paths that wound among the rubbish. She took him out of the way to show him a church, — evidently one of the ruins of which they were proudest, — where the blue sky was shining through the white arches. The Virgin stood with empty arms over the central door; a little foot sticking to her robe showed where the infant Jesus had been shot away.

"Le bébé est cassé, mais il a protegé sa mère," Marie explained with satisfaction. As they went on, she told Claude that she had a soldier among the Americans who was her friend. *"Il est ban, il est gai, mon soldat,"* but he sometimes drank too much alcohol, and that was a bad habit. Perhaps now, since his comrade had stepped into a cellar hole Monday night while he was drunk, and had been drowned, her "Sharlie" would be warned and would do

better. Marie was evidently a well brought up child. Her father, she said, had been a schoolmaster. At the foot of the convent hill she turned to go home. Claude called her back and awkwardly tried to give her some money, but she thrust her hands behind her and said resolutely, *"Non, merci. Je n'ai besoin de rien,"* and then ran away down the path.

As he climbed toward the top of the hill he noticed that the ground had been cleaned up a bit. The path was clear, the bricks and hewn stones had been piled in neat heaps, the broken hedges had been trimmed and the dead parts cut away. Emerging at last into the garden, he stood still for wonder; even though it was in ruins, it seemed so beautiful after the disorder of the world below.

The gravel walks were clean and shining. A wall of very old boxwoods stood green against a row of dead Lombardy poplars. Along the shattered side of the main building, a pear tree, trained on wires like a vine, still flourished,—full of little red pears. Around the stone well was a shaven grass plot, and everywhere there were little trees and shrubs, which had been too low for the shells to hit,—or for the fire, which had seared the poplars, to catch. The hill must have been wrapped in flames at one time, and all the tall trees had been burned.

The barrack was built against the walls of the cloister,—three arches of which remained, like a stone wing to the shed of planks. On a ladder stood a one-armed young man, driving nails very skilfully with his single hand. He seemed to be making a frame projection from the sloping roof, to support an awning. He carried his nails in his mouth. When he wanted one, he hung his hammer to the belt of his trousers, took a nail from between his teeth, stuck it into the wood, and then deftly rapped it on the head. Claude watched him for a moment, then went to the foot of the ladder and held out his two hands. *"Laisses-moi,"* he exclaimed.

The one aloft spat his nails out into his palm, looked down, and laughed. He was about Claude's age, with very yellow hair and moustache and blue eyes. A charming looking fellow.

"Willingly," he said. "This is no great affair, but I do it to amuse myself, and it will be pleasant for the ladies." He descended and gave his hammer to the visitor. Claude set to work on the frame, while the other went under the stone arches and brought back a roll of canvas,—part of an old tent, by the look of it.

"*Un héritage des Boches,*" he explained unrolling it upon the grass. "I found it among their filth in the cellar, and had the idea to make a pavilion for the ladies, as our trees are destroyed." He stood up suddenly. "Perhaps you have come to see the ladies?"

"*Plus tard.*"

Very well, the boy said, they would get the pavilion done for a surprise for Mlle. Olive when she returned. She was down in the town now, visiting the sick people. He bent over his canvas again, measuring and cutting with a pair of garden shears, moving round the green plot on his knees, and all the time singing. Claude wished he could understand the words of his song.

While they were working together, tying the cloth up to the frame, Claude, from his elevation, saw a tall girl coming slowly up the path by which he had ascended. She paused at the top, by the boxwood hedge, as if she were very tired, and stood looking at them. Presently she approached the ladder and said in slow, careful English, "Good morning. Louis has found help, I see."

Claude came down from his perch.

"Are you Mlle, de Courcy? I am Claude Wheeler, I have a note of introduction to you, if I can find it."

She took the card, but did not look at it. "That is not necessary. Your uniform is enough. Why have you come?"

He looked at her in some confusion. "Well, really, I don't know! I am just in from the front to see Colonel James, and he is in Paris, so I must wait over a day. One of the staff suggested my coming up here—I suppose because it is so nice!" he finished ingenuously.

"Then you are a guest from the front, and you will have lunch with Louis and me. Madame Barré is also gone for the day. Will you see our house?" She led him through the low door into a living room, unpainted, uncarpeted, light and airy. There were coloured war posters on the clean board walls, brass shell-cases full of wild flowers and garden flowers, canvas camp-chairs, a shelf of books, a table covered by a white silk shawl embroidered with big butterflies. The sunlight on the floor, the bunches of fresh flowers, the white window curtains stirring in the breeze, reminded Claude of something, but he could not remember what.

"We have no guest room," said Mlle. de Courcy. "But you will come to mine, and Louis will bring you hot water to wash."

In a wooden chamber at the end of the passage, Claude took off his coat, and set to work to make himself as tidy as possible. Hot water and scented soap were in themselves pleasant things. The dresser was an old goods box, stood on end and covered with white lawn. On it there was a row of ivory toilet things, with combs and brushes, powder and cologne, and a pile of white handkerchiefs fresh from the iron. He felt that he ought not to look about him much, but the odor of cleanness, and the indefinable air of personality, tempted him. In one corner, a curtain on a rod made a clothes-closet; in another was a low iron bed, like a soldier's, with a pale blue coverlid and white pillows. He moved carefully and splashed discreetly. There was nothing he could have damaged or broken, not even a rug on the plank floor, and the pitcher and hand-basin were of iron; yet he felt as if he were imperilling something fragile.

When he came out, the table in the living room was set for three. The stout old dame who was placing the plates paid no attention to him,—seemed, from her expression, to scorn him and all his kind. He withdrew as far as possible out of her path and picked up a book from the table, a volume of Heine's *Reisebilder* in German.

Before lunch Mlle. de Courcy showed him the store room in the rear, where the shelves were stocked with rows of coffee tins, condensed milk, canned vegetables and meat, all with American trade names he knew so well; names which seemed doubly familiar and "reliable" here, so far from home. She told him the people in the town could not have got through the winter without these things. She had to deal them out sparingly, where the need was greatest, but they made the difference between life and death. Now that it was summer, the people lived by their gardens; but old women still came to beg for a few ounces of coffee, and mothers to get a can of milk for the babies.

Claude's face glowed with pleasure. Yes, his country had a long arm. People forgot that; but here, he felt, was some one who did not forget. When they sat down to lunch he learned that Mlle. de Courcy and Madame Barré had been here almost a year now; they came soon after the town was retaken, when the old inhabitants began to drift back. The people brought with them only what they could carry in their arms.

"They must love their country so much, don't you think, when they endure such poverty to come back to it?" she said. "Even the old ones do not often complain about their dear things — their linen, and their china, and their beds. If they have the ground, and hope, all that they can make again. This war has taught us all how little the made things matter. Only the feeling matters."

Exactly so; hadn't he been trying to say this ever since he was born? Hadn't he always known it, and hadn't it made life both bitter and sweet for him? What a beautiful voice she had, this Mlle. Olive, and how nobly it dealt with the English tongue. He would like to say something, but out of so much . . . what? He remained silent, therefore, sat nervously breaking up the black war bread that lay beside his plate. He saw her looking at his hand, felt in a flash that she regarded it with favour, and instantly put it on his knee, under the table.

"It is our trees that are worst," she went on sadly. "You have seen our poor trees? It makes one ashamed for this beautiful part of France. Our people are more sorry for them than to lose their cattle and horses."

Mlle. de Courcy looked over-taxed by care and responsibility, Claude thought, as he watched her. She seemed far from strong. Slender, grey-eyed, dark-haired, with white transparent skin and a too ardent colour in her lips and cheeks,—like the flame of a feverish activity within. Her shoulders drooped, as if she were always tired. She must be young, too, though there were threads of grey in her hair,—brushed flat and knotted carelessly at the back of her head.

After the coffee, Mlle. de Courcy went to work at her desk, and Louis took Claude to show him the garden. The clearing and trimming and planting were his own work, and he had done it all with one arm. This autumn he would accomplish much more, for he was stronger now, and he had the *habitude* of working single-handed. He must manage to get the dead trees down; they distressed Mademoiselle Olive. In front of the barrack stood four old locusts; the tops were naked forks, burned coal-black, but the lower branches had put out thick tufts of yellow-green foliage, so vigorous that the life in the trunks must still be sound. This fall, Louis said, he meant to get some strong American boys to help him, and they would saw off the dead limbs and trim the tops flat over the thick boles. How much it must mean to a man to love his country like this, Claude thought; to love its trees and flowers; to nurse it when it was sick, and tend its hurts with one arm.

Among the flowers, which had come back "self-sown or from old roots, Claude found a group of tall, straggly plants with reddish stems and tiny white blossoms, — one of the evening primrose family, the *Gaura,* that grew along the clay banks of Lovely Creek, at home. He had never thought it very pretty, but he was pleased to find it here. He had supposed it was one of those nameless prairie flowers that grew on the prairie and nowhere else.

When they went back to the barrack, Mlle. Olive was sitting in one of the canvas chairs Louis had placed under the new pavilion.

"What a fine fellow he is!" Claude exclaimed, looking after him.

"Louis? Yes. He was my brother's orderly. When Emile came home on leave he always brought Louis with him, and Louis became like one of the family. The shell that killed my brother tore off his arm. My mother and I went to visit him in the hospital, and he seemed ashamed to be alive, poor boy, when my brother was dead. He put his hand over his face and began to cry, and said, *'Oh, Madame, il était toujours plus chic que moi!'*"

Although Mlle. Olive spoke English well, Claude saw that she did so only by keeping her mind intently upon it. The stiff sentences she uttered were foreign to her nature; her face and eyes ran ahead of her tongue and made one wait eagerly for what was coming. He sat down in a sagging canvas chair, absently twisting a sprig of *Gaura* he had pulled.

"You have found a flower?" She looked up.

"Yes. It grows at home, on my father's farm."

She dropped the faded shirt she was darning. "Oh, tell me about your country! I have talked to so many, but it is difficult to understand. Yes, tell me about that!"

Nebraska—What was it? How many days from the sea, what did it look like? As he tried to describe it, she listened with half-closed eyes. "Flat—covered with grain—muddy rivers. I think it must be like Russia. But your father's farm; describe that to me, minutely, and perhaps I can see the rest."

Claude took a stick and drew a square in the sand: there, to begin with, was the house and farmyard; there was the big pasture, with Lovely Creek flowing through it; there were the wheatfields and cornfields, the timber claim; more wheat and corn, more pastures. There it all was, diagrammed on the yellow sand, with shadows gliding over it from the half-charred locust trees. He would not have believed that he could tell a stranger about it in such detail. It was partly due to his listener, no doubt; she gave him unusual sympathy, and the glow of an unusual mind. While she bent over his map, questioning him, a light dew of perspiration gathered on her upper lip, and she breathed faster from her effort to see and understand everything. He told her about his mother and his father and Mahailey; what life was like there in summer and winter and autumn—what it had been like in that fateful summer when the Hun was moving always toward Paris, and on those three days when the French were standing at the Marne; how his mother and father waited for him to bring the news at night, and how the very cornfields seemed to hold their breath.

Mlle. Olive sank back wearily in her chair. Claude looked up and saw tears sparkling in her brilliant eyes. "And I myself," she murmured, "did not know of the Marne until days afterward, though my father and brother were both there! I was far off in Brittany, and the trains did not run. That is what is wonderful, that you are here, telling me this! We,__ we were taught from childhood that some day the Germans would come; we grew up under that threat. But you were so safe, with all your wheat and corn. Nothing could touch you, nothing!"

Claude dropped his eyes. "Yes," he muttered, blushing, "shame could. It pretty nearly did. We are pretty late." He rose from his chair as if he were going to fetch something. . . . But where was he to get it from? He shook his head. "I am afraid," he said mournfully, "there is nothing I can say to make you understand how far away it all seemed, how almost visionary. It didn't only seem miles away, it seemed centuries away."

"But you do come,—so many, and from so far! It is the last miracle of this war. I was in Paris on the fourth day of July, when your Marines, just from Belleau Wood, marched for your national fete, and I said to myself as they came on, 'That is a new man!' Such heads they had, so fine there, behind the ears. Such discipline and purpose. Our people laughed and called to them and threw them flowers, but they never turned to look . . . eyes straight before. They passed like men of destiny." She threw out her hands with a swift movement and dropped them in her lap. The emotion of that day came back in her face. As Claude looked at her burning cheeks, her burning eyes, he understood that the strain of this war had given her a perception that was almost like a gift of prophecy.

A woman came up the hill carrying a baby. Mlle. de Courcy went to meet her and took her into the house. Claude sat down again, almost lost to himself in the feeling of being completely understood, of being no longer a stranger. In the far distance

the big guns were booming at intervals. Down in the garden
Louis was singing. Again he wished he knew the words of Louis'
songs. The airs were rather melancholy, but they were sung
very cheerfully. There was something open and warm about
the boy's voice, as there was about his face—something blond,
too. It was distinctly a blond voice, like summer wheat-fields,
ripe and waving. Claude sat alone for half an hour or more,
tasting a new kind of happiness, a new kind of sadness. Ruin
and new birth; the shudder of ugly things in the past, the trembling image of beautiful ones on the horizon; finding and losing; that was life, he saw.

When his hostess came back, he moved her chair for her out
of the creeping sunlight. "I didn't know there were any French
girls like you," he said simply, as she sat down.

She smiled. "I do not think there are any French girls left.
There are children and women. I was twenty-one when the war
came, and I had never been anywhere without my mother or my
brother or sister. Within a year I went all over France alone; with
soldiers, with Senegalese, with anybody. Everything is different
with us." She lived at Versailles, she told him, where her father
had been an instructor in the Military School. He had died since
the beginning of the war. Her grandfather was killed in the war
of 1870. Hers was a family of soldiers, but not one of the men
would be left to see the day of victory.

She looked so tired that Claude knew he had no right to
stay. Long shadows were falling in the garden. It was hard to
leave; but an hour more or less wouldn't matter. Two people
could hardly give each other more if they were together for
years, he thought.

"Will you tell me where I can come and see you, if we both get
through this war?" he asked as he rose.

He wrote it down in his notebook.

"I shall look for you," she said, giving him her hand.

There was nothing to do but to take his helmet and go. At the
edge of the hill, just before he plunged down the path, he
stopped and glanced back at the garden lying flattened in the

sun; the three stone arches, the dahlias and marigolds, the glistening boxwood wall. He had left something on the hilltop which he would never find again.

The next afternoon Claude and his sergeant set off for the front. They had been told at Headquarters that they could shorten their route by following the big road to the military cemetery, and then turning to the left. It was not advisable to go the latter half of the way before nightfall, so they took their time through the belt of straggling crops and hayfields.

When they struck the road they came upon a big Highlander sitting in the end of an empty supply wagon, smoking a pipe and rubbing the dried mud out of his kilts. The horses were munching in their nose-bags, and the driver had disappeared. The Americans hadn't happened to meet with any Highlanders before, and were curious. This one must be a good fighter, they thought; a brawny giant with a bulldog jaw, and a face as red and knobby as his knees. More because he admired the looks of the man than because he needed information, Hicks went up and asked him if he had noticed a military cemetery on the road back. The Kiltie nodded.

"About how far back would you say it was?"

"I wouldn't say at all. I take no account of their kilometers," he replied drily, rubbing away at his skirt as if he had it in a washtub.

"Well, about how long will it take us to walk it?"

"That I couldn't say. A Scotsman would do it in an hour."

"I guess a Yankee can do it as quick as a Scotchman, can't he?" Hicks asked jovially.

"That I couldn't say. You've been four years gettin' this far, I know verra well."

Hicks blinked as if he had been hit. "Oh, if that's the way you talk —"

"That's the way I do," said the other sourly.

Claude put out a warning hand. "Come on, Hicks. You'll get nothing by it." They went up the road very much disconcerted. Hicks kept thinking of things he might have said.

When he was angry, the Sergeant's forehead puffed up and became dark red, like a young baby's. "What did you call me off for?" he sputtered.

"I don't see where you'd have come out in an argument, and you certainly couldn't have licked him."

They turned aside at the cemetery to wait until the sun went down. It was unfenced, unsodded, and a wagon trail ran through the middle, bisecting the square. On one side were the French graves, with white crosses; on the other side the German graves, with black crosses. Poppies and cornflowers ran over them. The Americans strolled about, reading the names. Here and there the soldier's photograph was nailed upon his cross, left by some comrade to perpetuate his memory a little longer.

The birds, that always came to life at dusk and dawn, began to sing, flying home from somewhere. Claude and Hicks sat down between the mounds and began to smoke while the sun dropped. Lines of dead trees marked the red west. This was a dreary stretch of country, even to boys brought up on the flat prairie. They smoked in silence, meditating and waiting for night. On a cross at their feet the inscription read merely:

Soldat Inconnu, Mort pour La France.

A very good epitaph, Claude was thinking. Most of the boys who fell in this war were unknown, even to themselves. They were too young. They died and took their secret with them, — what they were and what they might have been. The name that stood was *La France*. How much that name had come to mean to him, since he first saw a shoulder of land bulk up in the dawn from the deck of the *Anchises*. It was a pleasant name to say over in one's mind, where one could make it as passionately nasal as one pleased and never blush.

Hicks, too, had been lost in his reflections. Now he broke the silence. "Somehow, Lieutenant, *'mort'* seems deader than 'dead.' It has a coffinish sound. And over there they're all *'tod,'* and it's all the same damned silly thing. Look at them set out here, black and white, like a checkerboard. The next question is, who put 'em here, and what's the good of it?"

"Search me," the other murmured absently.

Hicks rolled another cigarette and sat smoking it, his plump face wrinkled with the gravity and labour of his cerebration. "Well," he brought out at last, "we'd better hike. This afterglow will hang on for an hour,—always does, over here."

"I suppose we had." They rose to go. The white crosses were now violet, and the black ones had altogether melted in the shadow. Behind the dead trees in the west, a long smear of red still burned. To the north, the guns were tuning up with a deep thunder. "Somebody's getting peppered up there. Do owls always hoot in graveyards?"

"Just what I was wondering, Lieutenant. It's a peaceful spot, otherwise. Good-night, boys," said Hicks kindly, as they left the graves behind them.

They were soon finding their way among shellholes, and jumping trench-tops in the dark,—beginning to feel cheerful at getting back to their chums and their own little group. Hicks broke out and told Claude how he and Dell Able meant to go into business together when they got home; were going to open a garage and automobile-repair shop. Under their talk, in the minds of both, that lonely spot lingered, and the legend: *Soldat Inconnu, Mort pour La France.*

XI

AFTER four days' rest in the rear, the Battalion went to the front again in new country, about ten kilometers east of the trench they had relieved before. One morning Colonel Scott sent for Claude and Gerhardt and spread his maps out on the table.

"We are going to clean them out there in F 6 tonight, and straighten our line. The thing that bothers us is that little village stuck up on the hill, where the enemy machine guns have a strong position. I want to get them out of there before the Battalion goes over. We can't spare too many men, and I don't like to send out more officers than I can help; it won't do to reduce the Battalion for the major operation. Do you think you two boys could manage it with a hundred men? The point is, you will have to be out and back before our artillery begins at three o'clock."

Under the hill where the village stood, ran a deep ravine, and from this ravine a twisting water course wound up the hillside. By climbing this gully, the raiders should be able to fall on the machine gunners from the rear and surprise them. But first they must get across the open stretch, nearly one and a half kilometers wide, between the American line and the ravine, without attracting attention. It was raining now, and they could safely count on a dark night.

The night came on black enough. The Company crossed the open stretch without provoking fire, and slipped into the ravine to wait for the hour of attack. A young doctor, a Pennsylvanian, lately attached to the staff, had volunteered to come with them, and he arranged a dressing station at the bottom of the ravine, where the stretchers were left. They were to pick up their wounded on the way back. Anything left in that area would be exposed to the artillery fire later on.

At ten o'clock the men began to ascend the water-course, creeping through pools and little waterfalls, making a continuous spludgy sound, like pigs rubbing against the sty. Claude, with the head of the column, was just pulling out of the gully on the hillside above the village, when a flare went up, and a volley of fire broke from the brush on the up-hill side of the water-course; machine guns, opening on the exposed line crawling below. The Hun had been warned that the Americans were crossing the plain and had anticipated their way of approach. The men in the gully were trapped; they could not retaliate with effect, and the bullets from the Maxims bounded on the rocks about them like hail. Gerhardt ran along the edge of the line, urging the men not to fall back and double on themselves, but to break out of the gully on the down-hill side and scatter.

Claude, with his group, started back. "Go into the brush and get 'em! Our fellows have got no chance down there. Grenades while they last, then bayonets. Pull your plugs and don't hold on too long."

They were already on the run, charging the brush. The Hun gunners knew the hill like a book, and when the bombs began bursting among them, they took to trails and burrows. "Don't follow them off into the rocks," Claude kept calling. "Straight ahead! Clear everything to the ravine."

As the German gunners made for cover, the firing into the gully stopped, and the arrested column poured up the steep defile after Gerhardt.

Claude and his party found themselves back at the foot of the hill, at the edge of the ravine from which they had started. Heavy firing on the hill above told them the rest of the men had got through. The quickest way back to the scene of action was by the same water-course they had climbed before. They dropped into

343

it and started up. Claude, at the rear, felt the ground rise under him, and he was swept with a mountain of earth and rock down into the ravine.

He never knew whether he lost consciousness or not. It seemed to him that he went on having continuous sensations. The first, was that of being blown to pieces; of swelling to an enormous size under intolerable pressure, and then bursting. Next he felt himself shrink and tingle, like a frost-bitten body thawing out. Then he swelled again, and burst. This was repeated, he didn't know how often. He soon realized that he was lying under a great weight of earth;—his body, not his head. He felt rain falling on his face. His left hand was free, and still attached to his arm. He moved it cautiously to his face. He seemed to be bleeding from the nose and ears. Now he began to wonder where he was hurt; he felt as if he were full of shell splinters. Everything was buried but his head and left shoulder. A voice was calling from somewhere below.

"Are any of you fellows alive?"

Claude closed his eyes against the rain beating in his face. The same voice came again, with a note of patient despair.

"If there's anybody left alive in this hole, won't he speak up? I'm badly hurt myself."

That must be the new doctor; wasn't his dressing station somewhere down here? Hurt, he said. Claude tried to move his legs a little. Perhaps, if he could get out from under the dirt, he might hold together long enough to reach the doctor. He began to wriggle and pull. The wet earth sucked at him; it was painful business. He braced himself with his elbows, but kept slipping back.

"I'm the only one left, then?" said the mournful voice below.

At last Claude worked himself out of his burrow, but he was unable to stand. Every time he tried to stand, he got faint and seemed to burst again. Something was the matter with his right ankle, too—he couldn't bear his weight on it. Perhaps he had been too near the shell to be hit; he had heard the boys tell of such cases. It had exploded under his feet and swept him down into the ravine, but hadn't left any metal in his body. If it had put anything into him, it would have put so much that he wouldn't be sitting here speculating. He began to crawl down the slope on all fours. "Is that the Doctor? Where are you?"

"Here, on a stretcher. They shelled us. Who are you? Our fellows got up, didn't they?"

"I guess most of them did. What happened back here?"

"I'm afraid it's my fault," the voice said sadly. "I used my flash light, and that must have given them the range. They put three or four shells right on top of us. The fellows that got hurt in the gully kept stringing back here, and I couldn't do anything in the dark. I had to have a light to do anything. I just finished putting on a Johnson splint when the first shell came. I guess they're all done for now."

"How many were there?"

"Fourteen, I think. Some of them weren't much hurt. They'd all be alive, if I hadn't come out with you."

"Who were they? But you don't know our names yet, do you? You didn't see Lieutenant Gerhardt among them?"

"Don't think so."

"Nor Sergeant Hicks, the fat fellow?"

"Don't think so."

"Where are you hurt?"

"Abdominal. I can't tell anything without a light. I lost my flash light. It never occurred to me that it could make trouble; it's one I use at home, when the babies are sick," the doctor murmured.

Claude tried to strike a match, with no success. "Wait a minute, where's your helmet?" He took off his metal hat, held it over the doctor, and managed to strike a light underneath it. The wounded man had already loosened his trousers, and now he pulled up his bloody shirt. His groin and abdomen were torn on the left side. The wound, and the stretcher on which he lay, supported a mass of dark, coagulated blood that looked like a great cow's liver.

"I guess I've got mine," the Doctor murmured as the match went out.

Claude struck another. "Oh, that can't be! Our fellows will be back pretty soon, and we can do something for you."

"No use, Lieutenant. Do you suppose you could strip a coat off one of those poor fellows? I feel the cold terribly in my intestines. I had a bottle of French brandy, but I suppose it's buried."

Claude stripped off his own coat, which was warm on the inside, and began feeling about in the mud for the brandy. He wondered why the poor man wasn't screaming with pain. The firing on the hill had ceased, except for the occasional click of a Maxim, off in the rocks somewhere. His watch said 12:10; could anything have miscarried up there?

Suddenly, voices above, a clatter of boots on the shale. He began shouting to them.

"Coming, coming!" He knew the voice. Gerhardt and his rifles ran down into the ravine with a bunch of prisoners. Claude called to them to be careful. "Don't strike a light! They've been shelling down here."

"All right are you, Wheeler? Where are the wounded?"

"There aren't any but the Doctor and me. Get us out of here quick. I'm all right, but I can't walk."

They put Claude on a stretcher and sent him ahead. Four big Germans carried him, and they were prodded to a lope by Hicks and Dell Able. Four of their own men took up the doctor, and Gerhardt walked beside him. In spite of their care, the motion started the blood again and tore away the clots that had formed over his wounds. He began to vomit blood and to strangle. The men put the stretcher down. Gerhardt lifted the Doctor's head. "It's over," he said presently. "Better make the best time you can."

They picked up their load again. "Them that are carrying him now won't jolt him," said Oscar, the pious Swede.

B Company lost nineteen men in the raid. Two days later the Company went off on a ten-day leave. Claude's sprained ankle was twice its natural size, but to avoid being sent to the hospital he had to march to the railhead. Sergeant Hicks got him a giant shoe he found stuck on the barbed wire entanglement. Claude and Gerhardt were going off on their leave together.

XII

A rainy autumn night; Papa Joubert sat reading his paper. He heard a heavy pounding on his garden gate. Kicking off his slippers, he put on the wooden sabots he kept for mud, shuffled across the dripping garden, and opened the door into the dark street. Two tall figures with rifles and kits confronted him. In a moment he began embracing them, calling to his wife:

"*Nom de diable, Maman, c'est David, David et Claude, tous les deux!*"

Sorry-looking soldiers they appeared when they stood in the candle-light, — plastered with clay, their metal hats shining like copper bowls, their clothes dripping pools of water upon the flags of the kitchen floor. Mme. Joubert kissed their wet cheeks, and Monsieur, now that he could see them, embraced them again. Whence had they come, and how had it fared with them, up there? Very well, as anybody could see. What did they want first, — supper, perhaps? Their room was always ready for them; and the clothes they had left were in the big chest.

David explained that their shirts had not once been dry for four days; and what they most desired was to be dry and to be clean. Old Martha, already in bed, was routed out to heat water. M. Joubert carried the big washtub upstairs. Tomorrow for conversation, he said; tonight for repose. The boys followed him and began to peel off their wet uniforms, leaving them in two sodden piles on the floor. There was one bath for both, and they threw up a coin to decide which should get into the warm water first. M. Joubert, seeing Claude's fat ankle strapped up in adhesive bandages, began to chuckle. "Oh, I see the Boche made you dance up there!"

When they were clad in clean pyjamas out of the chest, Papa Joubert carried their shirts and socks down for Martha to wash. He returned with the big meat platter, on which was an omelette made of twelve eggs and stuffed with bacon and fried potatoes. Mme. Joubert brought the three-story earthen coffee-pot to the door and called, *"Bon appetit!"* The host poured the coffee and cut up the loaf with his clasp knife. He sat down to watch them eat. How had they found things up there, anyway? The Boches polite and agreeable as usual? Finally, when there was not a crumb of anything left, he poured for each a little glass of brandy, *"pour aider la digestion,"* and wished them good-night. He took the candle with him.

Perfect bliss, Claude reflected, as the chill of the sheets grew warm around his body, and he sniffed in the pillow the old smell of lavender. To be so warm, so dry, so clean, so beloved! The journey down, reviewed from here, seemed beautiful. As soon as they had got out of the region of martyred trees, they found the land of France turning gold. All along the river valleys the poplars and cottonwoods had changed from green to yellow, — evenly coloured, looking like candle-flames in the mist and rain. Across the fields, along the horizon they ran, like torches passed from hand to hand, and all the willows by the little streams had become silver. The vineyards were green still, thickly spotted with curly, blood-red branches. It all flashed back beside his pillow in the dark: this beautiful land, this beautiful people, this beautiful omelette; gold poplars, blue-green vineyards, wet, scarlet vine-leaves, rain dripping into the court, fragrant darkness . . . sleep, stronger than all.

XIII

THE woodland path was deep in leaves. Claude and David were lying on the dry, springy heather among the flint boulders. Gerhardt, with his Stetson over his eyes, was presumably asleep. They were having fine weather for their holiday. The forest rose about this open glade like an amphitheatre, in golden terraces of horsechestnut and beech. The big nuts dropped velvety and brown, as if they had been soaked in oil, and disappeared in the dry leaves below. Little black yew trees, that had not been visible in the green of summer, stood out among the curly yellow brakes. Through the grey netting of the beech twigs, stiff holly bushes glittered.

It was the Wheeler way to dread false happiness, to feel cowardly about being fooled. Since he had come back, Claude had more than once wondered whether he took too much for granted and felt more at home here than he had any right to feel. The Americans were prone, he had observed, to make themselves very much at home, to mistake good manners for good-will. He had no right to doubt the affection of the Jouberts, however; that was genuine and personal,—not a smooth surface under which almost any shade of scorn might lie and laugh . . . was not, in short, the treacherous "French politeness" by which one must not let oneself be taken in. Merely having seen the season change in a country gave one the sense of having been there for a long time. And, anyway, he wasn't a tourist. He was here on legitimate business.

Claude's sprained ankle was still badly swollen. Madame Joubert was sure he ought not to move about on it at all, begged him to sit in the garden all day and nurse it. But the surgeon at the front had told him that if he once stopped walking, he would have to go to the hospital. So, with the help of his host's best holly-wood cane, he limped out into the forest every day. This afternoon he was tempted to go still farther. Madame Joubert had told him about some caves at the other end of the wood, underground chambers where the country people had gone to live in times of great misery, long ago, in the English wars. The English wars; he could not remember just how far back they were,—but long enough to make one feel comfortable. As for him, perhaps he would never go home at all. Perhaps, when this great affair was over, he would buy a little farm and stay here for the rest of his life. That was a project he liked to play with. There was no chance for the kind of life he wanted at home, where people were always buying and selling, building and pulling down. He had begun to believe that the Americans were a people of shallow emotions. That was the way Gerhardt had put it once; and if it was true, there was no cure for it. Life was so short that it meant nothing at all unless it were continually reinforced by something that endured; unless the shadows of individual existence came and went against a background that held together. While he was absorbed in his day dream of farming in France, his companion stirred and rolled over on his elbow.

"You know we are to join the Battalion at A——. They'll be living like kings there. Hicks will get so fat he'll drop over on the march. Headquarters must have something particularly nasty in mind; the infantry is always fed up before a slaughter. But I've been thinking; I have some old friends at A——. Suppose we go on there a day early, and get them to take us in? It's a fine old place, and I ought to go to see them. The son was a fellow student of mine at the Conservatoire. He was killed the second winter of the war. I used to go up there for the holidays with him; I would like to see his mother and sister again. You've no objection?"

Claude did not answer at once. He lay squinting off at the beech trees, without moving. "You always avoid that subject with me, don't you?" he said presently.

"What subject?"

"Oh, anything to do with the Conservatoire, or your profession."

"I haven't any profession at present. I'll never go back to the violin."

"You mean you couldn't make up for the time you'll lose?"

Gerhardt settled his back against a rock and got out his pipe. "That would be difficult; but other things would be harder. I've lost much more than time."

"Couldn't you have got exemption, one way or another?"

"I might have. My friends wanted to take it up and make a test case of me. But I couldn't stand for it. I didn't feel I was a good enough violinist to admit that I wasn't a man. I often wish I had been in Paris that summer when the war broke out; then I would have gone into the French army on the first impulse, with the other students, and it would have been better."

David paused and sat puffing at his pipe. Just then a soft movement stirred the brakes on the hillside. A little barefoot girl stood there, looking about. She had heard voices, but at first did not see the uniforms that blended with the yellow and brown of the wood. Then she saw the sun shining on two heads; one square, and amber in colour, — the other reddish bronze, long and narrow. She took their friendliness for granted and came down the hill, stopping now and again to pick up shiny horsechestnuts and pop them into a sack she was dragging. David called to her and asked her whether the nuts were good to eat.

"*Oh, non!*" she exclaimed, her face expressing the liveliest terror, "*pour les cochons!*" These inexperienced Americans might eat almost anything. The boys laughed and gave her some pennies, "*pour les cochons aussi.*" She stole about the edge of the wood, stirring among the leaves for nuts, and watching the two soldiers.

Gerhardt knocked out his pipe and began to fill it again. "I went home to see my mother in May, of 1914. I wasn't here when the war broke out. The Conservatoire closed at once, so I arranged a concert tour in the States that winter, and did very well. That was before all the little Russians went over, and the field wasn't so crowded. I had a second season, and that went well. But I was getting more nervous all the time; I was only half there." He smoked thoughtfully, sitting with folded arms, as if he were going over a succession of events or states of feeling. "When my number was drawn, I reported to see what I could do about getting out; I took a look at the other fellows who were trying to squirm, and chucked it. I've never been sorry. Not long afterward, my violin was smashed, and my career seemed to go along with it."

Claude asked him what he meant.

"While I was at Camp Dix, I had to play at one of the entertainments. My violin, a Stradivarius, was in a vault in New York. I didn't need it for that concert, any more than I need it at this minute; yet I went to town and brought it out. I was taking it up from the station in a military car, and a drunken taxi driver ran into us. I wasn't hurt, but the violin, lying across my knees, was smashed into a thousand pieces. I didn't know what it meant then; but since, I've seen so many beautiful old things smashed . . . I've become a fatalist."

Claude watched his brooding head against the grey flint rock.

"You ought to have kept out of the whole thing. Any army man would say so."

David's head went back against the boulder, and he threw one of the chestnuts lightly into the air. "Oh, one violinist more or less doesn't matter! But who is ever going back to anything? That's what I want to know!"

Claude felt guilty; as if David must have guessed what apostasy had been going on in his own mind this afternoon. "You don't believe we are going to get out of this war what we went in for, do you?" he asked suddenly.

"Absolutely not," the other replied with cool indifference.

"Then I certainly don't see what you're here for!"

"Because in 1917 I was twenty-four years old, and able to bear arms. The war was put up to our generation. I don't know what for; the sins of our fathers, probably. Certainly not to make the world safe for Democracy, or any rhetoric of that sort. When I was doing stretcher work, I had to tell myself over and over that nothing would come of it, but that it had to be. Sometimes, though, I think something must. . . . Nothing we expect, but something unforeseen." He paused and shut his eyes. "You remember in the old mythology tales how, when the sons of the gods were born, the mothers always died in agony? Maybe it's only Semêle I'm thinking of. At any rate, I've sometimes wondered whether the young men of our time had to die to bring a new idea into the world . . . something Olympian. I'd like to know. I think I shall know. Since I've been over here this time, I've come to believe in immortality. Do you?"

Claude was confused by this quiet question. "I hardly know. I've never been able to make up my mind."

"Oh, don't bother about it! If it comes to you, it comes. You don't have to go after it. I arrived at it in quite the same way I used to get things in art,—knowing them and living on them before I understood them. Such ideas used to seem childish to me." Gerhardt sprang up. "Now, have I told you what you want to know about my case?" He looked down at Claude with a curious glimmer of amusement and affection. "I'm going to stretch my legs. It's four o'clock."

He disappeared among the red pine stems, where the sunlight made a rose-coloured lake, as it used to do in the summer . . . as it would do in all the years to come, when they were not there to see it, Claude was thinking. He pulled his hat over his eyes and went to sleep.

The little girl on the edge of the beechwood left her sack and stole quietly down the hill. Sitting in the heather and drawing her feet up under her, she stayed still for a long time, and regarded with curiosity the relaxed, deep-breathing body of the American soldier.

The next day was Claude's twenty-fifth birthday, and in honour of that event Papa Joubert produced a bottle of old Burgundy from his cellar, one of a few dozens he had laid in for great occasions when he was a young man.

During that week of idleness at Madame Joubert's, Claude often thought that the period of happy "youth," about which his old friend Mrs. Erlich used to talk, and which he had never experienced, was being made up to him now. He was having his youth in France. He knew that nothing like this would ever come again; the fields and woods would never again be laced over with this hazy enchantment. As he came up the village street in the purple evening, the smell of wood-smoke from the chimneys went to his head like a narcotic, opened the pores of his skin, and sometimes made the tears come to his eyes. Life had after all turned out well for him, and everything had a noble significance. The nervous tension in which he had lived for years now seemed incredible to him . . . absurd and childish, when he thought of it at all. He did not torture himself with recollections. He was beginning over again.

One night he dreamed that he was at home; out in the ploughed fields, where he could see nothing but the furrowed brown earth, stretching from horizon to horizon. Up and down it moved a boy, with a plough and two horses. At first he thought it was his brother Ralph; but on coming nearer, he saw it was himself,—and he was full of fear for this boy. Poor Claude, he would never, never get away; he was going to miss everything! While he was struggling to speak to Claude, and warn him, he awoke.

In the years when he went to school in Lincoln, he was always hunting for some one whom he could admire without reservations; some one he could envy, emulate, wish to be. Now he believed that even then he must have had some faint image of a man like Gerhardt in his mind. It was only in war times that their paths would have been likely to cross; or that they would have had anything to do together . . . any of the common interests that make men friends.

XIV

GERHARDT and Claude Wheeler alighted from a taxi before the open gates of a square-roofed, solid-looking house, where all the shutters on the front were closed, and the tops of many trees showed above the garden wall. They crossed a paved court and rang at the door. An old valet admitted the young men, and took them through a wide hall to the salon, which opened on the garden. Madame and Mademoiselle would be down very soon. David went to one of the long windows and looked out. "They have kept it up, in spite of everything. It was always lovely here."

The garden was spacious,—like a little park. On one side was a tennis court, on the other a fountain, with a pool and water-lilies. The north wall was hidden by ancient yews; on the south two rows of plane trees, cut square, made a long arbour. At the back of the garden there were fine old lindens. The gravel walks wound about beds of gorgeous autumn flowers; in the rose garden, small white roses were still blooming, though the leaves were already red.

Two ladies entered the drawing-room. The mother was short, plump, and rosy, with strong, rather masculine features and yellowish white hair. The tears flashed into her eyes as David bent to kiss her hand, and she embraced him and touched both his cheeks with her lips.

"*Et vous, vous aussi!*" she murmured, touching the coat of his uniform with her fingers. There was but a moment of softness. She gathered herself up like an old general, Claude thought, as he stood watching the group from the window, drew her daughter forward, and asked David whether he recognized the little girl with whom he used to play. Mademoiselle Claire was not at all like her mother; slender, dark, dressed in a white *costume de tennis* and an apple green hat with black ribbons, she looked very modern and casual and unconcerned. She was already telling David she was glad he had arrived early, as now they would be able to have a game of tennis before tea. *Maman* would bring her knitting to the garden and watch them. This last suggestion relieved Claude's apprehension that he might be left alone with his hostess. When David called him and presented him to the ladies, Mlle. Claire gave him a quick handshake, and said she would be very glad to try him out on the court as soon as she had beaten David. They would find tennis shoes in their room, — a collection of shoes, for the feet of all nations; her brother's, some that his Russian friend had forgotten when he hurried off to be mobilized, and a pair lately left by an English officer who was quartered on them. She and her mother would wait in the garden. She rang for the old valet.

The Americans found themselves in a large room upstairs, where two modern iron beds stood out conspicuous among heavy mahogany bureaus and desks and dressing-tables, stuffed chairs and velvet carpets and dull red brocade window hangings. David went at once into the little dressing-room and began to array himself for the tennis court. Two suits of flannels and a row of soft shirts hung there on the wall.

"Aren't you going to change?" he asked, noticing that Claude stood stiff and unbending by the window, looking down into the: garden.

"Why should I?" said Claude scornfully. "I don't play tennis. I never had a racket in my hand."

"Too bad. She used to play very well, though she was only a youngster then." Gerhardt was regarding his legs in trousers two inches too short for him. "How everything has changed, and yet how everything is still the same! It's like coming back to places in dreams."

"They don't give you much time to dream, I should say!" Claude remarked.

"Fortunately!"

"Explain to the girl that I don't play, will you? I'll be down later."

"As you like."

Claude stood in the window, watching Gerhardt's bare head and Mlle. Claire's green hat and long brown arm go bounding about over the court.

When Gerhardt came to change before tea, he found his fellow officer standing before his bag, which was open, but not unpacked.

"What's the matter? Feeling shellshock again?"

"Not exactly." Claude bit his lip. "The fact is, Dave, I don't feel just comfortable here. Oh, the people are all right! But I'm out of place. I'm going to pull out and get a billet somewhere else, and let you visit your friends in peace. Why should I be here? These people don't keep a hotel."

"They very nearly do, from what they've been telling me. They've had a string of Scotch and English quartered on them. They like it, too,—or have the good manners to pretend they do. Of course, you'll do as you like, but you'll hurt their feelings and put me in an awkward position. To be frank, I don't see how you can go away without being distinctly rude."

Claude stood looking down at the contents of his bag in an irresolute attitude. Catching a glimpse of his face in one of the big mirrors, Gerhardt saw that he looked perplexed and miserable. His flash of temper died, and he put his hand lightly on his friend's shoulder.

"Come on, Claude! This is too absurd. You don't even have to dress, thanks to your uniform,—and you don't have to talk, since you're not supposed to know the language. I thought you'd like coming here. These people have had an awfully rough time; can't you admire their pluck?"

"Oh, yes, I do! It's awkward for me, though." Claude pulled off his coat and began to brush his hair vigorously. "I guess I've always been more afraid of the French than of the Germans. It takes courage to stay, you understand. I want to run."

"But why? What makes you want to?"

"Oh, I don't know! Something in the house, in the atmosphere."

"Something disagreeable?"

"No. Something agreeable."

David laughed. "Oh, you'll get over that!"

They had tea in the garden, English fashion—English tea, too, Mlle. Claire informed them, left by the English officers.

At dinner a third member of the family was introduced, a little boy with a cropped head and big black eyes. He sat on Claude's left, quiet and shy in his velvet jacket, though he followed the conversation eagerly, especially when it touched upon his brother René, killed at Verdun in the second winter of the war. The mother and sister talked about him as if he were living, about his letters and his plans, and his friends at the Conservatoire and in the Army.

Mlle. Claire told Gerhardt news of all the girl students he had known in Paris: how this one was singing for the soldiers; another, when she was nursing in a hospital which was bombed in an air raid, had carried twenty wounded men out of the burning building, one after another, on her back, like sacks of flour. Alice, the dancer, had gone into the English Red Cross and learned English. Odette had married a New Zealander, an officer who was said to be a cannibal; it was well known that his tribe had eaten two Auvergnat missionaries. There was a great deal more that Claude could not understand, but he got enough to see that for these women the war was France, the war was life, and everything that went into it. To be alive, to be conscious and have one's faculties, was to be in the war.

After dinner, when they went into the salon, Madame Fleury asked David whether he would like to see René's violin again, and nodded to the little boy. He slipped away and returned carrying the case, which he placed on the table. He opened it carefully and took off the velvet cloth, as if this was his peculiar office, then handed the instrument to Gerhardt.

David turned it over under the candles, telling Madame Fleury that he would have known it anywhere, René's wonderful Amati, almost too exquisite in tone for the concert hall, like a woman who is too beautiful for the stage. The family stood round and listened to his praise with evident satisfaction. Madame Fleury told him that Lucien was *très sérieux* with his music, that his master was well pleased with him, and when his hand was a little larger he would be allowed to play upon René's violin. Claude watched the little boy as he stood looking at the instrument in David's hands; in each of his big black eyes a candle flame was reflected, as if some steady fire were actually burning there.

"What is it, Lucien?" his mother asked.

"If Monsieur David would be so good as to play before I must go to bed—" he murmured entreatingly.

"But, Lucien, I am a soldier now. I have not worked at all for two years. The Amati would think it had fallen into the hands of a Boche."

Lucien smiled. "Oh, no! It is too intelligent for that. A little, please," and he sat down on a footstool before the sofa in confident anticipation.

Mlle. Claire went to the piano. David frowned and began to tune the violin. Madame Fleury called the old servant and told him to light the sticks that lay in the fireplace. She took the armchair at the right of the hearth and motioned Claude to a seat on the left. The little boy kept his stool at the other end of the room. Mlle. Claire began the orchestral introduction to the Saint-Saëns concerto.

"Oh, not that!" David lifted his chin and looked at her in perplexity.

She made no reply, but played on, her shoulders bent forward. Lucien drew his knees up under his chin and shivered. When the time came, the violin made its entrance. David had put it back under his chin mechanically, and the instrument broke into that suppressed, bitter melody.

They played for a long while. At last David stopped and wiped his forehead. "I'm afraid I can't do anything with the third movement, really."

"Nor can I. But that was the last thing René played on it, the night before he went away, after his last leave." She began again, and David followed. Madame Fleury sat with half-closed eyes, looking into the fire. Claude, his lips compressed, his hands on his knees, was watching his friend's back. The music was a part of his own confused emotions. He was torn between generous admiration, and bitter, bitter envy. What would it mean to be able to do anything as well as that, to have a hand capable of delicacy and precision and power? If he had been taught to do anything at all, he would not be sitting here tonight a wooden thing amongst living people. He felt that a man might have been made of him, but nobody had taken the trouble to do it; tongue-tied, foot-tied, hand-tied. If one were born into this world like a bear cub or a bull calf, one could only paw and upset things, break and destroy, all one's life.

Gerhardt wrapped the violin up in its cloth. The little boy thanked him and carried it away. Madame Fleury and her daughter wished their guests good-night.

David said he was warm, and suggested going into the garden to smoke before they went to bed. He opened one of the long windows and they stepped out on the terrace. Dry leaves were rustling down on the walks; the yew trees made a solid wall, blacker than the darkness. The fountain must have caught the starlight; it was the only shining thing,—a little clear column of twinkling silver. The boys strolled in silence to the end of the walk.

"I guess you'll go back to your profession, all right," Claude remarked, in the unnatural tone in which people sometimes speak of things they know nothing about.

"Not I. Of course, I had to play for them. Music has always been like a religion in this house. Listen," he put up his hand; far away the regular pulsation of the big guns sounded through the still night. "That's all that matters now. It has killed everything else."

"I don't believe it." Claude stopped for a moment by the edge of the fountain, trying to collect his thoughts. "I don't believe it has killed anything. It has only scattered things." He glanced about hurriedly at the sleeping house, the sleeping garden, the clear, starry sky not very far overhead. "It's men like you that get the worst of it," he broke out. "But as for me, I never knew there was anything worth living for, till this war came on. Before that, the world seemed like a business proposition."

"You'll admit it's a costly way of providing adventure for the young," said David drily.

"Maybe so; all the same . . ."

Claude pursued the argument to himself long after they were in their luxurious beds and David was asleep. No battlefield or shattered country he had seen was as ugly as this world would be if men like his brother Bayliss controlled it altogether. Until the war broke out, he had supposed they did control it; his boyhood had been clouded and enervated by that belief. The Prussians had believed it, too, apparently. But the event had shown that there were a great many people left who cared about something else.

The intervals of the distant artillery fire grew shorter, as if the big guns were tuning up, choking to get something out. Claude sat up in his bed and listened. The sound of the guns had from the first been pleasant to him, had given him a feeling of confidence and safety; tonight he knew why. What they said was, that men could still die for an idea; and would burn all they had made to keep their dreams. He knew the future of the world was safe; the careful planners would never be able to put it into a straight-jacket,—cunning and prudence would never have it to themselves. Why, that little boy downstairs, with the candlelight in his eyes, when it came to the last cry, as they said, could "carry on" for ever! Ideals were not archaic things, beautiful and impotent; they were the real sources of power among men. As long as that was true, and now he knew it was true—he had come all this way to find out—he had no quarrel with Destiny. Nor did he envy David. He would give his own adventure for no man's. On the edge of sleep it seemed to glimmer, like the clear column of the fountain, like the new moon,—alluring, half-averted, the bright face of danger.

WHEN Claude and David rejoined their Battalion on the 20th of September, the end of the war looked as far away as ever. The collapse of Bulgaria was unknown to the American army, and their acquaintance with European affairs was so slight that this would have meant very little to them had they heard of it. The German army still held the north and east of France, and no one could say how much vitality was left in that sprawling body.

The Battalion entrained at Arras. Lieutenant Colonel Scott had orders to proceed to the railhead, and then advance on foot into the Argonne.

The cars were crowded, and the railway journey was long and fatiguing. They detrained at night, in the rain, at what the men said seemed to be the jumping-off place. There was no town, and the railway station had been bombed the day before, by an air fleet out to explode artillery ammunition. A mound of brick, and holes full of water told where it had been. The Colonel sent Claude out with a patrol to find some place for the men to sleep. The patrol came upon a field of strawstacks, and at the end of it found a black farmhouse.

Claude went up and hammered on the door. Silence. He kept hammering and calling, "The Americans are here!" A shutter opened. The farmer stuck his head out and demanded gruffly what was wanted; "What now?"

Claude explained in his best French that an American battalion had just come in; might they sleep in his field if they did not destroy his stacks?

"Sure," replied the farmer, and shut the window.

That one word, coming out of the dark in such an unpromising place, had a cheering effect upon the patrol, and upon the men, when it was repeated to them. "Sure, eh?" They kept laughing over it as they beat about the field and dug into the straw. Those who couldn't burrow into a stack lay down in the muddy stubble. They were asleep before they could feel sorry for themselves.

The farmer came out to offer his stable to the officers, and to beg them not on any account to make a light. They had never been bothered here by air raids until yesterday, and it must be because the Americans were coming and were sending in ammunition.

Gerhardt, who was called to talk to him, told the farmer the Colonel must study his map, and for that the man took them down into the cellar, where the children were asleep. Before he lay down on the straw bed his orderly had made for him, the Colonel kept telling names and kilometers off on his fingers. For officers like Colonel Scott the names of places constituted one of the real hardships of the war. His mind worked slowly, but it was always on his job, and he could go without sleep for more hours together than any of his officers. Tonight he had scarcely lain down, when a sentinel brought in a runner with a message. The Colonel had to go into the cellar again to read it. He was to meet Colonel Harvey at Prince Joachim farm, as early as possible tomorrow morning. The runner would act as guide.

The Colonel sat with his eye on his watch, and interrogated the messenger about the road and the time it would take to get over the ground. "What's Fritz's temper up here, generally speaking?"

"That's as it happens, sir. Sometimes we nab a night patrol of a dozen or fifteen and send them to the rear under a one-man guard. Then, again, a little bunch of Heinies will fight like the devil. They say it depends on what part of Germany they come from; the Bavarians and Saxons are the bravest."

Colonel Scott waited for an hour, and then went about, shaking his sleeping officers.

"Yes, sir." Captain Maxey sprang to his feet as if he had been caught in a disgraceful act. He called his sergeants, and they began to beat the men up out of the strawstacks and puddles. In half an hour they were on the road.

This was the Battalion's first march over really bad roads, where walking was a question of pulling and balancing. They were soon warm, at any rate; it kept them sweating. The weight of their equipment was continually thrown in the wrong place. Their wet clothing dragged them back, their packs got twisted and cut into their shoulders. Claude and Hicks began wondering to each other what it must have been like in the real mud, up about Ypres and Paschendael, two years ago. Hicks had been training at Arras last week, where a lot of Tommies were "resting" in the same way, and he had tales to tell.

The Battalion got to Joachim farm at nine o'clock. Colonel Harvey had not yet come up, but old Julius Caesar was there with his engineers, and he had a hot breakfast ready for them. At six o'clock in the evening they took the road again, marching until daybreak, with short rests. During the night they captured two Hun patrols, a bunch of thirty men. At the halt for breakfast, the prisoners wanted to make themselves useful, but the cook said they were so filthy the smell of them would make a stew go bad. They were herded off by themselves, a good distance from the grub line.

It was Gerhardt, of course, who had to go over and question them. Claude felt sorry for the prisoners; they were so willing to tell all they knew, and so anxious to make themselves agreeable; began talking about their relatives in America, and said brightly that they themselves were going over at once, after the war—seemed to have no doubt that everybody would be glad to see them!

They begged Gerhardt to be allowed to do something. Couldn't they carry the officers' equipment on the march? No, they were too buggy; they might relieve the sanitary squad. Oh, that they would gladly do, *Herr Offizier!*

The plan was to get to Ruprecht trench and take it before nightfall. It was easy taking—empty of everything but vermin and human discards; a dozen crippled and sick, left for the enemy to dispose of, and several half-witted youths who ought to have been locked up in some institution. Fritz had known what it meant when his patrols did not come back. He had evacuated, leaving behind his hopelessly diseased, and as much filth as possible. The dugouts were fairly dry, but so crawling with vermin that the Americans preferred to sleep in the mud, in the open.

After supper the men fell on their packs and began to lighten them, throwing away all that was not necessary, and much that was. Many of them abandoned the new overcoats that had been served out at the railhead; others cut off the skirts and made the coats into ragged jackets. Captain Maxey was horrified at these depredations, but the Colonel advised him to shut his eyes. "They've got hard going before them; let them travel light. If they'd rather stand the cold, they've got a right to choose."

XVI

THE Battalion had twenty-four hours' rest at Ruprecht trench, and then pushed on for four days and nights, stealing trenches, capturing patrols, with only a few hours' sleep,—snatched by the roadside while their food was being prepared. They pushed hard after a retiring foe, and almost outran themselves. They did outrun their provisions; on the fourth night, when they fell upon a farm that had been a German Headquarters, the supplies that were to meet them there had not come up, and they went to bed supperless.

This farmhouse, for some reason called by the prisoners Frau Hulda farm, was a nest of telephone wires; hundreds of them ran out through the walls, in all directions. The Colonel cut those he could find, and then put a guard over the old peasant who had been left in charge of the house, suspecting that he was in the pay of the enemy.

At last Colonel Scott got into the Headquarters bed, large and lumpy,—the first one he had seen since he left Arras. He had not been asleep more than two hours, when a runner arrived with orders from the Regimental Colonel. Claude was in a bed in the loft, between Gerhardt and Bruger. He felt somebody shaking him, but resolved that he wouldn't be disturbed and went on placidly sleeping. Then somebody pulled his hair,— so hard that he sat up. Captain Maxey was standing over the bed.

"Come along, boys. Orders from Regimental Headquarters. The Battalion is to split here. Our Company is to go on four kilometers tonight, and take the town of Beaufort."

Claude rose. "The men are pretty well beat out, Captain Maxey, and they had no supper."

"That can't be helped. Tell them we are to be in Beaufort for breakfast."

Claude and Gerhardt went out to the barn and roused Hicks and his pal, Dell Able. The men were asleep in dry straw, for the first time in ten days. They were completely worn out, lost to time and place. Many of them were already four thousand miles away, scattered among little towns, and farms on the prairie. They were a miserable looking lot as they got together, stumbling about in the dark.

After the Colonel had gone over the map with Captain Maxey, he came out and saw the Company assembled. He wasn't going with them, he told them, but he expected them to give a good account of themselves. Once in Beaufort, they would have a week's rest; sleep under cover, and live among people for awhile.

The men took the road, some with their eyes shut, trying to make believe they were still asleep, trying to have their agreeable dreams over again, as they marched. They did not really waken up until the advance challenged a Hun patrol, and sent it back to the Colonel under a one-man guard. When they had advanced two kilometers, they found the bridge blown up. Claude and Hicks went in one direction to look for a ford, Bruger and Dell Able in the other, and the men lay down by the roadside and slept heavily. Just at dawn they reached the outskirts of the village, silent and still.

Captain Maxey had no information as to how many Germans might be left in the town. They had occupied it ever since the beginning of the war, and had used it as a rest camp. There had never been any fighting there.

At the first house on the road, the Captain stopped and pounded. No answer.

"We are Americans, and must see the people of the house. If you don't open, we must break the door."

A woman's voice called; "There is nobody here. Go away, please, and take your men away. I am sick."

The Captain called Gerhardt, who began to explain and reassure through the door. It opened a little way, and an old woman in a nightcap peeped out. An old man hovered behind her. She gazed in astonishment at the officers, not understanding. These were the first soldiers of the Allies she had ever seen. She had heard the Germans talk about Americans, but thought it was one of their lies, she said. Once convinced, she let the officers come in and replied to their questions.

No, there were no Boches left in her house. They had got orders to leave day before yesterday, and had blown up the bridge. They were concentrating somewhere to the east. She didn't know how many were still in the village, nor where they were, but she could tell the Captain where they had been. Triumphantly she brought out a map of the town—lost, she said with a meaning smile, by a German officer—on which the billets were marked.

With this to guide them, Captain Maxey and his men went on up the street. They took eight prisoners in one cellar, seventeen in another. When the villagers saw the prisoners bunched together in the square, they came out of their houses and gave information. This cleaning up, Bert Fuller remarked, was like taking fish from the Platte River when the water was low, — simply pailing them out! There was no sport in it.

At nine o'clock the officers were standing together in the square before the church, checking off on the map the houses that had been searched. The men were drinking coffee, and eating fresh bread from a baker's shop. The square was full of people who had come out to see for themselves. Some believed that deliverance had come, and others shook their heads and held back, suspecting another trick. A crowd of children were running about, making friends with the soldiers. One little girl with yellow curls and a clean white dress had attached herself to Hicks, and was eating chocolate out of his pocket. Gerhardt was bargaining with the baker for another baking of bread. The sun was shining, for a change, — everything was looking cheerful. This village seemed to be swarming with girls; some of them were pretty, and all were friendly. The men who had looked so haggard and forlorn when dawn overtook them at the edge of the town, began squaring their shoulders and throwing out their chests. They were dirty and mud-plastered, but as Claude remarked to the Captain, they actually looked like fresh men.

Suddenly a shot rang out above the chatter, and an old woman in a white cap screamed and tumbled over on the pavement,—rolled about, kicking indecorously with both hands and feet. A second crack,—the little girl who stood beside Hicks, eating chocolate, threw out her hands, ran a few steps, and fell, blood and brains oozing out in her yellow hair. The people began screaming and running. The Americans looked this way and that; ready to dash, but not knowing where to go. Another shot, and Captain Maxey fell on one knee, blushed furiously and sprang up, only to fall again,—ashy white, with the leg of his trousers going red.

"There it is, to the left!" Hicks shouted, pointing. They saw now. From a closed house, some distance down a street off the square, smoke was coming. It hung before one of the upstairs windows. The Captain's orderly dragged him into a wineshop. Claude and David, followed by the men, ran down the street and broke in the door. The two officers went through the rooms on the first floor, while Hicks and his lot made straight for an enclosed stairway at the back of the house. As they reached the foot of the stairs, they were met by a volley of rifle shots, and two of the men tumbled over. Four Germans were stationed at the head of the steps.

The Americans scarcely knew whether their bullets or their bayonets got to the Huns first; they were not conscious of going up, till they were there. When Claude and David reached the landing, the squad were wiping their bayonets, and four grey bodies were piled in the corner.

Bert Fuller and Dell Able ran down the narrow hallway and threw open the door into the room on the street. Two shots, and Dell came back with his jaw shattered and the blood spouting from the left side of his neck. Gerhardt caught him, and tried to close the artery with his fingers.

"How many are in there, Bert?" Claude called.

"I couldn't see. Look out, sir! You can't get through that door more than two at a time!"

The door still stood open, at the end of the corridor. Claude went down the steps until he could sight along the floor of the passage, into the front room. The shutters were closed in there, and the sunlight came through the slats. In the middle of the floor, between the door and the windows, stood a tall chest of drawers, with a mirror attached to the top. In the narrow space between the bottom of this piece of furniture and the floor, he could see a pair of boots. It was possible there was but one man in the room, shooting from behind his movable fort, — though there might be others hidden in the corners.

"There's only one fellow in there, I guess. He's shooting from behind a big dresser in the middle of the room. Come on, one of you, we'll have to go in and get him."

Willy Katz, the Austrian boy from the Omaha packing house, stepped up and stood beside him.

"Now, Willy, we'll both go in at once; you jump to the right, and I to the left, — and one of us will jab him. He can't shoot both ways at once. Are you ready? All right — Now!"

Claude thought he was taking the more dangerous position himself, but the German probably reasoned that the important man would be on the right. As the two Americans dashed through the door, he fired. Claude caught him in the back with his bayonet, under the shoulder blade, but Willy Katz had got the bullet in his brain, through one of his blue eyes. He fell, and never stirred. The German officer fired his revolver again as he went down, shouting in English, English with no foreign accent,

"You swine, go back to Chicago!" Then he began choking with blood.

Sergeant Hicks ran in and shot the dying man through the temples. Nobody stopped him.

The officer was a tall man, covered with medals and orders; must have been very handsome. His linen and his hands were as white as if he were going to a ball. On the dresser were the files and paste and buffers with which he had kept his nails so pink and smooth. A ring with a ruby, beautifully cut, was on his little finger. Bert Fuller screwed it off and offered it to Claude. He shook his head. That English sentence had unnerved him. Bert held the ring out to Hicks, but the Sergeant threw down his revolver and broke out:

"Think I'd touch anything of his? That beautiful little girl, and my buddy—He's worse than dead, Dell is, worse!" He turned his back on his comrades so that they wouldn't see him cry.

"Can I keep it myself, sir?" Bert asked.

Claude nodded. David had come in, and was opening the shutters. This officer, Claude was thinking, was a very different sort of being from the poor prisoners they had been scooping up like tadpoles from the cellars. One of the men picked up a gorgeous silk dressing gown from the bed, another pointed to a dressing-case full of hammered silver. Gerhardt said it was Russian silver; this man must have come from the Eastern front. Bert Fuller and Nifty Jones were going through the officer's pockets. Claude watched them, and thought they did about right. They didn't touch his medals; but his gold cigarette case, and the platinum watch still ticking on his wrist,— he wouldn't have further need for them. Around his neck, hung by a delicate chain, was a miniature case, and in it was a painting,—not, as Bert romantically hoped when he opened it, of a beautiful woman, but of a young man, pale as snow, with blurred forget-me-not eyes.

Claude studied it, wondering. "It looks like a poet, or something. Probably a kid brother, killed at the beginning of the war."

Gerhardt took it and glanced at it with a disdainful expression. "Probably. There, let him keep it, Bert." He touched Claude on the shoulder to call his attention to the inlay work on the handle of the officer's revolver.

Claude noticed that David looked at him as if he were very much pleased with him,—looked, indeed, as if something pleasant had happened in this room; where, God knew, nothing had; where, when they turned round, a swarm of black flies was

371

quivering with greed and delight over the smears Willy Katz' body had left on the floor. Claude had often observed that when David had an interesting idea, or a strong twinge of recollection, it made him, for the moment, rather heartless. Just now he felt that Gerhardt's flash of high spirits was in some way connected with him. Was it because he had gone in with Willy? Had David doubted his nerve?

XVII

WHEN the survivors of Company B are old men, and are telling over their good days, they will say to each other, "Oh, that week we spent at Beaufort!" They will close their eyes and see a little village on a low ridge, lost in the forest, overgrown with oak and chestnut and black walnut . . . buried in autumn colour, the streets drifted deep in autumn leaves, great branches interlacing over the roofs of the houses, wells of cool water that tastes of moss and tree roots. Up and down those streets they will see figures passing; themselves, young and brown and clean-limbed; and comrades, long dead, but still alive in that far-away village. How they will wish they could tramp again, nights on days in the mud and rain, to drag sore feet into their old billets at Beaufort! To sink into those wide feather beds and sleep the round of the clock while the old women washed and dried their clothes for them; to eat rabbit stew and *pommes frites* in the garden,—rabbit stew made with red wine and chestnuts. Oh, the days that are no more!

As soon as Captain Maxey and the wounded men had been started on their long journey to the rear, carried by the prisoners, the whole company turned in and slept for twelve hours—all but Sergeant Hicks, who sat in the house off the square, beside the body of his chum.

The next day the Americans came to life as if they were new men, just created in a new world. And the people of the town came to life . . . excitement, change, something to look forward to at last! A new flag, *le drapeau étoilé,* floated along with the tricolour in the square. At sunset the soldiers stood in formation behind it and sang "The Star Spangled Banner" with uncovered heads. The old people watched them from the doorways. The Americans were the first to bring "Madelon" to Beaufort. The fact that the village had never heard this song, that the children stood round begging for it, *"Chantesvous la Madelon!"* made the soldiers realize how far and how long out of the world these villagers had been. The German occupation was like a deafness which nothing pierced but their own arrogant martial airs.

Before Claude was out of bed after his first long sleep, a runner arrived from Colonel Scott, notifying him that he was in charge of the Company until further orders. The German prisoners had buried their own dead and dug graves for the Americans before they were sent off to the rear. Claude and David were billeted at the edge of the town, with the woman who had given Captain Maxey his first information, when they marched in yesterday morning. Their hostess told them, at their mid-day breakfast, that the old dame who was shot in the square, and the little girl, were to be buried this afternoon. Claude decided that the Americans might as well have their funeral at the same time. He thought he would ask the priest to say a prayer at the graves, and he and David set off through the brilliant, rustling autumn sunshine to find the Curé's house. It was next the church, with a high-walled garden behind it. Over the bell-pull in the outer wall was a card on which was written, *"Tirez fort."*

The priest himself came out to them, an old man who seemed weak like his doorbell. He stood in his black cap, holding his hands against his breast to keep them from shaking, and looked very old indeed,—broken, hopeless, as if he were sick of this world and done with it. Nowhere in France had Claude seen a face so sad as his. Yes, he would say a prayer. It was better to have Christian burial, and they were far from home, poor fellows! David asked him whether the German rule had been very oppressive, but the old man did not answer clearly, and his hands began to shake so uncontrollably over his cassock that they went away to spare him embarrassment.

"He seems a little gone in the head, don't you think?" Claude remarked.

"I suppose the war has used him up. How can he celebrate mass when his hands quiver so?" As they crossed the church steps, David touched Claude's arm and pointed into the square. "Look, every doughboy has a girl already! Some of them have trotted out fatigue caps! I supposed they'd thrown them all away!"

Those who had no caps stood with their helmets under their arms, in attitudes of exaggerated gallantry, talking to the women,—who seemed all to have errands abroad. Some of them let the boys carry their baskets. One soldier was giving a delighted little girl a ride on his back.

After the funeral every man in the Company found some sympathetic woman to talk to about his fallen comrades. All the garden flowers and bead wreaths in Beaufort had been carried out and put on the American graves. When the squad fired over them and the bugle sounded, the girls and their mothers wept. Poor Willy Katz, for instance, could never have had such a funeral in South Omaha.

The next night the soldiers began teaching the girls to dance the "Pas Seul" and the "Fausse Trot." They had found an old violin in the town; and Oscar, the Swede, scraped away on it. They danced every evening. Claude saw that a good deal was going on, and he lectured his men at parade. But he realized that he might as well scold at the sparrows. Here was a village with several hundred women, and only the grandmothers had husbands. All the men were in the army; hadn't even been home on leave since the Germans first took the place. The girls had been shut up for four years with young men who incessantly coveted them, and whom they must constantly outwit. The situation had been intolerable—and prolonged. The Americans found themselves in the position of Adam in the garden.

"Did you know, sir," said Bert Fuller breathlessly as he overtook Claude in the street after parade, "that these lovely girls had to go out in the fields and work, raising things for those dirty pigs to eat? Yes, sir, had to work in the fields, under German sentinels; marched out in the morning and back at night like convicts! It's sure up to us to give them a good time now."

One couldn't walk out of an evening without meeting loitering couples in the dusky streets and lanes. The boys had lost all their bashfulness about trying to speak French. They declared they could get along in France with three verbs, and all, happily, in the first conjugation: *manger, aimer, payer,* — quite enough! They called Beaufort "our town," and they were called "our Americans." They were going to come back after the war, and marry the girls, and put in water-works!

"*Chez-moi,* sir!" Bill Gates called to Claude, saluting with a bloody hand, as he stood skinning rabbits before the door of his billet. "Bunny casualties are heavy in town this week!"

"You know, Wheeler," David remarked one morning as they were shaving, "I think Maxey would come back here on one leg if he knew about these excursions into the forest after mushrooms."

"Maybe."

"Aren't you going to put a stop to them?"

"Not I!" Claude jerked, setting the corners of his mouth grimly. "If the girls, or their people, make complaint to me, I'll interfere. Not otherwise. I've thought the matter over."

"Oh, the girls —" David laughed softly. "Well, it's something to acquire a taste for mushrooms. They don't get them at home, do they?"

When, after eight days, the Americans had orders to march, there was mourning in every house. On their last night in town, the officers received pressing invitations to the dance in the square. Claude went for a few moments, and looked on. David was dancing every dance, but Hicks was nowhere to be seen. The poor fellow had been out of everything. Claude went over to the church to see whether he might be moping in the graveyard.

There, as he walked about, Claude stopped to look at a grave that stood off by itself, under a privet hedge, with withered leaves and a little French flag on it. The old woman with whom they stayed had told them the story of this grave.

The Curé's niece was buried there. She was the prettiest girl in Beaufort, it seemed, and she had a love affair with a German officer and disgraced the town. He was a young Bavarian, quartered with this same old woman who told them the story, and she said he was a nice boy, handsome and gentle, and used to sit up half the night in the garden with his head in his hands— homesick, lovesick. He was always after this Marie Louise; never pressed her, but was always there, grew up out of the ground under her feet, the old woman said. The girl hated Germans, like all the rest, and flouted him. He was sent to the front. Then he came back, sick and almost deaf, after one of the slaughters at Verdun, and stayed a long while. That spring a story got about that some woman met him at night in the German graveyard. They had taken the land behind the church for their cemetery, and it joined the wall of the Curé's garden. When the women went out into the fields to plant the crops, Marie Louise used to slip away from the others and meet her Bavarian in the forest. The girls were sure of it now; and they treated her with disdain. But nobody was brave enough to say anything to the Curé. One day, when she was with her Bavarian in the wood, she snatched up his revolver from the ground and shot herself. She was a Frenchwoman at heart, their hostess said.

"And the Bavarian?" Claude asked David later. The story had become so complicated he could not follow it.

"He justified her, and promptly. He took the same pistol and shot himself through the temples. His orderly, stationed at the edge of the thicket to keep watch, heard the first shot and ran toward them. He saw the officer take up the smoking pistol and turn it on himself. But the Kommandant couldn't believe that one of his officers had so much feeling. He held an *enquête*, dragged the girl's mother and uncle into court, and tried to establish that they were in conspiracy with her to seduce and murder a German officer. The orderly was made to tell the whole story; how and where they began to meet. Though he wasn't very delicate about the details he divulged, he stuck to his statement that he saw Lieutenant Müller shoot himself with his own hand, and the Kommandant failed to prove his case. The old Curé had known nothing of all this until he heard it aired in the military court. Marie Louise had lived in his house since she was a child, and was like his daughter. He had a stroke or something, and has been like this ever since. The girl's friends forgave her, and when she was buried off alone by the hedge, they began to take flowers to her grave. The Kommandant put up an *affiche* on the hedge, forbidding any one to decorate the grave. Apparently, nothing during the German occupation stirred up more feeling than poor Marie Louise."

It would stir anybody, Claude reflected. There was her lonely little grave, the shadow of the privet hedge falling across it. There, at the foot of the Curé's garden, was the German cemetery, with heavy cement crosses,—some of them with long inscriptions; lines from their poets, and couplets from old hymns. Lieutenant Müller was there somewhere, probably. Strange, how their story stood out in a world of suffering. That was a kind of misery he hadn't happened to think of before; but the same thing must have occurred again and again in the occupied territory. He would never forget the Curé's hands, his dim, suffering eyes.

Claude recognized David crossing the pavement in front of the church, and went back to meet him.

"Hello! I mistook you for Hicks at first. I thought he might be out here." David sat down on the steps and lit a cigarette.

"So did I. I came out to look for him."

"Oh, I expect he's found some shoulder to cry on. Do you realize, Claude, you and I are the only men in the Company who haven't got engaged? Some of the married men have got engaged twice. It's a good thing we're pulling out, or we'd have banns and a bunch of christenings to look after."

"All the same," murmured Claude, "I like the women of this country, as far as I've seen them." While they sat smoking in silence, his mind went back to the quiet scene he had watched on the steps of that other church, on his first night in France; the country girl in the moonlight, bending over her sick soldier.

When they walked back across the square, over the crackling leaves, the dance was breaking up. Oscar was playing "Home, Sweet Home," for the last waltz.

"*Le dernier baiser,*" said David. "Well, tomorrow we'll be gone, and the chances are we won't come back this way."

XVIII

"WITH us it's always a feast or a famine," the men groaned when they sat down by the road to munch dry biscuit at noon. They had covered eighteen miles that morning, and had still seven more to go. They were ordered to do the twenty-five miles in eight hours. Nobody had fallen out yet, but some of the boys looked pretty well wilted. Nifty Jones said he was done for. Sergeant Hicks was expostulating with the faint-hearted. He knew that if one man fell out, a dozen would.

"If I can do it, you can. It's worse on a fat man like me. This is no march to make a fuss about. Why, at Arras I talked with a little Tommy from one of those Pal Battalions that got slaughtered on the Somme. His battalion marched twenty-five miles in six hours, in the heat of July, into certain death. They were all kids out of school, not a man of them over five-foot-three, called them the 'Bantams.' You've got to hand it to them, fellows."

"I'll hand anything to anybody, but I can't go no farther on these," Jones muttered, nursing his sore feet.

"Oh, you! We're going to heave you onto the only horse in the Company. The officers, they can walk!"

When they got into Battalion lines there was food ready for them, but very few wanted it. They drank and lay down in the bushes. Claude went at once to Headquarters and found Barclay Owens, of the Engineers, with the Colonel, who was smoking and studying his maps as usual.

"Glad to see you, Wheeler. Your men ought to be in good shape, after a week's rest. Let them sleep now. We've got to move out of here before midnight, to relieve two Texas battalions at Moltke trench. They've taken the trench with heavy casualties and are beat out; couldn't hold it in case of counter-attack. As it's an important point, the enemy will try to recover it. I want to get into position before daylight, so he won't know fresh troops are coming in. As ranking officer, you are in charge of the Company."

"Very well, sir. I'll do my best."

"I'm sure you will. Two machine gun teams are going up with us, and some time tomorrow a Missouri battalion comes up to support. I'd have had you over here before, but I only got my orders to relieve yesterday. We may have to advance under shell fire. The enemy has been putting a lot of big stuff over; he wants to cut off that trench."

Claude and David got into a fresh shell hole, under the half-burned scrub, and fell asleep. They were awakened at dusk by heavy artillery fire from the north.

At ten o'clock the Battalion, after a hot meal, began to advance through almost impassable country. The guns must have been pounding away at the same range for a long while; the ground was worked and kneaded until it was soft as dough, though no rain had fallen for a week. Barclay Owens and his engineers were throwing down a plank road to get food and the ammunition wagons across. Big shells were coming over at intervals of twelve minutes. The intervals were so regular that it was quite possible to get forward without damage. While B Company was pulling through the shell area, Colonel Scott overtook them, on foot, his orderly leading his horse.

"Know anything about that light over there, Wheeler?" he asked. "Well, it oughtn't to be there. Come along and see."

The light was a mere match-head down in the ground,—Claude hadn't noticed it before. He followed the Colonel, and when they reached the spark they found three officers of A Company crouching in a shell crater, covered with a piece of sheet-iron.

"Put out that light," called the Colonel sharply. "What's the matter, Captain Brace?"

A young man rose quickly. "I'm waiting for the water, sir. It's coming up on mules, in petrol cases, and I don't want to get separated from it. The ground's so bad here the drivers are likely to get lost."

"Don't wait more than twenty minutes. You must get up and take your position on time, that's the important thing, water or no water."

As the Colonel and Claude hurried back to overtake the Company, five big shells screamed over them in rapid succession. "Run, sir," the orderly called. "They're getting on to us; they've shortened the range."

"That light back there was just enough to give them an idea," the Colonel muttered.

The bad ground continued for about a mile, and then the advance reached Headquarters, behind the eighth trench of the great system of trenches. It was an old farmhouse which the Germans had made over with reinforced concrete, lining it within and without, until the walls were six feet thick and almost shell-proof, like a pill-box. The Colonel sent his orderly to enquire about A Company. A young Lieutenant came to the door of the farmhouse.

"A Company is ready to go into position, sir. I brought them up."

"Where is Captain Brace, Lieutenant?"

"He and both our first lieutenants were killed, Colonel. Back in that hole. A shell fell on them not five minutes after you were talking to them."

"That's bad. Any other damage?"

"Yes, sir. There was a cook wagon struck at the same time; the first one coming along Julius Caesar's new road. The driver was killed, and we had to shoot the horses. Captain Owens, he near got scalded with the stew."

The Colonel called in the officers one after another and discussed their positions with them.

"Wheeler," he said when Claude's turn came, "you know your map? You've noticed that sharp loop in the front trench, in H 2;— the Boar's Head, I believe they call it. It's a sort of spear point that reaches out toward the enemy, and it will be a hot place to hold. If I put your company in there, do you think you can do the Battalion credit in case of a counter attack?"

Claude said he thought so.

"It's the nastiest bit of the line to hold, and you can tell your men I pay them a compliment when I put them there."

"All right, sir. They'll appreciate it."

The Colonel bit off the end of a fresh cigar. "They'd better, by thunder! If they give way and let the Hun bombers in, it will let down the whole line. I'll give you two teams of Georgia machine guns to put in that point they call the Boar's Snout. When the Missourians come up tomorrow, they'll go in to support you, but until then you'll have to take care of the loop yourselves. I've got an awful lot of trench to hold, and I can't spare you any more men."

The Texas men whom the Battalion came up to relieve had been living for sixty hours on their iron rations, and on what they could pick off the dead Huns. Their supplies had been shelled on the way, and nothing had got through to them. When the Colonel took Claude and Gerhardt forward to inspect the loop that B Company was to hold, they found a wallow, more like a dump heap than a trench. The men who had taken the position were almost too weak to stand. All their officers had been killed, and a sergeant was in command. He apologized for the condition of the loop.

"Sorry to leave such a mess for you to clean up, sir, but we got it bad in here. He's been shelling us every night since we drove him out. I couldn't ask the men to do anything but hold on."

"That's all right. You beat it, with your boys, quick! My men will hand you out some grub as you go back."

The battered defenders of the Boar's Head stumbled past them through the darkness into the communication. When the last man had filed out, the Colonel sent for Barclay Owens.

Claude and David tried to feel their way about and get some idea of the condition the place was in. The stench was the worst they had yet encountered, but it was less disgusting than the flies; when they inadvertently touched a dead body, clouds of wet, buzzing flies flew up into their faces, into their eyes and nostrils. Under their feet the earth worked and moved as if boa constrictors were wriggling down there—soft bodies, lightly covered. When they had found their way up to the Snout they came upon a pile of corpses, a dozen or more, thrown one on top of another like sacks of flour, faintly discernible in the darkness. While the two officers stood there, rumbling, squirting sounds began to come from this heap, first from one body, then from another—gasses, swelling in the liquefying entrails of the dead men. They seemed to be complaining to one another; *glup, glup, glup.*

The boys went back to the Colonel, who was standing at the mouth of the communication, and told him there was nothing much to report, except that the burying squad was needed badly.

"I expect!" The Colonel shook his head. When Barclay Owens arrived, he asked him what could be done here before daybreak. The doughty engineer felt his way about as Claude and Gerhardt had done; they heard him coughing, and beating off the flies. But when he came back he seemed rather cheered than discouraged.

"Give me a gang to get the casualties out, and with plenty of quick-lime and concrete I can make this loop all right in four hours, sir," he declared.

"I've brought plenty of lime, but where'll you get your concrete?"

"The Hun left about fifty sacks of it in the cellar, under your Headquarters. I can do better, of course, if I have a few hours more for my concrete to dry."

"Go ahead, Captain." The Colonel told Claude and David to bring their men up to the communication before light, and hold them ready. "Give Owen's cement a chance, but don't let the enemy put over any surprise on you."

The shelling began again at daybreak; it was hardest on the rear trenches and the three-mile area behind. Evidently the enemy felt sure of what he had in Moltke trench; he wanted to cut off supplies and possible reinforcements. The Missouri battalion did not come up that day, but before noon a runner arrived from their Colonel, with information that they were hiding in the wood. Five Boche planes had been circling over the wood since dawn, signalling to the enemy Headquarters back on Dauphin Ridge; the Missourians were sure they had avoided detection by lying close in the under-brush. They would come up in the night. Their linemen were following the runner, and Colonel Scott would be in telephone communication with them in half an hour.

When B Company moved into the Boar's Head at one o'clock in the afternoon, they could truthfully say that the prevailing smell was now that of quick-lime. The parapet was evenly built up, the firing step had been partly restored, and in the Snout there were good emplacements for the machine guns. Certain unpleasant reminders were still to be found if one looked for them. In the Snout a large fat boot stuck stiffly from the side of the trench. Captain Owens explained that the ground sounded hollow in there, and the boot probably led back into a dugout where a lot of Hun bodies were entombed together. As he was pressed for time, he had thought best not to look for trouble. In one of the curves of the loop, just at the top of the earth wall, under the sand bags, a dark hand reached out; the five fingers, well apart, looked like the swollen roots of some noxious weed. Hicks declared that this object was disgusting, and during the afternoon he made Nifty Jones and Oscar scrape down some earth and make a hump over the paw. But there was shelling in the night, and the earth fell away.

"Look," said Jones when he wakened his Sergeant. "The first thing I seen when daylight come was his old fingers, wigglin' in the breeze. He wants air, Heinie does; he won't stay covered."

Hicks got up and re-buried the hand himself, but when he came around with Claude on inspection, before breakfast, there were the same five fingers sticking out again. The

Sergeant's forehead puffed up and got red, and he swore that
if he found the man who played dirty jokes, he'd make him
eat this one.

The Colonel sent for Claude and Gerhardt to come to breakfast with him. He had been talking by telephone with the
Missouri officers and had agreed that they should stay back in
the bush for the present. The continual circling of planes over
the wood seemed to indicate that the enemy was concerned
about the actual strength of Moltke trench. It was possible their
air scouts had seen the Texas men going back,—otherwise, why
were they holding off?

While the Colonel and the officers were at breakfast, a corporal brought in two pigeons he had shot at dawn. One of them
carried a message under its wing. The Colonel unrolled a strip of
paper and handed it to Gerhardt.

"Yes, sir, it's in German, but it's code stuff. It's a German nurs-
ery rhyme. Those reconnoitering planes must have dropped
scouts on our rear, and they are sending in reports. Of course,
they can get more on us than the air men can. Here, do you want
these birds, Dick?"

The boy grinned. "You bet I do, sir! I may get a chance to fry
'em, later on."

After breakfast the Colonel went to inspect B Company in the
Boar's Head. He was especially pleased with the advantageous
placing of the machine guns in the Snout. "I expect you'll have a
quiet day," he said to the men, "but I wouldn't like to promise
you a quiet night. You'll have to be very steady in here; if Fritz
takes this loop, he's got us, you understand."

They had, indeed, a quiet day. Some of the men played cards,
and Oscar read his Bible. The night, too, began well. But at four
fifteen everybody was roused by the gas alarm. Gas shells came
over for exactly half an hour. Then the shrapnel broke loose; not
the long, whizzing scream of solitary shells, but drum-fire, continuous and deafening. A hundred electrical storms seemed rag-
ing at once, in the air and on the ground. Balls of fire were
rolling all over the place. The range was a little long for the

Boar's Head, they were not getting the worst of it; but thirty yards back everything was torn to pieces. Claude didn't see how anybody could be left alive back there. A single twister had killed six of his men at the rear of the loop, where they were shovelling to keep the communication clear. Captain Owens' neat earthworks were being badly pounded.

Claude and Gerhardt were consulting together when the smoke and darkness began to take on the livid colour that announced the coming of daybreak. A messenger ran in from the Colonel; the Missourians had not yet come up, and his telephone communication with them was cut off. He was afraid they had got lost in the bombardment. "The Colonel says you are to send two men back to bring them up; two men who can take charge if they're stampeded."

When the messenger shouted this order, Gerhardt and Hicks looked at each other quickly, and volunteered to go.

Claude hesitated. Hicks and David waited for no further consent; they ran down the communication and disappeared.

Claude stood in the smoke that was slowly growing greyer, and looked after them with the deepest stab of despair he had ever known. Only a man who was bewildered and unfit to be in command of other men would have let his best friend and his best officer take such a risk. He was standing there under shelter, and his two friends were going back through that curtain of flying steel, toward the square from which the lost battalion had last reported. If he knew them, they would not lose time following the maze of trenches; they were probably even now out on the open, running straight through the enemy barrage, vaulting trench tops.

Claude turned and went back into the loop. Well, whatever happened, he had worked with brave men. It was worth having lived in this world to have known such men. Soldiers, when they were in a tight place, often made secret propositions to God; and now he found himself offering terms: If They would see to it that David came back, They could take the price out of him. He would pay. Did They understand?

An hour dragged by. Hard on the nerves, waiting. Up the communication came a train with ammunition and coffee for the loop. The men thought Headquarters did pretty well to get hot food to them through that barrage. A message came up in the Colonel's hand:

"Be ready when the barrage stops."

Claude took this up and showed it to the machine gunners in the Snout. Turning back, he ran into Hicks, stripped to his shirt and trousers, as wet as if he had come out of the river, and splashed with blood. His hand was wrapped up in a rag. He put his mouth to Claude's ear and shouted: "We found them. They were lost. They're coming. Send word to the Colonel."

"Where's Gerhardt?"

"He's coming; bringing them up. God, it's stopped!"

The bombardment ceased with a suddenness that was stupefying. The men in the loop gasped and crouched as if they were falling from a height. The air, rolling black with smoke and stifling with the smell of gasses and burning powder, was still as death. The silence was like a heavy anaesthetic.

Claude ran back to the Snout to see that the gun teams were ready. "Wake up, boys! You know why we're here!"

Bert Fuller, who was up in the look-out, dropped back into the trench beside him. "They're coming, sir."

Claude gave the signal to the machine guns. Fire opened all along the loop. In a moment a breeze sprang up, and the heavy smoke clouds drifted to the rear. Mounting to the fire-step, he peered over. The enemy was coming on eight deep, on the left of the Boar's Head, in long, waving lines that reached out toward the main trench. Suddenly the advance was checked. The files of running men dropped behind a wrinkle in the earth fifty yards forward and did not instantly re-appear. It struck Claude that they were waiting for something; he ought to be clever enough to know for what, but he was not. The Colonel's line man came up to him.

"Headquarters has a runner from the Missourians. They'll be up in twenty minutes. The Colonel will put them in here at once. Till then you must manage to hold."

"We'll hold. Fritz is behaving queerly. I don't understand his tactics . . ."

While he was speaking, everything was explained. The Boar's Snout spread apart with an explosion that split the earth, and went up in a volcano of smoke and flame. Claude and the Colonel's messenger were thrown on their faces. When they got to their feet, the Snout was a smoking crater full of dead and dying men. The Georgia gun teams were gone.

It was for this that the Hun advance had been waiting behind the ridge. The mine under the Snout had been made long ago, probably, on a venture, when the Hun held Moltke trench for months without molestation. During the last twenty-four hours they had been getting their explosives in, reasoning that the strongest garrison would be placed there.

Here they were, coming on the run. It was up to the rifles. The men who had been knocked down by the shock were all on their feet again. They looked at their officer questioningly, as if the whole situation had changed. Claude felt they were going soft under his eyes. In a moment the Hun bombers would be in on them, and they would break. He ran along the trench, pointing over the sand bags and shouting, "It's up to you, it's up to you!"

The rifles recovered themselves and began firing, but Claude felt they were spongy and uncertain, that their minds were already on the way to the rear. If they did anything, it must be quick, and their gun-work must be accurate. Nothing but a withering fire could check. . . . He sprang to the fire-step and then out on the parapet. Something instantaneous happened; he had his men in hand.

"Steady, steady!" He called the range to the rifle teams behind him, and he could see the fire take effect. All along the Hun lines men were stumbling and falling. They swerved a little to the left; he called the rifles to follow, directing them with his voice and with his hands. It was not only that from here he could correct the range and direct the fire; the men behind him had become like rock. That line of faces below, Hicks, Jones, Fuller, Anderson, Oscar. . . . Their eyes never left him. With these men he could do anything. He had learned the mastery of men.

The right of the Hun line swerved out, not more than twenty yards from the battered Snout, trying to run to shelter under that pile of débris and human bodies. A quick concentration of rifle fire depressed it, and the swell came out again toward the left. Claude's appearance on the parapet had attracted no attention from the enemy at first, but now the bullets began popping about him; two rattled on his tin hat, one caught him in the shoulder. The blood dripped down his coat, but he felt no weakness. He felt only one thing; that he commanded wonderful men. When David came up with the supports he might find them dead, but he would find them all there. They were there to stay until they were carried out to be buried. They were mortal, but they were unconquerable.

The Colonel's twenty minutes must be almost up, he thought. He couldn't take his eyes from the front line long enough to look at his wrist watch. . . . The men behind him saw Claude sway as if he had lost his balance and were trying to recover it. Then he plunged, face down, outside the parapet. Hicks caught his foot and pulled him back. At the same moment the Missourians ran yelling up the communication. They threw their machine guns up on the sand bags and went into action without an unnecessary motion.

Hicks and Bert Fuller and Oscar carried Claude forward toward the Snout, out of the way of the supports that were pouring in. He was not bleeding very much. He smiled at them as if he were going to speak, but there was a weak blank-ness in his eyes. Bert tore his shirt open; three clean bullet holes — one through his heart. By the time they looked at him again, the smile had gone . . . the look that was Claude had faded. Hicks wiped the sweat and smoke from his officer's face.

"Thank God I never told him," he said. "Thank God for that!"

Bert and Oscar knew what Hicks meant. Gerhardt had been blown to pieces at his side when they dashed back through the enemy barrage to find the Missourians. They were running together across the open, not able to see much for smoke. They bumped into a section of wire entanglement, left above an old trench. David cut round to the right, waving Hicks to follow him. The two were not ten yards apart when the shell struck. Then Sergeant Hicks ran on alone.

XIX

THE sun is sinking low, a transport is steaming slowly up the narrows with the tide. The decks are covered with brown men. They cluster over the superstructure like bees in swarming time. Their attitudes are relaxed and lounging. Some look thoughtful, some well contented, some are melancholy, and many are indifferent, as they watch the shore approaching. They are not the same men who went away.

Sergeant Hicks was standing in the stern, smoking, reflecting, watching the twinkle of the red sunset upon the cloudy water. It is more than a year since he sailed for France. The world has changed in that time, and so has he.

Bert Fuller elbowed his way up to the Sergeant. "The doctor says Colonel Maxey is dying. He won't live to get off the boat, much less to ride in the parade in New York tomorrow."

Hicks shrugged, as if Maxey's pneumonia were no affair of his. "Well, we should worry! We've left better officers than him over there."

"I'm not saying we haven't. But it seems too bad, when he's so strong for fuss and feathers. He's been sending cables about that parade for weeks."

"Huh!" Hicks elevated his eyebrows and glanced sidewise in disdain. Presently he sputtered, squinting down at the glittering water, "Colonel Maxey, anyhow! Colonel for what Claude and Gerhardt did, *I* guess!"

Hicks and Bert Fuller have been helping to keep the noble fortress of Ehrenbreitstein. They have always hung together and are usually quarrelling and grumbling at each other when they are off duty. Still, they hang together. They are the last of their group. Nifty Jones and Oscar, God only knows why, have gone on to the Black Sea.

During the year they were in the Rhine valley, Bert and Hicks were separated only once, and that was when Hicks got a two weeks' leave and, by dint of persevering and fatiguing travel, went to Venice. He had no proper passport, and the consuls and officials to whom he had appealed in his difficulties begged him to content himself with something nearer. But he said he was going to Venice because he had always heard about it. Bert Fuller was glad to welcome him back to Coblentz, and gave a "wine party" to celebrate his return. They expect to keep an eye on each other. Though Bert lives on the Platte and Hicks on the Big Blue, the automobile roads between those two rivers are excellent.

Bert is the same sweet-tempered boy he was when he left his mother's kitchen; his gravest troubles have been frequent betrothals. But Hicks' round, chubby face has taken on a slightly cynical expression,—a look quite out of place there. The chances of war have hurt his feelings . . . not that he ever wanted anything for himself. The way in which glittering honours bump down upon the wrong heads in the army, and palms and crosses blossom on the wrong breasts, has, as he says, thrown his compass off a few points.

What Hicks had wanted most in this world was to run a garage and repair shop with his old chum, Dell Able. Beaufort ended all that. He means to conduct a sort of memorial shop, anyhow, with "Hicks and Able" over the door. He wants to roll up his sleeves and look at the logical and beautiful inwards of automobiles for the rest of his life.

As the transport enters the North River, sirens and steam whistles all along the water front begin to blow their shrill salute to the returning soldiers. The men square their shoulders and smile knowingly at one another; some of them look a little bored. Hicks slowly lights a cigarette and regards the end of it with an expression which will puzzle his friends when he gets home.

By the banks of Lovely Creek, where it began, Claude Wheeler's story still goes on. To the two old women who work together in the farmhouse, the thought of him is always there, beyond everything else, at the farthest edge of consciousness, like the evening sun on the horizon.

Mrs. Wheeler got the word of his death one afternoon in the sitting-room, the room in which he had bade her good-bye. She was reading when the telephone rang.

"Is this the Wheeler farm? This is the telegraph office at Frankfort. We have a message from the War Department, —" the voice hesitated. "Isn't Mr. Wheeler there?"

"No, but you can read the message to me."

Mrs. Wheeler said, "Thank you," and hung up the receiver. She felt her way softly to her chair. She had an hour alone, when there was nothing but him in the room, — but him and the map there, which was the end of his road. Somewhere among those perplexing names, he had found his place.

Claude's letters kept coming for weeks afterward; then came the letters from his comrades and his Colonel to tell her all.

In the dark months that followed, when human nature looked to her uglier than it had ever done before, those letters were Mrs. Wheeler's comfort. As she read the newspapers, she used to think about the passage of the Red Sea, in the Bible; it seemed as if the flood of meanness and greed had been held back just long enough for the boys to go over, and then swept down and engulfed everything that was left at home. When she can see nothing that has come of it all but evil, she reads Claude's letters over again and reassures herself; for him the call was clear, the cause was glorious. Never a doubt stained his bright faith. She divines so much that he did not write. She knows what to read into those short flashes of enthusiasm; how fully he must have found his life before he could let himself go so far—he, who was so afraid of being fooled! He died believing his own country better than it is, and France better than any country can ever be. And those were beautiful beliefs to die with. Perhaps it was as well to see that vision, and then to see no more.

She would have dreaded the awakening,—she sometimes even doubts whether he could have borne at all that last, desolating disappointment. One by one the heroes of that war, the men of dazzling soldiership, leave prematurely the world they have come back to. Airmen whose deeds were tales of wonder, officers whose names made the blood of youth beat faster, survivors of incredible dangers,—one by one they quietly die by their own hand. Some do it in obscure lodging houses, some in their office, where they seemed to be carrying on their business like other men. Some slip over a vessel's side and disappear into the sea. When Claude's mother hears of these things, she shudders and presses her hands tight over her breast, as if she had him there. She feels as if God had saved him from some horrible suffering, some horrible end. For as she reads, she thinks those slayers of themselves were all so like him; they were the ones who had hoped extravagantly,—who in order to do what they did had to hope extravagantly, and to believe passionately. And they found they had hoped and believed too much. But one she knew, who could ill bear disillusion . . . safe, safe.

Mahailey, when they are alone, sometimes addresses Mrs. Wheeler as "Mudder"; "Now, Mudder, you go upstairs an' lay down an' rest yourself." Mrs. Wheeler knows that then she is thinking of Claude, is speaking for Claude. As they are working at the table or bending over the oven, something reminds them of him, and they think of him together, like one person: Mahailey will pat her back and say, "Never you mind, Mudder; you'll see your boy up yonder." Mrs. Wheeler always feels that God is near,—but Mahailey is not troubled by any knowledge of interstellar spaces, and for her He is nearer still,—directly overhead, not so very far above the kitchen stove.

THE END

ENDNOTES

[1] The actual outbreak of influenza on transports carrying United States troops is here anticipated by several months.

SUGGESTED READING

ACOCELLA, JOAN. *Willa Cather and the Politics of Criticism.* New York: Vintage, 2002.

BROWN, E. K. *Willa Cather: A Critical Biography.* New York: Knopf, 1953.

HARVEY, SALLY PELTIER. *Redefining the American Dream.* Rutherford, NJ: Farleigh Dickinson University Press, 1995.

O'BRIEN, SHARON. *Willa Cather: the Emerging Voice.* New York: Fawcett Columbine, 1987.

ROSOWSKI, SUSAN J. *The Voyage Perilous: Willa Cather's Romanticism.* Lincoln: Nebraska University Press, 1986.